A LOVER'S QUESTION

Selected Stories

WORKS BY THOMAS FARBER

A Lover's Question

The Face of the Deep

Compressions: A Second Helping

Through a Liquid Mirror
(with the photographs of Wayne Levin)

The Price of the Ride

On Water

Learning to Love It

Compared to What?

Curves of Pursuit

Too Soon to Tell

Hazards to the Human Heart

Who Wrote the Book of Love?

Rag Theatre
(with the photographs of Nacio Brown)

Tales for the Son of My Unborn Child

A LOVER'S QUESTION

Selected Stories

∾

THOMAS FARBER

CREATIVE ARTS BOOK COMPANY
Berkeley ∾ California 2000

Copyright © 2000 by Thomas Farber

No part of this book may be reproduced in any manner
without the written permission of the publisher,
except in brief quotations used in articles or reviews.

For information contact:
Creative Arts Book Company
833 Bancroft Way
Berkeley, California 94710

The characters, places, incidents and situations
in this book are imaginary and have no relation
to any person, place or actual happening.

Cover Photo by Stephen Shames

ISBN 088739-298-9

Library of Congress Cataloging-in-publication Data
Farber, Thomas, 1944-
    A lover's question : selected stories / Thomas Farber.
      p. cm.
    ISBN 0-88739-298-9 (alk. paper)
    1. United States—Social life and customs—20th century—Fiction. I. Title
    PS3556.A64 L68 2000
    813'.54—dc21
                                 00-34611

Printed in the United States of America

To Norma Holzman Farber (1909–1984) & Sidney Farber (1903–1973)

"If the bread I broke with the world was music,
the cup I shared was words."
N.H.F.

The good singers of old time, Béroul and Thomas of Built, Gilbert and Gottfried told this tale for lovers and none other, and, by my pen, they beg you for your prayers. They greet those who are cast down, and those in heart, those troubled and those filled with desire, those who are overjoyed and those disconsolate, all lovers. May all herein find strength against inconstancy, against unfairness and despite and loss and pain and all the bitterness of loving.

—JOSEPH BEDIER, *The Romance of Tristan and Iseult*

My formula for the greatness of a human being is *amor fati*: that one wants nothing to be different, not forward, not backward, not in all eternity. Not merely bear what is necessary, still less conceal it...but love it.

—NIETZSCHE, *Ecce Homo*

contents

AUTHOR'S NOTE   *1*

Who Wrote the Book of Love?   *7*
STORIES

Hazards to the Human Heart   *83*
STORIES

Learning to Love It   *183*
STORIES

Author's Note

Still here. Two and a half decades in this Berkeley cottage. With absences: until the dying of a second parent in 1984, recurring extended visits back to Boston. Writer once more taking the measure of what he'd repudiated. Might yet attempt to repossess...Who knew what came next, what the story would be? Many selves; various, conflicted. Also, part of the late seventies and early eighties on a sheep ranch in Sonoma County. And, for years, ocean obsessions in Hawai'i, further west; several times, blue so deep, how could you leave? Still, now, here in Berkeley, at my desk. Destination familiar, footsteps away, oddly remote: where I again arrive at what Robert Adams terms the artist's "proper silence." The elusive Kafka to Felice: "...why one can never be alone enough when one writes...why even night is not night enough." For my own part, as it turns out I said "No thank you" to some other lives. Needed this one more, most. Insisted on, found, all the time in the world to read, write; read, write.

Still here, after a stretch of being posthumous. Heart: close call. I don't remember setting out to be a writer, just wanted very much to do a book. Then, later, another. Perhaps I was more stubborn than I realized I'd have to be, or more faithful. But how I worshipped the god of completion! A yearning for mastery; fear of falling short.

Going through my back pages, I'm startled, so far down this road, to find myself one of the readers I must have had in mind. Am struck by the ardor, repetitions, resolve. By the author's urge to move freely, learn what could be done without. No surprise, I'm also daunted by the worlds evoked. Consider a nineteenth-century photograph, a nude, young woman. Still beautiful, but...long gone. What to think of it all? I've argued that Geoffrey Fricker's photographs of dinosaur fossil assemblages—"death beds," they're called—are an effort to reconcile himself to Loss through Beauty. To compose himself, you might say. So: shape I bent myself into, song the singer became. "It's myself I remake," Yeats wrote.

Selecting: choices; rue. What's *not* here. My initial coming to terms with the ecstatic, perilous sixties, nonfiction published before 1975. In it, I learned revision, compression, how fictive nonfiction can be, came to hunger for truer lying. As for excerpting *Curves of Pursuit* (1984), a novel that both builds on and anticipates my shorter prose, contemplating such transformation induced vertigo. Nor have I included the past decade's nonfiction meditations on warm ocean, the tropics, death. (Pacific vast: not just play and light but *gravitas* in this water art.) I've also refrained from drawing on recent epigrammatic "stories," *very* terse explorations of the self, deceived; brevity driven to the margin of silence. (Who knows when the impulse to write will attenuate? Whether or not I'll look toward the hills and see "a beautiful crescent cupping and illuminating the globe of the moon, fist of Jupiter pulsing just above." See, and want—oh, need—to say so.)

What can be found here are fictions from 1974 to 1993 (author turning thirty, nearing fifty). To select is perforce to recontextualize: *Who Wrote the Book of Love?* (1977), *Hazards to the Human Heart* (1980), and *Learning to Love It* (1993) were envisioned as *books*, each achieved in a several-year tarantella. But the stories, sometimes untitled, were always meant to stand on their own, had their separate destinies. (Even Nefertiti was disinterred.) And though I did not include pieces from *Compared to What?* (1988), my third-person reflections on writing & the writer's life, some of its empowering tension between fiction and nonfiction—games of projected self as character, for instance—can be seen in the novella closing this volume.

The more one travels, Calvino's Marco Polo explains to Kublai Khan, the more he understands places left behind. Having resisted the enticements of the impulse to rewrite (authors: hostage to published work), what recurrences and obsessions do I see in these tales, fables, sagas? The apparently imperative leave-taking of Boston, childhood. All it required to settle, feel settled in, California and beyond. Men and women anxiously in and out of love; the implacable dislocations of "breaking up." My mother; mother tongue. The sometimes frightening disjunction between intended, actual. A yearning to name things, palpable pleasure in the crafting. An ever-more-explicit interest in narrative. In what the writer's metier allows, costs. "You do not know what life you live, or what you do, or who you are," Dionysius says in *The Bacchae*. I wanted to know, thought others should too.

So what's to come? The last few years, I've informed friends I felt the book then being published might be my last. "You've told me that three times," Terry said a few months ago. Ah, well: hooked. Kafka got *that* right, too: with or without audience, the hunger artist performs. Same here, despite the anomalies of writing—that it has little to do with being a better person, for instance. Author Leo Litwak, aware there are enough fools who are not artists, cheerfully reminds me my water books haven't saved anyone from drowning. Even if it's not good for the soul, then, what else might the writer-in-progress ask of prose? More of the epigrammatic. Essays on gossip, truth commissions—story's capacity to injure, reveal, redeem. A "sex and death" novel. Retelling the true legend of nineteenth-century Native Hawaiian "outlaws" Pi'ilani and Ko'olau. Further ocean collaboration with master photographer Wayne Levin. Alchemy: water and sky into syllables. Apologies, before it's too late, to those with whom I should have been more kind, more true, more...coherent.

"I have written a wicked book," Melville wrote to Hawthorne

about *Moby Dick*, "and feel spotless as the lamb." Most writers recognize that defiance—the mania of artistic effort and, after recklessly going one's own way, having to *submit*. But writers may also recognize something familiar in Robert Pinsky's reading of my *Compared to What?* as "the autobiography of one who has been saved from himself—though this is never quite said—by his craft..." If I have been saved, surely it's only at long last.

A Lover's Question. Song from my teen years performed by Clyde McPhatter. Summoning up another time and place, as well as the interrogatives haunting these stories. *"Really real?"* Well, yes, we'd all "like to know."

Thomas Farber
Berkeley, California, 2000

Acknowledgements

I'm indebted for guidance in culling from earlier work to Chester Aaron, Gavan Daws, Daniel Duane, Ella Ellis, Marion Faber, Helen Lang, Jeremy Larner, Laura Glen Louis, Leo Litwak, Joseph Matthews, Stephen Mitchell, Ken Pallack, and Anna Xiao Dong Sun. Special thanks to the journal *Manoa*, in which "Public Anatomy" first appeared. My gratitude also to Donald S. Ellis, without whom this volume would have been neither dreamed nor realized.

Who Wrote the Book of Love?

STORIES

Down at the Bay early that morning, southwest wind strong in his face, he passed a long hour watching the boats beat out toward the Gate. Cold and cleansed, he was on his way to work, moving slowly with the weekday traffic, when he spotted Ellen walking out of a market. Pulling up to the curb, he honked to get her attention, and she came over to the car. He hadn't seen her for more than a year, and had never really known her well. She and a friend of his had tried living together but separated after several months.

As she sat in the car, she did most of the talking, speaking intensely about her new career. "I like being a nurse," she told him. "I've always wanted to help people. But I've found, as I could have predicted, that most of their pain is beyond care. There are things I can do, of course, and I'm glad to know what I've learned, but the evidence of my senses only confirms what I've always believed: people suffer. Pleasure turns out just to be a brief deviation from the way things really are."

He felt tempted to laugh at her tragic view. There they were, in fine health, sun shining, wind strong enough to wash away all sorrows. It seemed an unnecessary act of will to insist there could be anything not consonant with the day itself. But he didn't laugh. Something in her tone, past the words themselves, summoned up despair, heartbreak, loneliness, loss. She was, he conceded to himself, speaking of what was also real.

As she talked, her incredibly thin and long lips occasionally curled into a tight smile, especially when she confirmed yet another bleak conclusion. "You know, people take years to die. After a while no one comes to visit. They can't do anything themselves. They can't even find the strength to give up." She looked at him hard, daring him to refute her point.

Her pessimism reminded him of the fifties, when it had been so much the fashion to identify with madness and isolation. But as she spoke, her enormous blue eyes taking him in, unblinking, he had no desire to mock. She was too beautiful.

"I have to get back to the hospital now," she said, checking her watch. "I'm in the phone book. Call me sometime. We all need people." She smiled, gathered her packages, and was gone.

Driving to his office, he grinned to himself at her seriousness, and wondered what she'd be like—with him—if she weren't bound to such severe truths. But there really was no point thinking about it. She regarded happiness as merely illusory, after all; any pleasures they shared would only make her uneasy. He wouldn't be able to win for losing. Even worse, however much she gainsaid her nursing career, her affection was clearly reserved for those most in need. Not ill, not broken, without enemies, needing no more than someone to love, he wouldn't have a chance with her. Again grinning to himself, he wondered if anyone had ever told her that a man can die of a broken heart.

Approaching his office, he dismissed the notion of asking her out. Finding the right person was hard enough without trying to argue someone into having a good time. Turning up the radio, he sang along. The lyrics had it right. Couldn't be with the one you love? Well, then, "love the one you're with…"

When he returned to his apartment that evening, it was nearly nightfall. Just as he entered, picking up the cat, turning on the lights, the phone rang. It was his brother calling long distance. "Listen," his brother said. "I have very bad news. Daddy is dead."

Hours later these were the words still in his ears, but long since he was saying them to himself, crying. After a while, walking from room to room still saying the words, he began to prepare to head home in the morning. He made a plane reservation, arranged to have his neighbors care for the cat, and spoke briefly to close friends to tell them what had happened. When they offered to come by, he asked them not to. He said he didn't know just how long he'd be gone.

Alone in the apartment, packed and ready to go, dazed, he wondered what to do until morning. Pacing, unable to settle, he looked up Ellen's number and dialed. When she answered he apologized for calling so late and then, finding no better words, said:

"My dad just died."

"Why don't you come over?" she replied.

Her apartment was small, spartan, and not very clean. It wasn't what he needed, he thought, as he walked in. And it was just too foreign, anyway. Of course she had no idea who his father had been, what their family was like, where he came from. He had made a mistake in calling, a mistake in coming over. This was no time for strangers.

She returned from the kitchen with a glass and a decanter of wine. "Drink," she said. He drank. And kept drinking.

"My dad's dead," he said after a while. "I don't usually drink much, and then not wine." He drank some more. "Do you think it's wrong to be getting drunk when your dad has died?" he asked her. She kept filling the glass.

"I have to be at the airport at nine," he said, absently, when the decanter was half empty.

"I'll set the alarm," she replied.

When the wine was finished, she guided him to the bed and helped him undress. Then she undressed and joined him under the covers.

"My dad died," he was saying. "Now my dad is dead."

She smiled a long, thin smile and took him in her arms. As they came close to each other he tried, through the alcohol, to ask himself if this was right. His dad had died, and here he was going to make love. Closing his eyes, he could see his father at the kitchen table, exhausted after a long day's work, soon losing the drift of the family's mealtime chatter, clenching and unclenching his fingers, staring at them as if still amazed that they could have lost their strength.

But then, coming back from so far away, he was in her, and could see her eyes staring up at him, enormous, blue, unblinking.

(1977)

Within days of their first meeting both felt they were playing for enormous stakes. The very pleasure they found in each other created anxiety: Was it "real"? Could it be sustained? Was there good faith? Relationships in flux all around them, the motives of others always mysterious, each imagined countless possible impediments. He took a first step, canceling a long-planned extended vacation. She was very glad he wasn't going, but didn't know just what had changed his mind. He didn't explain, and she decided it was too forward to ask. A week later, feeling overwhelmed, she went away for several days. He was devastated. There was no way for him to know how much she missed him. Or, rather, she told him so on her return, but he wasn't sure her words meant all he hoped they did.

Continuing to see each other, feeling elated but utterly exposed, they tried with questions to paint in the unknown terrain, as if the answers might somehow lessen the risk.

"Why did you quit school?"
"Do you like living alone?"
"Have you been in love many times?"
"Why did you two separate?"

And, late at night, when pleasure only heightened the understanding of how costly loss would be: "Who *are* you?"

One afternoon they went up to the park on the rim of the hills. Putting down their packs, they began what proved to be a long game of hide-and-seek, the chase and evasion increasingly intense as minutes passed. Successfully concealing herself behind a boulder, she waited till he passed and then shadowed him as he searched, barely muffling her laughter. But then she lost sight of him. He had sensed her presence, and, doubling back around behind her, suddenly came running, whooping as he closed the distance. Cornered, she picked up a branch. When he charged and wrestled her down, she fought back, flailing her legs, trying to bite his hands as he strained to pin her shoulders. Finally, exhausted, she bared her gums and hissed.

He rolled away. "I give up," he said, laughing. "No more, please, no more."

"Time out," she said. After all, it was only a game. Still, lying on their backs, they kept their distance from each other for a while.

Later, stoned, watching the sun sink in the sky, they spotted some hikers far below.

"Wouldn't it be fine to have some chocolate?" she said. "I bet those people have some."

"One of us should go find out," he replied.

"But which one?"

"Let's throw fingers to see," he said.

Because she didn't know what throwing fingers was, he explained that one of them would take "odds," the other "evens." They'd then count "Once, twice, three, *shoot*," each throwing one or two fingers on the word "shoot." The total number of fingers would be odd or even; one of them would win.

"But no flinching," he added.

"What's flinching?"

"Hesitating to see what your opponent does before committing yourself."

"Cheating?"

"That's it," he replied.

Each studying the other's face, second- and then third-guessing each other, finally they made their choices. She grimaced when she read the count.

"Head on down," he said, laughing.

She thought it over for a moment, and then said: "This is ridiculous. They won't have any chocolate anyway. And besides, they're almost gone. It's too far."

"None of that matters," he replied. "You lost. You have to go."

"I don't *have* to do anything," she said, watching the hikers disappear from view.

He was angry, but kept himself in check. They had made a bargain, he felt, and she was violating it. For the moment the game seemed a metaphor of all exchange between them. Without trust what was there? Further, he resented the way she had escalated the argument, implying that he was forcing her to go for the chocolate. Though he acknowledged to himself that he might have chosen his words more carefully, still he felt she was being capricious.

"You welshed," he finally said.

"What's welshing?"

"Backing out of a bet when you lose."

"It's your game, not mine," she replied.

They sat silent as the sun dropped behind the mountains on the far side of the Bay. "Time for us to go," he said curtly. She gave him a long look and then headed down toward the car.

In the months that followed they went abroad. Given the inevitable strains of travel, each worked to be as fair as possible to the other. Nor was this onerous, both repeatedly amazed at how quickly bad feeling passed, how their bond seemed of itself to be renewed each morning.

It was perhaps not strange that throwing fingers became part of their relationship. Instead of arguing about who would wash the dishes or fetch the laundry, they generally let the game settle the question. Trying to predict the other's strategy, thinking back to the previous time or the time before that, often hysterical with anticipation, they played over and again. Occasionally, hoping for reprieve, the loser would propose two out of three. Though the winner of course had no obligation to continue, there was on the other hand the lure of a more decisive victory. Only rarely did they play three out of five. And always, without question now, both honored the outcome.

After they had been together for more than a year, they crossed some invisible line of trust. Due to more than familiarity, the trust was warranted because each avoided compromising the other, offering apologies before conflicts went too far, for instance, or not making disagreements public. Though both were strong-willed, they collaborated on not being unreasonable.

One night they lay in bed together, both tired.

"Do you want to make love?" she asked him.

"I don't know," he said, "I'm pretty wiped. But maybe."

"Let's throw fingers," she said. They did, and he lost. Lying beside her, he didn't immediately move. Since an impartial mediator would surely have granted him a moment or two, this wasn't yet a violation of the rules of the game. But several minutes passed and still he lay on his back. Raising herself on her elbow, she looked down into his eyes. He returned her look. Clearly the stares contained an element of challenge, but she had no wish to force a confrontation. She lay down again. Both looked up at the ceiling.

"Well," she finally said. "Are you going to just lie there?"

She was being more than fair, he admitted to himself. She could have said something sharper, or remained silent, retaining the threat of all she might say. Certainly she was going out of her way to be conciliatory. She was making it easy for him, but he was surprised to find that, still, he wasn't moving. Though this was just the kind of minor betrayal he believed undercut the possibility of larger trust, he found himself on the verge of playing it out. Perhaps he'd provoke her to leave the bed. Then in the morning he'd come up with some lame explanation, or stomp out of the house, or insist hotly that it wasn't important. In any of these ways furthering his breach of faith.

Thinking all this, he had a moment of panic. Could it happen on even less than a whim? Could it be so almost inadvertent?

Throwing off the covers, he was relieved to find himself sitting up. He was that far, anyway. He took a deep breath, exhaled slowly. Closed his eyes, opened them, surveyed the room. Everything in its place? Ceiling above, floor below, bureau against the wall. Ah, well, he was himself again. He stretched, yawned, looked down at her. And then, reaching to embrace her, a kiss on his lips, he said:

"It's me; I'm here; here I am."

(1977)

They sit in her living room, the day waning. Pauline's an old friend and, in these hard times, a friend indeed. Someone to talk to, someone who'll understand, someone who knows them both. Solace, advice, affirmation, affection without demand, that's what he needs. Help.

Pauline makes herself comfortable in the soft chair, opens a fresh pack of cigarettes, lays several down before her in a neat row on the table. She pours a glass of wine, draws the bowl of crackers closer.

"You know," she says, looking at him across the darkening room, "you two should really have separated years ago."

"Why is that?" he says quickly, skin too thin to check his response, nearly any remark about their relationship promising new hurt, new guilt.

"Well," Pauline replies, drawing on her cigarette, laying it down carefully in the ashtray, "you and Dale really wanted different things."

Really wanted different things. He hears the words and tries to bring them to bear on the time they lived together. Of course they'd finished by wanting different things, but that was when they were separating. The words suggest a handle but don't really deliver any understanding of where and how the separation began. Weighing the phrase, irritated that it offers no saving formula, he is at the same time relieved to discover no new area of remorse.

"Not only that," Pauline goes on, "but Dale was too young for you." *Too young for you*. Is that it? But he was also young when they met; they met as equals. He'd been lucky to find her. Everyone had envied them. And, Jesus Christ, no older women were going around offering themselves to him.

Or were they? A year before he met Dale, he and Pauline spent a few nights together. But that was different; his heart never opened to her. Pauline had seemed to feel the same. Or had she?

The question takes him to dangerous ground and he backs off. He needs to work it through, needs friends. Pauline understands. She's been kind. She knows them both.

"She told me we never really knew each other," he says.

Pauline laughs. "You don't have to worry that one. People are always telling each other that kind of thing when they separate. It sounds much worse than it is."

"That's probably true," he says. "I'm trying not to read what we had between us in terms of the present. And I try not to listen when she does. I think I know her. I'm pretty sure we knew each other. We had something good together." He makes these last three assertions without much conviction, and looks to Pauline, hoping she'll nod.

"Of course," Pauline says, meeting his eyes, "everyone is capable of change."

Capable of change. The words sound fair enough. But capable of this change? Whatever had been between them, even the difficulties he initiated, he'd presumed that they were together. All disagreements—from each to other—had seemed to him to move out from that sure center. *Capable of change* barely hinted at the violence he felt in their separation.

"Anyway," Pauline continues, "the way it looks to me, she'll just play the two of you off, one against the other, as long as she can."

This he can't agree to, but Pauline isn't at fault, she doesn't know all the facts. There's much he hasn't told her. When Dale left him, she said she was sorry but she was following her heart. *Following her heart*. Who could argue with that? Could he tell Pauline he had used every cheap trick in the book to badger Dale into seeing him occasionally, that he had implored her, finally with success, to be unfaithful to her new lover? It was perhaps true that Dale now wouldn't mind having him on a string. But surely she hadn't set up the terms of the game—not by herself anyway.

What Pauline might tell him, what he might learn, then, is limited by how much of the truth he can stand to reveal.

"I wouldn't put it past her," Pauline adds.

And what Pauline can give him is limited also by what he'll allow her to say. He has no use for sharp words against Dale. Still she is primary in his life. These people he now talks to so much, needs so much, who are they? They were and are friends. No more, if no less. But what he had with her was beyond his feeling for all others. Now, in simply talking about her, these others seem to him to move toward occupying her space in his life. Imposing with even the most neutral words on what for him is still hers, between them, committed. He has in no way given her up, though everything his friends say to him presumes that she is gone.

"Did you hear me?" Pauline asks.

But he hasn't heard, he's somewhere else, working to remember a poem he once had to learn in school. Slowly he finds the lines:

> …Love is not love
> Which alters when it alteration finds,
> Or bends with the remover to remove.

(1977)

One day, late in the afternoon, she came up the stairs past the yellow blood roses to the porch where he was sitting in the sun. Down in the yard Al hammered on an engine.

"Hello," she said with a noticeable accent. "My name is Rita. Your sister gave me your address. She said to ask you if I could stay here when I passed through. We have mutual friends in New York City. I'll be here five days on vacation before I fly home to teach in Vienna."

"Sure," he said, "you can stay. There's plenty of room, see for yourself." They went inside the apartment, and he gave her the large back bedroom. Though clean, it was empty except for a dresser, lamp, and mattress on the floor.

"No one in this place but me," he said. "Not too much furniture either. But it's home. I camp up front in the little room by the porch. Right under the plum tree. Make yourself comfortable. Stay as long as you like. You won't bother me."

He made some sandwiches and, while they ate at the kitchen table, she spoke of the many places she had visited around the country. She showed him photos, too, most of the Southwest. He took his guitar out and was still playing when she went to settle down in her room.

An hour later he stopped by her door, knocked, and gave her some towels and a key to the house. Telling her to take anything in the refrigerator if she was hungry, he said he was going out.

When he returned late that evening, he saw her door ajar, the light still on. He sat in the kitchen for a few minutes playing the guitar, then put it away. Checking the front door, he washed up and got into bed.

Just as he was dozing off several minutes later, she appeared at the threshold of his room. Standing there, wearing a nightgown, she said: "Do you mind if I come in?"

"If you like," he replied.

She walked over to his bed and slipped in under the covers.

The next morning he was up early making coffee when she emerged from his room.

"Morning," he said.

"Good morning."

They sat in silence at the kitchen table, until finally she asked: "Where did you go last night?"

"To a party."

"You didn't think to invite me?"

"No."

"Why?"

"I wanted to go alone."

She smiled a weak smile and then, after another silence, asked: "Do women often come to your house like that and sleep with you?"

"I can't say it's a regular thing," he answered.

"Are you glad I came into your room?"

"I enjoyed making love with you."

"Do you like me?"

"I don't know you yet," he said.

Later that day they drove up into the dry autumn hills where they could see the sweep of the Bay below. Down at the harbor later, they walked out to the end of the long pier, watched the shark fishermen, got cold, and returned to the apartment. That night they made love again.

Life in the apartment the next three days was quiet. Each morning after coffee he sat in the kitchen playing the guitar. The phone rang, friends dropped by, he went out on errands. Late each afternoon he showed her other parts of the town, quietly describing the history, animal life, climate, and terrain. Each evening they watched the sun set behind the mountains at the far side of the Bay. And then each night, soon after dinner, she came into his room.

In the kitchen the morning she was to go she said: "You know, I think I'm in love with you." He said nothing in reply. "But, sadly," she then continued, "I have to go. School begins in a week." Still he was silent. She looked over at the clock. "I think we should leave now," she said. As they went down the stairs she took one of the yellow blood roses.

At the airport they had coffee in silence. When they reached the final check-in area she stood holding the rose, clearly hoping he would respond to what she had said. He looked at her carefully, trying to imagine how far away she would soon be, from how far away she had come. Wondering what she had to believe was between them. For him she had simply come out of thin air up the stairs, Al hammering on the engine below. She had stayed five days; they had shared some pleasures. And now, into thin air once more, she was leaving.

But seeing her standing there holding the rose, he decided to try. "Turn around," he said. She did. Then he whispered in her ear: "When you turn around again, I'll be gone." And he was.

(1977)

*W*hen she moved out, she packed up not only what she had brought to the apartment when they first decided to live together but also what she had acquired since. Quilts, rugs, pans, clothes, lamps, wicker baskets, paints, sheets, the stereo. Her things.

She also took those artifacts that, though "theirs," both tacitly agreed were more hers than his. Some bird nests, an old lute, most of the records. There was no quarrel over her choices. Finally out of words, he simply watched her, dizzied by the efficiency and apparent finality of her departure. She seemed in a very great hurry to begin her new life.

Alone in the apartment when she was gone, measuring what remained, his eye caught a hook on the wall. A woodcut had hung there, no larger than four by six inches, black and white. A bare tree with gnarled roots on a cliff just over the ocean; clouds edging past a moon setting into a too-close horizon; oversized stars sweeping through the branches down to the sea.

The picture had been a gift. Four years before, in Athens, they had been dinner guests at the family home of one of his old college friends. That night they learned that his friend's father, a surveyor, was also an artist. Completely unschooled, he had been painting for years. Blanketing the walls was an extraordinary sequence of watercolors of the planets, brilliant vistas of their surfaces as the painter imagined them, naïve and exuberant.

She had laughed with pleasure at the watercolors, repeatedly praising them. Later that evening his friend's father had given them the woodcut. At home they mounted it on the hook on the wall.

If, less taken than she with the visual arts, he had not fully shared her immediate delight with the paintings, if her enthusiasm was the probable proximate cause of the gift, the woodcut had nonetheless been given to *them*. Seeing it on the wall each day, he had come to treasure it and, through it, his memory of that evening.

As he thought about the woodcut, he was struck with the thought that it was not only these objects she had taken that were gone. Rather, because she was the only other witness to their time together, because without her there was so much he would not remember, that would have no further resonance, her departure threatened to cut him off from what they had lived between them.

This thought then crystallized in his mind, that she was the key to the door of his recollection of their shared past. Without her it was lost. And apart from the issue of their separation, he didn't want to lose those years, that life.

Because she had no wish to see him in the months that followed, he found himself looking for her on the street, at the market, in bookstores, at films. Occasionally bumping into her, reaffirming her sheer physical reality, he was able to renew his hold on the life they had shared. More often than not, however, he had to settle for glimpses of her as she drove by in her car.

The next year he lost track of her completely. Unable to find any listing for her in the phone book, desolate, he thought perhaps she had left town. It now often seemed to him that what they had experienced between them simply had never been. Whole sections—vital sections—of his life were disappearing.

Then one day, coming home from work, he saw her getting out from behind the wheel of a different car. He grinned with pleasure.

Contact had been reestablished. Once more he felt he had access to his memory. She was still real. He could touch the fabric of what they had shared.

Soon after, things improved even more. Apparently she had moved into his neighborhood, for he saw the car parked nearby each day. Try as he would, however, he couldn't match her schedule. Despite daily passes up and down the street, he never saw her.

As time passed he continued to look for her, but the door on what they had lived between them was shutting tight. He could now remember only the shadows of their shared past, as though it had been inhabited by others, if at all.

It was in this way, still more time passing, that when he tried to picture her, and so what they had experienced together, he could summon up no more than an image of the car.

(1977)

*T*his was a case of the child saving the parent. Several years before, the son not yet even a twinkle in his father's eye, the revolution had clearly been imminent, palpable if nonetheless just out of reach. Regulars on the block lived for, banked on, cataclysmic transformation. And then, just like that, almost faster than it had appeared, the wave of the apocalypse receded, leaving them high and dry. Like other regulars, Larry continued to stop by the cafés to take in the changes, he still hung out on the block to see what the street people were into, but it was over. Not only could the remaining fragments not re-create the whole, but, memory all too fallible, it was impossible to hold on to the feeling of collective power that had inspired them. So it was that the junkies, whose stylized suicide had only recently seemed both needlessly pessimistic and inexcusably private, now warranted another look. At least their days had an accessible pattern. They had a handle, if only the handle on death's door.

Nowhere to go, Larry took to living in his car, though like everything else that looked more or less the same as before, this was now no freedom. He felt more like a wino than a revolutionary, slept in vacant lots, walked the streets bouncing a rubber ball. He applied for Aid to the Totally Disabled, not as a shuck for easy money but because he was desperate. What was the job market for former revolutionaries? If he once wondered what would happen when the

Thermidorian reaction set in—governments seldom cherish anarchists, he'd often joked—at least then his life would have had a context, recognition, if only negative. But now, alone, he could barely connect his present to any past, least of all a heroic one. Nothing to do, he pored over the daily paper, averting his eyes from stories about suicides off the Golden Gate Bridge.

Then he met Sarah. While she herself felt shaky, having only recently won independence from her husband and his academic routine, she at least had the house from the divorce settlement. Larry soon moved in, and though he was often despondent, she valued him for being all her husband was not. Beyond the system, an outlaw, this even as he steadily berated himself for having wasted his life. If only he hadn't quit accounting school, he kept saying.

At his urging they sold the house and moved to the country. A new life, though the past followed them in the form of Sarah's ex-husband. Crazed since the day she met him, he plastered the rural community with flyers accusing Larry of woman-stealing. In spite of him, however, things quickly settled into place. Soon, at Larry's request, Sarah stopped using contraceptives. And then Glen was born.

Larry was elated. He wanted not only Sarah and Glen but all they implied. A wife and child to build his life around, to warrant and necessitate an entire range of commitments. He felt strange to have to be so intentional about what most people simply did, he knew there must be some middle ground, but for the moment it eluded him. He needed structure badly, could barely imagine how he'd once felt secure enough to mock all he now sought. He could occasionally remember the confidence of the recent past, but found no way to bring it to bear on the present.

Breadwinner of his family—and grateful to have the role—he attended night school at a local junior college and passed the real estate exam. Former compatriots on the block couldn't believe it, accused him of selling out. What could be more capitalist than a middleman in property exchanges? Could Larry have forgotten that "the land belongs to no one"? No, he hadn't forgotten, but he had to make a living. Had to support his wife and child. Yearned to support them lest he disintegrate completely. Jobs were scarce for the "unskilled." Real estate was at least open to anyone willing to work on commission. And while political rhetoric had once come easily to his lips, he'd never been an ideologue. The Vietnam War, the class war, racism, these had been real to him primarily as they referred back to the camaraderie of people working together, dreaming together, to make social change. If he had lacked the clarity and dedication of others in the vanguard, he was, on the other hand, not so different from "the people."

Working long hours, he began to earn good money. Throwing in his commission toward the down payment, he bought a home. Then, taking a second mortgage, he purchased a beach house, renting it out to build equity. He drove clients around in a new car, marveling at how easy it was to get credit. "All you have to do is play the game," he kept saying in wonder. When things were tough—commissions sometimes came few and far between; he pushed himself too hard; and clients often assumed he was their adversary—he'd think of going back on Aid to the Totally Disabled. But Sarah and Glen needed him. He kept at it. He dreamed of accumulating property, giving Glen a Frank Lloyd Wright for his twenty-first birthday. Maybe two Frank Lloyd Wrights.

Despite the pressures of work, he loved spending time with his son, watching him by degrees interact with and master the world around him. "Glen keeps me sane," he often said, laughing, changing a dirty diaper. And Glen kept growing, by age two strong and hot-tempered. Willful little fucker! Denied something, he'd give one angry look of warning, and, no concession forthcoming, would pee on the floor to get even. But nothing could dismay Larry: Glen was his reason for living.

In this period Sarah decided to move out and live by herself. Not that she loved him less, she told Larry, but she just had to give it a try or she'd always feel too dependent on him. There was little argument. Though an integral component of the life Larry had chosen so intentionally was being removed, Sarah was clearly speaking of a real need. How could he fight it? They found her an apartment, saw each other often and amicably, and shared care of the child.

Spending long hours with Glen, always confirmed and comforted by his sheer existence, Larry was repeatedly impressed by his son's straightforward—and undeniable—wants. Stoned, he'd watch Glen run naked around the living room, small penis bobbing up and down. No doubt about it, he often thought, Glen was a miniature adult. "Come here, little man," he'd call, laughing. Little man. And so it went, night after night, month after month, watching, learning, until Larry, whose understanding had once been couched in the language of revolution, now viewed life as far more elemental. Shit, piss, hunger, love, this is what he saw.

Time passing, he gave more and more consideration to these basic urges, which, he was sure, underpinned all social action. Selling a home, sneaking hits off a joint, he'd stand back and observe a couple as they argued about whether to take it, viewing them not as husband and wife but as two overgrown children. He could appreciate their needs, wasn't putting them down, but he just couldn't see them as they saw themselves. As for himself, he had ever less desire to clothe his own hungers in finery. "I'm just a little doggie," he'd say, laughing. "Any woman who loves me has to understand that. Watching me pee on some tree, sniffing someone's tail. Seeing it's no big deal. Just ol' Larry doin' his thing."

Spending time at a singles bar, initially hoping to replace Sarah, in time he came to enjoy just finding someone for the night. No pretenses, no promises. He wasn't averse to having things work out with Sarah, or anyone else for that matter, but it didn't have to happen. Or, if it did, he didn't have to confuse commitment with his simple needs. "Pussy!" he'd shout, walking around the house half naked. "Pussy tonight!"

As Glen continued to grow, the rural community boomed and began to suffer certain urban ailments. A pistol-carrying prowler terrorized the town with a series of rape/burglaries. Appointed block captain for the citizens patrol, Larry walked around at night with a flashlight and police whistle, on the lookout for a black man wearing a yellow cap.

Not surprisingly, while on patrol he came to know his neighbors better. Now they had good reason to talk to him; seeing him as their defender, they became more open. It was in this way that he found he didn't have to go to the singles bar to meet someone to spend the night with. Savoring the irony, he had to laugh. It made sense to him, son Glen his guru, that under any sky he would always find the earth.

(1977)

I was back in town for the summer wedding of a good friend. Relatives from both families stood under the elm, smiling at their in-laws-to-be, waiting for the music to begin.

Clearly pleased with the occasion, they were nonetheless surprised to find themselves under the canopy of the tree. Still, if having the ceremony outdoors was the greatest shock they were to receive from the young people—this in a time of couples living together without benefit of clergy—then so be it. It was, after all, a wedding.

How people point to the future, how they turn from the past! Surely the adults gathered there knew that the bride's parents had woven between them a web of intricate misery. That her mother, suddenly stricken with the new symptoms of a long-suffered neurosis, had asked the couple to postpone the wedding until she was healed. That, no delay forthcoming—her daughter was reaching for a star—the symptoms miraculously disappeared in time for the mother, too, to be present under the elm.

And surely the adults standing there knew the story of the groom's parents, how his mother moved to a remote town to share the life of her relentlessly pragmatic husband. How after ten years and two sons in that dreamless union she had taken her life.

But this day the past was to defer to the future. Beams of light worked down through thick leaves to the friends and relatives waiting below. Then, before any wicked witch could curse the match, guitar and flute struck up Vivaldi, and they were walking toward us across the green. Simple white brocade for her, a peasant shirt for him. Hand in hand.

The ceremony was brief, another blessing. When the glass broke under his shoe, her eyes had a wild look of triumph.

I was moved. Perhaps these traditional forms could carry them through the perils of the here and now. Perhaps the love they promised would endure. I wanted to believe that the clarity of their public statement would sustain them.

The marriage made, we all began to move back across the green for refreshments. I fell into step beside the groom's father. Since his wife's suicide nearly twenty years before, he had remained a bachelor. A successful small businessman, phenomenally uninterested in anything beyond his immediate circle, he played golf and bridge, had occasional girlfriends, and lived a life of easy routine.

"Well," he said to me, "you're his friend, what did you think?"

"A time for celebration, C.G.," I responded. "They looked wonderful."

"And what about yourself? A fella your age ought to be thinking about doing the same as my boy."

"But no one's asked me yet, C.G.," I replied, grinning.

"You'd best not wait for that," he said without a smile. "You're not getting any younger."

In his blunt way, unfortunately, C.G. had given voice to Truth. I wasn't getting any younger, and just then I was feeling my age. And of course the wedding left me sentimental for the fresh start I wasn't making, for the words of promise that weren't on my lips. It wouldn't take much of this kind of talk to make me blue.

"Someone your age ought to settle down, get married, raise a family," C.G. went on. "This is what a man needs."

"But why is that, C.G.?" I asked. "You seem to be doing pretty well on your own."

By now we had arrived at the bar and were both reaching for our drinks.

"I am doing pretty well," he said, "but that's different. Very different. You see, I've been through it. I know. I've got my boys. You need family, yes, you need family. Someone to bury you."

(1977)

*C*ompetitive, acerbic, and overweight, earning an almost-six-figure salary diminished somewhat by alimony payments to his first wife, he climbs heavily out of his BMW after a long day at the office. Coming inside the house, calling "Anybody home?" he walks back to the bedroom and lies down to watch Monday Night Football. Her husband.

Though now, after two years of marriage, much of what he is and does repels her, his second wife can make no claim that he misrepresented himself to her. That is to say, while courting her he never performed stoned late-night Charlie Chaplin routines, intimating some secret self only she could release. And, no Othello, he never wooed her with the hardships he had endured. Truth be told, he did little more than act naturally to win her, since she had been prepared to love him—or someone like him—well before they met. Like us all, she respected power, and was to some degree influenced by the opinions of those around her. Working in state government just after college, she could hardly remain unaware of the admiration he inspired in the bureaucratic world. In no time at all she saw him as others did.

Though no Adonis, he was decisive, confident of his acumen, and could defend even questionable decisions with real conviction. Nor in his meteoric rise as a technocrat did it discomfit him to dominate men of less power, intelligence, or certitude. Elected officials particularly were impressed by the brisk way he could list "the options."

When he met his second wife, she was committed to social change but pragmatic enough to try working within the system, bright, quick with words, and very good-looking. It would perhaps be unfair to suggest that he wanted her as a showpiece, but he seemed not to perceive that those qualities in her it gave him status to possess might also contain an essence capable of repudiating his own. Or perhaps he intuited that, already in politics, she'd be willing to let appearances stand for reality so long as others were impressed. Whichever, he bought the BMW to show her that he too was a free spirit, and proposed. Several important people attended their wedding.

Early in the marriage she had misgivings about certain things her husband did, small things to be sure, probably not even worth thinking about. His behavior at parties, for instance. There was something disconcerting about the way he'd stand clapping his hands to the beat while she did the latest step with some black man wearing platform shoes and a shirt split down to the navel. She admired her husband for not trying to be hip, was always flattered when he told her she was the best dancer on the floor. Yet particularly since he never seemed in the least bit jealous of her partners, she occasionally had the unsettling feeling that he found it too easy to say he couldn't dance, as if suggesting that such matters—the physical? the sexual?—were secondary to the real stuff of his life. But then, dancing by him, seeing his rumpled slacks and scuffed shoes, she'd again be charmed by his unfashionableness. He was what he was.

She was more troubled by the amount of traveling he did. He was always flying off to some conference for a day, often crossing the country and returning the same night. At first this had some allure: place names beckoned and the miles looked like freedom. But then they went abroad to three countries in five days. Though she met several cabinet-level ministers and their wives, she came home unconvinced that it made any sense. They had been exhausted from jet lag, the conferences on higher education were held in airport hotels, and this was just the moment when everyone was talking at cocktail parties about the fuel crisis and how to live more ecologically. Worst of all, her husband had put her on his payroll to write a memo on the meeting, but, going through her pages of notes, she could find little of value to report.

Soon after this trip she stopped working as a legislative aide, returning to painting and her old friends, though most of what entertaining she and her husband did together was for his colleagues. Back at a craft and spending time with people who lived more quietly, she was glad to be out of politics. If already she wished her husband had a different kind of work, she felt only more affection for him thinking of the price he paid. All those backbiting politicians and administrators, all that travel. Often he'd come home exhausted and fall asleep within minutes. But she loved him all the more; she rued the toll his job was taking.

Things began to change when they made a long-deferred trip to the mountains to visit some of her friends who were eking out a living as farmers. There her husband's verbal skill suddenly seemed only aggressive, and she found herself both admiring what her friends had created and wanting to explain or, even, apologize for her husband. Her embarrassment only increased when they went to a remote pond to swim. Compared to her friends, her husband was woefully out of shape, and, never having swum nude before, he couldn't stop joking. The more he talked the less her friends talked, until by the end of the weekend her friends were almost silent. When they finally headed back to the city in the BMW—which now looked opulent compared to her friends' battered Volkswagen—she sat in angry silence.

At the least her vanity was hurt. Though in the political world few men were more impressive than her husband, measured by the standards of those living simple physical lives he was hopelessly inadequate, and, worse, unable to grant such lives space to exist around him. He had been a lout.

Much as she had been taken with the rural calm, however, she was glad to be heading home. In the city, after all, important things were getting done, and they were at the center of it all. Yet for the first time she wished her husband less competitive, less rigid, less bureaucratized. Less himself. It did not soothe her when, sensing her unspoken criticisms, he began to mock her country friends.

As if to compensate for her thoughts, which she considered disloyal, she began almost without knowing it to defer to his judgment. Returned a sofa he didn't like. Phoned friends and canceled a dinner when he didn't want them to come over. Gave way whenever it seemed important to him to prevail. Much as all this pleased her husband, in terms of restoring her original feeling for him it was not an entirely effective strategy: the more she yielded the more peremptory he became. Or he would patronize her, explaining a political struggle, for example, as if she couldn't possibly understand.

As more time passed he came under enormous stress from work, and the attention he received—magazine articles, several prizes, an honorary degree—only took more time, more travel. They saw each other little, made love seldom. Speaking with her parents or friends, she occasionally hinted that she was displeased with the marriage, but carefully avoided blaming her husband, speaking rather of the pressures of his job, saying that a vacation would set things right.

In this period she began to resent driving him to and from the airport, not simply because he seemed to take her services for granted ("You're not doing anything, are you?" was how he'd put it), but because she'd come to abhor both the drive and the airport itself. All those cars on the freeway, going where? And all those planes hurtling so many miles at crazy speeds. Though he told her she was acting like a child, she was adamant in refusing to accompany him on any more of his work trips. She was beginning to want to function more simply, the road and the airport now epitomizing the aspect of urban life she wanted to distance herself from—and, increasingly, the aspect of her husband she wanted to distance herself from.

One night they were entertaining a group of foreign monetary experts. Just back from a long flight, totally exhausted, her husband kept addressing one official by his predecessor's name. Far down the table, increasingly exasperated, she repeatedly tried to get her husband's attention, but, engrossed as usual in what he was saying, he never noticed. She thought she'd explode.

Still angry the next morning, when a friend called she told her what had happened, not only giving the specifics but making no effort to excuse or soften her husband's error. When she hung up, she realized that it was the first time she had spoken against her husband to anyone. It didn't make her feel bad. Taking stock of her anger, she decided that most of all she was enraged at herself. She had made a terrible error. He had always been a boor.

That afternoon the doorbell rings. Deliveryman with a package. Young, hip, laughing, eager to talk. No, he knows nothing about politics. Likes to ski and—smoke dope. How her husband would sneer. A hippie! As she continues to talk with the deliveryman, she asks him if he'd like to share a joint back in the garden. Yes he would, he really would.

This is the night, then, that her husband comes home tired after another day of knocking heads at the office. Under the trees in the far corner of the garden she hears him pull into the driveway, slam the door of the BMW, enter the house, call "Anybody home?," and walk heavily back to the bedroom. "To watch Monday Night Football," she says to the deliveryman, pulling him closer.

(1977)

"Till death do you part." That's the way she often thought it would be, long after the divorce, every time her former husband showed up for his weekly visit with the children. She felt she'd never be rid of him, at least not for the eternity until the kids were grown up.

Typically he came early, came late, or canceled his plans at the last minute, leaving her to disappoint the children. Or he'd arrive with his latest lover, usually someone very young, making her feel old and dowdy as she got the kids ready to go. He loved to buy them expensive toys to make her look cheap, but then he'd be weeks late with the child support money, complaining he was broke, forcing her to call him again and again, then telling her to stop badgering him. When it suited him, finally giving the money as though she had no right to it, as though, suddenly, they were *her* children. "You're bleeding me to death," he liked to say. At long last putting the folded bills into one of the kids' hands ("Go in and give this to your mother") as he dropped them off after some pointlessly lavish spree. She didn't have to hate him to get clear of what they had created between them, but he made it hard not to.

Even so, she'd remind herself, he was still the children's father. Over and again she bit her tongue when they were in front of the kids, determined to play fair in their presence. She could still remember how, years before, he stood up to her parents when they first went out, frank about his interest in her, unashamed and unabashed. And brave enough, not long after, to announce to her father that they were engaged. He simply rejected all her father's opinions and threats: "Your daughter is twenty now," he said forcefully, "old enough to make her own decisions." Though it had been his decision, with which she concurred, though she hadn't really believed it could be done. He took her away from home in his sports car—"a dangerous luxury," she could still hear her father calling it—and as they drove off she felt free for the first time in her life. Now, years later, she could still thank him for that at least.

When things soured between them, she took the blame. He'd given up a fine job with Blue Cross to go into the health care business for himself. She should have stopped him, particularly since he kept saying he was doing it for her. After months of tension and fear the company was just holding its own, and seemed unlikely to improve. The whole effort had been pointless. But for too long in the marriage she'd been hard on him—as if, through her, her father still called the tune—just as she'd been too severe with their first child. Perhaps, responding to her expectations, her husband had tried to impress her. A bad idea, in any case: he worked long hours now, earned little money, felt like a failure. Twelve years married, seeing him struggle, she was full of regrets.

When he suggested a trial separation, she was afraid of losing him, but as she started dating—he'd been seeing other women for months, often pressing her to loosen up and take a lover—he went crazy, beating her, threatening to leave the state with the children. Initially intimidated, still feeling guilty, slowly she gained her distance from him.

Down to the morning of the divorce he contrived to procrastinate the hearings, repeatedly failing to appear in court after she had again jeopardized her job by taking another day off, advising her through his attorney that he'd contest custody of the children by documenting her "unfit moral behavior." He scared her with that, and she stopped going out for a while.

But finally they were both in the courtroom. "She called me and said that her husband had just thrown a kettle of boiling water at her," her sister testified calmly, "and she was very upset, crying over the phone." Of course it hadn't happened that way. Would that it had been so simple, some single act pushing them over a precipice clearly marked "Divorce." But this was law, not life; the court required a formula before granting a decree. "Something like boiling water is very good," her lawyer had told her, "if your sister will swear to it."

The lawyers huddled with the judge up at the bench, out of her hearing. "He'll agree to drop the moral behavior issue, in essence making divorce possible today, on two conditions," her lawyer came back to tell her. "First, no alimony."

"I've told him and I've told you all along, I don't want alimony," she said angrily.

"Keep your voice down," her attorney whispered. "That's fine, just fine. The other condition is that he pay only a hundred dollars a month for child support."

"A hundred dollars a month? For four children?"

"I know it's less than he should offer," her lawyer whispered, "but otherwise he insists he'll fight you all the way, and that could take quite a while."

"How long is quite a while?"

"A year, maybe more. You never know."

"All right, all right. Agree to his terms. I just want it to be over."

"You sure? You know what this means?"

"What choice is there?"

She went out into the gray winter day a single woman, and spent the next few hours alone, just walking. Finally, her feet long since cold and wet from the slush, she got into her car, some of her anger gone, still trying to impose order on all that had happened. "It'll take me some time to work out," was the best she could manage.

Her life as a divorcée was incredibly hectic. After she packed the children off to school in the morning, always a photo finish, she worked a full day as a social worker, did the shopping, came home to pay the baby-sitter, prepared dinner, cared for the inevitable daily catastrophes, got the children tucked into bed, and then, even when totally exhausted, went out as often as she could. She was determined to get back into the flow of life, to meet another—and better—man.

She suffered all the normal pratfalls: fell in love with a married teacher who, after endless agonizing, wouldn't leave his wife; dated an attractive high school baseball coach who was, finally, determinedly single; spent several months seeing a doctor who loved her but loathed children. The doctor even proposed, but she never really gave it a thought: she just couldn't imagine how he could be part of their family. In the wake of this relationship she became depressed. What, after all, were the odds on a single woman of thirty-three with four children finding a husband? Jimmy the Greek would just laugh. But for all the pressures and all the mistakes, still she felt herself coming alive again. The world wasn't the orderly place she once thought it was, but she felt better to know she could survive.

One night at a coffeehouse she met a quiet physicist who was also a folk music buff. It was hootenanny time, and he took the stage when his turn came, playing the guitar earnestly but so badly that she had to stifle a laugh. Several nights later he called and asked her out. Soon they were dating regularly.

Though for some time he hardly overwhelmed her, she found him candid and at ease with himself. Far from avoiding the kids, he enjoyed their company, seemed to take it as a given that they were part of her life. He'd had some rough times of his own, including a hard separation from his wife, but seldom wasted much time on self-pity or bitterness. There was a hard-won truthfulness in him that only grew on her. Nor did he bat an eye when her ex-husband came by to make a scene. Without compromising himself, he seemed to take it as a matter of course that people had pasts, possibly unpleasant pasts, yet never measured her except by what they had experienced between them.

What with jobs, commuting, errands, and the children, they had little time alone together, but instead of drifting apart or taking their anger out on each other, they slowly drew closer. Late at night, sharing one of the exotic drinks he liked to mix, they'd get tipsy and laugh at themselves and the world, always concluding with a toast they had discovered one drunken evening.

"To those who see straight lines in a crooked world," he'd say, "not to belittle curves, of course, beggin' your pardon."

"Little curves? Well then, to lovers and other fools," she'd answer as they emptied their glasses.

There were never fewer than a thousand possible grounds for going their separate ways. He got very sick for several months. She was fired from work and worried incessantly about money until, after weeks of anxiety, she found another job. And both former spouses seemed bent on doing all they could—short of collaborating—to make life unpleasant for them. The late-night drinks helped, they savored the quiet after the children were finally in bed, but nothing would have sufficed had not a genuine trust developed between them. She marveled at how seldom, even in the most confused moments, they attacked each other. The word "courtesy," which sounded almost archaic to her ear, kept occurring to her. It wasn't "manners" or "politeness" he was showing her: it was a steady respect she had never before been accorded.

Despite the hurly-burly of their lives, he too was at peace with himself, and together they only grew stronger. It was perhaps this newfound calm after so many storms that explains why they started putting on weight. Of course she was eating too many sweets and he had recently stopped smoking, but it went beyond that. Food was simply one pleasure they didn't have to deny themselves. Eating at a restaurant, beyond the reach of phones and calamities, they could be alone and have someone care for them for a change. They went out as often as they could afford to, buying drinks before dinner, wine with the meal, liqueur after. Time passing, standing in the bathroom together checking the scale, not believing the dial, or just looking at each other, they had to laugh.

They laughed on the day of their wedding, too, having overslept in a preconjugal bed, scrambling madly to get dressed, swerving from side to side through the unplowed snow to get to the church. When they finally arrived, it seemed to her that her whole life was passing before her eyes. Except for her former husband, who wasn't in the room?

There was her father standing off to the side, glowering, still certain his daughter had wasted her life, determined as always to let her know it.

"Let him go to the grave that way if that's how he wants it," she said to her husband-to-be. "I'm not going to shed any more tears."

"Neither am I, then," he answered, pulling her tight. But she did almost cry to see the kids, his and hers, one—if only one—with his arm in a cast, all with white shirts dirty long before the wedding anthem.

Standing in the congregation were their friends, a number of them, of course, their former lovers. Her sister, still calm, was also there, as was her attorney. *Not whispering now*, she thought to herself. The doctor who had once proposed to her was busy taking wedding pictures. And her husband-to-be's ex-wife, in an attempt to establish a better relationship with them, had insisted on doing all the catering for the reception.

So there they were in the old church, now almost man and wife, venerable bearded former ministers looking sternly down at them from their frames on the wall, organ rumbling, guests shifting restlessly in their pews. The lights were dimmed. Holding their candles, the children formed a circle, and then everyone joined in to sing "Amazing Grace":

> I once was lost, but now I'm found,
> Was blind, but now I see.

(1977)

*F*rom the time they were married they did little party-going, nor did they often seek out others for socializing. Tacitly they agreed that after his days at the hospital—he was a biochemist—and hers at the juvenile home—she was a counselor—they had had enough of people. Not that they didn't like both their jobs and their colleagues, but after work they welcomed the quiet of their home and each other's company. Walking through the snow to get the paper and some sweet rolls on winter Sundays, then returning home to savor the warmth, they particularly appreciated how comfortable they were with each other, remembered how very glad they were to have met. The radiator clanked; the days passed slowly.

They'd been married several years when she decided to see a psychiatrist. Far from having to straighten out something in their relationship, she felt that being so secure freed her to explore and make better accommodation with some bitter childhood experiences.

Trusting, as usual, his wife's judgment, her husband encouraged her even though the psychiatrist most highly recommended would be expensive. He knew her upbringing had been tough, and admired his wife for wanting to expose it to light and understanding.

The psychiatrist told her she could see him only if she would commit herself to a two-year program, four meetings a week. Since she worked and the doctor already had a full late-afternoon and evening schedule, she agreed to have her sessions at seven in the morning. Her husband was somewhat startled by the proposed regimen: she'd have to rise very early, make the long drive to the doctor's office, see him, work a full day, and then retire early. In addition, the cost of so many sessions would absorb most of her earnings, setting back for a while their hope of buying a home. In spite of these reservations he gave his approval.

The first few months she was in therapy seemed well worth the investment of time and money. She told her husband she was gaining access to some painful memories and was certain to profit emotionally in the long run. At the same time, he noticed that she was increasingly fatigued. Often unable to force herself to get to sleep early, she still had to rise by five-thirty in order to reach the doctor's office on time. When her husband suggested she cut her job down to part time, she insisted that she then wouldn't have enough money for the doctor, and that if she worked less she'd lose all hope of promotion. Seeing how exhausted she was, her husband for the first time wished she hadn't decided to see the psychiatrist.

A month later she came down with the flu. She missed work for several days and canceled her appointments with the doctor, but then, still not fully recovered, resumed her heavy schedule. Noticing how much weight she had lost, beginning to become very worried about the strain on her, her husband again urged her to cut down in some way, but again she refused. Thinking it over, her husband finally decided to call the psychiatrist.

"Hello, Doctor," he said. "As you know, my wife has been your patient for about six months now."

"Yes," the doctor replied.

"Well, I'm calling to say I'm concerned the combination of work and the early-morning appointments is putting her under too much stress, and I wonder if you have any suggestions."

"I don't know quite what you have in mind," the doctor replied.

"For instance, Doctor, could you meet her at another time of day, since I think having to get up so early is causing her to lose sleep."

"No; impossible. My schedule is quite full already, and I see no way to shift it around."

"Then how about seeing her somewhat less often? Would that make an enormous difference?"

"I'm afraid it would. I don't think I could recommend that."

"But when my wife came to you she had no particular disability, just a desire to work some things through."

"That's quite correct, but something important may well be at stake for her now, and she and I have made a contract to facilitate just that kind of process. Both the frequency of meeting and the guarantee of regularity are what create the possibility of progress."

"That makes good sense to me, Doctor, but the life she's leading now, between working and having her appointments, seems to me to be exacting a price on her that may be greater than whatever strain she was under before therapy began."

"Are you suggesting that your wife shouldn't be seeing me?" the doctor asked sharply.

"Not at all, not at all," her husband replied, startled by the doctor's tone. "I'm simply trying to say that my wife is not looking well, nor has she looked well for several months, and I think the source of her not looking well at this moment seems to be not so much psychic as physical. I'm hoping that you, as her doctor, will take cognizance of this."

"Well," the doctor said more calmly, "if you're really concerned, perhaps I could give her something to help her sleep better at night."

"That seems a rather indirect solution to this human problem," her husband replied. "Surely this is the kind of situation that can be better solved on its own terms, don't you think?"

"I'm afraid I can't be of any help to you in the way you suggest. I happen to believe it is most important for your wife that we continue things as they are. And frankly, if I were you, I'd reexamine your motives for this call."

Her husband was stunned. The conversation had gotten completely out of hand, and he saw no way to set it straight.

"Well, Doctor," he said, "that is most unkind of you. I had thought it all somewhat simpler, more mechanical. But thank you for speaking with me anyway."

When his wife returned home after her next session with the doctor, she was crying mad.

"You called my psychiatrist," she said to her husband accusingly.

"Yes, I did," he replied quietly.

"What did you say to him?"

"I told him I thought you were overextended physically, between working full time and your sessions with him. I was hoping that by explaining what I saw to him he might either change the time you met or else see you a little less often."

"What right did you have to do that?" she said bitterly.

"What right?"

"Yes. What right did you have to call my psychiatrist?"

"Hey, take it easy. I didn't mean to intrude in your life. I'm your husband, remember? I simply don't want to see you so overwhelmed that the cure becomes worse than the disease."

"It's not a disease!" she shouted at him. "I'm not sick."

"For Christ's sake," he said, "I didn't mean it that way. Calm down."

"You had no right!" she shouted again, and stormed back to the bedroom, slamming the door.

Time passing, she continued to look worn, but still she maintained her schedule. Weekends now were less pleasurable for them both; the issue of her seeing the psychiatrist had come between them, and neither could find a way back to the place they had shared before. Perhaps oversensitive because of her exhaustion, or, as likely, because of the intense feelings she was working through with the doctor, she couldn't forgive her husband for intruding into what was for her so private, for not supporting her fully in her choices. For his part, dating the tension in their relationship from the day she first saw the psychiatrist, he feared that soon there would be only hurt and hostility between them.

Hoping that going away might bring them closer together, he fought with his lab director for an extra vacation, and considered himself lucky to be granted one for two weeks in the early summer. Returning home that evening, he told his wife about his plan: they'd go to the ocean.

"It sounds good to me," she said, "but I have to see what the doctor says."

"You do?" he asked.

"Certainly. I have a contract with him."

"Doesn't he take vacations?"

"I assume so. At the end of the summer, I think."

"But I had to fight to get anything. I can't get one then."

"Well, I'll ask him, but I don't know what he'll say. You have to remember that the doctor and I have a contract. He doesn't renege on it, and I can't either."

"But we have a contract too," her husband said, frustrated by this now inevitable presence in their relationship. "Or have you forgotten it, and that it came before your contract with the doctor?"

"That was a cheap thing to say," his wife replied. "That was a very cheap thing to say."

"I'll tell you this!" her husband shouted. "If that's your response, then we might as well plan on divorce. Talk *that* over with your doctor."

Late at night, unable to sleep, watching his wife toss and turn, seeing her exhausted and drawn face, her husband shook his head as if to shake off all that had come between them. But nothing changed: he was no closer to deciding whether it was his concern or his rage he should be more ashamed of.

(1977)

*I*n the spring of 1950, turning fifteen on the farm in Montana, no longer willing to bear the scrutiny of her Mormon foster parents, who, from the time she approached puberty, appraised her every movement for signs of her mother's genes, she walked twenty-two miles through the night to the train station. Early the next morning she headed south to San Francisco to search for her mother the whore.

Finding her mother an aging alcoholic stranger who told her to go back where she came from, she determined to stay. Living in a rented room and working as an usher in a movie house, finishing high school, she enrolled in the university. Quickly meeting campus radicals, responding to their zeal, for the next four years she picketed nonunion industries, demonstrated against the House Un-American Activities Committee, protested the loyalty oath. Often broke, someone she loved always in court, still she felt she had finally come home.

Just completing her studies, she met a young doctor who was also devoted to "the people." A short, powerful man, always in motion, skilled pathologist, linguist, singer, and athlete, he dazzled her. Despite the shadow of a year-long FBI investigation—he had gone to grade school with a now-famous Communist, among other sins—they married.

As time passed, perhaps tired of always another set of martyrs, more defense funds, rent parties, and trials, her husband became more conservative. They argued often, among other things about her unwillingness to return to the university for a higher degree. Advancing rapidly in medical social life, her husband wanted someone he could show off, someone with credentials or at least a pedigree. She drove him wild by referring to herself as a "bastard child" when his colleagues asked about her background; by saying she came from a long line of "scrabblefarmers"; by listening attentively to the woes of yet another of life's stragglers. Not about to change, even after eight years of marriage and two children, she told her husband he'd have to leave her behind if he was so eager to get ahead. They separated.

Working full time since she would take no alimony, caring for the children, she was surprised to discover that a principal pleasure in her life was her new home. Though mortgages for single women were then hard to come by, she'd finally been able to make the purchase. If initially she regarded the house simply as an economy, paying herself instead of the landlord, in time she came to value it as a refuge from the outside world. She didn't admire her need for such distance, nor was she entirely comfortable with the idea of ownership, but the home gave her happiness: it was hers.

One night, more than a year after their divorce, her former husband invited her out to dinner. They talked about mutual friends, the days when they first met, the children, his career, each taking the measure of how much had been lost when they separated. He had roses for her, told her more than once how beautiful she looked, was clearly trying to recover the best that had been between them, and she felt tempted to pick up on his unspoken suggestion that they try it again. Who would she ever know as well? Who else had shared all that time? They cried that night when they made love, but the morning after he was all business as he put on his clothes, in her eyes quickly transforming himself into a man too hungry for success, too much in need of the confirmation of powerful others. Wearing a suit that was just too damn expensive. And as she dressed, she caught him looking at her as if still wondering why in hell she had to be so stubborn. He was family, she knew, one of them would be there to bury the other when the time came, but that was all.

Meanwhile other couples in her circle were divorcing, and more than one ex-husband came by to cry on her shoulder. She understood pain, they said, and she did, though with somewhat more distance than she'd felt when she was younger. She had heard the same stories too many times, understood that blame had to be shared, couldn't pretend not to know that for some misery there could be no solace.

One of these divorced men, by no means the most compelling, kept returning to visit her even after he regained his footing. He had never thought much one way or the other about social causes but was a good musician, loved jokes, cooked fine food. "We could look out for each other," he said.

She felt a fool. He was no one to marry. She wanted some deep commitment, some grace, some faith. But she was also tired of being alone; she needed someone there at night. Maybe she was asking too much. She remembered the animals on the farm in Montana, just coupling.

In this period she fell in love from afar with a young man who worked in her office. Genuinely open to life, eager for experience, undaunted by the criticisms of the older staff, he reminded her of radical friends at the university ten years before. The night he quit his job he came by her house to celebrate. Drunk on wine, against her better judgment, at his initiative, they made love. The next morning, early, he was gone. Knowing she wouldn't see him again, feeling thirty and foolish, she called in sick and sat alone with a bottle of bourbon. Not until she put on Al Hibbler singing "Don't Get Around Much Anymore" did she begin to smile.

Months passing, when the divorcé proposed a second time, she spent a weekend thinking it over and then accepted. At the wedding, however, she still had her doubts. Looking around at the familiar faces she couldn't help but see it was the second time around. But things changed, she thought; she'd just have to accept that. Some people were stronger than others, some had more clarity than others, but the absolutism was long gone. "Truth," "justice," "the struggle," these words were no longer the vocabulary of their lives. Or hers. Laughter, music, decency, just a body next to hers, perhaps this would be enough. Without it, in any case, she was only growing older. Her mother had died before they ever really spoke to each other, and she still had no idea who her father was, if her mother had even known. No, you couldn't get everything you wanted. You had to learn to take what life gave you.

Several days after the wedding her new husband moved his things into her house. She hadn't realized he owned so much. Racks of records, clothes, power tools, musical instruments, hi-fi components, gear for magic tricks, boxes of bric-a-brac, sports equipment, books, furniture.

Her kids were enthralled by so many possessions. She had to admonish herself—even as she was startled by so much that was his, thinking back to the poverty of her childhood on the farm—to be less severe. Though he wasn't yet aggressive enough physically for her, they *were* both laughing, and the kids seemed pleased. She thought it would work out all right. She made room for his things.

That afternoon he moved a soft chair into the living room. Right after he had carefully positioned it, just so, in the corner, her boy walked over to the chair and sat down to try it out. "No, no, not there," she heard her new husband say. "That's my chair."

She couldn't believe her ears, but there was no taking the words back. For the next few months she measured needs against wants, she tried the mathematics of small pleasures canceling out large hopes, she balanced what was at hand against what was beyond reach. But then one day as they argued, again hearing his words in her ears, willing now to settle for no more than what was hers, she said to her new husband: "Out, out, out of *my* house."

(1977)

From a poor family, his father a tailor, Al considered himself lucky to get a scholarship to a fine men's college. Though he excelled in his course work, he was often lonely, and studied as much for want of something better to do as for the rewards achievement might bring. He would have enjoyed the presence of women, but the nearest coeds were miles away; dating was for weekends, hours of driving through the snow. During the week, time to kill, he jogged and skied.

Getting his degree, having saved a little money by waiting on table, Al started to realize his dream of wandering through Europe, but the draft forced him home and back into school after two months. While interesting, studying law meant three more years in the kind of competitive environment he'd come to loathe. If he was angry that life had closed in, it was his style to stick it out: he was always skeptical of risk. Soon law school would be over, and then, he hoped, he'd have time to explore.

Anne came from a middle-class family that was always short of money. Speaking about growing up, she often criticized her parents for having seven children. Had there been fewer, she seemed to be saying, each would have had enough. An awkward if bright adolescent, she didn't come into her own until college.

Her posture was bad, her features irregular, but with long legs and a lean figure she was a very attractive young woman. Self-possessed and quick with words, eager for life, capable of both sharp insight and great warmth, she was sought out by many men. Now apparently compensated for any earlier deprivation, still she had enormous hungers, always ready for the admiration of others, the next party, more celluloid jewelry and flapper dresses.

Anne and Al met at a student-faculty dinner just before he started his last year of law school, as she was finishing college. That night he heard her before he saw her.

"You don't mean to suggest that the husband shouldn't have left his wife, do you?" she was saying to a professor.

"What I mean," he replied condescendingly, "is that of course love implies obligation."

"No doubt it does, Professor, but could you explain to me just how?"

The professor was becoming impatient. "I believe it is self-evident. In this context—a husband abandoning his wife and child—we needn't get too speculative about it. Obviously he should have been bound by the love he presumably once pledged."

"Incredible," she exclaimed, laughing, "the notion that love is in some way connected to action. But even if it is, shouldn't we ask first whether the obligation you speak of was explicit or implicit? And, if implicit, whether both parties were truly aware it existed?"

"My dear young girl," the professor retorted, exasperated. "Forget all your quibbling. A faculty member abandoned his wife and child. I hardly call that love, and, furthermore, I find it odd to hear you— a woman—defending such behavior."

"So I gather," Anne responded. "You might, however, find it less odd if you weren't so eager to dismiss my 'quibbling.' Think about it for a moment. Love's an emotion, a feeling. How can a mere feeling ever imply the existence of an imperative? Or, even if love does somehow imply obligation, when one stops loving, doesn't the obligation cease? X simply no longer loves Y. Besides, one can have obligation without love. Why not, then, love without obligation?"

"We could philosophize this way for hours," the professor said angrily.

"And perhaps even learn something," Anne shot back. "But in any case, I personally believe there's a love that has nothing to do with bargains or actions. A love that might, in this case, even keep a man with his wife and child."

Incredible, Al thought. Having escalated the discussion, then reversed her field, she'd emerged as the champion of "true" love, this while implying that her opponent would never be adequate to such emotion, not with her, anyway. An inflammatory argument, coming from a lovely woman, particularly one wearing next to nothing under her skimpy knit dress. She hadn't fought fair, Al knew, but the fool deserved no better. She'd been magnificent.

Waiting to introduce himself, he noticed she had little to say to the other women present. Still holding forth, surrounded by admiring men, nipples pressing at the fabric of her dress, she wasn't about to share the moment. She'd come to conquer.

When Al finally got to speak with her, he mentioned her argument with the professor.

"Oh," she said, smiling. "Such an unhappy man, don't you think? I have to learn to laugh at people like that. Sometimes life's just too serious to be taken seriously."

"But you do believe in love?" Al asked, grinning.

"With a capital 'L'? Of course. Isn't that clear? What else is there?"

Even after they were seeing each other regularly, Al couldn't help fearing she would leave him. Emphatically independent and still close to former lovers, Anne appeared quite capable of being on her own. Yet there she was, with him.

He felt no full commitment from her until her younger sister was lost at sea in a boating accident. Shattered, full of guilt, Anne had nightmares for weeks, crying out again and again in her sleep that her sister was drowning. Always Al was there to comfort her, wiping her face with a cloth, giving her sedatives, tucking in the blankets, keeping watch. He had never seen such suffering, wanted more than anything to spare her this pain. Often she woke in the middle of the night, sobbing, holding him, begging him not to go. "I won't leave you," he'd say, kissing her. "I won't ever leave you."

Slowly she recovered, and finally seemed to be herself again. Taking a vacation together, skiing every day, making love each night, they were both full of joy. Soon they were planning to marry. Though a wedding was surely appropriate to their happiness, it seemed a little strange at the time, for among their peers there was then little concern with traditional forms. Both Anne and Al said the ceremony was for their parents. As for themselves, if their feelings changed, they'd part.

It was a huge wedding. After the ceremony, family finally departing with last embraces and blessings, Anne drank champagne with her friends. "Marriage is a perversion of natural faithful affections," she said, laughing. "It's filled with hoaxes, falsehood, and guilt." Al laughed too. They were both very happy.

In the months that followed, the established order had ever less legitimacy in the campus community. No possibility now beyond reach, their friends increasingly defined themselves in terms of great causes. Moved by this public flux, Anne became restless with school. Though she was too interested in aesthetics to make any substantial commitment to social change, this was a moment when even taking drugs seemed a political assertion, when even the Left was swept aside by the rediscovery of license. It was this repudiation of the past and invitation to passion that moved Anne most.

Meanwhile Al struggled to hold himself in check. A little longer, a little longer and he'd be done. Law school was now worse than boring; at best attorneys seemed to be playing an outmoded and repressive game. Yet Al was on his own and knew it. The question of how to make a living was hardly the burning issue of the day, but he wondered what, if not law, he could do.

They'd been married no more than a year when Anne took a lover. Knowing Al would be devastated, she saw it as no small step. Yet the times were changing; all around her were men of restless raw power. She told Al that, not seeking it out, she'd fallen in love, that though she still loved him she was prepared to accept whatever decision he made. But because he himself yearned for more freedom, because her feelings were real, her confusion genuine, and because he simply wasn't ready to live without her, Al said he understood. When her lover soon left town, carried off by some new cause, Anne wept and Al sighed with relief. They resumed life as before.

Within months it seemed that the revolution was imminent, but already Al had moved up north to a remote town to take a job. Still in the city, to follow when she completed the course work for her master's, flattered by the attention of men she wanted to know better, inspired by the dreams around her, Anne denied herself nothing.

Given the times, no one she knew save her parents—and the part of herself they spoke for—would have disputed her desire to live as she wanted. But what, then, of Al? Wrestling with possibilities, she reasoned that she loved him no less, that, in fact, the richer her life the more she'd bring to him. Plural marriages, group sex, and free love now common in her community, these arguments didn't sound entirely implausible. Yet she doubted one could play it both ways, spoke sadly of separation, wistfully of accommodations that might be made. Al, meanwhile, was alone and working hard, still sending her money to finish school. Waiting for her, receiving her long letters, he thought she'd leave him.

Finally arriving, happy to see him, still Anne wasn't sure she'd stay. Cleaning house, shopping, running errands, isolated and resenting the drudgery, she kept noticing the many "freaks" doing odd jobs, dealing dope, living on welfare. She began to press Al to loosen up, to take more time off, saying he was a fool to spend so much time at the office. "What about pleasure?" she'd keep asking, certain his job was work, work *prima facie* painful.

He refused to listen. Despite the confining routine, he liked solid wages after so many years of scrimping. And though being an attorney was far from tapping the wild energy of the times, it was something he did well, even an opportunity to help others. Perhaps also, fearing he could neither keep Anne nor keep up with her, he sought out structure all the more.

So there they were, a couple, taxpayers, amortizing school debts while all around them people were openly "ripping off" the system. And because Al had little energy left after work, they usually paid cash for every good and service. House repairs, car repairs, medical bills, food, clothing: the money went out as fast as Al earned it.

Given Anne's dissatisfaction with such middle-class traps ("I don't think two is the perfect number," she told Al), their separation seemed imminent. But instead, blaming him for not spending more time with her, she began seeing other men, leaving for a night at a time, returning the next morning.

Sick at heart, Al said nothing. Perhaps he thought himself unnecessarily "uptight." The world had changed. How set the limits? Perhaps he believed negotiation impossible, that it would be Anne's terms or none at all. Or perhaps, whatever she did, he couldn't abandon the Anne he'd nursed when her sister had died.

Had he merely pretended strong interest in another woman, Anne might well have come home to stay if that was the goal. But Al couldn't play the game, didn't see it as a game, much less as war. Nor did it occur to him that alone he might find safer ground. As if believing that she had some special claim on life, he gave way.

Now only one of several men she loved, Al was still her husband, a professional man, crux of the life she felt she'd been told to live. Though she passionately advanced theories and admonitions about living for freedom and love, the real debate, which she had yet to resolve, was within herself. At each critical point, however, that internal argument reduced itself to resentment and anger. Who said she couldn't play it both ways?

Self-justification soon became her greatest labor. She liked to say, for instance, that Al chose to work. His earning power obviously greater than hers, it followed that there was no good reason for her to get a job. In fact, of course Al was too well paid for what he did. Were the world more fair, attorneys would earn far less, nothing at all if things were perfect.

A year of this married life passing, often alone for days at a time, Al began occasionally to spend the night with other women, always careful, however, to clear his choices with Anne. "Now he's living for pleasure," she announced triumphantly. Though she set his limits, she needn't have bothered: Al complied with her terms as if the miracle was in sustaining their relationship. As in a way it was. He worked hard, she played hard, but the real nub of their lives was Anne's refusal to have less than all she wanted. Al's willingness to let her try, however—to bind her to him with guilt?—served her badly: without a counterforce she was increasingly self-deceived, ever more ruthless.

In time a new phenomenon presented itself. Though she seemed beyond the rule of that kind of gravity, Anne was rebuffed by one of her lovers. While it was the hallmark of her relations with other men that she never had to play for full stakes—being married, after all—nonetheless she found the rejection galling. She also began to fear that she might "jeopardize the marriage." Her apprehension increased when a jealous neighbor, an older woman, told her she wasn't getting younger, that she'd lose her husband unless she settled down.

One evening soon after she was out dancing. Seeing her flirting with other men at the bar, her companion of the evening pulled her out to the street, knocked her down, and drove off. Alone in the night with a black eye, sure that the day of reckoning had come, Anne wept her way home to Al. But two nights later she was gone again.

To counter her fears, Anne advanced still more argument, like a Ptolemaic astronomer adding epicycles, until language finally lost all meaning. Long since, for example, pleasure required a capital "P". Now, though it was probably too much to have her lovers come by when Al was home, as "friends" of course they'd always be welcome. And how many "friends" she had! No doubt it was, as she argued, for the best. If life gave each of us all the warm bodies we needed, surely there'd be fewer wars, fewer Trojan wars, in any case. But through it all Anne kept her hold on Al.

One Sunday they drove to the beach. There Anne suggested they take LSD, something she had done many times, Al never. Those experienced with drugs might have counseled against it: there was trouble between them, and Al had to be at work in the morning. But perhaps eager to catch up to the Freedom she so often spoke of, he was game. Soon Anne was in the water, riding the waves, surfing from one tide pool to another, shrieking with laughter. Alone, up on the beach, mutilating women of the night, Al was certain he was Jack the Ripper.

Shortly after this debacle Anne found a cottage of her own, though resentful of being the one to move. She would, she decided, see Al several days a week, "friends" the rest of the time.

By now they'd lived in the country nearly three years. More time passing, she allowed one of her lovers to move in with her, dividing most of her energy between him and Al, though insisting—to her lover, now—that of course she retained the right to do as she liked. Even with Al as an exemplum her lover couldn't see it. There was no question that Anne cherished him—who could be more tender?—but at the point of exacting parity from her he, like Al, was helpless.

Nearly twenty-six, Anne began to talk about having a child. Lover sitting silent through her deliberations, she finally decided that Al would make the best father. They were already married, after all, she loved him, and he'd be able to support a family. Al apparently acquiesced, continuing to give her money and gifts, but he seemed at long last weary of what they had created between them.

Finally, inevitably, Al met another woman. Though he no longer cleared his lovers with Anne, his relations with them had continued to have at least a component of being done for effect. Now, however, a real alternative existed. Her worst fear confirmed, Anne came to his office daily, badgering him, saying it was time for the child, time to go away together for a long vacation. But because he wanted revenge, or because he simply had finally found Pleasure, Al told her he wanted a divorce.

"You'll have to pay alimony," Anne raged, bringing him to tears. "No amount can be too much for what I'm suffering. I'll show you

you can't abuse someone this way. I've given you the best years of my life. I'll stop you from doing the same to another woman."

Though she had always seemed untouched by time, ever capable of being nineteen again, there was suddenly no longer anything girlish about her. Hair cut short and curled, she took a part-time job and began to walk around town wearing a matronly dress and stockings, insisting on every bit of her age. And on something else. A working woman, that was her message, a woman struggling to make ends meet because she'd been wronged by her husband. Look what he had done!

Al now lived with his lover as Anne did with hers. Though he continued to speak of divorce, months passed and still no papers were filed. Anticipating a reconciliation, Love triumphant, perhaps even a second honeymoon, Anne pointedly maintained her marital status and obligations. Sending a Christmas gift to Al's parents, for instance, she signed herself "Al's wife."

And so it persisted, the two of them living apart, but, still, husband and wife. Not quite as they were when they first met, world exploding with discovery, nothing beyond dreaming, but as they'd already spent the years: staving off separation, clinging to their marriage like sailors to a spar, ship long since swallowed by the sea.

(1977)

He would have been hard pressed to precise what made him want to buy a house. Perhaps it began with the smog in the flatlands where they lived, particularly after the city diverted commuter traffic from shortcuts through neighborhood streets onto a main artery unfortunately close to the cottage they leased. Since they couldn't afford to rent up in the hills above the smog line, it made some sense to think about buying and fixing up a run-down house in an area they liked. Or he may have noticed, making out yet another monthly check to his landlord one night, multiplying it by twelve and then again by four or five, that he could have been paying all that money to himself.

Whatever the impulse for wanting his own home, it wasn't a bad thing that at thirty-three he was considerably older than his second wife. His first wife had left him because of his unwillingness to settle down, to "grow up," as she put it. If, however, he had once roamed far and wide, eyes lighting up at the mere mention of some foreign land, measuring his world in terms of islands, seas, and plateaus, he now felt, as the poet said, that he could scare himself with his own desert places. Though to think about owning a home suggested to him that his world had diminished, his second wife found the idea reasonable enough: she loved to make things, fix things, accumulate things. Having their own home seemed sensible.

The search wasn't easy. Real estate had tripled in value the last five years; now even a two-bedroom stucco was going for sixty thousand dollars. He winced to think of the monthly payments they'd have to carry, at least twice their rent, but on the other hand they'd have tax benefits and a growing equity, as well as the pleasures of the place itself. The more they looked, however, the more angry he was to think how easily he might have bought years before. Worse, the inflationary spiral made a mockery of all the small economies he had practiced.

One day their realtor called to say there was a tiny three-room cottage in a secluded area going for only thirty thousand dollars. It needed work, he told them, but the lot itself was worth nearly seventeen thousand. There was already a bid on it, but because the cottage was substandard both in size and construction, it seemed unlikely that the bidder would be able to arrange bank financing. If they could borrow enough for the large down payment, the owner would probably carry a note for the balance. He urged them to drive up and see it right away.

The neighborhood was unbelievably quiet, site of a former ranch, the old cattleman still living next door in what had once been the barn. As they inspected the cottage the old man came by to introduce himself. "My mother built this place, all by herself, for a friend paralyzed in the war," he told them. "She didn't want to see him go to a rest home. She cared for him ten years, feeding him, changing his linen, bathing him, turning him over several times a day. It may mean something to you if I say that never in all those years until he died did he have a bedsore."

The old man walked the property with them, talking about how much trillium there had been before the ivy took over, where the land was slide and where solid, pointing out the fruit trees—apricot, pear, plum, apple—showing them which were healthy and what care they'd need. He wouldn't be a bad neighbor, they both thought, not bad at all. And through the old bay laurel trees they could see clear down to the Bay. The house itself couldn't have been more modest, no more than living room, bedroom, tiny kitchen, and primitive bath, but it was charming, even more appealing given its low cost.

Nor did the obvious problems seem insurmountable. They could add on a room, perhaps something with two stories and lots of storage space. That would make a tremendous difference. Then they could open up the rear wall to enlarge the kitchen area and cut windows into the roof for more light. And they could buy a wood stove instead of installing space heaters. Fuel would be no problem: they could haul logs down from the mountains each time they went camping.

Later that day they learned the bid had in fact been withdrawn. Signing a check for the earnest money and handing it over to the realtor, he immediately suffered a bad case of buyer's remorse. Not that he didn't want the cottage, but look what he was tying himself into. Insurance, taxes, repairs, mortgage payments, the whole inevitable weight of the place, he who for so long had needed no more than his health and a pack on his back. Home ownership felt like just the kind of puddle a man could drown in. "Don't worry," the realtor told him, "you have a week to reconsider as you learn more about it. And you can't lose the deposit."

Bad news came fast. The termite inspector reported that the cottage was riddled with holes. And when the engineer met them up at the lot, he expressed surprise that they had asked him to come. "You don't need me for this," he said. "Basically the structure has value only if you plan to live in it as is. Or you could even rent it out, I suppose. But as soon as you apply for a permit to make improvements or additions, they'll condemn it."

One of their friends, a carpenter, also came up, and told them that they might be able to salvage the roof. But nothing more. "Look," he said, laughing. "No foundation, studs every four feet, plates rotted out, water leakage on the ceiling. This isn't even a shack."

Ever buoyant, the realtor told them it still had possibilities. If they bought the site and laid out another thirty or thirty-five thousand dollars—having talked down the asking price a little—they'd come out of it all owning a small house in a prime location without having spent much more than the cost of something ordinary in a less attractive neighborhood. And their place, the smallest in an expensive area, would have its value accelerated by the high prices of the surrounding homes. Nonetheless, the realtor conceded, it was of course not quite what they had thought it was, not really a house, actually little more than a very expensive building lot.

He found it painful to withdraw from the purchase. Already he had daydreamed about buying a piano now that they'd be really settled, had told his wife he'd get the last of his gear out of storage, for the first time in years having everything he owned in one place. What with these plans and the renovations they had imagined, he felt as if something already theirs was being taken away.

On the way down from their last—and saddest—visit to the cottage, they stopped at another listing the realtor had suggested. A small, dark house, new redwood shingles inflating the asking price another ten thousand dollars, neighboring homes crowding in on a postage-stamp back yard. They couldn't get out of there fast enough. Sixty-five thousand dollars.

So they were back to go. Minus a hundred and fifty dollars for the inspection reports.

That evening they went down to the Bay and walked out on the long fishing pier. Despite the cleansing north wind and the crescent moon setting over the Gate like Bojangle's smile, he was depressed. Just being up in the hills had forced him to realize how much money it would take to live there, money he wasn't ever apt to have, money the lack of which he had never quite noticed because they lived simply and among friends who, like them, rented. Despite all the freedom life had granted him, despite his wife, friends, and the many richness' available to him, all he could think of was that he wanted the calm and beauty of living in the hills for himself.

Seeing the houses, hearing the prices, understanding that they were beyond his means, all this catapulted him back to choices he had made long ago. Should he have been living differently all this time, earning more money, settling in sooner? Had he been a fool, had he failed to understand the game, was he now seeing the penalties for his actions?

While these questions rushed through his mind, his wife was nearby, talking to a fisherman who had just hauled in a small leopard shark. Though disappointed about losing the cottage, she seemed undismayed, apparently assuming something else would come along, or not minding at all if they had to move to the country to afford a place.

She was only several feet away, but he began to study her as if from a great distance. She had been a fine companion, had first traveled with him and then filled what homes they had with treasures. Plants, shells, rocks, nests, feathers. Fine meals. Love. She had shared and enhanced his life. He would have gone insane without her. But now, he thought, he was changing, even faster than he knew. He wished she had a source of income beyond the part-time jobs she took to pay her way. He wished she could bring as much to the purchase as he did. Then they could buy even in the hills.

Still looking over at her, he thought of the professional women he had once spent time with: filmmakers, lawyers, nurses, teachers. He thought of the kind of credit—not to mention savings—they must have had access to. He thought also of the heiress he had once lived with. In fact, he thought of all the women he had ever been close to who would have had the resources to help buy the house he now wanted.

As his wife continued to examine the leopard shark, waves breaking against the pilings, Pleiades running high overhead, he wished she had money, yes, he wished she had money. And, it occurred to him, since she had none he might be better off with someone who did.

(1977)

*T*hough surely they were always all around me, I never saw them until the end of a rainy winter, and really not until early one evening when at long last the sky cleared. And then, in the afterglow of the waning day, they came into my ken, came out like stars. An elderly woman walking home from market, pausing after achieving a block before attempting the next; two aged gnomes, him with cigar pulling the wife behind; a grandfather watching his heirs mortgage the home he paid for free and clear. And Rose. "Once an adult, twice a child," she cackled as she watered her garden, throwing snails out into the street. Her six cats watching.

Rose's garden. Anemone, crocus, marigold, primrose, iris. ("Iris makes you believe in God, doesn't it," she said.) Hyacinth, foxglove, tigridia, gladiolus, scilla, hollyhock. Black tulip, Johnny-jump-up, nasturtium, sweet William, columbine, verbena, phlox. Campanula. Cosmos. African lily, regal lily, black lily of the Nile. Canterbury bells. Snapdragons. Bird-of-paradise. Forget-me-nots.

"The *crocus flowers* very early," she said that evening. "When I was a child I couldn't find the verb," she told me, laughing, reaching for her baseball cap to see if it was still there.

When I stopped by her garden the next morning I said: "Hi, Rose. The crocus flowers very early." She jumped. "How did you know that?" she asked. "That one always gave me trouble. Never could find the verb. Was I embarrassed!"

Rose approaching eighty, at long last on her own. Stacks of clippings, books, and records against the day she becomes a shut-in. Diet of bananas, peanut butter, pure´ed vegetables, and ice cream. Afraid of dozing off into a dreamless sleep never to wake.

And Rose in her garden. Dove in the birdbath. Blackbird zipping up to a phone wire to shake and preen. Robin catching a worm. "Goodbye, worm," Rose calls out.

"I'm kinda lost in the world now," she says, cars roaring by the garden. "Old as I am, I can't really separate the dreams from the reality." Two white butterflies dance past her. "This is living," she exclaims.

"When I was a little girl, I had a mammy, Aunt Ruth, and she used to tuck me in every night. One evening I wandered down in the Negro section and there was a colored woman singing, sitting in a chair on her lawn, just singing. The sun went down and I stood there transfixed, I just stood there looking through the paling. And then a colored man, Jim, he came along and opened the gate for me—the latch was too high to reach—and he said: 'Now you go tell your mama I let you in, and don't you ever be out this late again.'

"Once I embarrassed my mother. Lord! We were sitting at table—I couldn't have been but three or four, still in the high chair—and when everyone was ready for the prayer, I lifted up my small plate and said: 'Here, Grandpa, read my plate.' I thought that's where he got the prayer, I thought he read it off the plate. Oh, my mother was so embarrassed.

"I never was afraid for anyone to see me with my shoes off. I always walked alone. I never was lonely. I danced naked in the wilderness. We had a cabin in the mountains when I was small and I played with hornets, wasps, and birds. I danced naked in the wilderness; everything was my friend. But then one day my mother found me and told me I had sinned. I never did undress again and dance around. Until that day I never thought of what other people were going to think or say. I just grew like Topsy.

"When they put me under ether it was goodbye, I thought. 'I'm gone,' I said to myself. 'I'm going down headfirst into a dark pit.' So I wiggled my finger to stop them from burying me. I felt like a house, and they were putting in doors and windows, just banging away.

"When I was a child, people believed old women were witches. They thought old women could turn themselves into cats, get into people's drawers, steal things. They believed this.

"I died on my grandfather's bed. Oops! I was just a baby then, he lost his foot in the Civil War. Tried to stop a rolling cannonball by sticking out his foot. I was wrapped up in a blanket on his bed when he finally died. I saw my grandmother die too, very calmly. 'Rest in peace' was her expectation. I have no fear of death. You may pick me up dead someday in the garden. I'm the last leaf on the family tree:

> "...if I should live to be
> The last leaf upon the tree...
> Let them smile, as I do now,
> At the old forsaken bough...

"If only we knew what the end of us was. Once I heard a voice, very steady and quiet. 'You are going to die,' it said. I didn't fight it. I was tired. It was like a realization."

Rose in her garden digging irrigation channels, passersby stopping to look or to ask for flowers, amazed at what she's made of the vacant lot. "I'm in hibernation now," she says, toes out, feet flat, cap on her head. "I walk alone. I told the children, 'Shoo, out of the nest.' I made a lot of mistakes. I don't think I'd have children again.

"My husband never meant that much to me. He was the same outside the family as inside, the same with everyone. He left me to care for things. My husband was a very popular man when we were young, an athlete, but three days after the wedding I rued it. I gave up my freedom, you see. 'After twenty-four, a girl no more.' You didn't divorce easily in those days. There were women and there were ladies. Ladies didn't divorce. There was another man who wanted to marry me, but he went into the Army and by the time he returned I was gone. After all these years he tracked me down. Called me up and said he still loved me, that he never had married. Wants to see me. On the phone he said: 'Is this Rose with the blue eyes and light brown hair?' 'Not anymore,' I told him. I never felt that kind of romantic love. No. I walked alone. I can't think of a thing on heaven or earth that could move me to remarry. My husband said that. 'You're a one-man woman,' he often told me. Patting himself on the back, I suppose.

"After my father died my mother married again. I set myself against her, told her not to. Do you know what she did? Just before the ceremony she switched me, three times in one day. I was a hard child.

"When I was at college, a professor wondered about me. 'Who is that girl who walks alone?' he asked. That was me. Now I walk alone. That fellow calls and wants to see me after all these years. Still loves me, he says. Well, it's too late.

"My grandmother was a fine woman. She was a tall person, from England, very beautiful. She lived by the Bible. When I was a child, I would put my head in her lap. 'Now, Rose,' she'd say, 'have you done anything wrong? Be sure to ask God for forgiveness or you'll be punished.' She never said what the punishment was. 'God is love, too,' she told me. Then Grandmother would tuck me into bed, snug and safe. As soon as she was gone, I'd pull the covers over my head so God wouldn't be able to see me."

One day the man who had loved her so many years drove up from Oklahoma in his camper. He stayed only several hours. "I made another mistake," she said after he left. "When he came in, I was surprised at the way he looked. I remembered him from way back then. 'Why, you're an old man,' I said to him. I guess that put him off."

On her own, Rose struggles to orient herself. "Which door did I come in?" she asks to get her bearings, constantly having to backtrack to discover what she was doing. Events merge, jump out of sequence, confuse, intimidate. As she works in her garden one day, there's a gunfight across the street. A man threatens to kill his child; police shoot it out with him. Hearing the shots, Rose is certain the sounds are either in her inner ear or else happened years ago.

A week later she sees a monkey in a tree and calls the police. The monkey turns out to be a cat. And late one night she sees a man feeding a raccoon right under her window. As she looks out into the darkness, the colors are phenomenally intense, her garden like a fairyland. She has no way to establish whether what she sees is real or not.

Thirty years ago, just out of the service, her son met a woman on the train and, within the day, asked her to marry him. Rose argued with her son, saying it was too precipitate, but to no avail. Years later her son's wife became epileptic. In a cruel trick of memory Rose now sees the two separate events as one. "Son," she has herself saying to him when they argued that day, "son, don't marry her. She's an epileptic." And what she remembers as her son's anguished reply keeps haunting her: "Mother, how could you say such a thing, how could you?" Her crime never having been committed—at least not in this form—there is no one to absolve her.

Each night Rose barricades the door. The cats take their places, one on the mantel, two by the heater, three on the bed. She drapes a black cloth over the songbirds' cage, and, suddenly, the din stops. Alone, adrift in the flow of the many people who have been part of her life, she reaches for something sure. Her grandmother. Wondering what will bloom in the morning, wondering if her sense of smell will return, struggling not to nod off involuntarily, she prays as she did as a child:

> Now I lay me down to sleep,
> I pray the Lord my soul to keep.
> And if I die before I wake,
> I pray the Lord my soul to take. Amen.

"I always add the Amen," Rose says.

(1977)

It was a slender thread, even as threads go, that he followed three thousand miles out to California. This is how it happened. Restless at nearly twenty-seven, a too-predictable life stretching out before him, he quit his job as a draftsman, abandoning career prospects in the vague hope of becoming an artist. Leaving town, he came down to Boston the Summer of Love, the summer she happened to be back east on vacation visiting friends. And looking for someone to have an affair with. Seeing her in a laundromat with her infant son, he soon discovered that she was divorced and invited her out for ice cream. He had a sports car but was nearly broke. She had some money but no car. He found her attractive and as shy as he felt; she thought he was carefree and a rogue. They spent the next month traveling around New England, and had a pretty good time.

When she headed west, he said he'd be out soon, without making explicit whether it was California or her that attracted him more. Three months passed and still he didn't write or call, but her heart wasn't broken: she was busy with teaching and her child. She had no way of knowing he was en route the whole time, more or less. Back home liquidating his belongings; parents tearfully urging him not to be foolish; former employer offering him his job back; coming winter filling him with old fears. But then one evening as she finished preparing dinner he appeared at her door. Expressing no surprise, saying only "Hello, how've you been?" she handed him a plate of food, which, stumbling as he reached for it, he dropped. Exhausted from the days of driving, thinking what an entrance he had made, all he could do was laugh. She loved him for laughing.

He stayed in her apartment nearly a year, and for each it went without saying that he did so at least in part to save money. Getting settled in his new life after a while, giving up the idea of being an artist, he did enough carpentry to earn the down payment on a ramshackle house near the Bay. It was a moment of change and possible commitment, which they almost wordlessly worked their way around by making her his tenant. She rented the front of the house for her son and herself; he took the back. The kitchen was hers. She prepared the meals, and, after some negotiation, he learned to do the shopping and wash the dishes. They split the food bill and made love in her sleeping loft, which he built.

Having tried it once, she had no use for marriage. As for him, still shaping a new life, cutting his teeth on the wide world, he didn't like to think of himself as being tied down. Landlord and tenant they were, then, and it suited them well enough, though they were as monogamous as any couple sworn to honor and obey.

After five years together they sought more distance from each other. A trip together to Europe only reinforced this desire: he spent the summer feeling that the austere romance of solitary wandering was being denied him, while she often thought of the men she might have been meeting. The trip wore them down, and it was all too easy to blame each other when they found themselves not so much travelers as tourists.

Back in California they agreed to part, after a fashion. That is, both continued to live in the house, but she had her lovers up front, while he built a separate entrance out the back. Even after he completed a kitchenette in his room, they still often ate together, and marked their changed relationship primarily by being more scrupulous about itemizing food expenses. Free of the burdens of intimacy, they were more polite to each other than they had been in several years.

Though her heart went out to an enchantingly impoverished young Talmudic scholar who finally left for the Holy Land owing her nearly a thousand dollars, after a while she had enough of romance. And her landlord/former lover, infatuation with a ballerina aside, logged enough hours sitting in bars sporting his new beard and pea jacket—lonely are the brave—to know what *that* life was like.

So once again they were alone together with her son in the house, but for a time simply as roommates and friends. Now less stifled by what they had created between them, life moving on, they were somewhat more gentle with each other. He no longer found it necessary to mock the affectations of her poet friends ("faggots," he'd once called them as he went out back to repair the septic tank); she got on him less often for drinking beer and watching sports on TV. Her son was old enough to shoot baskets with him, and he valued that. The house, which he never stopped improving, was steadily more comfortable, and they seemed, finally, friendly adversaries, a kind of family, which suited her. They spent many slow evenings together, preparing good dinners and entertaining company, without feeling the need to make each other over or deny each other any possibility. Things were okay for the moment, and who could pretend to know what would come next? They could have been sleeping together but weren't. As he said, she snored.

That summer a friend lent them a cabin in the mountains. They explored the area, climbed, swam, fished, camped out, chopped wood, watched the stars. For years strangers to small intimacies, they found themselves sometimes walking hand in hand or arm in arm, even occasionally kissing each other good morning. And they began to make love again.

For a time he thought she was putting on weight. Since she had always been trim, this surprised him, and of course in the mountains they were exercising heavily. He teased her about it, told her she must be getting older, but she simply smiled at him. One day, just before they were to return home, thinking it a foolish question and as always loath to play the fool, he asked her if she was pregnant. "I think I'm going to have it," was all she said, laughing.

When they came back to the city, he began converting the basement into a nursery, putting in paneling and insulation, laying a floor over the concrete foundation, drawing designs for a crib. As months passed and her stomach swelled he weighed names for the child. She wanted a boy, he wanted a girl. "Someone not like me," he said. She did exercises and watched her diet; he continued his carpentry, shooting baskets with her son after work. And up in her sleeping loft late one night before he headed back to his room, as she murmured that the baby was kicking too hard, he—surprising them both—told her he loved her.

(1977)

"So all in all," he's saying, "I think it's a good thing she didn't come. She really doesn't have any use for this kind of frenetic traveling, and of course at thirty-five I don't need to feel guilty about my style of doing things. Seeing her get exhausted and thinking it's a crazy pace. Which it is. Besides, we've barely been apart for four years. Good to separate for two weeks, just to be a little less taken for granted." This is a husband far from home talking with old friends, and, words just out of his mouth, a husband already ruing his suggestion that he and his wife need some time away from each other. An unfair dig at her, he thinks, so many thousands of miles away. Not really true, petty, pointlessly disloyal.

His trip is in fact incredibly hectic, and, though sure before leaving that he wouldn't think much about his wife, he often stops between meetings and friends to try to picture what she's doing at a given moment, careful always to allow for the difference in time zones. He sees her lying in bed, morning sun brightening the room, three cats for a blanket; bicycling off to dance class, closing the gate behind her; mixing grains for breakfast cereal. *She should have come*, he sometimes thinks, seeing a street entertainer, an interesting bookstore, a good friend. *She would have liked this.*

On the other hand, he has much to do, and there was in fact something arbitrary about taking the trip when he did, not to mention making it at all. At the least there was probably a better time, but he simply thought he wanted to go then, and committed himself. Though, as the time of departure approached, flying so far so fast seemed gratuitously violent, senseless, unnecessary. The morning he was to leave he and his wife sat out in the garden, cats chasing butterflies, birds at the feeder, squirrels scolding. Why go? But it was too late. "I suppose it's just as well she didn't come," he says to himself more than once.

Throughout the trip he has the sensation that traveling itself makes him unfaithful to his wife. Not because he left her behind, or because he's free of the domestic burdens they normally share. But because, out of his own environment, changing with each city and setting if only to adjust to what is there held to be real, he feels uncentered, unaccountable, not himself. In that sense, inconstant.

As he promised, he calls her often, and she seems eager to hear him say the trip will be shorter than the two weeks he had planned. But he tells her he's running hard and will barely return on schedule, feeling a touch of pique when she fails to applaud his efforts or to understand how much he's giving up—a trip to the country home of old friends, for one thing—to maintain his pace.

Lying in a hotel room one night, he dreams that all planes, cars, and trains have disappeared, that he must work his way overland on foot to get back to her. But there's some kind of war going on; he has to be careful. Towns burn; people are captured and killed. Lost and ill in his dream, he meets an old woman who gives him flower remedies: Pine, for those who blame themselves; Sweet Chestnut, for those suffering great anguish; Willow, for those who deny they deserved such adversity. And Holly, for those with no real cause for their unhappiness. "You'll find a home, never fear," the old woman tells him. "Some home. Does it really matter which?" In his dream he's ill for a very long time: at the moment before he wakes in the hotel bed, damp with sweat, he still has many miles to go.

Getting much business successfully accomplished the rest of his trip, he's ever more pressed and fatigued, but, the end in sight, he begins with relief to feel that of course it's the trip that is temporary, home of course that is permanent. The night before he's to return he calls his wife, trying several times but getting no answer. When, very late, he finally reaches her, she tells him she was out with a mutual friend.

"Where did you go?" he asks.

"To the movies."

"He just happened to call you?"

"He called and wondered if I wanted to go."

"Just like that? He never called to ask you when I was there."

"Of course not. He likes me, as you know, and thought I might be lonely with you away."

"That's consideration for you," he says sharply.

"Are you saying you don't think I should have gone?"

"No," he replies, suddenly exhausted, exhausted with himself, "no, I don't think you shouldn't have gone. What am I talking about?"

"Still love me?" she says, laughing.

"Yes, dammit, I still love you, but we're very far apart. Too far apart. Time to get back together, don't you agree?"

"I agree," she says. "Why don't you be sensible and come home?"

Just before he boards the plane, he sends her a card. Though he's mailed one each day during his trip, all have been notes. Seeing and feeling so much, shifting inner and outer ground so many times, he's been unable to find a point of purchase on all the changes, settling for doing what he could—saying hello. But writing this card, now a man returning to his wife, he has his voice:

"I thought I'd forget you while I was away, not having, as you know, much of a memory. And, as you also know, believing myself unwilling to live any life except the one right before my eyes. But I want to tell you that to my great surprise, over all these miles, I've seen you all the time. I hope you're still there."

On the plane he sits next to some newlyweds. "Going on our honeymoon," the bride tells him. "And you?"

"Oh," he replies, "I'm going home."

"How long have you been gone?"

"Two weeks today."

"Two weeks can be a long time, particularly if you have family. I'll bet you're glad to be getting back."

"Yes I am," he answers, "yes I am."

Hours pass. He watches the last range of mountains finally give way to the coastal plain, the seat-belt sign comes on, and they prepare to land.

His wife is at the airport to meet him. Extremely pleased to see each other, they embrace, get his bags, and drive home. Once there, all he so recently only imagined quickly paints itself in. The plants, the rugs, his books, the bed, a quilt, the cats. When they make love, far from feeling strange to him after his absence, his wife seems only more herself than he remembered.

Waking in the middle of the night, he walks restlessly around the house checking the doors. Seeing his wife in the bed, hair spread wide over the pillow, chin as always tilting up and away, he thinks, smiling to himself, that of course he who returns has never really left.

(1977)

Hazards to the Human Heart

STORIES

The Mad Dog Instructional League

"Mad Dog's back," my wife said, no trace of enthusiasm in the mother lode of her voice, a vein of pure reproach just beneath the surface. "I saw him crossing University down at San Pablo. He looks heavier, his hair is cropped, but it was Mad Dog."

"You positive?" I parried, trying in two words to express my hope that she was wrong, as well as to assert that of course I couldn't be held responsible. Christ, how much weight can two words take? I'd have liked them to convey that by mentioning his name she'd not only conjured up an image of him, but, for all I knew, had in fact caused his return. Had she not said his name, I wanted to suggest, Mad Dog might have been sitting in jail in Parrish County, Louisiana, desperate to be cut loose from a drunk and disorderly before the Feds could check out his prints and send a detainer. I could just see him sweating it out: shining on the guards, hustling the trusty, kissing the public defender's ass, swearing to the bail bondsman that he had a friend who would pay. Trying the line on anyone who'd listen, even his cellmates.

"Boy, let me tell you, if they allow me to go home I'm never coming back. I've learned my lesson. I sure hope they let me go home." Some prisoners hearing this craven bullshit shaking their heads in disgust; others venturing a smile, realizing that Mad Dog was just rehearsing—he'd con his way out.

Or, if only my wife hadn't said his name, possibly Mad Dog would have been just outside Denver, sprinting to his car for the lead pipe before surging back into the bar to crack that asshole on the head. To teach the fool a lesson: scare Mad Dog and he'll kill you. Or, maybe, he would have been in a coastal town not far north of Boston, home at last. Biting the nose off a to-that-moment belligerent unemployed teenager, only recently eager to test himself against the infamous Mad Dog.

"No question about it," my wife said flatly, straight-arming all my innuendo and speculation. "Your friend Mad Dog is back."

I don't really want to paint my wife as some kind of virago. She simply had the opportunity to say something critical, throwing in a little self-righteousness, and did so. We just weren't doing all that well together. Still partners, yes. Sparring partners. And I was looking—after what some refs might have ruled a low blow—to clip her one right on the jaw, so to speak. Forget the so to speak. I really wanted to let her have it, not so much for the way she was, but for what we now were together. At odds. Cross purposes. Out of step. All I seemed to hear from her was no. Her eyes half the time saying "I told you so." And when truces were sustained long enough to touch, maybe to make love, then her body was so sweet and rich that even as I was in her I'd become enraged to think how soon it would all be bad again.

At this marital moment, then, my wife wasn't much pleased by the prospect of Mad Dog coming around again, and I couldn't blame her. Why? Forget Mad Dog a minute. Try the times. Oh, this corpulent here and now, obliterating the past, numbing possibility, this pure present tense was on my nerves. Polyliberated Northern California had by this near-terminal point in the seventies reduced itself to flu and inflation. Too harsh? Unfair? Well, true, at least the drought had ended.

There had been almost no rain for two years. Reservoirs running on empty. Hillsides brown, burnt. Water rationing up here, while Southern Californians spewed water on the freeway shrubbery. Too many sunny days, no closure, no level of remove. No yesterdays. And then, finally, starting not long before Christmas, just about forty days and forty nights of blessed rain. Sewers gurgling, drainpipes leaking, ceilings staining. Green hazing the fields. Worms washed to the surface of the soil, fighting for air. And, of course, people—Mad Dog often said he'd sooner buy an American car than trust a human being—people complaining about gray days and getting drenched. Rush hour on the Admiral Chester Nimitz Freeway in the spirit of Corregidor. Numerous "rain-caused" fatalities.

So, drought over, bricks out of toilet tanks, complaints replacing hosannas, after a winter of rain spring had come. But even as wildflowers unfurled, nothing held together for me. One weekend I turned on the tube and saw, as I scanned the spectator sports, Joe Garagiola, Curt Gowdy, Bud Collins, and Howard Cosell. Grounds for massive depression.

I'm saying not only that this was no time for visionaries, but also that opportunists had run themselves ragged. Dreams hustled into so many marketable commodities you could get embarrassed for the species. And I kept hearing all the time, from walking shards, about therapy for the whole being.

As the Bay Area continued to sprawl, people in cars creating fumes to asphyxiate themselves, having no particular place to go (and afraid I'd still be me anywhere I went), I found myself at home. Liquidating ants, the Himmler of *Hymenoptera*, though they weren't even streaming in my direction. I believed, briefly, that a pasta machine would solve my problems. I bought a pair of electric-yellow track shoes—garish is too kind a word—and wore them everywhere but did no jogging. I had the inside of the house painted white. I read junk mail. I practiced disco dancing.

In this grim period I gave much thought to the word "flu," succored by the confident brevity of such euphemism. The big words, we're told, are always short, in this case a contraction for "influenza" ("contagious...general prostration...fever and accompanying depression...bronchial inflammation"). In the past, hundreds of thousands died in a single influenza epidemic. For the present, forget ex-President Ford's swine flu. What we now experience is seldom lethal, merely periodic. No big deal. But, truth be told, in sunny California people get flu all the time, often can't shake it, sometimes live with it for seasons. Few Californians under sixty-five are willing to speak publicly about this, particularly once winter wanes: lack of health in fine weather suggests characterological defects.

People are always slow to accept flu in others. Several years back, I shared an apartment with a carpenter friend who was incredibly strong. He could get hit on the back by a falling beam, come home, soak in the tub, do some yoga, and be out working the next morning. When I contracted the flu—ironic understatement for overwhelming dizziness, inability to walk a hundred feet, and a sense of utter desolation enhanced by a bill for the doctor's diagnosis that I "had the flu"—I say that when I got sick my carpenter friend wasn't long on sympathy. Invisible, no stigmata: the whole business smacked to him of hypochondria and malingering. Even the most gentle souls, I've found, can be like wolves if they don't understand what you're feeling. My carpenter friend thought that what was really wrong with me was "psychological." Or that if I improved my diet, jogged more, took vitamins—all within my power, you see—I'd improve. I cannot say I cried, then, when, like an elephant downed by pygmies, he got it bad.

Flu within was matched by inflation without. Prices in real estate doubling every third year, even near-Buddhas got greedy: surely this was no time to ignore the material plane. Failure to buy into the inflationary spiral would render one a peon for life. For lives to come.

As a corollary, it seemed that the entire bottom of the economy had disappeared. Almost no one spoke of the poor, particularly of helping them (the poor themselves were strangely silent, as if ashamed, or perhaps simply awed by the widening gulf between them and the middle class). Nor was there now any such thing as junk. "Nearly new" stores prospered, marketing items "new to you"; commodities depreciated not in price but in value.

Apparent to me also was a symbiotic relationship between condominiumization and the ecology movement. Those who could no longer afford a home, but paid seventy-five thousand dollars for ownership of a small apartment, had a keen appreciation of Spaceship Earth's limited resources. If there might not be enough room in the lifeboat for possibly recalcitrant fellow citizens—the choices would be terrible—at least whales could be saved. And given the difficulties of talking to those outside one's circle, interspecies communication looked both easier and preferable.

Working myself to a frenzy as I appraised all this, I sealed my fate by deciding to stop smoking. Phones rang incessantly in my pineal gland; I was a beached fish gasping in the sun. Snorting coke to suppress my nicotine craving (manifesting itself externally in budlike excrescences that I ascertained to be yaws), I ran through a thousand bucks, quick, and contracted a mild case of megalomania. My irritation increased as I saw subordinate sections of my psyche assert their primacy. I seemed to be at school in myself, majoring in four-letter words, minoring in scatology. Though intermittently aware of what my language sounded like, I was only the more depressed, perhaps because even when nothing seemed particularly wrong, I had the sensation that the depression lever in my cerebellum had been permanently tripped. I was forever on the verge of tears.

At long last, having absorbed an overdose of my vile language, my wife succumbed. "Your fucking dinner's ready," she said one night. "It's on the fucking table."

This exchange, once articulated, stopped the present tense from moving on to another present tense, as it had been doing so remorselessly. Having remembered almost nothing for weeks, I remembered this. And, dismayed, was left to measure it against my high resolve, when we'd first fallen in love, to never—no never!—say a sharp word to her.

But to return to Mad Dog. Why wouldn't my wife want to see him around? Why would I be eager to dissociate myself from his arrival? Well, there was a day, his previous trip through, that somehow seems typical. He came over to the house while I was out and hit on my wife for some money. Knowing I wouldn't have loaned him any more, knowing it was way out of line to be asking her. When she told him no as I'd instructed her, he stormed out, slamming the door behind him so hard that the knob fell off, locking her in.

Another time he met an old friend of mine, a man about six-foot-seven. Checking him out, Mad Dog, at five-eight, now without the suggestion of a smile, told my friend he hated tall people. Or Mad Dog would walk down the street, pass some black teenagers, and mutter, audibly, "jungle bunnies." He was like that his last run through town. And finally, cursing California, saying that everyone out here was "shallow," wishing us an imminent earthquake, he left. On to a Louisiana jail, that bar just outside Denver, and the coastal town, his home, not far north of Boston.

Let me conclude, then, that there was good reason not to be glad to see him. But absorbed as I was in making and then canceling appointments with my dentist, looking for something to change if not improve, needless to say I waited for Mad Dog's call.

To defend myself in this if I can, let me defend Mad Dog, or at least flesh him out. Once we were both in Boston the night of a real blizzard, and we trudged over to Cambridge, only a few cars left on the road. As we headed for Porter Square, we watched a cab turn onto Mass Ave. and get stuck in a drift. Mad Dog walked up to the elderly cabbie and said, "Hey, take it easy, we'll handle this. Got a shovel?"

An ancient matron in the back seat rolled down her window. "Thank you very much, boys," she intoned.

"Dig you out in a flash," Mad Dog replied gallantly. "Quick as we possibly can." He began shoveling at a ferocious pace and after about fifteen minutes shouted that it was time for a try. When the cabbie, who'd been standing beside me watching him work out, headed for the car, Mad Dog said, "Wait a second, hold it. I told you we'd take care of this. Gimme the key."

Sliding in behind the wheel, he told the matron to hang on, signaled us to push, and, rocking the car back and forth expertly, finally careened onto packed snow. Leaving the engine running, getting out from behind the wheel, he said to me, "Let's go, man."

"Hey," called the cabbie. "Wait a second. Let me give you something for all that."

"No way," Mad Dog answered, deflecting the man's hand. "This one's on us. Just be more careful in the future, and take it easy."

"All right," the cabbie said. "Thanks. Thanks a lot."

"Don't mention it," Mad Dog said. Waving to the cabbie and the matron, stuffing his hands in his parka pockets, he stalked off into the black night and white snow. Another save by Super Dog.

This was the noblesse oblige of an eight-bottle-of-beer-a-day man, a self-diagnosed paranoid schizophrenic. He knew what he was doing, however, in turning down the money: who needed five, or even ten, bucks? He was getting paid for just this kind of thing, three hundred and fifty a month tax free from the state, since it concurred in his diagnosis, considering him to have a "disability." And of course with that came free medical and dental. Further, if Mad Dog chose to live more expansively, still without holding a job, he had substantial resources: shoplifting food; stiffing restaurants, particularly ones that encouraged him to run up a big tab; or, best of all, collecting from the Catholic church. This last gambit was Mad Dog's bread and butter. He'd approach a priest, make his voice thick with submissiveness and shame, and say, "I'm sorry, Father, but my wife is really worried. The kids are sick and we're way behind on the bills. The pressure's building; I'm afraid she's going to leave us. Can you help? Fifty dollars would really give some breathing room." Mad Dog figured he batted .666 at this hustle.

Fortunately, both disability payments and these scams were portable, so he could move around. Without obligations, he had the freedom to be gone much of the time. No one could have been more local than Mad Dog until he started wandering. Poor Irish ("Resentful slobs," Mad Dog often described his kind, "resentful as a bastard"), he was raised in the small fishing town his grandfather had come over to, and for him this was the world. Playing guard on the high-school basketball team; wearing his letter jacket as he raised hell in local bars; following the Celtics and Red Sox. Always with people he knew, people he'd known all his life.

But home was also where his father, a construction worker, punched the hell out of him whenever Mad Dog (Michael to his parents) manifested willfulness, where his mother, often as drunk as her husband, would strike him in the face with a leather belt. Though he really left home for the first time at nineteen, off to prison for car theft, Mad Dog might have been lucky to get away at all. And lucky his crime wasn't patricide. Monumentally confused by his parents' crazy blend of love and violence, Mad Dog was hard on himself and wild with others.

In high school, for instance, he attended a basketball workshop staffed by professional players. Mad Dog's teammate one afternoon in a game of two-on-two was Jim Loscutoff, an enormous man, notorious enforcer for the Celtics during the Cousy-Russell-Sharman era. On the occasions Loscutoff came into a game, the Boston crowd roared for blood.

In this particular contest, which Mad Dog wanted very much to win, he terminated his dribble near the top of the key. Unable to move with the ball now, and without hope of throwing up a percentage shot, he had to pass and waited for Loscutoff to cut to the hoop. As if there was some way for Mad Dog to get the ball to him past two defenders, however, Loscutoff simply stood in the corner. Finally, enraged, Mad Dog heaved the ball over the backboard, screaming, "Damn it, you stupid bastard, when I tell you cut, you cut." Showing surprising speed and stamina for a man who spent much of his career on the bench, Loscutoff chased Mad Dog quite a ways.

Though Mad Dog continued to be dominated by his temper, in prison he found that things could have been worse. He played third on the softball team, batted .355 at cleanup, ran the laundry, and tailored his own clothes out of standard issue. The world within the walls, closed and slow, was a community; he liked the feeling of knowing everything that was going on. No, institution life wasn't completely different from the Navy career he'd often planned on, but of course in prison he never knew what crazy fucker would attack him next. And as one of the white minority inside, he had to learn much more about talking his way out of trouble, about biding his time to settle a score. He began reading psychology, the better to appraise others, to predict threats more accurately. In this he was only refining techniques he'd been shaping since childhood, when he carefully observed his parents each evening as they came home from work to see if they looked especially dangerous.

A quirk of his six-year "rehabilitative" sentence was that the time ran automatically to completion once it began, no matter what Mad Dog did. Hence, when he was paroled after two years inside, it occurred to him that if he disappeared for three years and three hundred and sixty-four days, he could come back, turn himself in for that last twenty-four hours, and tell them to shove it. Irritated with the restrictions his parole officer imposed, he picked up some phony ID and started hitching around the country, stolen official NBA basketball in the pack on his back.

Often he moved from college town to college town, becoming expert at walking onto a campus and, within hours, locating a dorm or fraternity house to sleep in. The next day he'd be playing ball at the gym. Frequently he'd stay for weeks, occasionally also auditing classes. At the University of Kentucky, which had backboards and hoops he liked, he became immersed in comparing different versions of the New Testament—King James, Living, and Amplified. His studies carried him on to Dante, and he particularly enjoyed John Ciardi's analysis of the *Divine Comedy*.

Meeting so many people in so many environments in his travels, always the outsider, he became ever more skilled at reading and manipulating others. He took pride in this, quick to try to peg where someone was from, what kind of work they did. Hanging around students, reading their books, he knew he had far more experience to chew on than they did. Yet he was still utterly confused about the relationship between love and violence. He had the savvy to continue to run down the clock on his sentence, he could con just about anyone, he always managed to be released from arrests for petty offenses before the authorities learned he was wanted, he had even begun to gain some perspective on what had shaped him, but he was no closer to self-control.

Isolated, without the sense of place his hometown had given him, bereft, really, arguing with parents who were of course miles away, who no one around him could possibly know, he was perpetually on the verge of rage. In Oakland one time, watching the Raiders on TV in a bar, perhaps jealous of the locals and their loud laughter, wanting some attention or recognition, the anonymity driving him insane, he felt impelled to say in a very loud voice that Kenny Stabler was just an overrated piece of shit. Left-handed shit, for that matter. Mad Dog won the fight—escalated first to a lead pipe, then ran faster—but he couldn't help himself. He longed to go home. Was dizzy with so many strangers, so many miles.

Finally, the clock on his sentence still running, he returned. Finding his younger brothers out in the yard, he was just calming down when his mother came out of the house.

"I knew you were back," she screamed. "I just knew it. What are you doing, you criminal? Haven't you screwed up your life enough? Now you're messing up your brothers."

"Hey, Ma, don't talk like that," Mad Dog said. "Especially in front of the kids. I'll be gone soon; I'm just here to see them. It's been a long time."

"Not long enough, you good-for-nothing. You can stay away forever for all I care. Get out or I'll call the cops."

"I heard her talking like that," Mad Dog once explained as we downed Irish coffees. "I saw her making me the evil heavy with the kids. Telling them I was a no-good slob. Shit. I knew what I was. Out of my mind most of the time. Half in the bag the rest of the time. But she didn't have to run me down like that. See, she had dominated me for years. She blinded me twice with that leather belt. She's sick but very, very bright. You can really dominate people when you're that sharp. And women are like that. Deviant."

"Devious?" I asked.

"Whatever. I mean you have to keep 'em in check or they'll spin these crazy webs. They're totally unpredictable. You can never tell what they're going to do next. Fortunately, most of them you can control by letting them do what they want, because basically they're not very aggressive people.

"But my mother, she was something else. She scared my moron father, and that's a fact. Anyway, there I was at home again after being away so long. It was really something to see my little brothers. I just about raised them, since she and my father were stinking blind drunk every day. I made dinner, sewed up their torn clothes, got 'em off to school, everything.

"So, there she is again, and I couldn't take it. I gave her a shot, broke her cheekbone. Then I guess I got a little crazy. Smashed all the windows in the house. I'll tell you, though, next time I saw her she was totally different. Totally polite. You know, if you really beat someone, wicked brutal and quick, a surprise, you stymie them. You take a piece of their life."

This, then, is the Mad Dog my wife wasn't eager to see around, the Mad Dog whose call I was waiting for. My wife wasn't wrong, of course, but she wasn't living inside my skin. She was, however, close enough to see me playing the soundtrack from *Rocky* for hours every day, earphones on my head, arms raised high as I jogged in place. A winner! And she did see me sitting at the breakfast table, grinning as I read in the morning paper that the federal government was financing sex changes for indigents. Nodding my head knowingly, as if another theory had just been confirmed.

Soon Mad Dog was stopping by nearly every afternoon. He'd come walking down the street sipping a "Tall Boy" can of Schlitz wrapped in a paper bag. Liquid brunch under wraps. Always he was careful to have me step outside immediately, afraid that if my wife saw him too often she'd find a way to set me against him. Usually we'd go play pickup half-court basketball near campus with the other unemployeds and unemployables, three-on-three or four-on-four. Or maybe we'd go one-on-one, Mad Dog showing me another move Cousy taught him or criticizing me for not protecting the ball better on the drive. Urging me to run with him in the mornings to build up my stamina.

He was a good teacher, carefully explaining a complex move, breaking it down into components, working steadily and quietly on each with me until he felt it was time to try the whole. Day after day he was methodical and persistent, if too quick with praise. But he wanted me to learn, to "reach my potential."

"With your height," he often said—I'm around six-one—"there's nothing you can't do in this game." And it seemed true. After a while he had me jumping out from a low post to take a pass, setting, and going way up in the air for my jump shot. Strength from underneath, soft touch on the release. By the time I thought I had it down he was waving a broom in the air in front of the hoop to force me to put more arc on the ball. And, amazingly, my shots were going in, the net giving that beautiful soft swish on the clean ones.

Despite the beauty of what I was learning and my rapid progress, both Mad Dog and I were of course begging a simple question: what sane man would be getting deeper into basketball—not to mention giving it the best energy of each day—at age thirty-three, just the time when most court heroes switch to tennis or concede to paunch, if they haven't long since. When the prospect of being clobbered from the blind side or twisting an ankle outweighs even the possibility of dunking the ball. But there I was, the hoop my Bodhi tree, a self-confessed space case my guru.

As a player Mad Dog was very good, no question about it, especially when he didn't flip out. Which, unfortunately, happened regularly. Someone wouldn't be passing to him. The game would get senselessly rough. There'd be too many big men on the court—Mad

Dog brooding about how great he could have been at six-three—clogging the middle, and no rule in half-court to make them move around, opening space for more agile players. Or he'd become despondent to think of how it was when he played full-court ball on a hardwood floor, banking shots off a glass backboard.

Not atypical was the day he simply quit playing defense altogether during a game. No one on his team noticed until they saw the man he was supposedly guarding drive in for a second uncontested basket. When his teammates, not unreasonably, asked him what he thought he was doing, Mad Dog exploded.

"Look, this maniac is clobbering me. I'm not going to get hurt just because he's out here."

"Then sit down and let someone take your place."

"To hell with that. Tell this fool to sit down. He doesn't know anything about the game."

"Fuck. What an asshole."

"Who's calling me an asshole? Come on, say it again and see if you can still remember your fucking name. Scumbag."

"Hey, man, be reasonable, will you? If you don't want to play why don't you be cool and sit down?"

"You be cool. You sit down. The man can't play ball. Get him off the court. I'm staying and that's all there is to it."

Though Mad Dog was not all wrong, since the man he was covering had no body control, of course he could have switched assignments with one of his teammates. Instead, enraged, he'd destroyed the game. It was, sadly, also true that he'd missed his first five shots. Had they gone in, he might have put up with almost anything for the chance to keep shooting.

Despite such explosions, when it occasionally all came together he'd be jubilant—achievement and community so clearly defined. Hitting his jump shot. Or faking it, waiting till he had his man up in the air, then driving all the way, sometimes finishing with a stutter-step underhand lay-up to rub it in. Or he'd hurry back on defense, intercept the ball, and set up a back-door play with sharp passing.

Such moments waned too quickly, however, and there was no film crew recording it all for posterity. Players could and did praise each other, one might sit for an hour after the game savoring what had happened, but it was often bad feelings that lingered longest.

At the least, the rules of the game were a source of endless conflict. Without the penalty free throws of organized basketball, there was little reason not to foul. The injured party could only stop play and take control of the ball. Further, in the absence of referees, disagreements over even these barely punitive calls were often resolved by sheer obstinacy and verbal violence: a man would insist he was right and hold up the game until he got his way. Such infantilism, surprisingly, was motivated less by a desire to win than by the endemic court affliction—a hopeless disparity between ability and self-image. Since many a player was in his own mind an undiscovered or former star, it followed that no one else could possibly know as much about the game. Certainly not the other players, obviously bums.

Much of this on-court autism and assertion of infallibility derived from the maxim "I shoot, therefore I am." Though aware that the great professional basketball dynasties subordinated individual virtuosity to team play, many pickup players seemed incapable of passing the ball once it came into their hands, as if it were thence irresistibly drawn up toward the hoop. The need here was not simply for the visible success of scoring but for a conclusive demonstration of dominance. To teammates, the message, "I'm the best, therefore I'll do the shooting;" to opponents, "Do you really think you can possibly stop me?" Strangely, off court many of these atavists—their hungers harkening back to an era well before the arrival of the hunter-gatherer—were reasonable men. The game, however, brought out the very worst in them. In most of us.

"I'm going to tear that asshole's larynx out," Mad Dog said one day as we walked off the court. He was speaking of a ball hog who had kept yelling for Mad Dog to pass to him. I could find no fault with Mad Dog's sentiment, particularly since we'd lost a close game that had been a hybrid of rugby and UN debate.

No doubt this depiction of the game's negative qualities is overdrawn. There was also much banter and camaraderie, savoring of skill and idiosyncrasy, respect for ability, and even gentility. Courtliness! Especially when one became a regular and, very important, played when there weren't too many men waiting. Then at least there wasn't so much competition for scarce resources, the court less a behavioral sink. Yet life in the game was often nasty, brutish, and—if you lost—short, a Hobbesian microcosm that only confirmed Mad Dog's world view.

Frequently all this would become too much for me, though I had nowhere better to go, really, and I'd swear it off. Only to return within a few days. At such times I was also avoiding Mad Dog, his possibly contagious violence, and the feeling that he was pulling me down. This was unfair, but he'd sense my distance and stay away for a little while. Knowing the weight he could impose, he never wanted to outlast his welcome. "I'm a loudmouth," he'd say. "Fucked up. That's the way it is."

On the court, in any case, he'd found his niche. Everyone knew him; it was acknowledged that he could really play the game. The court his community, he worked hard to ingratiate himself to the other regulars, particularly if he'd recently flipped out. As if in atonement, he'd then avoid argument—to general applause—the only catch being that he'd go to any extreme to agree with everyone, shining them on, flattering them, whatever was necessary. LSD, he told me, showed him that he should be less violent. But when his pendulum swung away from anger, often he could only play the fool, diminishing himself to make others feel life-size. Deeply skeptical of most people's motives and capacities, wanting desperately to count the court regulars as his friends, knowing the mayhem he could inflict on them if he only chose, Mad Dog alternated between blind rage and obsequiousness.

Life on the court, of course, hardly encouraged candor. I think of the time I watched Mad Dog play an attorney one-on-one. The man was good and incredibly competitive, going again and again to his two strong shots, taking no risks, concentrating on the game, grinning inadvertently each time he beat Mad Dog on the drive. He was, nonetheless, carrying an extra twenty pounds around his waist, had been smoking far too much, and was well past thirty. Mad Dog—basketball his vocation, always in training—had much more stamina.

Unlike the attorney, Mad Dog called no fouls, slacked off on defense, eased the pace. Threw the game, giving it away as one might when playing a child, only pretending to go all out. It was a convincing performance. Exhausted but still pushing himself on, the lawyer was elated when he won, gracious, if a bit condescending, in victory. Mad Dog, after all, was clearly lower class, uneducated, unemployed.

Why did Mad Dog let him win? Because he perceived that if the lawyer lost he'd be furious with himself, that soon his anger would be transmuted to an intense dislike of the man who'd forced him to confront those extra pounds, all the cigarettes, the years that had passed. The lawyer was a Princeton graduate—major league in the game of life—but had so little self-knowledge, and so primitive a faculty of generosity, that I stared at his hands to see if he had opposable thumbs. It was when playing this notable that Mad Dog, on his friendship-at-any-price kick, preferred to lose.

This lawyer was only one of the regulars. There were also some psychologists, teachers, and counselors, and a number of college students. Lots of men between jobs. About half a dozen ex-cons. A minister. A former city manager. A jazz drummer. And a radical doing a Marxist analysis of a local police force. Mad Dog snorted in disgust when he heard this player's politics and quickly forgot his no-argument program.

"You poor sap," he shouted. "You want to help people? You're dead wrong. Want to change the world? Just remember this: ninety percent of the people in this country are mean, dumb, selfish, and jealous. I know; I've been all over, every state and Canada. You've read too many books. The people you want to help would fuck you over in a minute if they could. As for criminals, I say shoot 'em, shoot 'em all. I believe in those police vigilantes. You know why? Because up until a couple of years ago I was a total maniac, pure and simple. If they had wanted to stop me they'd have had to kill me. No way around it."

As if to add emphasis to his point, that same evening in his skid-row hotel Mad Dog confronted a pimp who was making noise in the corridor. Mad Dog had warned him before, more than once sat up in bed shouting curses and threats after being wakened in the middle of the night. But this time, now also enraged at being underestimated, he reached for his lead pipe. When the pimp finally staggered off, bleeding badly, Mad Dog walked downstairs to the pay phone in the lobby, dialed the police, and reported that he'd been assaulted.

Phenomenally anxious, as usual, after losing control, still "wired as a bastard" the next morning, Mad Dog paced back and forth, reliving the confrontation, unable to shake the feeling that he might just as easily have killed the pimp. True to form, he decided that it was time to leave town.

More than a month passed before he showed up again, walking down the street, basketball in his pack, wearing his made-to-order "Don't Scare Me or I'll Pipe You" T-shirt. Apparently he'd been in Reno the whole time, visiting an old girlfriend. His story took some time to unravel, however, not only because he was knocking back the six-pack he'd brought with him, but because he took out his ball and played catch for a half-hour with the neighbor's five-year-old. Patiently explaining how to throw and hold it, steadily encouraging him, gauging the improvement judiciously, a little disappointed when the boy finally ran off. Like me, the kid had "lots of potential."

But Mad Dog really had important news. "Listen, man," he said, "my girl and I are dead in love. No shit. We already consider ourselves married. Fuck the government. We're going to love each other and raise our kids. That's going to be that. Nothing can separate us. But none of this modern shit. There are two roles: man and woman. Read the New Testament. Check it out. Everything has to be orchestrated by the man. You can't give women an inch. They're basically warped. Man sets the boundaries. Give them limits, they can function. But you have to be fair, too; you owe them answers. That's how it is."

If Mad Dog's philosophizing did not augur well for marital bliss, on the other hand he was looking pretty good. That he had chucked his favorite lead pipe seemed a fair indicator of emotional gain. Unwilling to go completely naked in this vale of tears, however, he carried with him a can of police Mace. "Just a squirt guaranteed by the manufacturer to blind you," he said. "But only temporarily."

If Mad Dog was making progress of sorts, so was I, and no longer by crawling on my psychic belly, whimpering. Or by shooting baskets. I could, however, regress to rage merely by wondering what was causing the improvement. Or, put another way, by wanting some explanation of my misery. Too much white sugar? Capitalism? Asbestos poisoning? Cocaine madness pure and simple? I seemed in any case to have stopped smoking (was that it?) but allowed myself an occasional hit, like a former junkie skin-popping. I did sit-ups each morning, ate vitamins C, E, and B-complex. I stopped drumming my fingers on the dinner table.

Late one night I went out for a walk. The city was strangely still: no dogs barking, not a car moving, no rock music carrying in on the west wind. Perhaps, for a change, no rapists at work. One of my cats wandered out to see what I was up to, wanting some company. When I picked him up he made a point of complaining, but I didn't mind. I'd been pretty peevish myself.

As I headed back inside, my wife was just finishing her day. Snails cleared from the garden one last time. Cod-liver oil—emergency treatment—on the roots of an ailing plum sapling. Cats inspected for fleas. Though I felt on the verge of satori, compared to the recent past, the change must not have been visible: I walked by, and my wife stared at me as if I were lucky not to be wearing a straitjacket.

I browsed around the house, letting my mind wander, trying to remember the part of myself that had once felt a kinship with so many others, that had held all our hopes in common. I couldn't locate the precise feeling, but at least it had occurred to me. I'd find it again, another time. I got into bed, turned off the light, looked out at the balmy darkness. I slept.

In the morning Mad Dog came by. He said he was getting ready to take off, going to Reno to pick up his girl, then on to Boston. Home again. We hadn't seen each other for almost a week. I was playing much less ball. It was just too piggish, and—the hideous truth hurt—I was shooting poorly. I'd also had enough of Mad Dog for the moment. He understood: long since, he'd had enough of himself.

We drank some beers, marveled at how well Yastzremski was hitting, and shared fears that the Red Sox pitching staff would fall apart in August. "Look for me on the tube when they play the Yankees," Mad Dog said. "Third-base side." Then he smiled, opened his pack, and handed me a present. It was a very expensive walnut plaque inscribed with my name, and, under it:

Most Improved Player
Mad Dog Instructional League

I knew without asking that he'd ripped off the trophy store near his hotel. But of course he'd paid, somewhere else, for the engraving. And the idea was his own. "From one madman to another," he said, and we both laughed. Laughed like a bastard, as he'd have put it.

(1980)

Whatever the Cost

Here was a man who thought his bride beautiful. If in the first weeks of their marriage he was, not surprisingly, consumed with desire for her nakedness, a corollary of the passion they shared was his awe at how fine she looked in even the simplest clothing. Studying her as if with new eyes, he was utterly overwhelmed by the gentle curve of her breasts under a tight sweater, the long line of thigh and shank in Levi's, the cascade of hair over a plain blouse's white collar. Oh, she had her flaws, he knew, but he no longer really saw them. Not even her crooked teeth.

Opting for a simpler life, they took up residence on a small farm soon after the wedding and dressed accordingly. Even so, catching sight of his wife bending to weed the garden or stretching on tiptoe to reach an apple, he marveled that the most functional clothing was never less than a foil for her beauty. He praised cotton, gave thanks to denim, no longer disparaged synthetics.

Of course the honeymoon came to an end. Giving her a down parka, he soon had cause for regret: what kept her warm also obscured, no, obliterated the lines of her figure. He couldn't stand it, tried to take the parka back. "You look like the Michelin tire man," he said. He was equally dismayed when she discovered sweat pants and began to wear them every day. She bought several pairs, dyed them various colors, even made some of velour. "I don't think they look good on you," he told her. "I don't care if they're functional. I know it must sound foolish, but can't you just humor me?"

Though he saw her in parka and sweat pants until he cursed winter, thought of moving to Hawai'i, he was solaced when they occasionally had reason to dress up. She'd go into the closet, rummage through her thrift-shop collection of dresses, choose a pair of heels, and emerge looking absolutely elegant. Torn between admiration (wanting to see her this way forever) and lust (eager to undress her immediately), he'd remind himself what a beautiful woman he'd married.

As they prepared for a friend's party one night, he suggested that she wear a black velvet suit he found particularly becoming. "I can't," she said. "I have no boots. I gave them away; they were worn out." A long silence followed her words. He was remembering that, years before he met his wife, he once gave his lover a very expensive pair of handmade shoes. He'd been working in the city then, bringing home good money. Now he had to watch what he spent.

His mind continued to wander. Did his wife know about those handmade shoes? Of course not, he told himself. How could she? He would never have mentioned it. Or had he?

"I don't really need them anyway," she said, interrupting his thoughts. "I'd almost never get to use them here."

"Maybe not," he responded, "but I just decided to buy you a new pair."

"You shouldn't; they'll cost a lot." She laughed. "You'll regret it."

"Hey," he said. "I'm going to do it. And that's that."

Several months later they flew to New York to visit some friends. Accustomed now to country life, he was both startled by the city itself and truly amazed at the clothing people were wearing. Even the men were into high fashion, dressed fit to kill. His roommate from college, for instance, had forty suits, countless monogrammed shirts, and twenty-five pairs of shoes. As for the women, obviously they spent much care and money on what they wore. In fact, only by reminding himself that he was just passing through town did he avoid feeling somewhat drab in his Abercrombie and Fitch Viyella shirts and baggy corduroy pants. No, the country squire look just didn't cut the mustard in the Big Apple. He was also chagrined to find that friends of both sexes admired his wife's velour sweat-pants creations, asked where she'd bought them.

One afternoon he suggested they go looking for boots. Since they were staying in SoHo, they began in the Village and walked down Eighth Street, where there were supposed to be some good buys. His wife saw one pair that interested her, but he found them inadequate. "They look cheap," he said. "If we're going to do this, let's do it right."

The next day they walked all the way up Fifth Avenue until they reached Saks. Though he was already tired, this trek proved only the beginning. Over the next several hours they tried Ferragamo, Bendel's, Bergdorf's, I. Miller, and Bloomingdale's. Rendered nearly catatonic by the crowds, the array of merchandise, and the prices, he persisted because he had in mind boots that were very simple, of obvious high quality—"classical," he kept telling his wife—but hadn't seen any. She, meanwhile, tried on a pair of green suede spike-heeled boots with turquoise embroidery; lace-up ostrich-skin ankle boots with detachable spats; and, completely forgetting their mission, pumps of silk crepe de chine.

As the afternoon ended they sat drinking coffee. "Sorry," he told her. "I have a headache. I'm exhausted. Let's call it a day." They were walking back toward Fifth Avenue looking for a cab when he stopped abruptly at a store window. His wife, who'd gone ahead several feet, turned and rejoined him. "Now this is what I meant," he said triumphantly. "Wasn't this worth waiting for?" The boots were both chic and austere, extraordinarily beautiful. And, he noticed, no prices were indicated.

The shop was small but luxurious, the chairs incredibly comfortable, the clerks dressed for disco dancing. As his wife tried on first one pair of boots and then another, his head began to nod. She poked him on the arm. "Do you like these?" He did, but, looking around at the displays, suggested she try several others. As his eyes closed again he heard the cashier tell a woman he'd seen trying on a pair of iridescent leather flats that it would come to one hundred and fifty-one dollars and thirty-three cents. Dear God, he said to himself, what will boots cost?

"Those are two hundred and ninety dollars, plus tax," the clerk told him as his wife walked back and forth in front of the mirror in a pair of burnt brown Spanish-style riding boots with contrasting trim. "They're designed by our experts here and then crafted in Milan. Each boot, of course, is handmade."

"Well?" he asked his wife as she sat down, beaming. "Should we get them?"

"They must be incredibly expensive," she said.

"Let me worry about that. Do you want them?"

"Who wouldn't? But do you really think they're worth it?"

As he took out his BankAmericard, hoping he hadn't already exceeded his credit limit, the cashier explained that they also had a selection of boots for men. "No thanks, not today," he replied. Not unless you take used Adidas in trade, he said to himself.

"Happy?" he asked his wife as they walked toward Fifth Avenue to find a cab.

"Yes," she said, "but I hope you won't regret it."

"Don't worry, I won't," he replied. Yet, even as they stood on the curb waiting for the light to change, he was translating the price of the boots into house payments (one and an eighth) and shaking his head. Come on, he told himself. This is something special. She'll have the boots for years. I'll love seeing her in them.

Nevertheless, he couldn't help thinking that it was a lot of money. Of course she'd hardly pressed him to spend it. He'd made the offer in the first place; he'd suggested that they go shopping; he'd found the store. Still, it was a hell of a lot of money for a pair of boots. No question about that. She knew it too. He wondered, accordingly, if she'd feel she owed him something for such a wonderful gift. He looked over at her, noticed her crooked teeth. No, probably not. She'd assume, not unreasonably, that he'd done what he wanted to do.

He kept thinking. Though the whole venture had been his idea, wouldn't it be something if there were a quid pro quo he could now expect from her that would somehow defray the expense? But what? He laughed to himself. What indeed?

The light changed; they moved with the flow. She took his arm, boots in a plastic bag dangling from her left hand. He kissed her cheek. What a beautiful woman, he thought. Really, what could he ask for? And if he were in fact able to find some way to broach so delicate a subject, what would she think the boots were worth? Could he, for instance, ask her to stop wearing sweat pants? No, probably not, not now that so many people had admired them. Too bad. Too damn bad. The boots would have been cheap at the price.

They walked on, her arm still in his, people streaming past in both directions. It began to drizzle. The sweat pants would certainly have been worth it, he told himself, worth every last penny. What a shame. Well, that was that. So what else could it be? And then, not only consoled but starting to grin, he remembered the down parka.

(1980)

The Material Plane

What's bothering Cecille? Why isn't she cleaning the ranch house the way she always does, sweeping the floors, washing the dishes, straightening up after the twins? Why didn't she make Gabe's sandwiches this morning at dawn before he saddled up? Why didn't she bake apple pie yesterday so there'd be some left over this morning for Gabe to take up to the high country? She knows how much he likes it. And why hasn't she fed the chickens, collected the eggs, milked the goats? Cecille knows that only work will make the ranch pay, Gabe's said so a thousand times, but still she's just sitting in the living room, Bach suites for cello on the stereo, looking out the window at the rain. She should be putting on her boots and foul-weather gear, but instead she's trying to imagine Boston, where she was headed the day she met Gabe.

There may be more direct answers to explain what's bothering Cecille, but one might begin with tansy ragwort. A tall weed with yellow flowers, tansy is pretty enough but, for ranchers, a persistent problem. When cattle are crowded on land or minerally deficient, they eat tansy and can be fatally poisoned by its alkaloids. Tansy is hard to eliminate, but it can be controlled. Even as Cecille sits staring out the window, the fields of tansy are under attack by striped orange and black cinnabar-moth caterpillars. Though voracious, however, the cinnabar can't keep up with the tansy's awesome seeding. Yet it happens that sheep seem to be able to eat tansy without danger. By methodical cross-fencing, enough sheep can be contained on any given section of pasture to both clear out the tansy and keep down poison oak, bracken fern, and greasewood. Meanwhile, if properly constructed, the fences may also deter coyotes, thus saving lambs.

This isn't, as they say, the half of it. If you're into progressive pasture-management techniques the way Gabe is, you take cognizance of what's called the nitrogen cycle. Consider a legume like clover, which fixes nitrogen through nodules in its roots. Bacteria in the nodules put that nitrogen into the soil. As the clover develops, it provides enough nitrogen to make rye, fescue, and orchard grass produce well. If sheep are then grazed intensively, they not only crop the grasses, which thrive on being driven hard, but their manure—more nitrogen!—keeps the clover and grasses growing. This means winter pasture growth; just what the ewes need when lambing. Richer milk. Healthier lambs. Ultimately, not only is nothing lost, but a self-tending system of ever-greater plenitude develops.

But the fencing, the fencing. Much of the expense and labor comes from trying to make the fence coyote-proof. Strychnine now banned, a four-foot swath of woven wire is topped with two strands of barbed wire, then sealed at the bottom by a two-foot wire apron. The fence route is leveled into a road, the slope of the hill cut back to prevent easy leaps over the barbs. Whenever he can spare the time, there Gabe is, fencing and cross-fencing. Scuttling uphill on foot, fast, looking—pudbar in hand and construction helmet on his head—like a Spartan hoplite, four sticks of dynamite and some nitrogen fertilizer tamped into a stump below. About to go off. The explosion waits, waits some more, and finally crackles like a thunderclap through the background drone of the flies. A cloud of dust rises and, slowly, settles. But already Gabe is back on the huge D-8 Cat (from any distance no more than a toy, cute, and yellow like tansy), feet pumping the two brakes, hands flying from Johnson bar to blade-control lever to clutches as he surges forward, backs, wheels, and screeches, forcing his way down the slope at an impossible angle. Time passing, other tasks cared for, the seven-foot treated fir posts will be driven in with a rammer on the back of a John Deere. The wire will be laid out, stretched, and tightened with the Cat. Stapled, hog-ringed, and, at long last, done. One step toward improving the ranch.

Gabe, you see, has a dream. He wants to make this place show a profit, and then he wants to buy another. Two, in fact. One for each of his young sons. He doesn't want to end up like his father, too broke to go into town for a meal, owing bills at the feed store. Fences in disrepair, animals sick and lost. Drinking whiskey to start the day. Botching everything, finally getting his skull staved in by his own horse. No, at thirty Gabe's willing to work for what he wants, unwilling to let anything stop him.

To make the ranch pay, Gabe goes flat out all year round. Doing mechanical work in the winter when getting around the hill country becomes too treacherous, tearing down and rebuilding engines; putting out hay to help the stock resist the stress of cold, frost, and occasional snow. Lambing in January, calving in March. Doctoring and marking by the end of May. Shearing in June. Preparing for market, haying, fencing, and logging through the dry summer and fall. Doctoring the cattle again, and weaning calves, before the rains return.

Consider just the logging, one task of many. Always short of cash because he reinvests the money from the sale of lambs and yearlings back into his flocks and herd, Gabe logs as much timber each year as he can. Setting out early in the morning, always, to avoid the heat of the day, chain saw slung up on his shoulder, three-foot blade cushioned on a folded burlap sack, gas can, oil jug, and ax in his free hand, Gabe trudges up through alder, poison oak, myrtle, and cedar, looking for trees to fell. Picking one, deciding where he wants it to land, studying curves in the trunk that suggest it will split and shoot back when cut, checking wind direction and force, Gabe grunts as he jerks the starter cord on the saw. He places his undercut, knocks it out with the ax, and steps around the tree. Sawdust now shooting back from under the blade, foul-smelling water pouring out of the white ("piss") fir, Gabe slices into the rear side, perhaps making additional cuts to stop the trunk from pinching the blade. And then, moving away quickly, he watches as the tree tilts, creaks, breaks, rips, and crashes.

For a moment, saw stilled, there's quiet. Sunlight filters down, air full of the myrtle's aromatic smell; the northwest wind soughs through the branches. But Gabe has his rhythm and, gear gathered, is already moving on. Later he'll return to trim the trees and haul them out with the Cat, then buck the logs into standard lengths for the mill. All this is hard and dangerous work. Stories of loggers being maimed and killed are common. But for Gabe, timber is money, and money buys him time to increase his stock and finish the fencing.

A little more than six years have passed since the day Cecille first drove up the four miles of unpaved road to the ranch in Gabe's battered '52 pickup. Hitching through the Northwest, in no hurry at all, she was on the first leg of a trip cross-country from San Francisco to visit her brother in Boston. She was twenty then, about to begin her sophomore year of college, and tired of feeling too well protected. She'd traveled, even to Europe, but always with her parents or as part of an organized group. Her parents had objected vehemently to her plan to hitchhike alone, but she'd told them, quietly, that she could take care of herself. Her confidence was confirmed in the first four days on the road: rides came quickly, one after another; everyone was friendly. She stayed overnight with some musicians in Eureka, camped with a family in a VW bus on the beach in Southern Oregon. The proprietor of a roadside café offered her a job as a short-order cook.

The morning Cecille met Gabe she'd taken a ride inland with some longhairs. They left her off in a small town that it seemed to her was in the very middle of nowhere, flat green country with clusters of dairy cows standing under isolated shade trees. She'd walked on past town about a mile when Gabe drove up and stopped. He didn't say a word, simply leaned over and punched the door, hard, throwing it open. Cecille climbed in, smiling and saying thanks, but Gabe only shook his head as she tried several times to close the door. Then he leaned past her, grabbed the handle, and slammed the door shut. Cecille's initial impression of Gabe was of disparate parts: his straw cowboy hat, shocks of red hair pushing out from under; his silence; his long legs folded under the steering column; and his right hand, nails filthy and broken, skin scarred. An old man's hand, Cecille thought, though Gabe was obviously in his early twenties.

As they drove along, his silence was so profound that she couldn't think of a way to break it. She failed even to ask him how far he was going or what road would connect with a major highway. In another context, hitchhiking alone, she might have found such silence menacing, but Gabe simply seemed remote. After about ten miles, as he approached a crossroads grocery and post office, he said, "This is as far as I go." It was high noon, hot. Not a car in sight. Cecille began to gather her pack and jacket.

"Have you ever done ranch work?" Gabe asked, looking straight ahead out the dirty windshield.

"No," Cecille said quickly, assuming now that she'd misread him, that he was making some kind of advance. "I'm on my way to Boston to visit my brother. Then I go back to school."

"People learn a lot on a ranch," Gabe said, still looking straight ahead.

Cecille couldn't control her laughter. He had to be putting her on, she thought. The taciturnity, the avoidance of eye contact. It was surely a parody of rural style.

"People learn a lot in school," she said, still laughing.

"Maybe," Gabe answered, now looking toward her but not quite meeting her eyes. "Maybe. But I'm getting a ranch going. I'm looking for someone who can cook and clean and garden. Fifty dollars a month and room and board."

Cecille laughed again. This really would be a story to tell her family and friends. "Woman's work, is that it?"

"That's right," Gabe said, apparently missing her sarcasm.

"Well," Cecille replied, thinking it had gone far enough. "I'm not looking for work right now. I have plans."

"Ever see a ranch?" Gabe asked, as if she hadn't just rejected his suggestion.

"No."

"Why don't you visit one before you make up your mind?"

Cecille looked down the road. Still not a car in sight. Sun hot and high. "How far is it?"

"Four miles."

"You promise to drive me back down?"

Gabe nodded, and, before Cecille could say anything else, shifted into first gear and headed up the dirt road, a plume of dust streaming out behind each rear tire. Finally they approached the ranch house, which sat tucked in a hollow, a creek flowing behind it past corral and barns.

"This is beautiful," Cecille said, surprised. But Gabe seemed not to hear her, or to speak right past her words.

"I'm alone here. I need someone to help."

"For the woman's work?" Cecille asked, again sarcastic, thinking that her friends would never believe someone his age could be so out of date.

"That's right," Gabe said, apparently missing, or ignoring, her tone.

Weeks later, Cecille learned how Gabe's father had died, that his mother had run off years before, and that Gabe had been in the merchant marine, traveling all over the world, so his country manner was at least partly a matter of intent. But that afternoon she had little to go on. Marveling at the beauty of the land, however, she decided to stay for several days. Another adventure. Yet, strangely, Gabe did nothing at all to encourage her, going off on horseback without inviting her, saddling up as she watched him, without a word about when he'd return. It was nightfall before he came in, clearly exhausted, only nodding his head to acknowledge her presence. Breaking out a can of franks and beans with a look of reproach, as though he'd expected her to have dinner prepared.

While he'd been gone that afternoon, Cecille had inspected the ranch house, startled to see how dirty it was, the absence not only of order but of any softening touches. He really did need someone, she thought. She'd also walked out to the barn and corrals and had seen the dogs.

"Why do you keep the dogs like that?" she said when they sat down to eat.

"Like what?"

"Chained up."

"So I know where they are."

"All day?"

"They're here to work. They're not pets."

"But why do you need so many?"

"Two for sheep, three for cattle. Two growing up to replace the ones that get hurt."

"I think it's horrible," Cecille said self-righteously.

"I'm running a ranch here," Gabe responded. "I don't have much time to play."

When he fed the dogs later that night, however, Cecille was surprised to see him let them off the chain. Was he doing it for her? He spoke quietly to them, teasing them as they swirled around him, a kaleidoscope of black and white, shooting up at his face over and again like porpoises. Seeing Cecille watching, Gabe said, "They're Border collies. Purebred. Expensive. And it took a lot of time, too much time, to train them. But they're good dogs."

That night Gabe showed Cecille a room, empty except for a mattress on the floor, a bare bulb hanging from a cord in the ceiling, and gave her a few blankets. No sheets, no pillow. Cecille had trouble sleeping, heard two owls hooting back and forth for hours, woke frequently. In the middle of the night she opened the window and looked out. There was no light in the sky, the fog in low, air moist and absolutely still. Past the outlines of the myrtle, oak, cottonwood, and maple she could just make out the barn roof's sharp slope.

When Cecille came down in the morning Gabe was gone and didn't return until late afternoon. Though she had considered staying several days, she was piqued by his lack of attention.

"I thought you were going to drive me to the road," she said, feeling slightly foolish as she heard herself.

"Sorry. I had trouble in the high country."

"You should have taken me along. I'm a good rider."

"We'll see, then. I have to go back up tomorrow."

The next morning at six he knocked on her door, and by the time she came down he was outside, sitting on his horse and holding the reins of another. This is more like it, Cecille thought. For nearly an hour, dogs running on ahead, they climbed slowly through the ground fog, sun finally breaking through. As they came over a rise onto the high south-facing prairies, they saw several elk. Cecille was elated.

"I wish I had my rifle," Gabe said.

"Why would you want to shoot them?" Cecille asked.

"I don't hunt," Gabe said, "but elk destroy the fencing. They don't even try to jump the fences sometimes, just plow on through. You don't know this country or what it's like to run a ranch. You can't imagine how much work they cause. They're beautiful, but I wish I'd brought a gun."

Cecille knew that she should say something more, that no one should kill such animals. They were wild, free, had to be saved. But what Gabe told her made sense, given his perspective. At least he wasn't glad to shoot them. That was in his favor. As they rode on, time and again Gabe sent the three dogs into the brush to drive out the groaning cattle. "Way 'round now," he'd shout, and the dogs would surge off in a wide circle to get past the cows and calves and stop them. Once this was done, Gabe would call "Get in behind" to bring the dogs back, cursing under his breath if they were slow to respond. Then he and Cecille would canter along to another area. Finally they drove the stock they'd gathered down to the corral behind the ranch house.

Though she'd loved the riding, Cecille was exhausted and quickly depressed both by Gabe's obvious intention to continue to work and by the corral itself. The bare muddy ground and weathered gray planks had escaped her notice the day before, but now she began to appreciate the relentless progress of the pattern. The main corral fed into a small corral, which opened into a holding pen, which in turn funneled into a narrow walkway down which Gabe drove the cattle with an electric prod. Cecille thought of pictures she'd seen of Bull Connor and the marchers in Alabama.

Gabe forced each animal into the inverted V of the squeeze's bars. The opening behind clanged shut each time, and, as the cow or calf lurched forward, the front gate caught it at the neck and shoulders. Tongs Gabe placed in the nostrils jerked the head up. And then, depending on what he decided had to be done, Gabe cut ears and tagged them, branded, vaccinated, wormed, fluked, castrated, dehorned, checked for pinkeye, and, finally, with another clanging, released the terrified animal to a holding pen. Her stomach turning, Cecille forced herself to stay. But Gabe was too busy to notice, his bloody hands reaching for drench gun, hoof trimmer, prod, branding iron, worm gun, knife, Elastrator, syringe, dehorner. "I'm sick," Cecille finally shouted and ran up to the ranch house, sure she'd leave in the morning.

She didn't leave, of course. Perhaps because Gabe made no advances. Cecille couldn't even take it as a sign of respect; he just didn't try to sleep with her. And her admiration for his drive and skill was growing. The next day she rode with him again and watched him separate a bull from some cows. Cantering through the pasture, rocking easily in the saddle, Gabe brought his gelding next to the bull and guided him—both animals now thundering along—flank to flank, buffeting the bull over and again, forcing it yard by yard up the hill. It was a dangerous job, done well, but Cecille gave Gabe no praise, still annoyed by his apparent lack of concern about whether or not she'd stay.

That afternoon she watched him fix one of the gelding's shoes, taking the hoof and putting it up on a broken axle that functioned as a makeshift stand, deftly tearing off the shoe, cleaning out mud and rot, cutting back the nail with rippers, and filing the hoof smooth. Then, having straightened the shoe on the anvil, Gabe turned his back to the gelding's head, bent over, took the hoof through his legs, and supported it on his knees. The gelding shifted his weight restlessly, tossed his head. "Way, way, come on now," Gabe said softly. Towering over him, the gelding pulled back. "Take it slow, come on," Gabe said. Grunting with exertion, he drove eight nails into the shoe, cut off the ends, and filed them down. Cecille was moved, the same way she'd been when Gabe let the dogs off the chain the first night. He was incredibly gentle with the gelding. The work was rough, often cruel, Cecille thought; but Gabe wasn't.

The next day she began to clean up the house and cook the meals. She started by washing the walls and floors, finally, after a week, feeling ready to paint. Each evening Gabe came back filthy, fed the dogs, and sat down to eat. "You're on the payroll," he'd said that first evening, "but spend as little as you can. You'll have to put in a garden. I'll slaughter an animal for some meat." He seemed pleased that the house was cleaned but said nothing at all about the painting, as if he simply tolerated it. When Cecille gave him the bill for the paint and brushes, he raised his eyebrows and stared but didn't stop her. Merely left the suggestion that she was doing it for herself, not for him.

Cleaning out an upstairs closet about a week later, Cecille came across a box of books. There were many paperback Westerns and, to her surprise, the collected works of Joseph Conrad.

"Whose books are those?" she asked when Gabe came in that evening.

"Upstairs? The Westerns belonged to my father."

"Who read all the Conrad?"

"Me."

"Why such an interest in him?"

"I wanted to get away from home. And I did. I joined the merchant marine when I learned that Conrad had left Poland, a landlocked country, and become a sailor. I figured if he could do it, then I could at least make it fifty miles to the coast."

Cecille was elated. No one at home would believe it. A cowboy who read Conrad and had been to sea!

Soon Cecille had been on the ranch a month, having written her brother several times to say she'd been delayed. As weeks passed, she was aware that it was almost time to return to San Francisco to get ready for the fall semester. On the whole, she was pleased with herself. She knew she'd helped Gabe, she'd learned a great deal about ranching, and she'd have incredible stories to tell. She hadn't reached Boston, but she'd get there next summer, or maybe even at Christmas. The only thing that bothered her was that she and Gabe hadn't made love, hadn't kissed or even touched for that matter. She just couldn't figure him out.

Then one day she got chilled swimming in the creek. It was her own fault. She'd been taking a dip late each afternoon, both to bathe, since the shower was broken, and in the hope that Gabe might see her as he returned to the ranch house. Still she was irritated by his apparent lack of desire for her. There was no sun that particular afternoon, and even as she got dressed she was shivering badly. By the time Gabe came back she was in bed. He felt her forehead, made her some tea, covered her with extra blankets. She tossed and turned all night, but each time she woke she saw Gabe sitting in a straight chair beside her bed, dozing, long legs stretched out before him, bits of hay in his red hair.

She came into his room one evening not long after she recovered. It was transformed now that she'd cleaned and painted it. Walls white, floor bright blue, small throw rug on the floor, wildflowers in a vase. She got into Gabe's bed and stayed the night.

"Why did you make me wait so long, and why did I have to come to you?" she asked when they woke in the morning. "You know you're my favorite cowboy."

"I guess I'm shy," Gabe answered.

"Is that really it?" Cecille said, only half joking, thinking that maybe he just hadn't wanted her, hoping to be reassured.

"I guess I don't like fast women," he said. He was smiling; he had his arm around her.

"You know, the trouble is that I think I believe you."

"There's more."

"What?"

"I wanted to see if you really liked the ranch."

"I should sleep with the ranch then."

"I'm serious."

"You're strange. Or maybe just straighter than straight. I thought your type was dying out."

"It probably is. But before I'm gone, let's make love one more time."

About two weeks later, Cecille told Gabe she'd have to leave soon to arrive at school in time for registration. By now she didn't want to go but had no idea what Gabe was thinking.

"Of course there's a lot to learn at school," Gabe said, grinning. "Then again, there's a lot to learn on a ranch."

"So?"

"But if you stay and live on the ranch like this, people will talk."

"I want to stay. Let them talk."

"No," Gabe said quietly, "I don't think that's the way to go about things around here."

"Then what?" Cecille said, about to cry, thinking Gabe was telling her to leave.

"Well, I think we'd have to be married. I think that would pretty much shut people up."

Gabe didn't want a big wedding, no ceremony at all really, so they settled on a justice of the peace in the small town where he'd picked Cecille up on the road. They took no honeymoon, however: Gabe said he just couldn't leave the ranch with market time coming right up. A month later Cecille rode by bus down to San Francisco, startled, once there, by the crazy variety of life, the light, the laughter, the numbers of people, the choices of ways to be. She was sorry Gabe hadn't come, but she returned to the ranch full of energy, thinking of the many changes she'd make. Friends would visit, her parents too. They'd all love Gabe. She'd get a car, so as not to have to depend on Gabe's schedule. And she'd find a stereo. She did in fact receive a stereo from her brother as a wedding present, but friends came seldom and usually stayed no more than several days. Always Cecille felt abandoned as they drove off. As for the car, when her parents gave her their old station wagon she got the feeling that Gabe was displeased. She asked herself repeatedly if she wasn't mistaken, but it was true. Gabe didn't want her to be able to leave the ranch whenever the spirit moved her. He considered the ranch his world, got uneasy when any part of that world wasn't under his control. This was something that called for understanding, Cecille told herself. Gabe's mother, after all, had run off. In time Gabe would see; he'd learn to trust her.

Now that she had the car, however, she decided to visit her sister in Seattle. She urged Gabe to come, pointed out that the neighbors' son could do the chores for a week, but Gabe insisted he had no time to waste. He could still get some logging done, he said, before the heavy rains began. When Cecille responded that she'd have to go herself if that's how he was, he simply refused to discuss it further. Clearly he felt betrayed. Cecille made the trip, finally, driving away from the ranch in a rage, but she was gone less than a week, worrying about Gabe the whole time. When she called from Seattle, she told him she was sorry. He didn't make it easy for her to apologize.

As that first year passed, she learned more and more about ranch life. How to start the pickup—putting a heel on the floor starter as you gave it gas with the toes of the same foot—was the first lesson, then how to drive the tractors. With Gabe's help she put in an enormous garden and carefully planted rows of marigold and mint against insect predators. She began baking loaves of bread each week, and pies. She learned how to repair engines, sharpen tools. She got goats and ducks for milk and eggs. She canned and dried fruit and vegetables. When lambing began, she learned how to put her hands deep in a ewe's womb to help a breech birth, and soon had ten motherless lambs—bummers—feeding in the living room. She kept so many bummers alive, in fact, that Gabe made no objection when she insisted on keeping one, marking it with red dye so it wouldn't be carted off to market by mistake. The lamb followed

Cecille around like a pup, even went swimming with her in the creek.

Cecille would not, however, help Gabe butcher the animals they consumed themselves. She knew it was inconsistent—she ate lamb or beef almost every day—but she couldn't, not after the time she watched Gabe slaughter four wethers. He put them in the front yard that morning, closed the gate, and shot two, a bullet apiece. Once more Cecille had to admire Gabe's skill. Then he raised them off the ground with the tractor lift and quickly bled, beheaded, skinned, gutted, and halved the carcasses. He returned to the front yard, took up his rifle again, and dropped the third wether. The fourth, now alone and smelling blood, surged from end to end of the yard. Waiting patiently for a good target, Gabe finally fired. Blood spurted out of the wether's mouth, but, crazily, it came right at Gabe, then broke past him across the front porch and down the road. Cursing, Gabe chased and at last downed it, slitting the throat as he broke the neck. The sun eased through the clouds; yellow jackets gathered on the wheelbarrows teeming with innards. Though she knew Gabe hated what he called "false sentimentality," Cecille began to cry.

Perhaps she was overwrought because she was pregnant. For months before the twins were born, in fact, she wondered if she'd been right to marry Gabe, and now to have his children. Her parents had come up to meet him and see her new home, but though they'd said how beautiful it was, clearly the life seemed harsh to them. Her father, a doctor, was an opera buff, her mother a singer of lieder music. For them the ranch was a place to visit, but no more. When Gabe, trying to be polite, expressed sympathy that they had to live in a city, her father corrected him, going on at length about the riches of urban life. Inviting Gabe, pointedly, to come and see. Sometimes, reading the weekly letter from her mother, thinking of the concerts her parents were going to, of the incredible mix of her parents' friends, Cecille would find herself ground down by the practicalities of the ranch. And by Gabe's monomania. Everything had its function. Animals were raised to be sold or consumed. Fruits and vegetables too. Pups that didn't show promise were shot. And, it occurred to Cecille, she too had her place on the ranch. To cook, to clean. And to breed.

She chastised herself for such thoughts, felt disloyal to Gabe. He'd never dissembled; he was just as he presented himself. A man building up a ranch. His aspirations had moved her; she'd responded to his dream. More, she knew how vulnerable he was, the shame he'd felt for his father, how he'd suffered when his mother ran away. But understanding Gabe didn't always help. Still she could find no way to make him compromise. She'd been certain when they married that she'd be able to enhance the gentleness that was clearly in him, to get him to ease his pace. But now, with her help and presence, he seemed only more driven. And life on the ranch was all on his terms, his personal preferences buttressed by the demands of two-thousand acres, seven-hundred and fifty animals, and loan payments. Cecille began to feel that she could argue with Gabe but not with the whole damn ranch. She kept the bummer lamb, built hummingbird feeders, put candles on the table at dinner, bought linen napkins, all to insist that not everything had to be functional. She did all this but felt as though she was only losing ground.

During her pregnancy, sometimes scared of what she had set in motion, she'd laugh bitterly to herself. Visitors found the ranch so romantic, but they knew little of the reality. Of course there was the branding, the castrating, the butchering, the endless dirty and dangerous work. But beyond that, seeing the ranch as remote, visitors failed to understand how exposed it was. At the least, much of Gabe's land was unfenced, and in any case all fencing was porous. Elk and bear flattened it at will; nothing could keep all the coyotes out. More, even on horseback with the dogs, working the heavy timber and brush of the high country, Gabe could never be certain he'd gathered all his stock. Was it just the inevitable four percent wandering around up there, or had someone been rustling?

Reinforcing this sense of permeability, and far more intrusive, were the hunters. Both Gabe and Cecille dreaded deer season. Some hunters moved with caution and respect for land not their own. But others, crazily overarmed, drinking heavily, crossed property lines at will. Skidding and winching up impossible slopes, eroding prairies and rutting out roads, loaded rifles pointed out the windows. Eager for their quota, often shooting even in a heavy fog at any sound of movement. Gabe could post the land, of course, but legal proceedings suggested only wrath incurred, and cattle were simply too easy to pick off. Ultimately there was no obstacle to determined hunters. Gunfire echoed in the hills. Resting in the afternoons, Cecille often pulled the pillow over her ears, but there was no escaping the sound.

Sometimes even the language of the ranch country drove Cecille wild. At first the economy of gesture, composure, and taciturnity seemed quaint, almost comic, to her, but slowly she sensed that it was all structured for an avoidance of direct requests and refusals. No one wanted to give offense. A grudge might develop, a barn might be burned. Cecille knew that Gabe was comfortable with the circumlocutions, found protection in them. And she often loved him the more as she watched him talk to other ranchers with an abiding reserve that Shane or the Virginian would have grudgingly admired. Yet no matter how much it suited Gabe, this was also the mode of people who had something to lose. No one, she thought, was "up front." Women on ranches nearby spoke with her frequently, were generous and helpful, but remained neighbors. No more, if no less.

Just before the twins were born, another rancher's stray cow was hit by a car on the road near the house. Though the animal was suffering, Gabe refused to shoot it until he could reach the owner and get his approval. Cecille listened, hour after hour, as the animal groaned in pain. She begged Gabe to put it out of its misery. Surely, she argued, the man would understand. But Gabe waited a day and a half.

Once the twins were born, Cecille had little time to wonder if she'd chosen the right life. Between caring for the boys and her endless round of chores, questions were a luxury she couldn't afford. Spring, summer, and fall she and Gabe went flat out, and winter never seemed long enough for a real rest. She made one trip each year with the twins to visit her parents but had little energy for exploring the city.

As the boys grew and she watched Gabe initiating them into ranch work, she began to feel that already they were not hers. What could they know of the world she'd come from? Perhaps, she told herself, they could spend time with her parents when they were older, summers, or even go to boarding school in San Francisco. It would be a battle with Gabe, of course, and she was glad such a possibility was years off. Meanwhile Gabe still drove himself, though by now the cross-fencing was finished, tansy under control, stock increasing each year. Other ranchers, doing less well, took vacations in winter when things slowed down, hired foremen, but Gabe was looking for another ranch. Since Cecille met him he'd gone no more than the fifty miles to cattle auction.

The fall the boys were five they went off to school. Suddenly, after years without a moment to herself, Cecille had time to daydream, to simply look around her without trying to get something done. She began to relax, no longer feeling that she was always behind, struggling to catch up. Hungering for something new in her life, wanting to see the world outside the ranch, she signed up for an ecology course at the regional junior college fifty miles away, planning to make the trip two nights a week. Far from supporting her in this, however, Gabe argued that the hundred dollars for the course was a waste of hard-earned money, not to mention the cost of gas and wear and tear on the car.

"But this is something I want to do, Gabe," she said, struggling to control her anger.

"Nobody gets everything they want."

"You do," Cecille suddenly shrieked. "You do."

"Lower your voice," Gabe said. "The boys can hear."

"Let them. It's about time they heard me say something. You wanted another ranch, so you put us in debt all over again. No questions asked. You wanted another tractor, you bought it. Did you ask me about that? You wanted to increase the flocks again instead of keeping the money. Who asked me? When is it ever not what *you* want? And now you tell me, the first time I've done something like this, that a hundred dollars is hard earned? I know what it took to get that money. What do you think I do around here all day? I know it was hard because I earned it. Over and over and over again. And don't you dare tell me I didn't."

Cecille shouted these last words at Gabe's back as he slammed the front door behind him. He said nothing more about her taking the class, but neither did he apologize. If anything, she thought, he was harder than ever, less open, more set against any manifestation of her autonomy. If she hadn't had the car her parents gave her, she was sure, Gabe would have made it impossible for her to go.

At class she met students who worked in the mills or at various small businesses in town. Their wages were small, they had no hope of better jobs, but to Cecille they seemed remarkably free from care. Despite Gabe's silent opposition and the long drive, she looked forward to each class. Only twenty-six, she'd begun to think of herself as an older woman, no longer young in any case, in part because of the twins. Her classmates, however, simply assumed that she was more or less like them. Several men at school asked her to join them for drinks, and though she begged off, she was flattered. Gabe had for some time seemed to take her for granted, and the few males she saw at the ranch—other ranchers, the cattle buyer—were always ponderously careful to treat her less as a woman than as Gabe's wife. She felt younger each week the semester passed, laughed more. Maybe, she thought, she could even loosen Gabe up a little.

One day when the twins were off at school, Cecille stepped out on the front porch and saw a hunter only several yards away. Bowie knife and pistol on his belt, rifle in hand, wearing fatigues and an Army jacket. Beside him was a dead buck, clearly underage. She felt the hunter watching her as she looked at the deer. This kind of thing had happened before, many times, and Gabe liked it no more than she did. Over and again she'd seen Gabe check his temper, forcing himself to be civil, waiting until the hunter left his land. But this time Cecille couldn't do it.

"That buck is too small," she heard herself saying. She knew Gabe would be furious if he learned.

"Oh, I don't know about that," the hunter said easily, meeting her eyes. "I'd say it's okay. Wouldn't you, now that you think about it?"

Cecille heard the threat but was so angered by the very presence of the hunter that she was unable to stop herself. "No," she said. "Count the points for yourself."

"Oh, that," the hunter replied, grinning. "That's nothing we can't fix." He pulled out his pistol and fired four times, blowing the antlers to bits. "There now," the man said, holstering his gun. "No more problem."

"But I saw it," Cecille said, her ears still ringing from the shots.

"Well," the man responded, "I guess you might have made a mistake."

"No," Cecille said, "I didn't make a mistake." Scared, she went inside and locked the door. Finally she heard the man drive off.

Late that afternoon, walking the bottom land on her way to check the apple trees, she heard several shots back toward the ranch house. More hunters, she thought. When she returned from the orchard, passing the barn, she saw a bull on its side, still alive but slowly bleeding to death from a gunshot wound. There was no way, Cecille realized, not so close to the house, that the shooting could have been accidental. The hunter must have returned to teach her a lesson. Cecille went inside, got Gabe's rifle, placed a shell in the chamber, and walked out toward the barn. Putting the muzzle against the bull's head, she pulled the trigger.

She was still there, sitting beside the bull, when Gabe came down from the high country. She'd thought of lying to him, but when he reached her she told him about the hunter and what she'd said. She waited for him to explode, but he just nodded his head as if he'd expected as much. As if she really had no place on the ranch. Still silent, he walked over to the shed, backed out the small tractor, and hauled the carcass into the barn.

For several days not a word passed between Gabe and Cecille. She stopped baking bread, made no pies. Then the winter rains began in earnest, and her depression deepened. It would be cold and gray for months. She thought of visiting her parents but had no energy for the trip. She'd gone through it all too many times. Packing up, going to the bus station, riding all those miles. Seeing her parents, having to answer their questions, knowing they always worried about her. Being overwhelmed by the city. Only to return to the ranch to find Gabe the same, herself the same. Each morning she packed the twins off to school, but each day she spent more time letting her mind wander. She stopped canning and drying fruits and vegetables. She had to force herself to milk the goats. She missed one class, then another. Days passed, a week, but still Gabe didn't speak to her. He was freezing her out, she thought, and she was turning to ice. Was this what Gabe's father had done? Was that why his mother had run off? Cecille stopped cleaning the house. Dishes piled up in the sink. There were no clean clothes. The twins complained. Still Gabe said nothing. Without a word, finally, he did a wash but left the dirty linen napkins in the hamper.

Late each afternoon now, when the twins came home, Gabe returned from whatever work he was doing, got them into their rain gear, and took them out with him. He began to make them breakfast and supper. Each day, watching this, Cecille spent more time thinking. When Gabe rounded up the cattle from the high country, bringing them down to the corrals, she played Bach cello suites on the stereo to drown out the sound of the cows and calves calling to each other. Did the cows know the separation was final? she wondered. Did the calves know it was time to die?

Cecille felt herself losing control but could think of no one to ask for help. She gave up altogether the idea of going to class. What was the point? She had endless bitter imaginary arguments with Gabe, screaming at him to say something, to leave the ranch, to come with her to San Francisco. To show her some love. Convinced suddenly that he would try to sell her bummer lamb, she closed it in the barn. She sat for hours in her workroom, returning again and again to the day Gabe picked her up on the road. The longhairs who had given her a ride that morning. The spot where they'd left her off. The feeling of being in the middle of nowhere, clusters of dairy cows standing under isolated shade trees. The heat of the sun. What would have happened, she kept wondering, if she hadn't taken the ride? If she hadn't gone up to the ranch? If she hadn't stayed? What if she'd continued on? Where would she have gone? Who would she have met? Where would she be now? Would she be different? How? Who would she be? What would Boston have been like?

(1980)

The Tom in Particular

The cats were pushing for dinner as though they had God on their side, making no allowance for the shift the night before off daylight saving time. The orange tom, having earlier suffered the ignominy of being shooed out for nagging, dropped off the garage roof (from which he could survey most of the human movement in the cottage) onto the redwood fence, sailed to the ground when he reached the gate, and sprinted through the cat door into the kitchen. Arriving at the threshold of the living room with heartfelt urgency, convinced at the very least by his own velocity: surely it was time to eat.

Though the two other cats—the huge tortoiseshell female and her much smaller black-haired mother—spatted obligingly as the tom made his entrance (their strategy being to demonstrate that only hunger pains could drive them to such uncharacteristic squabbling), their mistress was too preoccupied to pay them any mind. She was unpacking, finally, the trunks, bags, and suitcases she'd brought back from her parents' home, the welter of childhood baubles, inherited valuables, and flea-market finds she'd left there for the nearly ten years she'd been on her own.

She'd always insisted that nothing of hers be thrown out, arguing long distance more than once against her mother's resolve to "clean up the children's rooms once and for all." It was not until her parents announced their decision to give up the house for an apartment, however, that she'd gone to fetch what was hers.

Of course she had always kept with her some few treasures. A black cashmere overcoat, once her mother's. Two Mesopotamian spun-gold earrings that tinkled like bells when she wore them. A necklace of black seed pearls given to her grandfather by fishermen on the river Don. And several silver buckles from a belt of her grandmother's, each engraved with a maiden in profile (right hand cradling a crescent moon, left bearing a garland of lilies).

But at last, now twenty-seven, she finally had all her things again. "Market value four hundred dollars, tops," her husband said from the soft chair in the corner. Newspaper in his lap, shaking himself awake to survey the unpacking.

"Oh, stop it, will you," she said, thinking she'd just as soon be alone. "You don't even know what these things are."

"Artifacts from a previous incarnation? Salvage from Pompeii?"

"Is that supposed to be funny?" she responded sharply. "I don't need to hear it." Just looking at the work ahead made her want quiet and space; she found her husband's voice particularly intrusive. It would help considerably if he—and the cats—just disappeared for a while.

"Sorry. No offense," he said.

Unable to tell from the tone of her husband's voice if he meant it, or if his grin was really apologetic, wondering why she even had to try to figure him out, she glared in his direction. Even this took her far from her thoughts.

"I said I'm sorry. I meant it."

"Okay, okay. Forget it. I'm busy."

Shaking her head, finding none of her husband's tricks amusing, her mind teased by the rush of associations each object summoned up, she walked over to the stereo. Putting on her father's favorite, Stravinsky's *Firebird*, which she'd heard so many times as a child, Pachelbel's Canon in D Major ready to follow, wearing white tights, a black leotard, and black tooled cowboy boots, she began to cull the jumble into three categories.

Clothing

A gray linen schoolgirl's jumper, at least fifteen years old, which still fit her. A sleeveless cotton tennis shirt. A poor-boy sweater with jewel neckline knitted by her sister. Two pairs of straight-leg corduroy pants. "Way too short for my father. Mother got them in a thrift shop."

"What?" her husband asked, busy in the sports page, unable to tell if she was talking to him or to herself.

"Nothing."

Jodhpurs with leather kneepads. A visored riding helmet covered in black velvet. Leather pants. *Ruined,* she thought, remembering how years before she'd waded into a saltwater pond when the family's German shepherd had fallen through the ice. And then stood shivering in the cold, watching the dog, memory so short, chasing a cormorant down the beach, while she'd wondered if the pants could be saved. Now, holding them up, inspecting them carefully, she was sure they were finished.

She pressed on. A sky-blue velvet dressing gown with an Elizabethan collar. Two mutton-sleeved bodices: one red silk, the other forest-green taffeta with ivory cuffs and dickey. Anderson tartan Bermuda shorts. A silk Anderson dress-tartan scarf, with bits cut from it. Rosettes for her grandmother's grave.

A skirt of French grosgrain ribbon. A mustard seersucker peasant skirt and blouse. Pleated cream crepe evening pants. An English wool houndstooth jacket. A pair of turn-of-the-century silk ladies' drawers. Her mother's old bathing suit: flowered pleated rayon with full skirt and fitted bodice. Bright pink.

A pinafore with whale spouting. A brick-red Ferragamo knit suit, never worn. A white terrycloth beach jacket. A pencil-cut purple raincoat. A natural raw-silk overcoat, also her mother's.

Chartreuse linen shorts. A Georgian flannel dress with lace collar. An A-line unbleached muslin wraparound skirt, with buttonholes in the shape of dolphins. A velour hat, cabbage green. "I'd never wear something like this, would I?" Her husband, dozing off again, was slow to respond. "Would I?"

"Would you what?"

Material

Black crepe with embroidered silver clouds. Strawberries, lots of them, on a circular flowered patchwork. Organdy and piqué patchwork, all in different whites. Swatches of voile and poplin. French silk organdy, cloud blue with salmon polka dots. *The color of St. Joseph's Aspirin for Children*, she thought. Blue cloth flowers. Satin ribbons. Sequins. A lace butterfly.

Several yards of Chinese linen, small golden horses crossing at full gallop. "It hung over my bed when my room was yellow. I was a horse maiden."

"How old are horse maidens?"

"Are you awake now?"

"More or less."

"I was eleven or twelve. That's horse-maiden age. I had to ride an enormous pinto. Cherokee. He was almost impossible to control. He gave me nightmares. He had a hard mouth."

"What's that?"

"You could rein in hard, but he'd keep on going, biting the horse in front of you. Then that horse would wheel or kick. Cherokee was more like a pony."

"What's wrong with ponies?"

"They're vicious and ornery, cunning, they don't respond easily. Cherokee was full of tricks. He'd rear when you put a foot in the stirrup. Or try to nip the person who was giving you a leg up. When he got too far out of control, my teacher would come over and poke at him with a pointed stick."

"Why did you ride him, then?"

"I had to. It was my teacher's way of making me learn not to give in to a horse. I was always scared of Cherokee, but even so he was a beautiful animal. I loved him."

"Prepubescent maidens turned on by their noble steeds?"

"Very funny."

Usables (and some other things)

Damask curtains. Moss-green linen sheets, soft and worn like flannel. A wicker laundry hamper. "I'm going to paint it white. It should be white." Several silk lamp shades. Red tumbleweed from the Mojave Desert.

Bags of metal shavings (curls of copper and brass). Scissors from Finland. All sorts of biscuit tins, tall and cylindrical, from Fortnum and Mason's or Jackson's of Picadilly. Three Dundee marmalade jars. A picture frame of plaster—painted to look like wood—set on wood, with ailanthus leaves engraved. A pair of finger cymbals for belly dancing. An ornate silver pomegranate.

"What can you do with that?" her husband asked.

"With what?"

"The artificial fruit."

"The pomegranate?"

"If that's what it is. Why does it go with the usables?"

"It's good for storing things in. Like hairpins."

"Oh."

A needlepoint pincushion, filled with sand. Eaton's cards, embossed with her name, for thank-yous her mother had to force her to write. A box of Norell perfumed dusting powder, with puff.

Ernest Thompson Seton's *Rascal*. *The Peregrine*, by J. A. Baker. A guide to ferns. *The Art of the Japanese Kite*. Four books on coyotes. And an enormous index, with watercolor illustrations, of North American wildflowers.

Cans of oatmeal, a gift from her mother. Not to be eaten, but to be used instead of soap (packed with a bottle of vinegar for restoring the pH balance to the skin). And from her father, a recording of Donizetti's opera *Betly*.

"Betly's a beautiful girl who spurns her lover."

"Sounds depressingly familiar."

"But she accepts him finally."

"Then there's hope?"

She paused in her sifting, exhausted. Too much of the past had been opened up, and, with her husband in the room, the present was too well represented. She'd have to take it much slower. In the morning, when he was out of the house. As it was, she'd made it through less than half her things.

Still in the corner in the soft chair, newspaper at his feet, her husband was staring at the disorder as if trying to find something—negative, she thought—to say.

"What's the matter?" she asked.

"Nothing. I was just wondering when you're going to have this mess cleaned up."

"Is that really what's on your mind?"

"No."

"Then what?"

"I've given you lots of things too."

"I know that," she answered, startled to find tears welling in her eyes.

"Well, I forgot. Particularly looking at all your stuff."

"I'd never forget any of your presents."

"Listen. Let's pile everything I've given you in the living room too."

"What? Now?"

Her Husband's Gifts (a partial list)

Three authentic Indian baskets. A treadle sewing machine. One pair of Red Wing Irish Setter work boots. A book of plates of Georgia O'Keefe's paintings. One down parka, one down sleeping bag. A set of foul-weather gear, including Captain Courageous rain hat. An electric juicer. One rigging knife, one Swiss Army knife. An oriole's nest. A wasp's nest. A duck's wing. A set of salmon's teeth. The soundtrack from *Saturday Night Fever*. "And there's lots more," he said as the pile grew, "not counting the roses for your last birthday. Let me think."

Still not fed, the cats practiced the feline equivalent of Zen meditation: tortoiseshell haunched on the wicker hamper; her black-haired mother curled on the damask; orange tom camped on the chartreuse shorts. The tom in particular despaired that the inventory would ever end.

(1980)

Certainties

At thirty Ralph wasn't really what you'd call a happy bachelor, though like many former husbands he'd gone after what he perceived to be greater freedom. His married friends at work envied him, and he played the game, just winking when they asked what he'd been doing the night before, why he was looking so worn out, but for nearly a year he rued his divorce. Chastised himself, catalogued the many wrongs he'd done his wife, tried finally to win her back, starting with flowers on her birthday. This though he'd in effect forced her to leave him, ever more curt and abrupt, verbally abusive, lacking the courage to come out and tell her he wanted a separation. His mourning, nonetheless, was as heartfelt as it was self-deceived.

Part of the problem was that he was alone too much. He had vast reaches of time to fill, almost daily had to plan what he'd do for an evening, for the coming weekend. Nothing just happened; everything became intentional. He feared if he stopped extending himself, making calls, getting out and around, he'd just spend another night, another weekend, by himself. Watching TV.

It took a while, but after that endless first year on his own he felt better. He'd enrolled in a cooking class to keep himself busy and now could prepare a range of interesting meals, could invite dates to join him for dinner at his place. He began to enjoy shopping, too, for the first time, deciding carefully what he'd have for dinner, where he could get the best produce, what wine would be appropriate. He put on weight and then began playing more tennis to keep himself in shape. He had to look good, care about himself. He also began to enjoy seeing different women, feeling privy to some larger mystery just by getting to know his lovers' idiosyncrasies. What gave pleasure; what the limits were. Who could have imagined? One woman served him steak and potatoes but liked him to dominate her sexually, pin her down and take her, so to speak, against her will. Another woman, with Michelangelo's Adam in the heavens above her bed, kept saying she wanted something permanent, but never suggested it should be him. Meeting these women and others, Ralph tried to suspend judgment: here at long last was the wide world; now he was part of it. He was learning something all the time.

He was bothered, though, that coupling seemed to have to precede friendship, if friendship in fact ensued. "I hope you can get it up," a woman he met at a bar said to him on the way to her place. And often, waking beside a semi-stranger, Ralph felt he was sowing his seed at random. Not that he wanted children, or marriage again—God forbid!—but surely there could be some continuities. One night, going to see *Last Tango in Paris* with a woman he'd recently met, Ralph smiled as Brando thundered "No names, no names" at Maria Schneider, insisting they know as little as possible about each other. Still amused by the hyperbole of the scene, Ralph suddenly realized he couldn't think of his date's name. He struggled the rest of the movie to remember it. They spent the night together, and before falling off to sleep he planned to check her purse in the morning. She got up before him, however, and it wasn't until hours later at work that he finally remembered.

Though often flattered by his successes, sure he understood women better all the time, several incidents persuaded Ralph that the single life wasn't for him. First, he slept several times with the wife of one of his tennis partners. He liked the man well enough—a decent person, a bit dull, but nobody's enemy. Nobody but his wife's, that is. She took to dropping by Ralph's place, always to complain about her husband. Though it was clearly to Ralph's advantage to be sympathetic, he found it hard: she was pretty, but a shrew. When, one night, she said she wanted to stay over, Ralph could have been more enthusiastic. He simply fell asleep with her beside him, determined not to be forced to take on every woman who came his way, but by morning they were making love. Such as it was.

The next time they saw each other she asked him when he was leaving on his vacation to Hawaii. Though she and her husband were supposed to be going to the Sierras together, she said Ralph's plans sounded more appealing. Could she come along? Her husband wouldn't object, she assured him. Hearing this, a little high on white wine, Ralph sobered up fast. Was such weighing of small advantage all one could expect? Could he hope for more? Angrily, he told her he was going by himself. Which he knew he'd regret, since he'd be lonely the whole time.

Still chewing on all this several days later, he went to visit his friend Bruce. A confirmed bachelor for years, Bruce had the game down pat, presiding over sunbathing in his back yard and a small sauna he'd built in the basement. Indeed, Ralph considered Bruce a genius at getting women to undress. Part of his skill was in making nudity seem cosmopolitan, as if only a crude soul could find anything offensive in it or suspect some ulterior motive. What, indeed, could be more natural?

That particular afternoon Ralph was hoping to meet Bruce's new woman, since, untypically, Bruce was saying seriously that he was in love. As Ralph came down the driveway to the back yard, he caught sight of two naked bodies. Approaching closer, he could see Bruce hurriedly covering his lady friend with a robe. Protective, proprietary. The afternoon passed; Ralph never did see her naked. It gave him pause.

Finally, he came home from work one evening to find yet another note from a woman he'd met only once, at a party. Since then she'd been writing him almost daily or coming by to leave flowers, messages, love poems, small gifts. Loneliness had driven her crazy. Knowing almost nothing about him, she was certain he was the man she wanted. "Love is what's important, Ralph," this note began, "and I want you to know that I love you. As a human being you make sense to me intellectually, intuitively, and sexually. Why should we hold back? Time is short. Call me tonight." He didn't call. Her desperation, parodying his, only made him sad.

He was particularly susceptible to depression because he'd met a woman he was very attracted to. They'd gone out a few times and had wonderful lovemaking. She was a filmmaker, and he was fascinated by her interests and ambitions. But when he called her up to go out again, she said she couldn't see him anymore.

"I like you," she told him, "and I had a great time in bed with you, but I'm emotionally overextended. I'm seeing someone already, and a man I used to live with is coming into town again. I just can't handle it all." Ralph wanted to protest, to tell her how much he liked her, but what she'd said sounded fair. And final.

Months later, thinking back to all this, Ralph sighed with relief: he'd fallen in love. Though Anna was a little young, still finishing college, he was sure she was all he wanted. The only problem was to win her. But even that went more easily than he could have hoped. They got drunk on Scotch and laughed all night the first time they went out, both swearing in the morning that they never touched hard liquor. Which was pretty much true until they got into it together. Ralph, in any case, kept asking her out, and Anna kept accepting. One of her former lovers frequently called, and occasionally she had long phone conversations with him when Ralph spent the evening at her place, but she said she wasn't seeing him anymore, and apparently she wasn't.

Finally, a month after they met, Ralph and Anna were comfortable enough together to venture out of Berkeley. He'd told her about his old friend Gail, and, nearly three hundred miles of highway behind them, they pulled in the long dirt driveway. Easing down, they checked out Gail's beehives, goats, chickens, and ducks while she regaled them with tales of her belly-dance students and her performances in local bars.

"I'll bet you're a Sagittarius," Gail suddenly said to Anna.

"How did you know?" Anna asked, startled. "Did Ralph tell you?"

"He doesn't believe in the stars," Gail replied, "but all the women he's really loved have been Sagittarius."

This talk made Ralph uneasy. He felt too predictable, to begin with, nor did he like it said that he'd loved other women. Had Anna been put off? he wondered. Apparently not. As they moved into the house to inspect Gail's collection of thrift-shop Orientalia, their eyes met. Abruptly excusing themselves, hurriedly closing the door of the spare bedroom, they made sweet and noisy love for what seemed like hours. When they finally emerged, heading for the tub with a sheet around them to cover what was left of their modesty, Gail laughed. "I guess you two are sexually compatible," she said. "You're one lucky man, Ralph. You don't deserve her. But don't you just love his legs, Anna?"

"Did you spend time with Gail?" Anna asked when they were in the tub.

"We're old friends," Ralph said, begging the question.

"Were you lovers too?"

"A couple of times," Ralph answered reluctantly, afraid of what might follow.

"You have good taste. Gail's very beautiful. I'm glad we came up here."

"Good," Ralph said, enormously relieved. Maybe he never would understand women, he thought.

The next night, Gail out dancing, Ralph and Anna drove down to the beach north of Arcata. Walking a mile or so in the heavy fog, they pushed on, though both were tired, until Anna located a spot she deemed appropriate. Rejecting Ralph's suggestion of a hollow in some marsh grass on the edge of the dunes, carefully considering a driftwood fort (only to dismiss it when she noticed some beer cans nearby), she finally chose an enormous redwood stump that had washed down Mad River into Humboldt Bay. Cold wind whistling through their legs, bark damp beneath her, sand blowing on his back and behind, their bellies joined. They felt no pain.

Years later, well after they were safely married, when they had long since created between them a sorrow for nearly every joy, Ralph was nevertheless not nostalgic for the early days of their relationship: the state of falling in love had been nerve-racking. Just before that trip to Kneeland, for instance, they had a date to meet at his apartment at midnight. As usual, Anna planned to study at the library until closing time. At one, however, she had still not arrived. Ralph had told her several times that it was pointlessly dangerous to bike around Berkeley late at night, but she'd only laughed. "I can take care of myself," she'd told him.

Indeed, Ralph believed her, feared, in fact, that she was young enough and independent enough not to need him. Not as he needed her, in any case. Though as time passed he was increasingly anxious, phoning her apartment several times, he was not at all certain his concern for her safety was warranted. To this point they were, obviously, lovers. But only that. Perhaps Anna had decided to be alone. Or to see someone else. The passion they shared seemed to give him no claim on her reliability, not to mention fidelity. It did seem totally out of character for her to be late, or for her not to call. They'd been together nearly every night since they'd met; but still he felt he had no real claim on her.

After calling her apartment every few minutes from one to one-thirty, Ralph decided to go over and take a look. In case her phone was out of order, he told himself, or because she might have stopped there and fallen asleep. Though aware that he might learn more than he wanted to, he went downstairs and got into his car. Following the route across town she usually biked, hoping to spot her, he saw only some stray dogs, several cats, and two street people with backpacks moving silently up to the hills to camp for the night.

When he reached her place no lights were on; his knocking drew no response. Jumping back in his car, he dismissed the thought that she'd been inside, listening. Running stop signs all the way back to his apartment, he took the stairs two at a time, hurried in the front door toward the phone—wondering if he was insane to be calling the police, or insane not to have called them sooner—and nearly jumped out of his skin when Anna leapt out from behind the bookcase as he rushed past.

Ralph could have throttled her. Not for scaring him, though she continued to laugh uncontrollably for several minutes at how startled he'd been, how successfully she'd surprised him. No, even after she explained that she was sure she'd told him the library was open late during exam period, he had to fight to control his rage. He kept seeing himself driving across town to her apartment: racking his brain to see if he'd said or done something to offend her; unsure of what he'd find, utterly unable to decide whether he should be sick with worry or wild at being treated so shabbily.

The night passed—ended with them curled in each other's arms—but he was left thinking that what they shared might be no more than ephemeral. Another affair. Desperate for substance, he pushed hard the next months to normalize their relationship, to be able to take it and her if not for granted, then as a given. Yet it was more than a year before he stopped believing that he had to be on his best behavior, that if he were "himself" Anna would have good reason to leave.

Ralph's quest for certainty, as it happened, took him through a number of emotional mine fields. Toward the end of their trip to Kneeland, very happy, for the first time he told her he loved her.

"Don't say that," she responded sharply.

"Why not?" he answered, hurt.

"I hate it. People use the word 'love' so carelessly. Everybody does."

"But I mean it."

"Maybe you do, but you don't have to tell me. When you say it, then I'm forced to say the same thing. And I don't like to."

"You don't love me?" he said too quickly, knowing as he heard himself that he'd willfully misread her, was being coercive.

"Did I tell you that? Can't you understand what I'm saying?"

"For Christ's sake," he muttered, unwilling not to have the last word but feeling more precarious than ever.

On another occasion, snuggled dreamily next to her, Ralph said he hoped they'd be together forever. She laughed.

"Is that what you told your ex-wife?"

"What's she got to do with us?"

"It seems obvious."

"Not to me. That wasn't the same thing. Not at all."

"No?"

"I'm telling you no. I was much younger then. She's not you. She and I together weren't the same as we are together. I don't even want to think about it."

"*That* I can believe," Anna said.

Or, when from time to time Anna spoke of her travels in Greece and North Africa, Ralph always fell silent, wearing a hangdog expression that might have silenced someone less strong. When, finally, she called him on it, he tried humor but was obviously serious.

"Who wants to hear about your infidelities?" he said.

"Infidelities? You mean when I was with Rick?"

"I don't particularly want to hear his name, thank you."

"How was that unfaithful? Come on, explain yourself. How was I unfaithful when I was with Rick?"

"You weren't with me, were you."

"Of course not. We hadn't met."

"I know that."

"Then what? Should I have been waiting for you? Is that what you mean?"

"You could have thought about it at least."

And then late one night, after they'd made love and were still drunk enough to be lapping Johnny Walker Black out of each other's navels, Anna asked him if he didn't mind "being imprisoned in monogamy." Ralph again felt an enormous gulf between them. Of course she was young, he thought. She'd want to try out a lot of different things. He barely slept that night.

Months passing, however, he learned to let her actions speak instead of the words he wanted to hear. Not so very hard, since most of the time they were happy together. Proud, he knew he was overcoming a failing in himself and was particularly satisfied with what he gleaned from rereading Saint-Exupery's *Le Petit Prince*: "*S'il te plaît...apprivoise-moi*," the fox tells the prince. *That's what it is*, Ralph thought, marking the page. *She's just telling me how to tame her. Fair enough. Why didn't I understand?*

Despite his self-congratulation, it was perhaps simply the passage of time that made him feel more at ease. Slowly, shared history superseded the unknown; what they had between them now was grounded in specifics. And a past, particularly one full of pleasure, suggested to him that a not dissimilar future could be inferred. An innocent bystander might have poked holes in Ralph's logic, of course. Didn't he remember his first marriage? But his memory was selective. He felt good.

Since they were both now working, her studies completed, routine also gave him the pleasant sensation of predictability. Life had boundaries; even passion had to fit its forms. If this meant that their lovemaking slowly lost the abandon of their early days together, Ralph felt it was not too high a price to pay. Nothing was perfect, after all.

There was nonetheless one recurrent phenomenon that, though predictable, never failed to undermine his need for certainty. Whenever he and Anna were separated for any substantial length of time, more than a week, say, at the moment they were reunited it was—it seemed to him—almost as if they were strangers. They always recognized each other, never for a moment stopped being man and wife, but always he felt Anna merely going through the motions of greeting him, holding her body back, her embrace only formal. Each time, miles successfully spanned, after phone calls every day, a vast distance remained to be closed.

It was just once, after their first separation when he visited his family by himself, that Ralph carried Anna up to bed as soon as they reached home, insisting by his actions that intimacy was of course in order. From that time on, however, whenever they were reunited hours would pass before they made love, the small familiarities of the prosaic finally reinforcing a sense of shared lives. But even then, like animals checking scents before mating, they would move warily toward each other.

Always this made Ralph feel that what bound them was, after all, quite fragile. And, further, that it had been some deception on his part, or some kind of psychological violence, that had domesticated Anna. He had obviously pursued her relentlessly, leaving her no time or space to be with anyone else. He'd contrived every kind of pleasure for them he could: long walks on the pier on the Bay; hikes in the hills; visits to a friend's place at Stinson Beach; good meals at Japanese restaurants with lots of sake; films. And their lovemaking. Of course their pleasure in each other had astonished them both. But often, when they could easily have slept, he'd come in her again, once more bringing her to climax, as if, were her pleasure great enough, she would lose all reason. And want to stay with him.

Or, Ralph often thought, coercion aside, if she had in fact committed herself with what could be called her own free will, then she just hadn't been able to foresee the consequences. Perhaps because he withheld the truth. When they first met, for one thing, Anna didn't realize he was napping after work each day to be able to sustain their all-night lovemaking. In a confessional mood some months later, Ralph told her, and he was amazed that she didn't feel defrauded. Similarly, after he proposed he told her that she could make a better match. She simply stared at him, stared until he felt compelled to defend himself. "I'm older than you are, Anna. I know about these things."

They had nonetheless married, and five years together brought them a not abnormal mix of pleasures and pains, though probably less strife than many couples experience. She compulsively complained about his driving, to the point that Ralph often threatened to run them into a pole. But late at night she'd search his skin for blemishes, like a chimp delousing its mate. He nagged her almost daily about not closing doors behind her, or not dressing up enough, but frequently said how happy she made him, and often soaped her back when she took a bath.

In that fifth year, however, Ralph began to complain that they weren't making love often enough, though he'd long since found such direct challenges counterproductive: Anna simply got her hackles up. Still, he couldn't stop himself, perhaps because one night she'd asked him if he wasn't bored with her sexually after so long together. He had thought many times that he'd take lovers if he weren't afraid of losing her. He understood that she might just be searching for a compliment or some affection, but her words unsettled him. Her question suggested the possibility of enormous changes, and who knew what would happen? Thinking it over later, he concluded she was really saying he didn't satisfy her anymore.

On this slim evidence he built his case; that same night he began to argue it. Telling her again and again that all he needed was real responsiveness from her, though of course he couldn't speak for what she was after. As he could have predicted, Anna only grew more remote, while he felt like a fool for trying to bludgeon her with accusations into, as he'd put it, "being more loving." Yet he persisted. He couldn't stop himself. He slept alone that night on the living room couch.

The three following nights he also slept alone, and poorly, angry at her, angry at himself. He was tired of women, he told himself over and again. Tired of being with them, tired of being afraid of being without them. After five years with Anna, after his time as a bachelor, after his first marriage, he was sick of making things work, worrying they wouldn't work. Exhausted by all the possibilities, all the ambiguities. His needs, his responses. He wanted an end to it; didn't want to be reasonable anymore; didn't want to understand; didn't want someone understanding him. For once in his life, he kept telling himself, he just wanted things his way. Period.

Still on the living room couch that fifth night, he kept thinking how incredible it would be to once and for all end Anna's capacity for withdrawal. For disagreement, for change. He lost more sleep fantasizing victories over her. Taking a lover, someone with the kind of olive complexion she always envied. Watching Anna beg him to come home. Refusing to go to bed with her when, crying, she tried to make it up to him. Spurning her apologies again and again.

As their war of attrition went a sixth, seventh, and then an eighth day, however, Anna gave every sign of being able to outlast him. "She doesn't need me," he thought morosely. "She doesn't even need to fuck. She could go on this way for years. For centuries."

"You have to woo me and win me," Anna said, laughing, on the ninth night. Right in the middle of his complaints, as though he was just being foolish. Though now nearly exhausted, he worked himself into another rage. He'd get her to acknowledge she was wrong, somehow he would. He'd show her. But later that night, confronting the living room couch yet another time, he made a series of bleak admissions to himself. One: he'd be better off alone, but wouldn't be able to stand it. Two: without him she'd flourish, and his best friends would be the first to come around. And three—most bitter of all: he just was never really going to get his way.

Full of self-pity, his mind spinning with resentment, he paced around the house until he finally settled at the kitchen table. Still looking out the breakfast-nook window into the blackness at three-thirty, utterly spent, he heard a door open upstairs. Several moments later Anna came into the kitchen.

"What are you doing up so late?" she asked, a thin, but not tight, smile on her lips.

"What do you think?" He studied her smile, trying to figure out what it was for. She didn't dare believe she'd won, did she?

"I'm sure I don't know." Still smiling.

Now Ralph was up against it. Was he going to keep fighting for some acknowledgment that he'd been right all along? Or, after nine nights, was he going to bite the bullet? Worse than that—woo her and win her. Otherwise, if things kept on going, one of them, probably him, was going to have to pack up and take off. Oops. There was the void again. Scary. Very scary.

He stared at Anna. Still that same smile. Inviting, he had to admit. She looked good, very good indeed. No wonder everyone told him he was lucky to have her. He certainly wanted to hold her, to open her robe and kiss her breasts, to have her holding him. Christ, he wanted her.

"It's late," Ralph said noncommittally. Pleased at how long he'd let the silence run, how long Anna had been standing there. Smile or not. Congratulating himself for not having given away any more. Maybe he could still salvage something.

"It certainly is," she said.

Another long silence. He thought of several strategies, options, possibilities. What to say, with what inflection, at what speed. With what tone of voice. The choices were tough.

"I've been acting a little crazy, I guess, lately," he finally said, throwing in the "lately" at the last possible moment to add some ambiguity. And then, not satisfied, continuing on. "Not sleeping enough probably, that must be part of it." There, he'd said it. A mixed bag. She'd have to make of it what she could. She'd have to take it or leave it. And if that smile turned smug he'd stay up all night just to show her he wasn't finished. Not by a long shot.

Her response, which he listened to very carefully, was—and he analyzed every nuance—"Let's go to bed." He gave her a long searching look, weighed her words another time. She smiled again. He got up. No irretrievable commitment yet. Or was there? Quite suddenly, it seemed to him, though it could have happened at normal speed, she turned, crossed the kitchen, and headed for the doorway.

His move now, but with very limited options. Very limited indeed, he thought. Alone, on his feet, he shook his head. Grinned foolishly. Shrugged his shoulders. Said, out loud, "Fuck it." There really was no point: one way or the other, he'd just have to follow her up the stairs.

(1980)

The Price of Song

Startling, the enormous valley far below, an almost-mirage sighted from the high country of the Sierras, a vast bowl perhaps twenty by ten miles. At its eastern verge a crossroads ranching community, population two hundred, elevation five thousand feet. Two cafés, a general store, post office, and grade school. Perhaps thirty homes, many owned by offspring of the Italian-Swiss who came to find gold but stayed on to log and work cattle. Immigrants whose arrival terminated the annual summer migration of Indian bands to the valley, their traditional trek up from winter camps in the foothills.

Summer in the valley. A short growing season, too brief for most fruits and vegetables, killing frosts early and late. Powerful sun blasting stillness into each endless day, until, long overdue, a rising west wind rustles the leaves of cottonwoods towering over homes in town and farmhouses remote on the plain. Nights cold; floorboards chilling bare soles in the morning. Ground fog engulfing all but the very peaks of the barns' pitched roofs.

Summer. Early and late the sound, often from miles across the bowl, of logging-truck gears being double-clutched; or the rattles of an old pickup just down the way. Cattle fattening for market, wood being corded, all scheduled against the coming winter. Lightning storms, hard rain, hail. Cumulus clouds paralleling the valley floor, so close and seeming substantial that one could climb just a few rungs of Jacob's ladder to walk that higher plateau. Keeping an eye out, of course, for patches of cirrus.

Summer. Bats after sunset sweeping back and forth near the houses as if begging to be admitted. And a hummingbird, trapped inside, beating all night against the pane.

This very small community, still often unreachable for days during the winter, even in fair weather nearly an hour from the county seat. Off the tourist track: no lakes, no skiing, no Victorian storefronts. A hard place when it was settled. *Emma. Died June 1, 1896. Age 22 years and 4 months. Also our twin sons Edward and Erwin. Age 3 weeks.* And still a hard place, the low taxes and quiet notwithstanding, despite the good hunting and creek fishing. Winters just too damn severe. No work anywhere, particularly with the log mills shutting down. Too many old people. Always a backwater, but now without a promise even of continuing what was. A future only in rumors—scientologists planning to buy the old Vinelli place down the road; golf course developers envisioning the valley as one enormous fairway.

It must have been thirty-five summers ago, not long after World War II, that young Albert House and his bride Mildred first passed through town with a logging gang, mostly his brothers and cousins. The men cut, she cooked and cleaned. They lived in tents in the mountains and stayed until snow threatened. Then, following the rhythms of Albert's people, headed down to the foothills.

The next summer Mildred found a place to rent on the outskirts of town. Albert refused to let her come up to the mountains again: the crew was too rowdy this year, he said; he'd be afraid for her. Each Sunday he came in from camp to leave his dirty clothes and pick up the food she'd prepared. Loaves and loaves of bread. Cakes, doughnuts, dried fish, dried fruit. Sometimes he'd bring down a deer he'd taken out of season, leaving it with her to dress and jerk.

Mildred was in that house nearly four months and just about went insane. Each day she walked to the store and back, maybe two miles in all, always buying something—butter, thread, a candle, fishhooks—but often doing so only to justify her trip. She needed human contact; the isolation was driving her mad. Each day she'd walk slowly, very slowly, along the unpaved shoulder of the road, looking for anything that might be a distraction. A rancher baling hay, neck burning, massive belt buckle disappearing under paunch. A coyote crossing the field, bold as you please. A turkey vulture wheeling, soaring higher, red skullcap leading the spirals.

Each of these empty days, four months' worth, Mildred passed the silent and staring locals sitting on their front porches under the cottonwoods and willows. None of them ever said a word to her: no one wanted to speak to the white woman who was married—she said!—to that Indian fella.

As they were packing up that autumn, Albert saw a notice on the telephone pole outside the general store, an announcement of a job opening at the grade school in town. Wanting year-round employment, realizing that if he logged long enough he'd lose a leg or his life, Albert went in to talk to the school-district man. And, to his surprise, got the job. Scored higher on the test than the other applicants. "Custodian, Step One": salary, such as it was, every two weeks, fifty-two weeks a year; pension; health and insurance benefits. As Albert likes to say, still grinning after countless repetitions of the line over the years, he's been at school ever since.

Summers are the slow time, polishing floors, repainting walls. When school's in session, kids in perpetual motion, he settles for keeping the classrooms, corridors, and bathrooms clean, or moving furniture around. Setting up folding chairs in the auditorium/gymnasium for assemblies, then clearing it completely and lowering the backboards for basketball games. He also drives the school bus, circumnavigating the valley twice each weekday. Starting out at five-thirty, after milking, returning twelve hours later. Time for milking again.

Their own children are long gone now, and, with Albert at school so much, Mildred tends to wake late. In no hurry to face the day, chain-smoking as soon as she's up, turning on the TV, she drinks cup after cup of black coffee. She eats in the morning if at all, for despite the array of platters she sets on the table for Albert or for guests, no one ever sees her take a bite. If with his black hair and smooth weathered skin Albert seems more fifty than nearly sixty, Mildred—gaunt, face incredibly wrinkled—carries the weight of all her years.

Perhaps life with Albert wore her out. Not that he's a bad man, quite the contrary; nor is he a hard husband. He's always been willing to go out and work, has "always done what had to be done," as Mildred puts it. But early on he knew he'd have to fight. Stood next to his brothers and cousins as a child, taking on attackers; traded punches and kicks after tackles when he played football in high school; more than once stepped outside the bar to settle things when he was in the service. Fought to win Mildred. It may be that, so much behind him so soon, he accepted what people can be like. Acquired early on a certain bemused tolerance for their stupidity and cruelty. Or perhaps just exerted tremendous self-control, imposing will on a natural taciturnity. Watching and waiting. Never letting on, possibly even to himself, exactly what he felt.

But not Mildred. Raised by her grandparents, at an early age she was taking cattle to the back country on her own, spending days out there. She could ride, brand, doctor animals, repair fences, take care of just about anything. Though she had to tell her grandfather to go to hell when he objected to Albert, she was used to being able to improve something, make a change, work it out. Prejudice, however, bamboozled her.

Even Albert's name gave her trouble. *House*. What could be more ordinary, more prosaic? Less Indian. Albert said he'd never thought about it, had no idea where the name came from. It was just there, a word. But when Mildred first came to the valley, every time her signature was required—to register to vote; at the doctor's; at the electric company; at the hospital the day she broke her hand—every time, she'd see the clerk's face change, as if she had somehow tried to deceive them. Hell, they knew better, she was the Indian's wife. As if Albert should be wearing loincloth and feathers and calling himself Sitting Bull. *House!* She came to hate the name, but what could you do?

Actually, short of changing it, she and Albert did quite a bit, all they could. Sometimes, looking back over the years, reappraising one of the countless small victories, Mildred marvels at what they achieved. They could have lived down in the foothills with his people or kept to themselves in the valley, but instead, never discussing it together, not once, they determined to win the respect of those who held them in contempt. And, on the basis of that respect, to be accepted.

For instance, once they settled in the valley Albert never again took a drink. Not just hard liquor, either, but, even after cutting firewood on a stinking hot day, sweat running down through the grime on his chest, horseflies biting, never even a sip of beer. He just wasn't going to be the drunken Indian, or give anyone room to suggest he was. In sympathy, though Albert never spoke of it, Mildred stopped using alcohol too. They'd both be beyond reproach.

The achingly slow process of acceptance: in unspoken accord, Albert and Mildred kept at it. At the local store they made it a point not to run up a bill. Each and every time, they paid cash, just to show they could take care of themselves. Not like some others, as Mildred often said. To supplement Albert's small salary, Mildred worked part-time as a waitress, also baking the café's pies. They always managed to set a little more money aside.

After Albert had been at the school three years, a storeowner in the market town on the far side of the valley suggested that they take advantage of the special price he was offering on new refrigerators. Mildred really wanted one, but Albert told the man they just didn't have enough saved up. "You got a job, don't you?" the man asked. "Over at the primary school?" Albert nodded. "Well then," the man said, "as I see it, you're a whole lot better off than most around here. I don't mind carrying the loan. Not one bit."

Mildred often tells this story, always as if it was some special act of generosity to allow them to pay eighteen percent on the note. "I still put flowers on his grave," she says fiercely. "I'll be doing it until the day I die, too, if I have my way."

Later, when this same man became the Ford dealer, he told them they deserved a better vehicle. Soon Albert was driving over on the first of each month—proud of his new pickup—with money for both payments in his wallet.

Slowly, slowly, they became part of the community. Got a bank loan for a home. Worked to keep lawns neat, trim painted, wood corded cleanly. Lots of wood, for that matter, sometimes fifteen cords out back. "To show we weren't afraid of work, that we were the kind that planned ahead," Mildred says. And, on the chance that someone would come by to visit or, on the pretext of a visit, to snoop, Mildred kept the house spotless, going over it again and again until every surface sparkled, until Albert complained that there wasn't a place dirty enough for him to step or sit down on.

Through these years, Mildred always thanked God that the nearest reservation was seventy miles away. It would be easier, she was sure, for people to relate to Albert as an individual. And she was glad he worked at the school, drove the kids. People got to see him around, had to concede he did a good job, clearly enjoyed the children. But still it wasn't easy. Every year the principal had the teachers for dinner. There were just two teachers, Albert the only other adult in the school. Though as years passed teachers came and went, though Albert was always there, the principal never invited him to come. Mildred never stopped believing that the new year would be different; Albert never spoke about it.

Far from passively hoping for change, however, Mildred did everything in the community she possibly could. Baked for the various Grange sales, bazaars, and picnics. Visited the sick and elderly; gave blood; brought blankets, clothing, and food to the victims of flood and fire. It took time, but the local women, seeing her efforts, began to invite her to participate. Mildred knew they spoke against her behind her back, even whispered that she wasn't really married to

Albert, but she realized they did that kind of thing to each other. At least they were calling her.

The children were another blessing. Mildred never had any, and if over time she made peace with the fact, she perceived that to be childless set her apart from the other women in town, made it harder to share their lives or conversations. But then Albert's brother and sister-in-law died in a car crash, and they decided to take in the three boys. Mildred loved them as her own, but also never minded at all that they made her seem more normal, even if everyone in the valley knew just how they'd come to her. And, fortunately, they were obedient kids, better-than-average students, fine athletes. One even became vice-president of his class at high school. Mildred was certain her strict discipline was at least part of the reason the boys did so well. Not like so many of the other kids.

Albert, meanwhile, had himself found some acceptance, invited after about eight years of working at the school to join the local sportsmen's club. Though he had stopped hunting by this time, Albert enjoyed the monthly meetings, the pounding of the gavel, the parliamentary protocol, seeing his name in the mimeographed newsletter they printed up each month with the minutes of the meeting. "Albert House suggested the deer quota should be increased this year on account of the heavy rains last fall." Or, "Albert House says the old logging road to Mill Lake should be graded or shut down otherwise, since even four-wheel drive can't get you through those mud slides."

In time, in fact, Albert was elected treasurer of the club. His picture appeared in the valley weekly, a shot of him dressed, as always, in a green Sears work shirt (top of a white T-shirt visible at the collar) and green work pants, tips of his cowboy boots protruding from under the cuffs. His mouth slightly open, not to talk but, as usual, to listen. Oh, Albert says things to people, and not just at club meetings. But it's remarkable how little a man has to speak to get by. The talkers always talk anyway, their salutations almost invariably the same, barely requiring a verbal response. A smile, particularly from a man understood to be both gentle and quiet, does it all.

"Hey, Albert, how's it going?"

"Kids ganging up on you, Albert? That why you're looking so whupped?"

"Hell, Albert, if I was you I'd risk a speeding ticket just once in that damn school bus. Crank her up and see what she'll do, for God's sake."

"What's new, Albert? How's Mildred?"

Now long since accepted, Albert seems essentially unchanged. Still laconic, still smiling, though his reserve as always leaves one to speculate on what he really feels. But particularly when one sees him with the school kids or at work around the house, he seems a man satisfied with what he does, where he finds himself; a man without terrible scars. And Mildred? "Oh, those hippies," she says, lighting another cigarette. "I heard they're back at the hot springs, running around naked, doing God knows what. Right out in plain view. Some people have no shame. I hope the sheriff gets down there quick and moves them on. Or else. They're offending a lot of decent people, people who live here."

At some level, Mildred surely remembers swimming naked with Albert up in the small freezing lakes where they logged, laughing as he chased her through the reeds and mud and pulled her down. Neither of them worrying, at those moments, about mosquitoes or leeches. Mildred also knows that no one has gone near the springs for years except to make love in the back seat of a car, that if anyone can see the hippies they'd have to have driven over to take a look. But she's said this kind of thing far too many times. Her words have a life of their own, and live it.

So Mildred's down on hippies. Votes Republican and tells you why. (Too much government interference. Too many laws. Russians getting too powerful. Bureaucrats spending money on the kind of people who won't help themselves.) She was truly sad to see Reagan leave office, would vote for him again. Any time, any place.

More, she has a sharp word for the loose men and women in town, particularly the divorcees. Did they think it would be all roses? Is that what they figured? They just didn't try hard enough to make the marriage work, did they? And what about all the drinking going on? And the kids? Running wild, not like they used to. Need more discipline, that's what they need. A little discipline never hurt anybody, did it?

And the new Indian movement? Well, particularly in recent years Mildred has made sure everyone remembers that Albert is an Indian, has even claimed a little Indian blood for herself. Not long ago she put several Washoe baskets on the mantle, some Pueblo concho belts and Plains Indian beadwork up there too. A Navajo rug on the floor. And when a Western is on TV she watches it critically, quick to tell guests that of course that wasn't the way it was at all. "But these militants," she says, "occupying that island and things like that. Shooting at the police. That's not right. They should watch out. They'll get the taxpayer mad, and then where will they be? I ask you. Who's going to bail them out then?" Albert, who has forgotten all but a very few words of his people's tongue, sits silent.

By staying on so long in the valley even as the town has been dying, Albert and Mildred have outlived many of their adversaries to assume a position of importance in the tiny community, in part because there simply is no one else. The children of most of the Italian-Swiss families are long gone, and though Albert and Mildred are relative newcomers, they are at least old enough to understand the world of the remaining ranchers, to have been shaped by it. Just down the road from their place, Ed Martini still lives on his enormous ranch. But he's crippled, and his wife is perennially ailing. They don't like nurses around, so the Houses—as neighbors, as people who have known them a long time—help out. Fetch the firewood, shovel the snow, bring in the mail. If for years Martini and his wife made no overtures, treated Albert and Mildred as though they didn't exist, now things are different. It almost seems that Albert and Mildred were always the Martinis' friends.

For seventeen years Albert has milked his cow Juniper twice a day, and recently, since he's at the Martinis' so much, he keeps her in their barn. Someone else could of course do the milking, but

Albert thinks he should. Juniper knows him. Albert could also let her dry up: neither he nor Mildred drinks milk—digestion troubles—and he usually can't even give it away. But, needed at Juniper's side morning and evening, the farthest he's gone in seventeen years is day-hunting or over to the county fair.

Each time, he enters the barn through the windowless anteroom where milk used to be stored. Like many ranch structures in the valley, it's in disrepair, light filtering through gaps in the roof. Coming into the central portion of the barn, a vast room perhaps sixty feet high, Albert walks along the string of stalls. Forking some hay into the manger, Albert opens a side door for Juniper, who's been waiting, lowing, outside. Though she must be twenty, she's fat and glossy, her hide still shines. By this time all the cats and kittens, some four families, have gathered up from their hiding places under the floorboards. Juniper goes right into her stall and starts eating. The cats wait. Squatting beside Juniper on the milking stool, Albert slides in the pail, and, a dug between each thumb and forefinger, quickly milks her dry with firm rhythmic pulls.

Pail foaming, he pours perhaps a gallon of milk into various bowls, which he places in different spots in the hope that all the cats will get some. Then, though as always Juniper would prefer to stay and eat, Albert shoos her out the door. Getting back into his pickup, Albert drives the three hundred yards up to his place. He could walk, of course, but few men in town walk when they can drive. And Albert is proud of his new truck, its winch and oversize cab. Working at school so much, he just doesn't get to use it enough.

Home again, he puts another log in the stove and turns on the TV. The Olympics are on, a young Russian girl walking the balance beam, an American boy holding an iron cross on the rings. During the ads Albert turns away from the screen, not wanting, he says, to fill his head with garbage. "I like to let my mind wander," he explains. But how far? Mildred lights yet another cigarette, talks on the phone to her best friend about the upcoming benefit for the volunteer fire department, their conversation moving quickly to the latest local scandals. Tuning her out too, looking at the waxed floors, no dust visible, does Albert think of the cabin he was raised in, accessible only by foot, with its packed dirt floors and handmade shingles? Where he and his brother were horses, tin cans for hooves, switches for tails?

It's never easy to tell what Albert is thinking: he's passed most of a life without saying. And besides, the commercial is over. If, lips parted, Albert wasn't just listening to the announcer's voice, if, looking past the plaque he received for twenty-five years of service at the school, he was about to speak, now he keeps his thoughts to himself. As he always has.

(1980)

Let Nature Take Its Course

In high school Jack got by on sheer luck, God only knows how. The girl he was going steady with looked, his closest friend told him knowingly, as if you could blink and she'd conceive. Not until they made love the first time, after a year's passionate everything-but, did Jack, shuddering involuntarily as he pulled up his pants, recall his friend's words. She was eager to get married, too, an aspiration that perhaps assuaged her fear of pregnancy.

Amazingly—and happily, as far as Jack was concerned—nothing happened. Though no longer "pure," as she put it, she still wore the gold circle pin Jack had given her. But when spring came, instead of announcing their engagement they quarreled. She accused him of wanting her only for sex, and, though he protested that she was wrong, they broke up just before the prom. Even then Jack sensed that he'd been spared.

His first semester of college, in 1960, he got off to a good start, doing well on his hour exams and meeting lots of girls at the dances held on campus each week. Around winter exam time, however, just when he should have been in the library cramming morning to night, he began to date a woman who worked as a research assistant for one of his professors. Nearly twenty-five, she seemed to Jack incredibly mature. Far from being a student, she'd dropped out long since, explaining to Jack that one could of course accomplish more outside academic routines. Indeed, she hardly had time to pursue her various interests. "I just can't allow myself to read periodicals," she told Jack, who, seldom having ventured past the sports page of the local daily, nodded knowingly.

Their first night together they went out to dinner. Normally voluble, Jack sat silent as she spoke about Mozart, Bach, Mann civil rights, the Rosenberg case, Chagall. He recognized the names but couldn't, so to speak, place the faces. At her apartment later, as they listened to some John Fahey, she rolled what he thought was a cigarette, inhaled deeply, and offered it to him. "No, thank you, I don't smoke," he said, not realizing that she was passing a joint.

It was by this time nearly midnight, and Jack was agonizing about the studying he should have been doing. His friends would just now be packing up their notes, signing out reserve books to take to their rooms, planning to be back at the library when it opened at eight. He'd flunk out, he thought. Finally, heart beating from anxiety about unread pages, he said he thought he should go. Instead of getting his coat and walking him to the door, however, she embraced him, kissed him very gently, and guided his right hand between her legs.

If all this surprised Jack—he'd taken her out on a dare from his roommate, who'd bet she wouldn't accept, much less spend the night with him—he was startled when she suddenly pushed his hand away. Had he done something wrong?

"I have to put the diaphragm in," she said.

"What?" Jack said, associating the word with gym class and correct posture.

"My diaphragm. Unless you have some better idea."

"Oh, no," Jack answered, hoping he sounded nonchalant, watching her carefully as she took a small plastic case from her purse and went into the bathroom.

"All set," she said when she returned, now wearing a bathrobe. As they began to make love, Jack wondered what she'd done. It took some discreet inquiry, but by the end of exams he had a fair idea.

That summer Jack went to France and had the good fortune to meet an Austrian girl. Conversation, unfortunately, was limited: he spoke no German, she only halting English. What words they could exchange were in French, which they were both there to study.

Jack understood her intentions well enough that first night, however, to head down the four flights of stairs two at a time to find a pharmacy. Entering the store out of breath, he waited until the few customers left and then pretended to be browsing, hoping the proprietor's wife would go in the back room. Finally Jack walked up to the counter.

"*Je vous en prie*," he began. He liked the phrase anyway, and this time, he thought, he really had something to beg of someone. But even as the words left his mouth he realized that he lacked the crucial noun. *Condom?* Just didn't sound as if it would translate well. Certainly not *frenchy* or *French letter*. He'd heard that, returning the English compliment, the French called them *capots anglais*, but wasn't sure this was true.

What to say? The proprietor was still waiting. Cognates. Over and again Jack had been amazed at how well they worked. Administration? Nothing to it: *l'administration*. But in this case nothing came to mind, until suddenly he had a flash of inspiration: prophylactic. A ringing polysyllable, certainly deriving from Latin, probably surfacing in all Romance languages. A good risk. All he had to do was give it a little twist at the end for the sake of phonetics. "*Je vous en prie*," he began again, now with some confidence. "*Est-ce que vous avez des prophylactiques?*"

The proprietor just stared at him, clearly didn't understand. Jack looked around the store again in the faint hope that some would be on display, but of course not, not in this Catholic country. Not, in 1961, even in the States. His eyes met the proprietor's. An impasse. Several interminable—in French, *interminable*—moments went by. But then, conspiratorially, the man looked over his shoulder toward the back room, as if to make certain his wife was out of hearing. Raising his eyebrows questioningly, making sure he had Jack's full attention, he extended the forefinger of his right hand and drove it savagely through a circle formed by the thumb and forefinger of his left.

Jack nodded vigorously. "*Pré-serv-a-tif*," the man enunciated, as if teaching a language class. Jack repeated it, grinning, pleased with success, the prospects of the evening, and the linguistic sense of it all.

Later that summer, though they had used the prophylactics he purchased that night and quite a few more, the Austrian girl missed her period. Now the croissants and petits fours tasted less sweet; the professor's orations on the existentialists failed to impress; they stopped memorizing lists of new words. What were they going to do? Days passed; they waited. And then one morning as she stood by the bidet, she started laughing. "Jack, Jack, *je ne suis pas avec ta babée*," she shouted, unconcerned about the nosy concierge, utterly without interest in searching her mind for the correct idiom.

By the time Jack finished college he'd spent time with a number of women, considered himself a freethinker, frequently said he believed in free love. By this he meant sex without obligation, physical pleasure not burdened with what he liked to call "outmoded beliefs." These were high aspirations, to be sure, but often he found himself still hemmed in by the dead hand of the past. Once, for instance, he spent the night with a woman he met at a party. When they woke in the morning, painfully hung over, she accused him of having gotten her drunk to seduce her. This kind of accusation, however, like the issue of loss of reputation, disappeared as quickly as the risk of pregnancy when the Pill came into use. Just in time for the madness of the mid-sixties, if, as Jack often speculated, the Pill hadn't caused it all. So quick were the changes that soon Jack could hardly remember those "outmoded beliefs." Hadn't there been a time—no more than a moment ago—when he'd had to talk women into going to bed, when at least the charade of male as aggressor had been required? It was a new world, Jack thought; the game had changed.

Within a few years, however, other effects of the Pill had been catalogued. Nausea, bloating, vomiting, high blood pressure, headaches, blood clots. And IUDs, another technological wonder, could be expelled, or cause bleeding, cramps, pelvic infection.

It had been nice while it lasted, Jack thought; all he could have asked for and then some. But, on the other hand, so many private and public passions were playing themselves out. World turning, after such freedom he himself began to yearn for some limits, for something certain. Spending time with a woman he liked very much, he wanted to invest more in what they had between them, didn't want to share her affection or attention—not to mention her body—with anyone else. Became downright possessive, and liked it when she said she felt the same about him. Whatever he'd once believed, he saw no anomalies when he asked her to marry him.

If for Jack promiscuity was now something of the past, he had still to confront the problem of contraception. His wife had gotten off the Pill soon after they started seeing each other ("Too dangerous," she said) and stopped using the Dalkon Shield shortly before it was banned by the FDA. They were left, accordingly, to consider the alternatives short of celibacy. Neither liked diaphragms, and that was that. They tried spermicides for a while, but the foam, a mighty deterrent to oral-genital sex, burned her vagina. They read up on postcoital contraception, but this too seemed to have dangerous side effects. Jack could have solved the problem with a vasectomy, had friends who boasted of theirs, but he was, finally, reluctant to tamper with his manhood. Further, thinking that he might want children some day, he refused to trust a sperm bank. What if the refrigeration broke down?

Having determined that coitus interruptus was no more than a variation on Russian roulette, they were down to prophylactics and the rhythm method. They used the prophylactics, which neither of them much liked, whenever they thought she might be ovulating. This could have worked reasonably well, except that her periods were wildly irregular. Calculating safe days was difficult, conservative reckoning mandatory. In an attempt to be more precise, Jack's wife charted her daily body temperature over a number of cycles but concluded that early ovulation is always possible, that one knows only in retrospect when it has taken place. Not surprisingly, Jack became a frequent purchaser of Trojans, ruled a bathroom-cabinet domain of Sheiks and Ramses.

Thinking about the precautions necessary to avoid impregnating his wife, Jack occasionally asked himself the obvious question—why not children? For many years the answer had seemed absurdly simple. Children meant settling down, a loss of freedom. Jack had wanted to live his life a while, see what he thought of it, make choices, before continuing the cycle. If at all. Even in the sixties, when some considered making babies a wondrous affirmation of the life force, Jack held back, though there had been women who asked nothing more of him as potential father than his sperm.

When Jack met his wife he was thirty-one, she twenty-four. She told him several times before they married that she'd probably never want children. Having worked as a governess during college, she had no illusions about how much time and care children required, how the world could diminish to their scale. "If we have money for a nanny," she said, "I might do it. Or if you want to stay home and raise a child. But otherwise, I don't think so." Though what she said had both conviction and reason, Jack tended to discount her words. Whether it was culture or biology that had such force, he'd met too many women who, turning thirty, believing it was then or never, decided to have just one child. He concluded that his wife might well feel the same someday and prepared himself to face the question when and if it arose. Besides, he was curious to see what he'd want. His parents had had him—their only child—quite late. There was plenty of time.

Of one thing Jack and his wife were sure: not another abortion. She'd had it about a year after they married. Though quick and painless, apparently traumatic neither surgically nor psychologically, she was left feeling that she should have been more careful, that she'd forced herself into a set of choices she had no wish to make. Of course it was her body, she wasn't going to be a child-producing machine, she never really thought about not going through with it, but she was angry at herself for having created the beginning of a life only to terminate it. Bad business, she thought. Unnecessary.

Jack concurred in her decision to have the abortion but without enthusiasm, though as they spoke of it the issue seemed ultimately practical. They didn't want a child just then, if at all; an abortion was merely minor surgery; the capacity to abort a fetus was, apparently, part of life. Still, Jack was unsettled. Of course, he told himself, there were peoples that practiced infanticide—had to, just to survive. And he'd seen too many unwanted children to believe that life was in and of itself sacred. Hell, the people at Zero Population Growth knew what they were talking about too. Even so, Jack was disturbed. Like his wife, he wished they'd been more careful. He made a kind of peace with himself when, leafing through a book on Indian myths, he read that once a given soul tries to enter this life, it perseveres until it succeeds.

Few people who knew Jack would have accused him of being sentimental about children, "dwarfs," as he often referred to them. If he saw no automatic virtue in parenting, so he reserved judgment on children, easily charmed by them but just as easily put off if they were spoiled or out of control. "Haywire," his mother had always said to describe him when he was confused or hysterical as an adolescent. He'd never liked the word, but could appreciate his mother's feeling now that he was an adult.

On the other hand, Jack was sometimes surprised. A couple he knew had a baby, and Jack predicted, correctly, that the husband would never change a diaper, never get up in the middle of the night if the baby cried. He could not have imagined, however, the child's beatific smiles of discovery and delight as she and her father pushed a beach ball back and forth. Nor did he foresee the compassion and vulnerability that emerged in his friend when the child became ill.

As he reached his mid-thirties, Jack's hunger for success was easing. He'd been making good money as a journalist for some time, had won several professional awards. His life was in order, he thought. Yet he found himself ever less interested in the flow of larger events. He'd interviewed too many politicians, been at the scene of too much mayhem, described too many wrongs. He was, finally, sick of the news. He began to spend more time at home, working in the garden, walking with his wife, building a toolshed, reading. These things were real, he thought. The rest was just a very intricate masquerade.

In this period Jack's father died. He'd had a long life, and a good one. Many people mourned his passing; for Jack the loss was assuaged by pride. As he measured the impact of his father's death, it registered on him that, neither of his parents having siblings, their bloodlines could end with him. He was too much a skeptic now to feel messianic about perpetuating himself through progeny, but he did feel that he'd just as soon not be the last of his particular kind.

Increasingly often, it seemed to him, the question of having children came up. A close friend had her second child twelve years after her first and, though cursing the endless diapers and sleepless nights, was clearly happy. A painter he knew married a woman with three children, worked hard to support his new family, gave up enormous amounts of the private time he'd for years so zealously protected. His life was richer now, he told Jack.

Another friend, a longtime bachelor, expressed the fear one night that he'd pay for not having children, that he'd end up alone in some skid-row hotel. Was this, Jack wondered, an argument in favor of having children? To protect oneself emotionally, if not financially? He recalled that, fighting with his parents when he was thirteen, enraged, he'd asked why they'd had him. They were silent, Jack remembered, as if wondering themselves. Years had passed, but Jack still felt he was unwilling to risk a similar question from a child of his own. Or to have to respond that he'd just gone ahead and done it. What kind of answer would that be?

And then at a family reunion one of Jack's cousins asked him when he was going to have kids.

"Probably not for a while," Jack said, tossing off a quick answer to what seemed a perfunctory question.

"You're right," his cousin replied. "We had too many too fast. Never should have done it." Jack didn't know quite what to say. Finally, he asked his cousin why they did.

"Tell you the truth," his cousin said, "once we had the first, we figured why not the whole bunch."

"But why the first?"

"Well," his cousin answered, "I could tell you my wife wanted it, and she did. Then too, people expected us to have a family. That's the way it was. But even so, that doesn't explain what was going on. There was just some point when we decided to go ahead, both of us. A feeling, that's all. That's how it was."

For years Jack had worked hard to shape his life, to free himself of what might confine him. So many times, he thought, he could have been snared. What if he'd married his high-school sweetheart? And professionally Jack saw many of his colleagues just marking time, going through the motions, all he'd fought not to do. If he'd intuited early on that many things simply happen, nonetheless action, effort, making change had been his way. Yet now, gaining perspective on needs once so urgent, he began to feel that his younger self had been someone else entirely. Same name, same limbs and organs, but little more. Pulling out an old photograph of himself one night, he studied the twenty-year-old in the picture. Lean and hungry. Cocksure. His wife loved the picture, the black T-shirt, cigarette dangling from his lip, the James Dean/young Brando look, told Jack she wished she'd known him then. But for Jack the photograph was of someone else. He'd changed, had lost the illusion of having control of his life. And like his cousin, he thought, he was responding to feelings he could in no way justify. Not even to himself.

Feelings. Sifting through his life from time to time, Jack wondered if there was a thinness in the world he and his wife had built. He loved her more all the time, in part because he knew too well how easily things could be destroyed, in part in response to her deepening love for him. But was it not, he asked himself, affection that would have gone to their children? Did his wife not sense this? Was their home so spare, so ordered—too immaculate? They had peace, but wasn't it in some way sterile? They ate no red meat, drank bottled water, took vitamins, got the best organic vegetables. Had they cared for themselves too well? So many questions; Jack was glad at least to be old enough not to expect immediate answers. If any. He'd just see what happened. What else was there? How could he have once believed he knew it all?

"I think I'm going to go ahead and apply to law school," his wife told him one morning at the breakfast table. She'd been thinking about it for nearly a year, tired of her part-time job as a commercial artist. She wanted power to influence things, she'd said several times, wanted to be able to affect the real world. Her ambition had more than once brought a wry smile to Jack's lips. Even as he felt that he'd just as soon never have to deal with that world again, his wife wanted to get further into it. The era of women, Jack thought, and he hoped they enjoyed their shot at opportunity and power. They couldn't do worse than men.

"Good," Jack said that morning. "Go ahead. I'll work for a few more years, expose some more bastards, and then I'll retire."

"To do what?" his wife responded, laughing. "You'll go crazy."

"No I won't," Jack said testily. "I'm changing. I'll find something. Maybe I'll just be a house-husband. Aren't they coming into vogue?"

"That won't be enough for you and you know it."

"It might, it might, particularly if we had kids."

"But we don't. Remember?"

"You're absolutely right," Jack said. "But anyway, you're going to law school."

"Wait a minute, not so fast. If you were going to be a house-husband, that might make things different. I wouldn't have to miss more than a semester to have a baby. It's not impossible."

"I'll keep that in mind," Jack replied, reaching over to kiss her. "Watch out."

The next morning he went to the public library. Looking under embryology in the card catalogue, he soon located a shelf of volumes dealing with conception, pregnancy, and birth. In one book, he saw incredible color photographs shot inside the womb, read that at eleven weeks the fetus, "like an astronaut in his capsule...floats in its amniotic sac with the villi of the placenta around it like a radiant wreath." He was amazed to see the closed eyes of the fetus at five months, the "unearthly calm" of the face.

Picking up another book, he learned about the potential hazards of labor and about the trauma of birth—what the writers described as entry into the "kingdom of opposites." It was when Jack read that the child's first breath feels like fire, sears the lungs, that he decided he'd absorbed enough for one day.

In bed that night, his wife woke to find Jack sitting up against the headboard counting on his fingers.

"For the love of God," she said, "what are you doing?"

"Arithmetic. You made me lose count."

"Of what?"

"I'm trying to figure out what astrological sign a child conceived now would have."

"Well?"

"Wait a second. Okay. Scorpio."

"No thanks," his wife said. "No thanks."

"Why?"

"I don't know any Scorpios I like, that's all."

"Fair enough. How about Sagittarians?"

"Much better."

"Careful. I'll remember that in a few weeks."

"You be careful," she said, kissing him. "You're the one who'll end up changing diapers. Ca-ca."

"Ca-ca?"

"Absolutely right. Think it over, house-husband-to-be."

"I can't be scared," Jack said, grinning. "I'm a hard-bitten journalist. I've seen it all. A little crap isn't going to intimidate me."

"Whatever you say," his wife replied. "Now, if you don't mind, I'm going back to sleep."

As Jack finally dozed off, right palm on his wife's belly, he was smiling. Not at the prospect of dirty diapers, it should be said. No, future coming into focus, he could just make out a recently conceived Sagittarian. One-fifth of an inch long. Sex not yet apparent. Vestigial gills. A tail. No more than a newt—and his, by God!—but taking shape, recapitulating the evolution of the phylum. Gaining strength. Preparing to be born.

(1980)

Passion's Duration

You should have seen them when they first met. God, they couldn't get enough of each other, making love until all hours of the night, on the phone if separated for even several hours, thinking of each other whenever they passed beyond the reach of still another sweet embrace. This was, truly, the passion of which the poets sing.

Skeptics, rest easy; romantics, stand and be counted! Ponder this: sustained passion is similar to perpetual motion, a perfection inexorably denied by some almost negligible friction. Why talk of blame, character, choice? There are laws. We can even attempt the thermodynamic, something like "Passion is inversely proportional to familiarity." (After an initial period of grace, of course.) Think of it. Perhaps passion, like other forms of energy, can be neither created nor destroyed. Merely found, and lost. Perhaps also this constant amount of passion in the atmosphere is not quite enough to go around, must therefore be kept moving for the benefit of the species as a whole. How else would people ever get together?

If such speculation seems too mechanistic, let us examine the facts. To begin with, our lovers so exhausted themselves in bed that one evening she suggested they sleep apart a night, just to get some rest. She put down several cushions on the living room floor, brought out another set of sheets, and was dreaming—of him—by the time her head hit the pillow she'd taken from the double bed. He, too, quickly fell asleep. But, waking several hours later, cold north wind shaking the windowpanes, he got up, shivering, and came into the living room. He told himself it was wrong to disturb her, yet, grinning to imagine himself Prince to her Sleeping Beauty, brushed her lips with his until she reached out for him. They woke, very late for work, utterly exhausted.

The next night they tried it again, but this time he promised to let her sleep. In the morning both felt better and made love with renewed vigor. Several days later, sensibly enough, they purchased a second mattress and springs. If they spent nights in the same bed, both agreed, their passion would utterly consume them.

How to calibrate change? This nocturnal separation was merely an attempt to be reasonable, an acknowledgment that there could be too much of a good thing. Led to nothing more serious than arguments about who would come to whose room to make love; who, passion spent, would have to traverse the ice-cold floor back to an unwarmed bed. No, though a bit odd, this arrangement was hardly remarkable, nothing to misconstrue. On the other hand, after they'd been together nearly a month he developed an allergic reaction to the hair of her blue-eyed Samoyed. His own eyes began to water if she embraced him without washing her hands after petting the dog. Sometimes, approaching him for a kiss, she'd realize that her hands weren't clean and would have to control her impulse. And, not surprisingly, sometimes she just didn't feel like washing her hands yet another time. He went to the doctor for shots, never blamed her or the dog, but there it was, a small impediment to the direct flow of feeling. A little something between them.

Though their passion continued unabated, a constant miracle they created together, there were several other minor problems. She complained that he failed to clean the dishes carefully when he washed them. After starting to protest once that no one else had ever mentioned it, he caught himself, smiled, and promised to be more thorough. Meanwhile, he found that he didn't much care for her closest friend, who seemed to him to be displeased that they were living together. He even got into the habit of going out "on errands" when the friend came by. Though he never mentioned it, he was irritated by feeling compelled to leave his own house. But, of course, he'd been the one who'd insisted she give up her apartment.

None of these problems, really, affected the great desire they had for each other. In this period, however, having experienced a series of debilitating stomach ailments (which, she noted, began right after she moved in with him), she decided to go on a strict organic and meatless diet. For nearly a week he shared her new regimen, eating large salads, much fruit, tofu, and various kinds of nuts, but then announced one evening that he'd bought a steak. Sitting alone at the dining room table after he'd broiled it, he ate with pleasure and noisily drank the juice from his plate.

That night he also told her that organic produce was just too expensive. Soon, accordingly, they purchased their food at different stores to prepare separate dinners. Initially, one cooked and then waited for the other to do the same so that they could dine together. But sometimes one of them had an appointment or a class in the evening, and, kitchen so small, the process of making two dinners took time. Before long they often ate separately. Further, she'd found that the sight of raw meat now made her nauseous, that even the smell was more than she could bear. Trying to be considerate, she said nothing, but of course he noticed that she'd come into the kitchen when he was cooking to throw the windows wide open.

In the ensuing weeks she purchased a number of books on organic diets and pored over them, occasionally explaining to him, for instance, the mucus-inducing potential of the foods he consumed. He was more sarcastic than he intended one night when he told her that even if organic food was becoming her metaphysic, he preferred to be an agnostic, if need be even to have his soul end up in some charbroiled hell. Sensing immediately that he'd gone too far, he tried to retreat to the solid terrain of fact, and pointed out that she still drank countless cups of coffee each day and smoked cigarettes. If he thought that demonstrating an anomaly would stave off her anger, however, he was sadly mistaken.

Her smoking was in fact a real problem for them. He'd stopped five years before, after a tremendous ordeal of depression and what he remembered as near insanity. He'd actually told himself before meeting her that he'd never live with a woman who smoked. The sad truth being that he still yearned for a cigarette and didn't need the stress of constant temptation. He finally asked her not to smoke in the house but relented when the winter rains came. Instead, he posted a No Smoking sign on his bedroom door and kept it closed all day.

She told him she understood, even tried to cut down on her smoking, but something about the closed door exasperated her. Often he'd return from work and, an avid reader, would stay in his room with a book for hours, keeping out of the living room both because she smoked there and because her Samoyed liked to curl up on the sofa. Sometimes, looking down the hall toward his bedroom door, she couldn't help feeling that he was closing her out.

The problem of her cigarettes was finally solved, after a fashion, when he began to smoke again. Soon he was up to more than two packs a day, while she found that her own consumption quickly doubled. Feeling pains in his legs and chest, he couldn't stop himself from blaming her; while she, now suffering from a hacking cough, insisted that until he began again she'd always smoked in moderation. Every few days he'd try to quit, growing more irritable as the hours without a cigarette passed, until, seeing her light up, he'd grab the pack, glaring at her.

Could anything else, one wonders, come between them? Well, yes. She frequently suffered from insomnia, while he had an obsession about burglars. Often her restless pacing in the middle of the night would snap him out of a deep sleep, his hand groping in the dark for the can of Mace he kept by his bed. Worse, perhaps, he played the flute. Badly. An accomplished pianist, she not only quickly abandoned the idea of accompanying him but grew to dread his practicing, the same mistakes repeated over and over again. Finally, her checks often bounced. If she thought nothing of it, he, coming from a poor family, had grown up forever in shame about the dunning of creditors. He knew it was none of his business, but just to see her leafing absentmindedly through a stack of unpaid bills set his teeth on edge.

What, then, of their passion? Strange as it may seem, even after bitter argument they could sometimes work their way back to each other by making love. By this time, of course, it was quite different than when they met. So much to ignore; so much to forget; such deep breaths to take simply to exhale the rage. Just to decide who would come to whose room required careful negotiation and diplomacy: someone had to concede. And even then her hands had to be washed clean of the Samoyed, he had to brush his teeth to eliminate the smell of cooked flesh. Nonetheless, on rare occasions, so much dangerous terrain finally spanned, their loving would be almost sweeter than before. Tinged, now, with the fear of loss; with self-reproach; and, in the small hours of the night, once in a very great while, with a piquant sadness for all that had come between them.

(1980)

Mad Dog, One More Time

No, these were hardly high times. Chain letters and pyramid schemes proliferated; money, various entrepreneurs said, was love. The bodies of Reverend Jones and his followers were finally tallied and shipped home from Guyana. Coca-Cola established an exclusive contract with China, and Chinese technocrats arrived in the United States to see what we had to sell. A new market, almost a billion potential consumers: new hope for our way of life. Weapons for oil; straight business. So much for Mao.

Late one autumn afternoon, nearly a year after he'd piped the pimp and left for Reno and points east, Mad Dog wheeled his battered VW bug up my driveway. It turned out that he and his "wife"—though he frequently used the word, I gathered that no clerk or cleric had tampered with their vows—were already settled in town. She'd found work in a fabric store, while he'd come up with a job in an auto repair shop. He was learning a lot, he told me, and had even arranged to be paid under the table. No withholding, no retirement, and, declaring no income, he could still draw his monthly check from the state for being a basket case. What with his medical benefits and food stamps, they were already setting money aside to buy land up north.

Scams notwithstanding, Mad Dog was genuinely pleased to be working again, had cut down to six beers a day, and looked fine. A sergeant perennially searching for the right army, Mad Dog respected his new boss and was determined to do a better job than anyone could have asked. This was quintessential Mad Dog, playing a strong supporting role in some World War II movie that never stopped running in his mind's eye. Given half a chance, he'd be the tough bastard who always chewed everyone out but who then used his body to smother the live grenade, saving his buddies by sacrificing himself.

If I was pleased to find Mad Dog looking good, I was particularly glad to see him because I'd been playing a lot of basketball. When we reached the court that afternoon, he was duly impressed with how much I'd improved, and I felt that my labors in life had not been entirely without reward.

During the past year I'd not only learned more about basketball but had come to know the regulars on the court, though it had taken me several months to get used to spotting them around town in street clothes, to believe that they actually had lives outside the game. They'd stare at me too, as if, not wearing my shorts and high-top sneakers, I was in costume. If I saw them when I was with my wife, I'd notice them appraising her, perhaps wondering how a twenty-five percent outside shooter could score so well in the game of love.

Spending so much time playing basketball, I found that having to wait for another turn when my team lost became less onerous. The men in line to play would sit on the side of the court against the wall, catching the weak warmth of the setting sun. Resting, loosening up, maybe taking hits off a joint, they'd hoot when someone on the court was beaten badly, laugh when a prayer shot dropped in, applaud a fine move, jeer when a player they disliked was shooting well. What a different sport it was from the sideline! How obvious the mistakes, how manifest the hungers. A man would make an incredible shot, one the gods might never grant him again, and show no expression, as if nothing could be more normal, more true to his capacities. Players on the sideline would cackle.

Always there was talk, this other level of the game. If you played well you wanted to savor the moment, to get others to relive it with you before, so ephemeral, it was gone forever. If you looked bad, you wanted to be sure to let everyone know that you were just coming off the flu, that you hadn't played for three weeks, that your bad heel was acting up. And, finally, since everyone on the court periodically lost his temper, argued maniacally over nothing, played the prima donna, just plain blew it, talking it over was not only a search for concurrence but a form of apology. No one was ever right enough to stay silent for long.

The talk: stories, character analyses, apologias. Subjects of interest included why Big D always called out the score incorrectly (and in his favor); why Danny shot so much even when he was missing; how Lonnie managed to keep the game so free of argument when he played. Nor were matters beyond the court off limits. Why did Rick Barry pout? Was *Invasion of the Body Snatchers* as good as *Carrie?* Would the Warriors get Bill Walton? Couldn't the deaths in Guyana have been averted if Reverend Jones had been into basketball? The sideline consensus on this point was that the game would have turned Jones's paranoia to nothing worse than what we all experienced: occasional rage and an endless desire to run it again. If power was what Jones had wanted, after all, nothing could compare to looking good at pickup ball. And as for killing himself, well, it was widely understood that no one had ever willingly stopped playing the game.

There was the story, often recalled, of the player who sold forged football tickets to all the regulars, and no doubt made a nice piece of change at his hustle. But he then had to stay away from the court. What a price he paid.

As it turned out, Mad Dog became one of the sideline regulars' great topics of discussion. This is how it happened. He'd been working long hours, but generally managed to get up to the game just before nightfall, usually polishing off a beer as he arrived, often exhausted, sometimes drunk. More than once, when he seemed to forget to play defense, his teammates would get on him, but Mad

Dog would just laugh or, smiling, tell them to fuck themselves. He was feeling good, working; the game just wasn't going to get to him, even if he messed it up for others.

Going to work one morning, he showed up at seven as usual to open the shop. He liked being there alone for a while each day, was flattered that his boss trusted him with the keys. When the parts man arrived on time at seven-thirty, Mad Dog took his normal break for his first cup of coffee. A few minutes later, as always, he realized that he'd better get to a toilet quick. That's just the way his system worked.

When Mad Dog asked for the key to the bathroom, the parts man started to pass it to him but then dangled it just beyond reach. Mad Dog didn't much like the game, feeling as though his sphincter would give way at any moment, so he told the parts man to stop fucking around. When Mad Dog reached for the key again, the parts man slapped his hand away. A big man, he'd been on Mad Dog's nerves for some time, always giving him a hard tap on the shoulder when he passed, just playing, of course, but treating Mad Dog as if it were clear that he could push him around.

"Look, asshole," Mad Dog finally said. "If you don't give me the key I'm going to split your fuckin' head open."

"Try it, sucker," the parts man responded.

Mad Dog didn't want to blow his job, but he had to have the key. What was he going to do, shit in his pants? He gave it one more try, hoping to shine the parts man on. "C'mon," he said, "enough's enough. Give me a break. I gotta go real bad."

"Tough titty," the parts man said, and laughed. He was still laughing as Mad Dog gave him a kick that shattered his kneecap. Then Mad Dog hauled him to his feet, broke his nose with a judo chop, dropped him, and picked up the key. Mad Dog was crying: he knew his boss would be upset by the violence, would see no percentage in keeping him around.

Mad Dog was half drunk when he showed up at the court that afternoon, and really hurting, feeling he'd betrayed his boss, mourning the respect and affection he'd lost. It had been a strange day even before he arrived: too many men waiting for their turn, tempers flaring on the court, the action rough and sloppy. When Mad Dog finally got his game there were repeated arguments, but he just waited each one out, saying nothing. He played listlessly, without heart.

Over on the sideline we were talking, as usual, when the fight began. Big D threw a punch at Mad Dog and drew first blood. Apparently they'd collided with each other, hard. Already enraged by the arguments, and having missed all his shots, Big D decided to take it out on someone. He and Mad Dog had exchanged words before.

Giving away eight inches and fifty pounds, too drunk for strategy, Mad Dog stood toe to toe with Big D. They traded punches fast and furious, but Mad Dog couldn't get anything past Big D's long arms, kept taking shots to the head and chest. Both because most of the players had no use for either man, and because all the evil of the day seemed to be working itself out in their combat, no one made a move to break it up, no one said a word.

Finally Mad Dog stepped back, shook his head a few times as though stopping himself from saying something, and then walked off the court toward his car. Catching up with him, I checked his cuts, but, blood aside, he was okay. I was more concerned with keeping him from getting a pipe or some Mace and coming back to settle with Big D. "Don't sweat it," Mad Dog said. "I'm not going to do a fuckin' thing. If I get him now there'll be twenty witnesses to assault with a deadly weapon. I'd get sent away forever. I had my shot at him but was too loaded to bring him down. You lose a fight every once in a while. That's just the way it is."

The game resumed that day, everyone quiet, chastened by the fight, seeing in it the worst of what they themselves so often expressed on the court. Big D showed up again the next afternoon, apparently without understanding that his life had been spared through no fault of his own, but Mad Dog stayed away. Job gone, game gone, he drank himself silly the next few weeks. Then one day I got a call from his wife. Mad Dog was in jail, arrested for shoplifting a pair of pants at a suburban shopping mall; the bail was five hundred dollars. Weeping at the appropriate moments, his wife conned a bondsman into putting up the money, though she must have known that Mad Dog had no intention of ever showing up in court. A convicted felon, he'd face a "petty with a prior," would stand to do real time even for a fourteen-dollar pair of pants.

Mad Dog knew it was time to go. This would be the fourth state he was wanted in, but, he laughed, there were plenty still to go. Warning him not to run through them too fast, I watched his VW bug pull off into the night. I haven't heard from him since.

The day after Christmas that year I shot better than eighty percent for five straight games. The next afternoon, sad to say, I was back to normal. Players who had seen my moment soon forgot it, and I had no proof for those who hadn't been there. What could I do but keep playing? Winter continued, but even on the cold gray days, whenever it didn't rain, I changed into my basketball gear, pulled on two pairs of sweat socks, laced up my high tops, and headed for the court. Of course the game went on.

(1980)

Learning to Love It

STORIES

"A Land of Men & Women Too"

What a world, she thinks, reading the morning *Chron*, both girls already off to preschool. Random shootings on freeways, condoms for prisoners, free needles for junkies. Trapped in forty-mile-long fishing nets, whales are not only dying but perceived to be competing with humans for scarce resources. We have no visitors from outer space because as a culture achieves space travel it simultaneously overruns the capacity to control its technology. I'm taking in too much data, she thinks, doing the dishes. The homeless, Tiananmen Square, cold fusion, the ozone layer, and, for a moment, peace breaking out: Gorby, the Berlin Wall. We don't build elaborate tombs for our dead in California, a priest is quoted as saying, because cemeteries are really for the living: a transient people, we'll soon be moving elsewhere. My soul/my suburb, she thinks, putting in a wash after going out for diapers. Sitting down to check out the Yankees box score in the Sporting Green, still following the daily fate of a team her father grew up watching in a city three thousand miles away. Scanning the stats for the hint of another Mantle, Ford, DiMaggio. Is Don Mattingly, for instance, an Immortal?

Though most weekday nights the four years they were married, running the household with first the one baby daughter and then the second, she cooked her husband dinner from yet another recipe out of *Sunset Magazine*, when the good life palled he broke her jaw.

She'd had an affair to compensate for his increasingly staccato gruffness, rudeness, belligerence, testiness, ever more monosyllabic lack of grace. *Staccato*—his normal cadence, a kind of verbal karate chop, only adding insult to injury, though she savored the onomatopoeia when the word first conjured itself up in her mind to describe how he spoke. This at a time she was taking ballet twice a week not just to get in shape, sweating in leotard and tights, but for the *adagio* of dance, the *duende*. She'd had an affair, in any case, nothing to really write home about, as she told her girlfriend next door, though sex and sinsemilla in the hot tub at his place in Muir Beach, on the cliff with a view down the coast the ten miles to San Francisco, was picturesque, and then she told her husband she'd had the affair, not exactly to get even but to let him know there was some kind of equal something at work in the world, at which point, girls upstairs sleeping, he broke her jaw with one punch. And then stormed out of the house and, soon after, sued for divorce. Did all the paperwork himself, the cheapskate, though of course for propriety's sake—and attorneys always had to be proper, he'd conveyed so many times—he filtered it through the office mail under his partner's signature.

Which brings up the first thing she had to learn about men: never, ever marry an attorney, because if and when you divorce (as you may well, despite or because of TV/nouvelle cuisine/cappuccinos/postmodernism), your former spouse will kill you in the property settlement. Which brings up the second thing she had to learn about men: never, ever marry an attorney and have children with him in this dolphin-loving/rain-forest-saving nation of recyclers. Particularly not girl children, because if and when you divorce, your former spouse will kill you forever and ever, not only turning the children against you, suggesting explicitly and implicitly every second weekend when he has custody (except for when he doesn't want to see his daughters whom he loves more than any father could because he has to go to Tahoe to ski or has important business—*everything* being business, actually, that fraud invented by men for men), but intimating that they, his daughters, can love and please Daddy as

Mommy never had the legs/hips/lips to. Nor, she learned, should you let an attorney father your children because then, every inch of the way, on issues of child support/shared medical bills/custody time/fees for swim class, etc., etc., then all that accredited legal training and member-of-the-bar dues-paid and socially condoned killer instinct will be brought to bear on...*you*. "Mammas, don't let your babies grow up to be cowboys," she heard Willie Nelson sing. Oh, it made her laugh and then made her cry: Mammas, don't let your little girls grow up to marry attorneys.

Attorneys: she got murdered by hers in the divorce, a woman, framed sheepskins on the wall, suit like a man's, incompetent or co-opted by the opposition she could never quite tell. But at least finally she had the divorce. Called herself a widow, for the laugh—would that it were true—but of course now she was a divorcée at twenty-six, damn it, a kind of failure, single parent with a bad alimony and support settlement, and even if they'd stayed married the fucker would never have predeceased her. She thought of remarrying, but then decided there had to be something more, so she went back to school part time. Finishing her BA would lead her toward a job eventually, she figured, a teaching credential or something on that order. But, she noticed, nothing in the least bit contemporary in the catalog much interested her: no deconstruction, no women's studies, no ethnic studies, no psychology. She was after what had survived. Fell in love with Blake, Rembrandt, with the words Apollonian and Dionysian, with the sounds Daphnis, Chloe, and Persephone, spoke of one of her professors as "my mentor."

Also, despite her bias against self-help books and/or the notion that we are all victims, nonetheless, reading a magazine article on BART one day, she decided she had low self-esteem. Of course she did: her father had wanted a boy, had told her so, and her mother had always been cold as ice. Not antagonistic, just not warm. She'd once thought it was because her parents loved her sister more. Her sister, six years older, understandably unhappy once a sibling arrived. But then, when her sister killed herself in a car crash at nineteen, into drugs and a bad love affair, she thought her parents somehow blamed it on her. Another eight years later, however, when her father died her senior year in college, looking down at him in the coffin and accepting that he never wanted her, she said to herself, "Goodbye, Daddy, you asshole." Thought of the dead Yankee greats. Wept. And then accepted her boyfriend's offer of marriage, impelled by the fact that she was already two months pregnant.

Time as a widow passed. She framed her daughters' finger paintings. Picked nasturtiums in her garden. Heard the phrase "Kyrie eleison" as if never before, though in choir in high school she'd often sung the words. "Lord have mercy," she muttered, putting away leftovers, not about to start going to church again. Stood in the mirror examining her breasts, wondering who should hold them. Saw the paint peeling in the living room, behind the rabbit cage. Her mentor, the classics professor, tumbled out of the crown of a huge redwood—she never did understand what he'd been doing up there, but gathered it had something to do with Art—and then, still wearing a cast on his arm, he tried to get her to sleep with him, wouldn't see her in office hours after being rebuffed. But still she continued to feel exalted by what she was reading. Kafka, Virginia Woolf, Confucius, Rilke, Beckett. There were secrets out there, something truer, The Truth. Felt she was getting closer when she produced a term paper on baseball and hubris.

She met a guy she liked at a dinner party, liked him from the start because he ignored her date completely, talked to her as if they had every right to talk because theirs was a true meeting of the minds. So they left the party together, drove to her girlfriend's. Just in time, because there was a potluck in progress for Sensual Suburbia, a kind of Tupperware party scheme for neighbors to merchandise sexual paraphernalia to neighbors, with the result that before they ever went to bed they were examining "Anal intruders," "Ben Wa balls," cock rings, vibrators, body oils, and "edible undies" for both men and women. Passing up "Nympho Cream" and "Joy Jell," settling for incense and a tube of KY jelly, they headed over to her place, where she told him the story of her divorce: "I'm a widow; my husband beat me," she began, and then did a hula for him. A real hula, since she'd taken classes as a girl. After which she explained how Kyrie eleison would come to mind, how she felt like Odysseus, like Sylvia Plath, like Frida Kahlo, like Thurman Munson.

Later, when they were in bed, she told him, "Pretend you're saying you love me."

"Pretend I just was," he responded, and they both laughed.

She licked the small of his back, sucked the toes of his right foot, thought of a line from the fragments of the Greek poet Archilochus: "the seam of/the scrotum."

"Who's Thurman Munson?" he finally asked, which greatly increased her respect for him.

Somewhat later, just as he began to enter her, she'd been about to say, "Can you believe my life?"

(1993)

Learning to Love It

Ray was a great athlete in high school and college. Massachusetts schoolboy record for the high hurdles. Star shortstop. AA and AAA minor league ball before knee injuries ended his career at twenty-four. Then two packs a day and enough beers to take the edge off, this plus an insistent refusal to reminisce about the glory days, not simply with semi-strangers but even with close friends. Ray did, however, take into the future several imperatives from what had been the passion of his life: bend your knees; keep your eye on the ball; always be moving forward.

Ray often said he'd die young—"Who cares, I'm going to die young anyway," was how he usually put it. This verbal tic stemmed from an assortment of impulses and insights: from self-reproach for the smoking and drinking; from an attempt at a reverse curse, in effect asking God to give him a break since Ray was taking the risk of saying God wouldn't; from a simple reading of the medical odds; from a weakness for the maudlin; and from what proved to be a quite accurate bone marrow intuition about his fate. Also, Ray was driven by a genuine if intermittent desire to be free of all that bound him. Think of him as the first male in his family since the great-grandfather from County Kerry not to fight in a war in the U.S. Army: baseball injuries spared him Vietnam. Think of him as the first male in family memory to hold a job in peacetime, go to college, to stay this side of alcoholism, not to take the occasional swing at his wife. All this despite his father, Ray I (Ray himself being Ray Jr., his own firstborn being Ray III). A father who, unemployed with spouse working two jobs, had the capacity to watch Ray compete in the high hurdles as a high school sophomore and then tell Ray he'd shamed him by finishing second. When the drunk teenage driver's van hit Ray's car, therefore, there was irony—in high school, Ray often drove while half in the bag—and for Ray at least some element of relief. His parents imposed a Catholic funeral on his wife, who was in shock, his unemployed cousin lying by arguing that Ray had only recently talked about wanting to start going to Mass again. When the funeral procession left the church in Charlestown, the line of mourners' cars became separated from the hearses and limousines, took a wrong turn on the Southeast Expressway, and never did arrive at the gravesite. Keep your eye on the ball, Ray might have said, suppressing what kids in New England continue to call a shit-eating grin.

~

Ray, married with two children, in his late thirties, one more blue Monday heading for work in downtown Boston. Another gray December morning, cloud ceiling low. At Park Street Station, off the T and up the ancient escalator—out of order yet again, so hustling up two steps at a time, trying to beat his previous personal best. A guy coming down the stairs past him wearing a kelly-green sports coat with brass nautical buttons. "Jesus, Mary, and Joseph," Ray says to himself, "does nothing ever change?" And then mutters, "Screw it, I have no problem with that."

Off the escalator onto Tremont Street, past Bailey's, where his grandmother once worked serving ice cream sundaes to Brahmin matrons. Tan cloth raincoat, hod-carrier's cap, black rubbers over penny loafers, tweed sports coat, regimental tie, gray slacks. Camouflage. Protective coloration. In this environment, absolutely ordinary. The coat and tie an effort to mask the rapaciousness of the species, Ray often thought, watching proceedings over at the State House.

The legislators, that band of male primates, distance between rhetoric and reality rivaling *Animal Farm*. Ray's own costume belied, or made irrelevant, by the speed at which he walked. He couldn't help it. In the office he'd go from cubicle to cubicle at an incredible pace, arriving at someone's desk like a skater braking to a halt—*whoosh*—just in front of the goal. He'd do this perhaps twenty times a day. Or he'd finish a meeting at another agency's building and walk—churn—back to the office with members of his staff struggling to keep up. "Bend your knees," he'd tell them, though they always received the line with a slightly puzzled look, having no reason to read it as metaphor, and though it wasn't fair anyway, since Ray's fuel was anxiety, of which he had so much that he'd arrive at the office not only not winded but soothed.

Ray's bag lunch, peanut butter and jelly sandwiches he made for himself each morning at five-thirty. In by seven, long before his employees. Reading the *Globe*, having the first of maybe fifteen cups of coffee. Then out for another to one of the croissant shops proliferating in the downtown, though the idea that croissants were so saleable in Boston drove him crazy. *"Buy American,"* he used to mutter—growl—as he stood waiting for change.

Lunch was usually at eleven-forty, once a week over at the Fatted Calf, a burger and beer joint for politicos and lobbyists at the foot of Beacon Hill, hard by the government offices. Conspiracy stories. Political gossip. Ratio of men to women nine to one. Ray eating his burger, generally the first person in, waitresses still gearing up, and then heading back to his office at a ferocious clip, shooting a glance at King's Chapel as he turned right onto Tremont, tooling past the Old Granary Burial Ground, Park Street Church, cop on horseback, Salvation Army bell-ringers. Maybe having another lunch around three, pulling out the paper bag from home.

Sometimes, feeling all he'd done was create yet another bureaucracy, one more indispensable layer of civil service workfare for people like himself, after leaving the office Ray would head over to the Museum Bar on Huntington Ave. It always made him laugh: right up the road from the Museum of Fine Arts and Symphony

Hall, just a joint with its hookers and street alcoholics of various races and ethnicities, equal opportunity and affirmative action in action, cabbies and dispatchers between shifts from the garage around the corner, booths along the wall with roaches to whack, floor of the men's room flooded, somebody passed out with his head on the bar, no hassles, nobody giving a shit—no one unmasked, exposed—all this with a mural depicting some South Seas paradise on the rear wall. So Ray would be there—"Anybody's lookin' for me, I'm over at the Museum," he'd call to the night desk man as he went out the door, the guy just nodding, leaving Ray to wonder—putting away a beer, another, another, eating dozens of crunchy orange goldfish, all salt and "cheese-flavored," until finally the thought of even one more made him sick, often not getting home until nine, nine-thirty, driving through the sleet, wipers clacking, prying off his rubbers on the back porch, dinner cold on the table, boys already down, Barbara not saying anything but making him feel bad.

∼

One of the things that disturbed Ray was Miss C, as he called her. C for Cabot. When she first came to work for him he was just starting out and she was already eligible for Social Security. Driving a hard bargain and proud of it, he offered her eighty a week to be executive secretary. Soon she pretty much ran the place. Wrote most of the grants, the annual report, hired, fired. After a while he raised her salary to one-fifty, but more than that she wouldn't take. The deal was, he realized, she wanted somewhere to be.

Every day, accompanied by her Border collie, she came in from Hyde Park on the T. About five-one, eighty-five pounds soaking wet. (Ray tried not to picture her naked.) Pure will. Never sick, incredibly sharp. A spinster, had perhaps never been kissed. Her mother married a Brahmin, whose family, appalled that his bride was Irish, cut him off completely. Then her father's business went under and he began to drink, finally disappeared. Miss C—Emmie to her mother—took a job while still in high school, and soon the routine was that she worked while her mother stayed home. At the end of the day Emmie would return, having also gone shopping, to make dinner for both of them, and then she'd wash up. Her mother kept her from dating, which perhaps suited Emmie: men seemed only coarse to her. ("I've never really understood what kind of beauty artists see in the proportions of the male nude," she once said to Ray.) This, in any case, is how things went until she was nearly sixty-five, when her mother died. Miss C thought then that she too would die, but when she didn't she bought the Border collie and got in the habit of walking it every morning in Arnold Arboretum. That first April after her mother was gone she watched spring come in: crocus through the late snow; witch hazel; some early tulips; forsythia, jonquils, daffodils. Not long after, she applied for the job with Ray, the proximate cause being that her old boss got angry because she bought a Chrysler. "You don't need a Chrysler," he shouted, knowing that she rode the T, that she never went anywhere. It infuriated the man, all of it, including that she'd saved money on the pittance he paid her. So she took a job with Ray. Which was fine with him, given her extraordinary competence and loyalty, but on the other hand she seemed too typical an aspect of the city, another life shaped by denial, loss, sacrifice to family/prejudice/economic exploitation. Ray didn't really believe revolutions would change the world—the first thing he'd noticed about Castro was a brother well up in the hierarchy—but perhaps, he'd think, hearing Miss C in the next office, perhaps a revolution might be worth a try.

One time Ray arrived at Miss C's house to visit—she was seventy-five by then—as she was coming down the ladder after putting up the old wood storm windows. Later she cooked a full dinner for the dog, pot roast/lima beans/mashed potato. Another time Ray came out, Miss C was down on all fours cutting the back lawn with hand clippers. She cackled: "The lawnmower's broken." He used to wait for her to complain, but she wouldn't. That is, he waited for her to complain about her fate, as opposed to tirades about this employee or that one, but she never did, even when the surgeon decided to amputate a breast though she'd been in perfect health her whole life, even though the surgeon later conceded the growth was benign. Miss C's only real problem, it seemed, was who to will her house to, but then she found an organization that pledged to care for her Border collie until its death if she left adequate resources. Ray had it checked out—Miss C had gone through a period of getting burned by contractors, benefitted from three new roofs in three years—but everything seemed for real.

∽

The kid who killed Ray. He came around the curve on the wrong side of the road. No surprise: he'd been drinking Scotches straight up at a local bar for more than an hour. O'Malley. Twenty-four, unemployed, a mother who couldn't say no. Her van. He attended Suffolk University for a semester, then quit to work for an uncle at Wonderland, the dog track out in Revere. Liked both uppers and downers. Liked to bet the spread against the Celtics/Sox/Patriots. A would-be bully who'd never moved out of the family home. A type utterly familiar to Ray, so that if at the moment of the crash he beheld death's visage, saw the kid through the two dirty windshields, Ray would have had to laugh. Nothing more exotic than another thwarted local loser? Merely the naked face of homegrown violence? The New England fan equivalent of skinheads out at NFL games in Foxboro if you were black and made the mistake of needing to go to the men's room; the umpteenth teenager to smash your car window to get the tape deck while your car was parked illegally when you went to the movies and decided to risk the ticket to save being gouged at the garage; or that representative of the lumpenproletariat in Dorchester who smoked angel dust and then ripped the face off an eighty-year-old for her wedding ring. Going on to serve a life sentence, all of it pointless except maybe for the fee to the court-appointed lawyer, salaries of the judge/bailiff/cop/stenographer/guard/warden/counselor/parole officer.

Being good. Ray was good in part because he was afraid not to be, afraid he'd become an alcoholic, be unemployed, be like his father/grandfather/great-grandfather. Beyond this, Ray thought that whatever Dionysius spoke for in other cultures, in Boston the god spoke not for freedom but for mayhem. Child abusers; tax evaders; politicians fixing a deal with contractors, hospital walls crumbling; state police cheating on promotion exams; star guard fixing the basketball game; victory being not joy but tearing down goalposts. Those with means moving out to the suburbs, then deploring urban violence.

Car windows. A friend put a sign in her Honda: No Radio. Came out one morning to find the windshield smashed, a different sign taped to the dashboard: *Get One*.

Ray did cut loose, once, right after leaving baseball. This was in '69, the whole world going crazy. He went to Europe, read books on the beach in Italy, smoked hash, thought he might just figure out how to stay a while. He knew a little of the history of the continent, it seemed nothing if not a record of war after war, one population being exterminated, yet another springing up in its place, the castles were fortresses, all this was clear. Nonetheless, in Italy for some reason Ray could imagine a middle ground, there governments seemed the danger, individuals and clans endowed with an instinct for peace, for savoring, nurturing. But in Boston, Ray felt, in Boston you really had to choose which side you were on.

One night he was out with his old friend Brian, drifting down Exeter Street. He and Brian played ball together in grammar school and high school. Baseball had saved Brian from two alcoholic parents, especially from a father who liked to beat the shit out of him. Now, a gambler and occasional coke dealer, Brian was drinking heavily. As they passed one of the fern-bar singles places, Brian saw a guy playing Asteroids by the window, pushed his way through the crowds at the door, walked up to him, and said, "I want to play," which the man correctly understood to translate as, "Get out of my way," to which he responded, "Fuck you," after which Brian took a swing, so Ray tried to ride his back to slow him down. Hard to do, since Brian was a bull. In fact, Brian once said to Ray's wife, "What fucks like a bull and winks?" and then winked.

The next day, Brian hung over and sober, Ray asked, "What was that about?"

"Come on," Brian said, "the guy was just another Carolan or Hoolihan or whatever. I didn't like his attitude. Tryin' to be a fuckin' preppy or something. Thinkin' his shit doesn't stink. Fuck him." The accent on "fuck," not "him."

Being good. Ray was good to his wife Barbara because he knew her, because he felt gratitude, because he felt obligation, because she was an extraordinary person—bright, giving, beautiful, loyal— because he was afraid of the wider world—AIDS increasingly crossed his mind as an argument for monogamy—because she put up with him, because he loved her even though he was certain that to love is to coerce. As for the kids, Ray was good to them because he couldn't help it, because when he first held Ray III in his arms he experienced a hormonal change, felt himself in that instant an utterly different person. Juices reconstituted, as he put it to himself, grinning. This was beyond choice: he just wasn't about to let anything hurt his child. A sensation that only deepened as he watched Ray III grow with an openness and trust that amazed him. Sitting in the rocking chair in the living room one night, studying his infant son, it occurred to Ray that he'd had to teach himself everything, everything. He'd been lonely all through his childhood, a very, very long time. Tears came to his eyes; he shook his head. Maudlin while sober, he thought. And envying my boy. Pathetic. What's become of me? He wiped his eyes, inspected Ray III's diaper. "A bean's a bean," he then said to his son, "but a pee's a relief."

∼

When Ray returned from Italy—Barbara wrote that if he didn't come home soon she'd start dating other guys—he took a job working for a church-sponsored recreation program in Roxbury helping inner-city kids. That is, housing-project blacks. Ray did so well the board encouraged him to set up a halfway house for ex-convicts, and he did so well with that that soon he had two halfway houses and fifteen employees, not to mention a roster of pacifist volunteers doing alternative service. His system then began to attract notice because it had no therapy. Non-therapy, Ray called it, that is, nothing more than job counseling, use of existing social services, a place to stay, and a few rules to offer some structure during the transition from prison. Remarkably effective without any talk of rebuilding the soul of the convict, not to mention consonant with Ray's skepticism: no unnecessary assumptions. Please.

There were only two problems for Ray. First, as the organization grew his salary grew, and as his salary grew he kept thinking he was overpaid; and second, his fear that the whole network might fold and he'd be unemployable. After all, what he had was a BA and some expertise on the baseball diamond. Barbara would say, "Fine, you want security, go work for the State Department of Corrections, Department of Youth Services, whatever," but they both knew he wouldn't. This though she shared Ray's amazement that a career line could be built out of so little. So it was that despite praise from people in the human services community, Ray felt he was doing it with smoke and mirrors. Wasn't it just common sense, really? To hold all this together, he came in at seven, left at seven, brought paperwork home for the weekends: the only way he could carry it off.

Actually, sometimes Ray knew he had special gifts. Blarney, for instance, being able to bullshit people, set them at ease. He and all the kids he knew growing up could do it, but out in the world it was apparently a scarce commodity. Then too he understood loyalty, or, loyalty was for him not an ethical imperative but, rather, like being able to play the ball on the short hop, something he didn't remember learning. So Ray was constantly surprising people by his loyalty, which, briefly, kept him surprised. As for the ex-cons, they were dazzled by freedom, which they failed to comprehend in all its complexity, coming as they were from the intricacies of not-freedom, and in part they saw Ray as responsible for their freedom, though he never claimed such power. Beyond this, Ray had no need to dominate the men, simply talked in practical language about the choices available to them. Perhaps too they sensed Ray wasn't physically afraid. He was, actually, if he thought about it; of course some one nut was capable of going crazy and pulling a gun. But day to day, because the men often had less self-control than other people, they seemed to Ray refreshingly direct, not nearly so menacing as some bureaucrats he'd encountered.

If the ex-cons were street-smart but not educated, Ray found his staff overeducated but not smart. Which was fine, since it left him some place to operate out of. Further, many of his employees, even the ones older than he was, seemed to need a father, would place him in that role whether or not he wanted to be there. That's just the way it was.

～

Barbara. Considering everything she could have been worse off. They'd bought the house when the market was still down; now it was worth a fortune. More, to everyone's surprise Ray had actually acted on his words about dying young and taken out a big life insurance policy.

These practicalities aside, Barbara had the benefit of not wishing she'd just had one last chance to talk to Ray. They'd known each other fifteen years, had been married for ten. They were best friends, long since familiar with each other's sorrows. Often he'd wake her in the middle of the night. "Babs, I can't sleep," he'd say mournfully, and, now wide awake, she'd console them both.

Barbara failed to wish she had one more chance to talk to Ray even though he didn't really speak to her the last six months before the accident. His silence—except for the absolutely necessary words—began after Ray III, age two and a half, came home from the hospital. It was a miracle, what the surgeons had done, but as Barbara saw it Ray was irreparably altered, finally just shut her out.

The nightmare started after Ray III had a cold for several days, but then instead of recovering kept vomiting, began to seem increasingly unresponsive. At the hospital, delirious, he was taken to Intensive Care. "Now we know what we're dealing with," the doctor finally told them after the blood test. "The high level of ammonia in the blood is diagnostic. This syndrome is rare, and poorly understood. Not genetic; usually comes after a viral infection. There's swelling in the brain, so we're going to begin medication to reduce it."

The next morning Ray III was still comatose. "What we have to do now," the surgeon told them, "is check the spinal fluid pressure so we can determine just how much medication can be safely used." The surgeon seemed to be planning to leave it at that, but Ray insisted on knowing more. "All right," the surgeon replied impatiently. "I understand. Informed consent. Well, we use a bone saw to remove a section in the skull, making a kind of window, then cut through the membrane below, the dura mater, after which we guide an ICP monitor to the ventricle of the brain to measure intracranial pressure."

This alone could have sent Ray over the edge, Barbara believed, but the surgeon, apparently feeling Ray had goaded him, wasn't finished. "If the swelling continues, the medicine isn't working. What happens then is the liver continues to turn to fat, and the brain swells until the brain stem, which controls breathing, is pushed through the bottom of the skull. This—herniation—is terminal. If the medicine does work, however, we operate again to take out the monitor and replace the bone square. There'll be no anesthesia when we begin, since your son is in a coma and feeling no pain."

It was too much for Ray, Barbara thought. Not that he'd been great even at her deliveries. "I gotta go now," he kept saying when she was in labor, and he'd head out for yet another cigarette. He just didn't know how she could stand it. But with Ray III, he crossed into some other zone completely. Perhaps, Barbara thought, perhaps because for weeks after the miracle of Ray III's survival, scar slowly disappearing as hair grew back, Ray III had terrible nightmares. The staff in Intensive Care restricted his movement and bound his wrists in gauze to keep the bandages from being disturbed, which appeared to explain why after he came home you could see him in a yet another dream wringing his hands, moaning, shifting, trying to escape. Nor would he cry: perhaps from his point of view he'd cried at the hospital, and all that had happened was someone then came and hurt him again.

Ray knew it was wrong, he felt terrible guilt, but even so he stopped talking to his wife. The deal they'd made, Ray seemed to be saying, was that he'd work and she'd raise the children. *Protect them*, he'd apparently understood that to mean. So he turned on Barbara, something he'd never done before. Emotionally spent after the operation, getting almost no sleep for weeks because of Ray III's nightmares, she decided to wait until spring to talk to Ray about it. But then he was killed. The short-term effect was that life became easier, his anger now absent. Nor did she have to deal with his insomnia/fear of being found out/anxiety about money/tirades about nepotism and patronage. His reflexive or genetic need to establish some security, his rage at being vulnerable to such a need.

∼

A few months before the kid killed him Ray suffered the paralysis of one side of his face. "An aberrant response of the immune system to a viral infection," the specialist explained, "always affecting just the right or left seventh cranial nerve." Not life threatening, but also there was no treatment. The paralysis almost always ended, eighty percent of the time within several months. Ray badgered the man. Was it stress? Smoking? Diet? In fact he wasn't about to change his life, but he did want some explanation. "Listen," the specialist replied. "It's just random. No cause, no blame, no nothing. Not something you did or didn't do. The nervous system—the brain—tells itself a story about whatever it encounters, which is to say, it looks for a pattern. But this phenomenon has none. Not everybody gets this viral infection, and of those who do, only a very small number get this paralysis. The impulse of the nervous system to find order is its nature, but in this kind of situation such an impulse just cannot be successful."

As for the level at which the phenomenon could be described, if in no way instrumentally affected by the capacity to describe it, one side of Ray's face retained its mobility while the other was unable to move. Along with hyperacusis, that is, increased sensitivity to sound, which only made Ray's insomnia more frequent and severe, and beyond the fact that he had to tape his eye closed at night to protect the cornea since the lower lid sagged, and after you noted that his forehead was furrowed on only one side, the paralysis gave his smile an odd quality, a kind of wryness even when Ray was most happy, one corner of his mouth drooping slightly, and also endowed even his scowl with an adjoining neutrality. So it was that when the kid's van barrelled around the curve on Ray's side of the road, when he saw it coming right at him, Ray began to grimace and was saying to himself, "I know Babs understands why I've been hurting her," and thinking, "We really don't need any more time to set it straight," and wondering if the new corrections grant would come through from the Feds and whether Miss C would be all right and Jesus, Mary, and Joseph, who's going to be there to teach the boys how to play the game, and even at the moment of impact—"Always be moving forward," were Ray's last words to himself—he also appeared to be sporting some kind of a grin.

(*1993*)

Song of the Self-Made

Silicon Valley, not far south of San Francisco, only two decades ago still semi-rural, and, back before the orchards and walnut groves, Franciscans and Jesuits vying to alchemize Ohlones into Christians. "Silicon," however, not like Mississippi/Massachusetts/Susquehanna—no shard of an indigenous tongue—but, via Latin, denoting the wafers used in semiconductors. Valley of the computers.

Not visibly drowning in all this history, Michael at forty-five, vice president in charge of appraisals at Golden Northern California County Bank: eighty-seven K per annum plus bonus plus car for the commute. *Ecce* Michael: heading left down the corridor away from his desk, destination a meeting with a VP two doors to the right, circumnavigating the entire floor in order to avoid passing the president's office, which, of all the luck, is just next to his. Low profile. Upper middle management. Appropriate stratagems, learned by fourth grade, *mit* appropriate disguise—Mr. Middle America, Bay Area style. American flag pin, nice touch, in the lapel of the black pinstripe suit. Club tie. Think Yiddish/dress British. Suit more stylish than it would be in Peoria, cordovans more expensive, face more lined. Face more lined? Oh yes, more lived history here in this golden state in the land of the free. Forty-five in '88? Twists and turns. That would make Michael twenty-five in '68: draft eligible/dope smoking/

203

venereal-disease prone. Traveling around the world on "liberated" airline tickets when not protesting the war. Right in Johnson's and Nixon's face: one of The People. Selling the occasional lid.

Where have all the flowers gone? Visiting our rawboned democracy in the 1830s, Alexis de Tocqueville observed that where class is not rigidly defined, status becomes an incessant anxiety. *Any* man a king? Though as a revolutionary Michael feared the Thermidorian reaction, was too interested in sex and drugs to be more than intermittently swayed by his own commitments, though he experienced a mean period of living in his car while waiting for some new communal vision to inspire him, by 1971 he'd successfully retooled, quickly enough to be deemed an apostate by radical friends still waiting for the apocalypse. He studied for the real estate broker's exam at a local community college (never did finish the B.A.), took on family in the form of a wife he didn't actually marry and her child by a previous (state-and-church sanctioned) marriage before they had one of their own. A boy. Glenn with two n's. Accumulating a small paper fortune in the late seventies inflationary spiral in housing—no laws in California against realtors speculating—and then losing it when, right in step with the times, Michael developed an interest in cocaine and started milking the properties for cash until interest rates went up, money got tight—he was using his bank cards as a source of credit by then, eighteen percent plus per—and the property was... gone. All this culminating in bankruptcy proceedings, which turned out not to be as bad as he'd feared.

By then his non-wife wife, heading in a somewhat different direction, had taken up with a victim of the sixties. Talk about vectors! Here was Michael, aspiring middle class right down to his coke habit after the lost years of civil war and revolutionary dreams. And there was his wife, who though she had no trouble ingesting the coke was nostalgic for some larger freedom, freedom others had tasted while she was stuck raising her first child as a high school principal's spouse, enraged by the inevitability of another day of school for her daughter, another day of school for her husband, another day of obedience classes for the dog, just wanting Something Outside The System. Finally, after long-term passive resistance in the face of Michael's decade of relentless upward mobility, encountering Harry: brilliant but too unstable to work, deeply troubled, living on Social Security. Which is to say, free! Or, she liked coke but wanted to deal it, not buy it: that way it too would be free.

Meanwhile, coming back one night from their cabin at Muir Beach, traversing Mount Tamalpais, a watershed in the coastal range just north of San Francisco, finishing yet another joint of sinsemilla, Michael crossed a watershed so to speak. "Screw it," he muttered, "she and I are history." Sucking on the roach, he pondered the idiom. *She and I are history*. It suggested, he concluded contemplatively, that he and his non-wife had *become* what they'd once simply been living between them. "That is," Michael said to himself, advancing his line of reasoning, "we are what we were, which, if you think about it, means that now we aren't anything at all." Accelerating down the last section of curves leading to the freeway, taking one last toke, Michael began to laugh. *"All right,"* he shouted, *"all right."*

Not more than several months before this moment, he'd had a true sign. He'd been taking prescription pain medication, had then belted back some Scotch, and was driving the Volvo he'd bought his pregnant non-wife. (Buying a Volvo for the mother-to-be of your child: an apparently inevitable hormonal response for middle-class males.) Michael was in Oakland when he hit the wall. Totaling the car, nearly killing himself. And as the dust settled he'd realized the significance: he'd *hit the wall*. Decided to put down the drugs/change his life/save his non-marriage, or, as it turned out, cut back on drugs a little and end his non-marriage. Whatever.

In the wake of the accident he also suffered a conversion to a new superego in the form of General Douglas MacArthur. He'd been on MacArthur Boulevard in Oakland when he crashed, you see. Suddenly, in the living room with the redwood paneling he'd installed at such great cost because of the repose it was to induce, there appeared framed photos—two by three feet—of young MacArthur, all puttees and swagger stick, and soon The General was consulted on Michael's every move. This had to be some kind of a joke, but there Michael was, yet again going into the next room to ask The General's advice in private. And The General's usual response? Well, he tended to point Michael back toward the dreams of the teenager Michael had been. Toward West Point. A cadet's life, though in good conscience Michael could never remember whether he'd arrived at the Academy straight out of high school or after coming up through the ranks. The intervening twenty years of national and personal life—total chaos on all fronts—somehow airbrushed away in the process.

∼

Michael in the health club at his stress doctor's behest, staring. Transfixed. A naked old man, checking his hold on the stainless steel railing, descends into the pool a step at a time. Legs hairless, flesh off-white, breasts enlarged, penis all head and no shaft. Standing waist deep in the green water, adjusting black goggles and red bathing cap, the old man hyperventilates, splashes water on his chest, and then falls forward, beginning an achingly slow crawl, shoulders heaving out of the water each time his head jerks up for air, legs twitching sporadically. Holding on to the edge at the end of each lap for several seconds before again pushing off. "That's okay," Michael tells himself, "only a stickler would call it cheating." Michael's vantage point on all this? His exercycle. Pedaling in place, he's done two miles, has three to go.

About a mile later he shakes his head, realizes he's been spacing out. The murder of Martin Luther King, his funeral. Coretta King in a pew. Dylan's "All Along the Watchtower," sung by Jimi Hendrix: "There must be some kind of way out of here…"

Nearby, some older men are at the Nautilus machines and weight benches. "Yes," comes a voice, "I commuted twenty-five miles each way, two hundred and fifty miles a week, twelve thousand miles a year for twenty-five years. That's…"

"Three hundred thousand miles," Michael mutters.

"Three hundred thousand miles," the voice continues.

"He's a self-made man," another voice is saying.

Bell ringing on the exercycle, Michael dismounts and walks past several men who, pedaling furiously while wearing the diaperlike shorts issued by the health club, for a moment appear to Michael to be wizened infants in some kind of tricycle race. Shaking his head, Michael enters the locker room, where Sam is talking about his plans. Same old thing: he and the wife play bridge every evening. Marty, meanwhile, still smarting from being defeated by Sam in racquetball, says he lost because he had sex recently. Sam's rejoinder? "Marty, if you remarry you won't have to worry about that anymore," a line that leaves Michael squinting.

Michael shrugs, composes himself, pulls it all together. Adjusts his tie, slips into a blue blazer. This to round out gray flannel slacks, argyle socks, and saddle shoes.

∼

Work. After bankruptcy, a period as a freelance appraiser, dunning clients for checks. Then a headhunter—"my guru," Michael calls him—gets Michael his first job at a bank. A Vietnamese-owned bank, whose directors, having been so kind as to ignore the missing years on Michael's resume, frequently try to get him to "be reasonable before the place goes broke." Michael never fails to hold his ground, but the struggle wears him out, the problem being that a good appraiser should be a kind of in-house cop, challenging loans on property he considers overvalued, the salesmen and, sometimes, upper management arguing that the appraiser's estimate is too low.

After the Vietnamese-owned bank goes under, the guru finds Michael a position that's more businesslike but still not corporate enough for what's proving to be Michael's taste, that is, the new bank lacks the structural dignity and gray hum of layers of employees far removed from any bottom line, a row of elevators to the 17th/29th/

38th floor. This though Michael likes being a vice president, liked it enough to empower his guru to trade two thousand a year in salary for the honorific when his contract was being negotiated. But beyond this Michael wants to manage, not do the task itself, and there are just not enough Indians here. Worse, the company is too entrepreneurial, raw, a one-man show. Of the president and founder Michael says: "I speak only when spoken to." And, "If you move, he may mistake you for wild game."

Notwithstanding these shortcomings, the job's of course an enormous step forward. By the time he settles into his new office, Michael is sobered only when his guru calls with news he thought Michael should hear from him. "You remember," his guru says, "we were wondering why such a fine position came free. Well, the long and short of it is, your predecessor apparently jumped off the Golden Gate Bridge."

∼

Crazy Davy comes by, throws a rock through the window. In 1966 Davy was going with Anne. Michael slept with Anne a few times, it meant next to nothing to him, Anne had had enough of Davy, but Davy went crazy, so Anne used to let Davy come around as a friend, so Davy got to know Michael. Davy hung around Michael in the antiwar groups, but already seemed to be losing hold. Even his major was all wrong. Psychology in a department of behaviorists, all those experiments on rats, endless journal articles to read, never a book. Then Davy began to smoke dope, but it overwhelmed him, and even behind the dope he wore coat and tie, as if afraid to let the clothes go lest his entire persona disappear, which only made him seem odd to other girls, though Anne seemed to understand. Part of the problem was that Davy's parents were Romanian royalist refugees. Irredentists, never not planning to return the day the Russian tyrants were overthrown. Davy was raised in a suburb, won a varsity letter on the swim team, engaged in heavy petting in his '55 Chevy, but he just couldn't quite get in synch with the land to which his parents had been exiled.

Now, twenty years after losing Anne, Crazy Davy's never put it together. A brief period selling real estate. Small annual guilt stipend from his parents. Some time as a cab driver. Hours every afternoon in the cafés. No girlfriends. An occasional impulse to let Michael have it for ruining his life. The occasional call to Michael in the middle of the night, just breathing into the phone. And, once in a while, something more.

When Michael hears the crash, he knows what it is. "Davy," he says to himself, getting out of bed, walking into the living room. Seeing the glass, he heads back to the kitchen for a dustpan and broom.

∼

In the wake of hitting the wall, after The General becomes part of his life, before he meets his wife-wife, Michael solves weekends. He'd always hated them. Vacant, empty, too open to self-criticism. Now, on Sundays, he goes to church. Gets up, gets organized, puts on coat and tie. The only problem being his mother, since he was born and raised a Jew, if by quite secular parents.

"I'm pretty comfortable," he said after joining a local congregation, the middle-class members' focus less the hereafter than good works in the company of similar others—ecology, women's rights, the homeless. "I'm trying it on, like new clothes. I didn't want to spend the rest of my life as a brunette." Grinning, Michael adds, "The minister's name is Gipper."

∼

Marriage. "Do nothing irrevocable," friends and therapist said when things were going bad with his non-wife. Nonetheless, at a time when Michael was aching for stability, she seemed to him to have come up with the analogue of the Symbionese Liberation Army in her friendship with Harry. So it was that ten years after they met, the morning after he crossed Mount Tamalpais, Michael suggested they separate.

A week later, at a realtor's office planning to list his house, Michael started chatting with one of the brokers. Sally: strawberry blonde, going on twenty-seven, never married, bright, straightforward, eager to start a family. "Want to make a deal?" Michael asked her, and she laughed. The next weekend, singing Sinatra—"If you think I'm only foolin' 'bout the French Foreign Legion, think about that uniform with all its charm…"—Michael went shopping for an engagement ring. In one store, the proprietor argued that antique rings were no good because they were "worn out," but Michael had a vision of something with history. Also in this period he developed a kind of tic, a chronic manic laugh, as if to say, "I know this seems crazy, but here I am doing it." Or, as Michael acknowledged to his mother, "It kind of takes your breath away." Adding, "But I'm not going to let this opportunity go by." When he phoned with the news he'd begun by saying, "Mom, sit down."

At the wedding, Michael's son by his non-wife was ring bearer, and Gipper, the minister, managed to make no audible reference to Jesus, apparently out of consideration for Michael's mother. Just before the ceremony, Michael inspected himself in the men's room mirror. "It looks like me," he said. "It must be me."

∼

Some years before, Michael decided that TV was the cause of his problems. Too powerful, too many fantasies. Too many simultaneities implying the possibility of participation. Not diverting but confusing. Threatening, actually. One morning, therefore, right after Glenn left for school, turning off the *Today Show*, feeling both courageous and at risk—he was giving up a way of life—Michael loaded the four sets into his car, drove to a pawnshop in Oakland, and sold them.

When Glenn got home that afternoon he immediately phoned his father at work. "Dad, something happened to all the TVs." Hearing what Michael had done, his son started punching the phone buttons in anger. "Electronic rage," Michael said later, describing Glenn's response.

~

Learning that his father died when he was nine, Michael's therapist tells him he has no father figure, does nothing to discourage Michael's interest in General MacArthur. Reading Manchester's *American Caesar*, Michael finds that MacArthur all his life tried to measure up to his father's example, that for MacArthur the word "gentleman" had a religious meaning "higher than any title, station, or act of Congress." "Think of it," Michael tells himself, "the humiliation he suffered when they abandoned the Philippines."

As Michael experienced his own life, there was always an enormous amount to forget:

"If the sixties was a time of judging for me personally, the seventies was a time of trying to find out who I was as a man and as a human being. And now, in the eighties, I want action…without power, nothing is accomplished. The key to power in the eighties is money, and that was not the key in the sixties…"

In the barbershop Michael had picked up a *Playboy*, came to Jerry Rubin's words, read them, felt tears welling. For the love of God, there he was, waiting for a by-appointment-only haircut; he had a pinstripe suit/wife/kid/mortgage big enough to crush an elephant. And working in a bank, yes, you made a living, but was it something to boast about, was this the stuff of dreams?

A few days later Michael read an account of the murder of former Congressman Allard Lowenstein by Denis Sweeny. Brave, idealistic, and primed for sacrifice, Sweeny gave all he had to the civil rights movement. By the end of the sixties, however, he'd become a drifter, sure his life was manipulated by unseen others, feeling enormous guilt for sins only he knew of. Lowenstein, the charismatic left-liberal who'd helped inspire Sweeny, who had perhaps also been his lover years before, was, Sweeny finally concluded, allied with the parties monitoring his mind.

Michael read about Lowenstein's death, Sweeny's madness. He winced: how close he'd come. A Beatles line occurred to him: "Once there was a way, to get back homeward..."

∽

The job. "I love to delegate," Michael says. The joys of delegating undercut only by the president's penchant for humiliating his employees. "Well," Michael says, trying to be positive, "at least they've done away with public hangings."

∽

When Michael married his wife-wife, the question was whether or not to fight for custody of his son. His new spouse understood, he wanted to raise his child, that was a clause in the deal they made, but another part of him wanted never again to see his non-wife or any aspect of her in his son's eyes, mind, spirit. Nonetheless, Michael decided to try, and to his surprise Glenn made it clear to the court that he wanted to live with his father, though the school he'd be attending would be strict and his father's demands about homework severe. Perhaps it had to do with the fact that his mother and Harry were living in a teepee in Ukiah.

One problem was that Michael's wife understandably rued the constant presence of an adolescent not her own, another that because Glenn spent alternate weekends with his mother plans had to be made for the pickups and dropoffs, but Michael's non-wife frequently lost or confused the schedule. Finally Michael installed a separate phone in Glenn's room, said, "I don't want to speak to your mother anymore. You love her, be a good son to her, but otherwise think of me as the quarterback and you're on the offensive line. If the quarterback gets sacked you're on the bench. Up to the teepee."

Passing one year at his father's house and then another, full on into puberty, Glenn developed a terrible case of acne on his face and back. Having had acne himself, Michael couldn't just stand and watch. So it was that each night he'd apply the medicine to Glenn's back, kept at him about diet and washing and sweating and exercise, went to the therapist with him from time to time to talk about the problems of having a stepmother who wasn't always enchanted with her stepson, Glenn having protected the quarterback very well indeed.

∽

These are words that had once motivated Michael, made him feel he was marching in the Army of the Just:
"...the people of this country must take possession of their lives... the oppression of any people in the world is our oppression...the hope for a situation of equality and justice in this country and the world rests on our being free in the face of America." Inspired, surrounded by thousands of inspired others, Michael heard in his inner ear the soundtrack from *Victory at Sea*.

∽

Though Michael had a gift for knocking girls up in high school and college, though Glenn was conceived for want of a condom and under the influence of various nonprescription drugs, Michael and his wife-wife had trouble making a baby. Which, he soon concluded ruefully, was not the same as making love. He'd return from work on the given days for what he called his second job, her temperature having been taken and taken again, they'd tell Glenn to enjoy a night off from doing his homework and go to a movie with the boys, but month after month there was no good news. They saw the doctor, learned about hormones/motility/implants/artificial insemination, spent some weekends off together just to relax, but when at long last she finally conceived Michael attributed it to the fact that he'd stopped wearing jockey shorts.

Meanwhile, in the corridor outside his office one day, Michael stood listening as the president prepared to tell a joke. "Or are you too busy, Mr. Vice-President-In-Charge-of-Appraisals?" the president asked. Smiling benignly, all ears, Michael imagined a response: "Excuse me, sir, but can you tell me how to spell, uh, *wazoo?*"

The president's joke, meanwhile, was about the accountant, lawyer, and chief appraiser who were being considered for promotion to CEO. In turn, the board chairman asked each one to estimate the value of a building the bank was considering financing. To make a long story short, the accountant behaved as accountants will, crunching lots of numbers in his estimate, while the lawyer split hairs and cited relevant statutes. As for the chief appraiser—now the president was laughing, could barely get the words out, forcing Michael to make sounds of appropriate concern—when it was the chief appraiser's turn he walked to the door of the boardroom, looked around carefully, and closed it. "And then," the president told Michael, getting a grip on himself, "then the chief appraiser replied, 'What's the building worth, Mr. Chairman? In my view it's worth whatever you say it is.'"

∽

Glenn continued to thrive, apart from an incident of streaking while pledging for a high school fraternity. Apprehended by the local police, he ended up volunteering fifteen hours of community service, Michael disturbed less by the offense than by the fact that Glenn was the only boy who got caught. "Point of information," Michael said to his son. "Does naked mean barefoot?"

One evening soon after, Glenn borrowed his father's car. Worried that the emergency brake was still on several minutes after leaving home—"It felt real stiff, Dad," he said subsequently—Glenn pulled the release so hard that it broke. When he came home everyone was asleep, not that he was eager to discuss what had happened, so he went to his room. The next day, about to head to the bank at six-thirty, well before the rest of the household roused itself, as usual moving the gear shift to neutral and setting the brake before getting out to raise the garage door, Michael watched the car slowly roll back through the worktable and washer-dryer.

∼

A call from Crazy Davy at three in the morning, weird but not too menacing: Davy's version of a bouquet for Michael's impending forty-fifth. Michael's mother in town for the occasion, comfortably housed at his mother-in-law's apartment, the two old moms, as they call themselves, doing fine. Seventeen-year-old Glenn and two-year-old Alice also doing fine. Wife-wife once again very pregnant. With twins, according to the amnio. Homemade carrot cake on the dining room table.

Toupee slightly askew, the gay pianist from down the block plays "Happy Birthday." Beholding the cake, The General standing at parade rest on the wall behind him, Michael smiles, says, "I want to thank my wife, my mother, my friends, my agent—"

"What is this, the Academy Awards?" someone shouts.

Before Michael blows out the candles, he pretends to faint.

(1993)

Zenobia in New York

*L*ate May in Manhattan, overcast, very humid, and very hot, the threat of rain. Walking through Central Park beyond the Metropolitan toward the reservoir by the Guggenheim, sky ever darker, Zenobia—Zeno, for short—thinks, "Time to find shelter" as she sees two Rhodesian Ridgebacks go by, says to herself, "They belong on the veranda of some farm in the veldt." Right after which several horsemen pass, putting Zeno in mind of how she almost got a job driving a carriage around the park. That is, Zeno met a woman in a diner over on Ninth Avenue who was a driver and offered to introduce her to the owner of the stable. Something Zeno gave thought to before deciding against it by not deciding, balked primarily by the image of horses laboring on asphalt in the summer heat.

Nearby, several kids torment a squirrel, but Zeno's attention is diverted by a passing golden retriever. Just then a jogger steams past with an aging German shepherd on leash trailing miserably behind. "That's simply not right," Zeno says out loud, as if to an assembly of fair-minded observers, and adds, "Shepherds are very loyal." Staring for a moment at the bend around which dog and man have disappeared, thinking this mistreatment of a noble animal must be stopped, she takes off after them just as the downpour begins, flashes of lightning and several claps of thunder for a moment stilling the sirens, horns, and undifferentiated roar of the city.

Later, soaked, passing the Senegalese street vendors selling fake Rolexes, after stepping into the Greek joint on the corner near her apartment for some souvlaki, Zeno takes the subway downtown, holds on to a strap and sways as the train accelerates, as a bare-chested black man in dreadlocks, torn shorts, and bare feet comes through the rear door of the car carrying a paper cup. "I need some money. I don't want to rob, but I am hungry. I don't want to hurt nobody. Just give me some money." Teenage black girls snickering, as if his pitch just doesn't cut it.

~

Living room of an apartment on the Upper West Side, Zeno maid of honor at the wedding of her friend Flo. Flo's third marriage, this time to an investment counselor who's had trouble with alcohol and drugs. On their first date, resolved to seduce him, Flo left the front door ajar, placed herself in the bath. "Come on in," she shouted when she heard the doorbell. Reaching the doorway of the bathroom, her husband-to-be fainted: when he was three, Flo later learned, his mother died of a heart attack while bathing him.

Now Flo stands with him under the huppa, hip rabbi performing the ceremony before the thirty guests. "Kiss the bride," the rabbi says, but, when Flo and her husband embrace, adds, "I told you to kiss, not consummate." After the ceremony, quite sure the rabbi's used the line before, Zeno confronts him, says, "That was cheap, very cheap. Shame on you."

Later, Flo's mother-the-psychic, adding hors d'oeuvres to her enormous girth, observes, "Perhaps now my daughter Flo's finally learned to find peace in herself." Then, wiping her mouth with a napkin, she grabs Zeno's right hand, inspects the palm. "This is serious," she says. "Come see me soon."

"You must get outside yourself," Flo's mother tells Zeno the following week. "Your biggest trouble is, what do you really want? You've already lived more than a quarter of a century. You're ravenous but you forget to eat. You sought your freedom, and now you have it. *Use it.*" And, pausing: "What did you say your sign is?"

∽

One of Zeno's many returns to Manhattan. The jet's long slow glide up the west side of the island above the Hudson, then a languid right turn toward La Guardia above Columbia University. Sunset, the buildings like dominos, World Trade Center/Chrysler Building/Empire State Building. Zeno—so close to the ground now, approaching human scale—no longer afraid of being airborne.

Back in New York. "Sometimes I'm frightened," Zeno tells her mother on the phone. "I get on the subway and want to bolt like a horse. Why me, here? What journey am I on?"

"Don't be theatrical," her mother says theatrically.

Good thing I'm not in need of protection, Zeno thinks.

"And try to dress up more," her mother adds. "I really wish you'd work on it."

∽

"If I can't have boys, then for the love of God give me a warrior queen," Zeno's father always said. Septima Zenobia, ruler of Palmyra, who conquered several of Rome's eastern provinces before being subjugated. According to the '39 Encyclopaedia Britannica, family reference work during Zeno's childhood, Zenobia was a "remarkable woman, famed for her beauty, her masculine energy and unusual powers of mind…" who "exceeded her husband in talent and ambition." And, "The queen refused to yield to Aurelian's demand for surrender and drew up her army at Emesa for the battle which was to decide her fate. In the end she was defeated, and there was nothing for it but to fall back upon Palmyra across the desert. Thither Aurelian followed her in spite of the difficulties of transport, and laid siege to the well-fortified and provisioned city. At the critical moment the queen's courage seems to have failed her; she and her son fled the city to seek help from the Persian king, they were captured on the bank of the Euphrates, and the Palmyrenes, losing heart at this disaster, capitulated..."

Zeno grew up with this version of her namesake, and though inspired by the tone, of course she had questions, continues to wonder. *"Her courage seems to have failed her..."* In the 1979 Brittanica's version, for example, which Zeno peruses at the public library on Forty-second Street, Zenobia instigated the assassination of her husband and stepson, then "styled herself queen."

"Zenobia's career made a deep impression on the Roman writers of the collection of biographies known as the *Historia Augusta* ("August History," probably fourth century). They compared her to the Egyptian queen Cleopatra (first century B.C.) and recounted—not always reliably—stories regarding her dark beauty, chastity, learning, and fabulous wealth. She is known to have studied Greek literature with the philosopher Cassius Longinus. According to some sources, she saved her life at the time of her capture by blaming Longinus and her other advisers for Palmyra's aggression, and they were subsequently executed."

"Revisionist!" Zeno says out loud, stalking out of the library.

∽

New York City, 1986. *Littering is dirty and selfish and don't do it.* A street sign à la Mayor Koch. New York as Calcutta. Primal soup. The homeless and other euphemisms. Investment bankers all the rage. The realm of the fiscal being extended, Zeno observes, transactions not previously seen as monetary now part of the cash economy. Used cardboard fruit cartons being sold at the Korean fruit markets, for example. Potential mates calibrating each other's net worth. A city of certainties. Everyone knows what's what, what they want: *more; out.* Zeno long since familiar with the nuances of finance, daughter of parents raised in wealth who managed to disinherit themselves of everything but their social status, the "wherewithal" to maintain that status perennially a concern, if unmentionable.

Zeno's New York. Biking home through the park from fabric design work on her used white Raleigh three-speed against a steady stream of joggers, skaters, and cyclists, past Cleopatra's needle and the model boat basin. Papers and empty beer cans flying up eleventh Ave., icebergs floating out to sea on the Hudson. Ballet class. Yoga class. Capoeira class. Christmas Eve at the cathedral of St. John the Divine. Chestnut and pretzel vendors loading up their carts on Ninth Ave. Down to the food stalls under the overpass for Yugoslavian goat cheese, Amish chickens, celery root and apples, sake and Italian bread. Ailanthus tree budding in the courtyard, gutters swimming. Parrots in the oaks, blown up on a hurricane.

Zeno's fifth-floor apartment in Hell's Kitchen. Rent controlled. One seventy-two/month. View of the river. Ten units, no elevator. A steal. Her building part of a blue-collar New York fast disappearing, developers fighting for it, neighborhood going upscale fast. Soon to hold no more workers, dancers, actors, musicians.

Her apartment: living room, bedroom, small kitchen, tub across from the stove, tiny bathroom. Air shaft, diesel fumes, noise of many households. (Zeno rescuing a pigeon trapped in the air shaft by someone who nailed a screen over the opening.) Pile of lumber for the bookcases she's building. Self-designed cotton sleeping bag. Pair of light green corduroy pants in progress. Swaths of quilt material under the sleeping William-the-Cat. (Abandoned in the subway; saved by Zenobia.)

E. B. White's *Charlotte's Web* on the floor beside her, Zeno reads Vicki Hearne on language, interspecies communication, and *virtu*, Hearne arguing that "a story about how what appears to be horse insanity may be...evidence of how powerful equine genius is, and how powerfully it can object to incoherence...The stories we tell matter..."

Zeno, reading this, feeling elevated, confirmed.

Zeno on her childhood. "Once we were down by the boathouse and a bobcat came up. A bobcat! That's a kind of lynx, a wildcat. It had tufted ears, it was the size of a dog, something like an Border collie. It was just standing there, looking hungry, so I fed him my sandwich. Then I went back to the house for more food and turned to find him trailing behind me. A bobcat! There was also a pair of ravens that sat on a railing. I'd put my eyes to my hands when they passed. Of course there were raccoons, possum, rabbits, garter snakes, orange newts, toads, box turtles, what-have-you.

"There were always fireflies. Sometimes you'd see one caught in the spider's web in the back room.

"There'd be sun in the meadow beyond the trees, daylilies and butterfly weed in bloom, fresh-cut cherry wood stacked by the shed, hornbeam and wild swamp azalea. Moss. Lichen (a word I've always loved)."

And once, at her family's summer place, Zeno lay spread-eagled in the pasture surrounded by the neighbor's five cows. Their white faces lowered over her, she says years later, remembering, "the heat of their exhalations very moist, gossamer wisps of saliva falling. Tears in their eyes." Later, the five of them sat circled around her, "shoulders and spines visible above the waves of grass like the humps of five russet whales."

Zeno at nine, yearning. High up on the four-poster in the lavender bedroom that faces out to sea, venetian blinds softly rattling in the offshore breeze, long lavender curtains stirring fitfully. Zeno sprawled on a white cotton sheet, drinking goat's milk from a monogrammed glass. Thinking of how, that morning, an enormous blue heron stared as she pretended to be very busy collecting sand dollars.

A childhood dream. Great white osprey soaring with Zeno on its shoulders, small feathers cascading down with each pulse of wings. Zeno putting the feathers in her jewel box, "to show—like milk teeth, or Grandmother's Mesopotamian spun-gold earrings that ring like bells—to strangers."

Zeno tells these stories to Jacques, a Haitian from her capoeira class, whose heavily accented English is less than fluent. At her invitation he spends the night on a mat in the living room instead of going all the way back uptown to his place, but not as her lover. Or, not yet; Zeno's thinking it through. She likes Jacques in part because he excels at capoeira, in which the Portuguese verb for fighting is *jogar*, to play. Zeno also has the feeling that Jacques understands play in the sense that animals understand it: frisking, butting, just pronging along on all fours, skedaddling; the sheer sport of being alive. But in her mind she also pictures going to Jacques's home in Haiti with him, falling off the map of the known world, being lost to all she's lived thus far, like the great European women explorers of the nineteenth century. And this she has to think through.

Play. Animals. Often Zeno sees people as animals, wishes them more like animals or that they'd admit the resemblance. Humans, Zeno thinks. Reluctant to acknowledge any essential connection to behavior routinely manifested in the "lower" world: cannibalism, infanticide, fratricide, parricide, the impulse to dominate. And as for sex, people seem determined to diminish the power of what's involved, the insanely volatile mix of fear and attraction, the threat of mutual aggression. What Zeno loves in the animal kingdom are the rituals of courtship, the chases—dances!—of cheetahs, for example, female with harem of males in pursuit before she exhausts all but the one with whom she'll copulate. Play-fighting, play-biting, pouncing: courtship to moderate tensions of conflicting desires. Females at the penultimate moment raising one leg as if to ward off danger; males and females sinking their teeth into each other's necks, drawing blood. Or the male spider working hard to convey to his potential lover that he's a mate, not dinner. Or screams modified into songs: the complex morning duets—calls and whoops—of gibbon pairs, audible for miles across Southeast Asian forests as they announce the dawn.

~

Zenobia as her own doctor, practicing without a license, working not just for health but for regeneration. A diet of live fresh foods and sprouting seeds. Garden essences for balancing, cleansing: celery, to restore the immune system; cucumber, for reattaching to life during depression; dill, to assist in reclaiming power one has released to others; okra, for returning the ability to see the positive; and comfrey, to repair soul damage in a past or present lifetime.

Sure, it sounds ludicrous, Zeno acknowledges, measured by the standards of Western science. But what, she asks, what has that science produced now? Besides the threat of nuclear war/chemical poisons in our food/endless torture of animals?

And to whom does Zeno say this? To her father, of course, university researcher, expert on light coherent and incoherent, romantic whose song is the song of science. Her mother chiming in, "Oh, Zeno, do leave the poor man alone." Zeno then announcing plans to be in Central Park for the Harmonic Convergence, the organizers' intent to have at least 144,000 humans get together around the world to hold hands and chant—"to resonate in harmony." The idea being to help Earth synchronize itself with the rest of the galaxy. Thus to prevent extinction of many species, including humans.

"Oh," her mother says. "Must you?" Zeno thinking of the various phyla in which mothers are known to sacrifice their children. Remembering being in the back of the Volvo station wagon yet again as a child, being taken somewhere, somewhere, by her mother. Realizing how much she resembles her mother. Her father pouring himself another shot of Glenfiddich, asking, "Have you bought health insurance yet? You must have health insurance."

"Yes, Daddy," Zeno replies, thinking of the mice, monkeys, and cats on which his lab performs research. The word "abattoir" coming to mind.

"You don't want to end up an eccentric spinster, do you?" her mother adds. "Well, do you?"

∼

"I'm struggling with what I want to commit to and what is possible," Zeno tells Flo, whose marriage to the investment counselor is already in trouble. Zeno thinking it might be easiest—having been up at The Cloisters earlier, looking at the medieval tapestries—if someone simply gave her a castle for which she could be chatelaine. Where she could wait for her unicorn.

Zeno deciding she's not ready for Jacques, the Haitian. That Harry, the film editor who's been wooing her with travel and jazz, just doesn't have any idea who she really is, doesn't want to know, that a match with him would be "wildly inappropriate." That he can't see beyond her blond hair. ("What's the matter with liking blond hair?" Flo shouts.) That having two sexes for reproduction in mammals may simply have been an evolutionary wrong turn. "Parthenogenesis," Zeno says to Flo. "Hermaphrodites!" Suddenly thinking of a quilt with a flying goose pattern, or perhaps something with giraffes.

"Well, I want a *man* in my bed, thank you," Flo says, "not just some cat." Zeno not reminding Flo that at least feline testosterone levels seem immune to fluctuations in the stock market.

∿

Zeno up late, pulling out her Halliburton's *Book of Marvels*. "In affairs of state [Zenobia] astonished the ministers with her wisdom. In the army the generals marveled at her bravery... Astride her white racing camel, her purple cloak flying, she led her Arab cavalry back and forth across the desert from battle to battle, from victory to victory... The world had never before seen such an all-conquering woman warrior.

"...One story tells that when she heard Palmyra had been destroyed she refused to touch food for thirty days, and killed herself by starvation.

"But another story says Aurelian carried her, very much alive, on to Rome. And there, bound in gold chains, the unhappy queen was forced to walk behind Aurelian's chariot as he rode through the streets in triumph..."

∿

Zeno with William-the-Cat. Trying to figure out what's bothering him. Combing him for fleas. Certain that if she just pays enough attention, he'll convey exactly what's on his mind. In idiomatic English, perhaps. And why not?

∼

Zeno, depressed. By the daily illegal eruptions of no-doubt-poisonous soot from the chimneys of neighboring buildings. By Homo sapiens' relentless destruction of loggerhead turtles, the true Ancient Ones. "I'm leaving New York," Zeno tells Flo the night before her twenty-eighth birthday, suddenly afraid she's one of those people who always say they're going to leave New York but never do. Adding, "Winter is my favorite season. The seed beneath the snow."

(1993)

Citizen Mad Dog

Three years of prison in his early twenties for motor vehicle theft, known as Mad Dog: too violent when provoked to bother with. Thriving despite being one of the small minority of whites inside. Bad break, to be busted in the South. Promoted to running the laundry long before he got a release date, impeccable in his upgraded prison issue, resplendent in starched shirt and tailored pants. The unspoken logic of so hostile an environment something like: Care for yourself and so be worthy of being cared for by others, were they only here to care for you, though of course they're not.

Finally out on parole, Mad Dog immediately disappeared, basketball in his pack, wandering the country shooting hoops in college towns, always reading another book—especially the latest Updike, when the setting was coastal Massachusetts—until after three years and thirty-five states the clock on his sentence expired and, turning twenty-seven, he was a free man.

Returning to Boston, he went right up to the North Shore, to Ipswich, bars full of the Poles and Greeks he came of age drinking with. Bannon's at Depot Square, then the Choate Bridge Pub ("Oldest stone arch bridge on the North American continent," people would say when he was a kid). Waiting around town most of the day until his father finally walked by.

"Hey, what do you know? Shit floats to the surface. My own lost son Richard."

"Nice to see you too, Dad."

"So what do you want?"

"Nothin'. Really. I come back to give you somethin'."

"You can try." Mad Dog's father was forty-eight, five-nine/two-fifty, a hod carrier. Strong as a bastard, to use the local vernacular. Never known to back away from a fight, graced with an amazingly high tolerance for physical pain. And, in a way, prudent: armed. For a long time he carried a gun, once pulled it when Mad Dog tried to settle things between them.

"No firearms today, Dad?" Mad Dog said, studying him carefully. "Tough luck. Anyway, I got a short speech prepared. Which is: you fucked over me and Danny and David and Ellen with all that brutal shit. I could let it go, smoke some dope, say, 'That's just the way it was,' but you wouldn't, would you, Dad? Or I could say, 'The poor alkie stumblebum couldn't help himself, if he had just gotten better medical help...' Blah, blah, blah... But that's fuckin' liberal bullshit meaning take it in the ass again. Right, Dad?"

"You been takin' it in the ass, jailbird? Convict cocksucker."

Mad Dog nodded: his father was helping. Just to see his father after so long clarified things, not to mention being reminded of his father's special way with words. So Mad Dog feinted with a left jab and shot out a short kick to the right knee, hearing it crack, and as his father went down Mad Dog kicked him in the stomach, then real quick grabbed his hair, slamming his head against the pavement. His father lying there groaning, spitting blood, the barfly unemployed Greeks and Poles watching as Mad Dog pulled down his zipper and pissed on his old man.

"Farewell, Updike Country," Mad Dog shouted as he walked away. He'd had a job mowing the writer's lawn one summer years before, felt a connection. Humming "California Here I Come," he went down South Main Street past the old Town Hall to Argilla Road. He just really needed one last look at Crane's Beach before heading west, before the Ipswich police could catch up with him.

∽

There are people who have a bad childhood and want to get started on children of their own as soon as possible. And then there are people who have a bad childhood and want never to bring a child of their own into this vale of tears. Mad Dog, despite having raised and loved his younger siblings, protecting them when his parents were "blind, stinkin' drunk," being of the latter persuasion. And that would have been it, except for his non-wife Rita. Who, after nearly ten years with Richard, decided she wanted kids. Insisted she wanted them right now, since she was turning thirty. That if not, she'd leave him. All of which he failed to take seriously until Rita had the locks changed and got a restraining order from the court to keep him away. From his own fuckin' apartment! Pissing him off mightily, but in the end he went with Rita to see a therapist—a lesbian, he was certain—and had to sit there and promise not to hit Rita ever again and not to drink so much and to be more sensitive to her needs and to try to get her pregnant.

"Hey, one question," Mad Dog interjected. "Do I have to sleep with her?" Adding, "Just kidding" when the therapist scowled. "Joke. Joke." Holding up his hands as if the therapist had him covered. So he and Rita did sleep together, for the first time in months, since Richard was usually dead drunk when she came home from work, but though it was just once, once was enough.

"Our love is not to be denied," Mad Dog said some months later, contemplating Rita's swollen belly. Knocking back another beer for medicinal purposes.

∼

Rita. Richard had argued that he actually was a Buddha in dealing with her, even if he did occasionally get rough, since she was bedeviled by both premenstrual syndrome and post-menstrual syndrome: headaches, short temper, disorientation, peevishness. "What it comes down to," Richard told the therapist, "is you have maybe five days a month when she's herself, or, put another way, when she's a fuckin' human being. You want to know who's the victim here, *I'm* the victim. Plus," he added, "she's redneck white trash. You're still stuck with some Eleanor Roosevelt bullshit you learned in social work school: everyone the same, Family of Man. Well let me tell you. What bein' redneck white trash in America means is that her whole family is vicious, alcoholic, and stupid. That her parents came from parents who were vicious, alcoholic, and stupid. It means she can't help bein' vicious and stupid herself a lot of the time even if she's dead cold sober, pushin' me, tryin' to make me mad. Takin' a swing at me. You have any idea how many times I haven't hit back? Such as, ninety-nine point nine percent of the time?"

Mad Dog stared at the therapist. "Really, lady, these ideas of yours, they're how things *should* be, maybe. Well here's a should: you should try walkin' a mile in my shoes sometime. I just look like a fuckin' monster."

∽

Hair cropped, jowls enormous, no neck in sight. Not really a monster, though you will concede that the bloom of Mad Dog's youth does seem to have departed. He was five-nine/one-seventy when he took on his old man that day in Ipswich. Now, thirteen years later, turning forty, he's fifty pounds heavier. His father's size. "The fruit always falls close to the foot of the tree," Mad Dog opines, putting down another beer, one of his ten a day. Eight to ten being what it takes to maintain. This in conjunction with the prescription antidepressants.

And if the social worker ever takes up Richard's challenge to walk a mile in his shoes, it will have to be with arch supports—all those years of jump shots on asphalt playgrounds. Yet even then the question will arise, Which shoes? since at any given moment Richard owns perhaps thirty pairs of sneakers. Three new pairs of The Pump: the Imelda Marcos of basketball footwear.

∽

Mad Dog as house-husband, taking care of his son—Danny, named after his brother—five and a half days a week. Rita working at the restaurant four days a week, getting one and a half days off, then taking over with the kid. Richard endlessly patient during what he calls "my shift," wanting to be there for his son. No day care, no babysitters: he'll take care of it. Putting another wash into the machine. Mopping the floor. Doing the dishes. Taking out the trash. Bringing Danny with him everywhere, all day. Tucking him under his arm like a loaf of bread when Danny's small. Determined to stay put for at least five years to give him the security and continuity Richard deems essential to trust. What Richard himself never received. Giving Danny as much freedom as possible, trying to keep the boundaries simple and clear. And for Rita one rule only: nobody hits the kid, no matter what he does. Send him to his room, fine, tap him on the butt, but that's it. Period.

∾

Ipswich. Crane's Beach, miles of shore and dune running up from the river. Fried clams in summer, fresh corn on the cob, blueberries. Taking the train into Fenway or hitching in to see the Sox. The town's colonial homes, Mad Dog growing up in a house that was rundown but built before 1800. Liking the idea so many people had lived there before. Shooting hoops over at Linebrook playground in summer, inside the Episcopal church gym when it started to get cold. Pellucid autumn days, the intensity of the turning leaves often making him nod in appreciation, as if watching virtuosi, sobered only by the threat of the coming interminable winter. Depressing perhaps because of the relative absence of light, or because it was the season his father would really get mean.

Just one time was Richard surprised when his father hit him. That is, usually Richard could figure out the sequence in his father's mind. Not that it was fair or right, but it could be divined. Once, however, right after they left his grandmother's, as they got in the car his father wacked him behind the head very hard, knocking him into the dash, breaking his nose. Richard must have been nine. It took him a while, but finally it came clear. Of course: his grandmother had showed him affection.

∾

Mad Dog's economics. The rent-controlled apartment is two-hundred a month plus utilities, two bedrooms with a view of the hills. Five-fifty a month tax free from Social Security for having convinced them he's crazy—which on the other hand he is—plus free medical and dental plus food stamps. Then Rita earns maybe twenty K working as a waitress four days a week. And after that there are the credit cards. Sit still long enough, they start coming in: Richard has five in his name, five in Rita's. Then occasional construction work under the table—another five K per annum, maybe—and the gambling. Despite some heavy losses at blackjack up at Reno, Richard does know sports. In 1988, for instance, during spring training, he took the Dodgers to win the Series. A twenty-five to one shot, but at season's end there was gimpy-legged Kirk Gibson hitting that home run off Dennis Eckersley and young Orel Hershiser having the week of his life. Mad Dog, looking like a genius, immediately buying two reclining chairs for the living room, new washer-dryer, and video cam to film the kid. All quality stuff.

Add to this the occasional shoplifting of expensive records, then returning them to the store for a credit slip to sell at a discount for cash, or the weekly prime beef lifted from the yuppie market down on Telegraph, and the stolen gear available on a regular basis over at People's Park, and you have...well, something resembling a lower-middle-class standard of living. "Figure the equivalent of forty-five K per annum," Mad Dog says, doing his books. "Maybe thirty-two K tax free."

∾

California. Mad Dog hates it. Perhaps because having found some place he can survive, he's constantly reminded he'd have been dead if he'd stayed in Ipswich like his brother Danny. Or his sister Ellen, a drug addict who might as well be dead. David having gotten out too, living in a van somewhere up in Oregon, a small-time burn artist. So while California has given Richard shelter, it's exile. A place he's not from, where people just don't understand where he's coming from, what might have shaped him. Why he's there at all. Which is to say, what's true. "Phoney, stupid, know-nothing, no-class motherfuckers," Mad Dog often says, speaking of Californians. "Superficial. Bigoted. Slime. Shallow scumbags."

∼

Mad Dog on his day off from Danny, over at the Bear's Lair on the Cal campus knocking back a few beers, one of the football players aching to push him around. Mad Dog simply giving the would-be stud a two-handed shove on the chest, hard, sending him across to the wall, leaving it at that. But why not teach the dumb fuck something more? Why? Because Mad Dog can't risk being sent away from Danny. Shit: ex-con non-student? Assault with intent? C'mon, they'd throw away the key. "Cramps my academic freedom, havin' a kid," he says thoughtfully as he sips his beer, looking over at the football player, thinking what else he could teach him.

Mad Dog as instructor, a role he savors. Working with Danny on each new skill, always patient. Or trying to show some teenager on the court how to improve his jump shot, willing to stay there for hours if need be. Or Mad Dog in a bar, telling the man on the next stool—"I ain't shittin' you, buddy"—that he just doesn't know what he's talking about. About the prospects for a given year's phenom hitting fifty home runs, for example. "But he's already got thirty-one and we're not even at the All-Star break," the man says. "So put your money where your mouth is," Mad Dog replies, as usual not unwilling to inform. "Give me two to one on a hundred?"

Mad Dog also gets into it with one of the local cops. The problem starts one night when the man pulls him over for rolling through a stop sign, then cuffs him with his hands behind his back, concluding by roughing Mad Dog up for mouthing off about being cuffed with his hands behind his back. "Fuckin' dwarf," Mad Dog shouts when the cop tells him to put his hands behind his back. "Fuckin' Puerto Rican dwarf," though he knows the man is Chinese. The cop responding by punching him in the stomach, then kicking him in the small of the back.

By the time a second officer arrives, Mad Dog is more than ready to explain where it all went wrong. "See," he says to the black lieutenant, a former Cal linebacker who's something like six-five, "this little prick has a complex. Too short. You know I'm no trouble to any cop who plays by the rules. But this mini-dirtbag's on a trip. Maybe this is the only way he can get it up. You oughta buy him elevator shoes."

"Cut him loose," the lieutenant tells the cop who cuffed Mad Dog, trying not to smile. "Cut the crazy bastard loose."

Which would have been it, except that on his days off from Danny Mad Dog follows the Chinese cop around town with his video cam, just waiting to document his next mistake. "Bill of Rights," he often shouts at the cop. "Bill of fuckin' Rights, little cocksucker."

~

Mad Dog's mother. Though she was also a drunk, though she frequently beat him when he was young, he settled things with her early on, cracking her jaw when he turned thirteen, one quick punch that completely changed the balance of power between them. More, whatever made her tick was so alien to him that he regarded her as another species, beyond understanding, to be judged only by her behavior. She was a lush, she was bitter that Mad Dog's father had abandoned her for a younger woman she always called "The Thing," she was utterly selfish and seemed to have no instinct to love or to protect her children. That's all Mad Dog could figure out, and, really, all it seemed necessary to know.

Nonetheless, having been out of touch with his mother for years, as Danny turns two Mad Dog has the impulse to try to salvage something for him. Some predecessors to identify with, lineage, history, continuity. Something more than the Cal ring Mad Dog wears, class of '72. Authentic, but of course not his. Who wouldn't want this for his child? Nonetheless, when Rita asks if he's thinking of inviting his mother to come out to California, he replies: "Are you crazy? How could we ever trust her around Danny? We couldn't."

"But don't *you* want to see her, Richard?"

"You know, Rita, my mother could eat shit and die as far as I'm concerned. No offense, but as far as that goes I have no regrets your father died last year and that your mother's too weak to get on a plane. No disrespect, but she has the mind of a five-year-old."

"Don't talk about my parents that way," Rita shouts.

"Right," Mad Dog responds. "Right. I know what you mean. The truth really hurts."

∼

Mad Dog and insomnia. Since he was a child, he's frequently been unable to sleep through the night. Maybe it began with waiting for his father to come home, to see if his father would be looking for someone to knock around. Whatever the reason, frequently Richard's up late, TV on, sitting there alone, and often he thinks of The National on Fourth Street in St. Petersburg. A place he discovered years before while running out his parole. A drunk box, dollar a shot, nice and dark in back, easy on a drinker's tender eyes, several pinball machines, pyramid of hard booze bottles behind the bar. "When I'm upset about my lot," Mad Dog says, "when I truly despair of my condition, when I think it wasn't fair what happened to me or my brothers and sister, when I get my father on the brain,

I try to make myself change the station in my mind, so to speak. And then I think of The National in St. Pete's." He laughs. "You know," he adds, "if I ever disappear, if I just can't take it anymore, give me a week or two, then look for me down at The National. Most days I'll be comin' in around noon."

(1993)

Public Anatomy

"Part of my cure is interminable waiting," the writer's mother says. She's propped up on pillows in her hospital bed, one tube running into her forearm, another snaking in under the sheet. Hand trembling, knuckles enormous from arthritis, his mother struggles with a piece of the chicken he's cut up for her. Finally she raises the fork, but it begins to tremble and twist; the chicken drops. With insistent control his mother sets the fork back down, as if now it's trying to levitate or escape. "This must be disturbing for you to see," she says.

Brain-stem stroke: oxygen-rich blood cut off en route to brain tissue, nerve cells unable to function. Effects slight or severe, temporary or permanent. Over the last few months the writer's come to construe his mother's stroke as a blast of lightning, smells the burn, tastes the ozone. "Will you endorse this check, Mother?" The writer places a pen in her hand. She tries to sign her name, can't. "You're making things too hard for me," she cries. "You're forcing me to struggle with my mind."

∽

In *The Mountain People,* Colin Turbull writes of the Ik, an African tribe in the mountains beyond Lake Rudolf, whom he observed in the early 1970s when their traditional culture was breaking down.

Survival of the individual was all; cruelty replaced love; the Ik were mean, greedy, selfish. Children left to fend for themselves, the old abandoned to starve.

The writer also reads an article about a tribe of nomads that in the course of its annual migration encounters a large river. It seems that anyone not an infant has to cross under his own power or be left behind. Thus it happens that an old person is given blankets and food, and sits alone, watching, as the rest of the tribe departs.

∽

Some months after his mother's death, the writer has this dream: he's back at the house where he grew up, which in the dream is where she died, though of course his parents sold the house years before even his father's death, which itself was more than a decade before hers. In the master bedroom in the dream, in any case, there's the familiar double bed covered with white chenille, chaise lounge in the corner, writing desk by the windows, elm trees just outside, large and leafy, willows and pond on the far side of the park below. Everything in its place, an Ur reality for the writer, dating from, defining, the very beginning of memory and then confirmed, unchanging, for years and years.

Also in the writer's dream, right in the middle of the room, though of course it shouldn't be there, was never there before, is an old trunk with a rounded top—wasn't it in the basement or the attic when he was a child? And now, feeling a sudden surge of anguish, the writer sees that the trunk has been opened by strangers, who've gathered around it, who've discovered what the writer and his siblings never knew existed: packets of letters tied in ribbons, diaries with locks on them. His mother's secret life.

∽

The writer comes into the hospital room at a brisk pace, only to be brought up short: the nurses are changing and turning his mother. In an instant the writer averts his eyes, backs out through the doorway, but images are already recorded: zipper of terrible scars on her stomach from the most recent surgery; catheter; thatch of pubic hair.

One doctor, a former pupil of his father's, tells the writer there are many people who simply cannot make themselves go into hospitals to visit family members. The doctor means well, the writer knows, but this idea seems like self-indulgence. Seems like self-indulgence even as he stands in front of the outpatient entrance staring at the electric sliding door, watching it go back and forth again and again as people arrive, depart, as he concludes that each trip inside eats away another crucial quantity of bone marrow.

Up on the ward, the writer stares at the nurses, so young, so healthy, so ready to love, have children, buy a car, find a house, plan a vacation. To go to Filene's Basement, the Cape, Pops, the Bruins. He also plays pickup basketball on the asphalt court across the street, often with residents and interns he sees on the corridors inside. One of the court regulars is a tall half-Japanese woman from Hawai'i, Michelle, a UPS delivery person, who tells him she had a year on the varsity squad at USC. Whenever possible the writer gets on Michelle's team, frequently passes off to her, both to admire her moves on the court—Michelle can really play, runs effortlessly—and to see her breasts lift as she brings the ball up and over her head before releasing a jump shot.

∼

A week after his mother's death: where has winter gone? Out on the Charles, thirty/fifty/one hundred eight-man shells stroke by, scores of individual sculls. The many runners on the banks are in shorts and T-shirts, spring not only possible but here.

The writer and his friend Paul sit on a bench on the Memorial Drive side of the river. Down from Vermont to visit before the writer heads back west, Paul appraises his old friend's face. "Middle age comes in on crow's-feet," Paul says.

∽

Her dying changes the writer in ways he cannot control. Whenever he sees an illness or death on the TV news or in a movie, almost any representation, no matter how mawkish, tears come to his eyes. His mother always howled with derision at sentimentality, wanted her emotions hard-won, precise. Even when the writer's alone now, his responses embarrass him: inadvertently, he looks around to see who's watching.

After his mother dies he thinks the truth must be told: he'll do a book of nonfiction on five, ten absolutely ordinary deaths, the statistically most likely. A quiet book, just spare portraits of terminal cancer, heart disease, etc., etc. He'll show people what awaits them. News of the planet: two hundred thousand people dying per day; seventy million plus per year.

He also begins to shed certain friends and acquaintances. Almost always, before, he'd been redeemed by irony, could savor even folly and foible if only for the sake of story. God's world, such as it was. Now, however, he hears himself passing judgment all the time, relentlessly, priggishly. He can't stand it, but there it is. "*Treyfe*," he often mutters: against all odds, against his own capacities, he wants it clean.

At a party the writer encounters a professor of comparative literature he's met once before. In his mid-forties, single, no children, the professor's defending Rilke against the charge of narcissism or cannibalism. Rilke was right, the professor says: he could be "true and fundamental" not by seeking to enrich the beggar or straighten out the cripple, but only by singing the "incomparable fate" given them by the "God of completeness."

Suddenly dizzy with rage, unable to speak, the writer hears the woman beside him begin to respond. "But isn't it being able to cel-

240   *Thomas Farber*

ebrate your own suffering that's the real test?" she says, the writer's grimace now transformed into a grin.

"I have to go," the professor says, turning away, the woman who'd spoken then moving toward the table of hors d'oeuvres, leaving the writer staring down a long tunnel in his mind's eye, seeing himself very far down the tunnel, windswept, buffeted, without protection. The sensation that he is greatly threatened, a threat to himself, a threat to others. It also comes to him that he knows this tunnel; with its walls of white tile it's the route under Boston Harbor his family always took to the airport, to the beach. Place and time thus defined, however, the writer experiences no consolation.

In this period an old friend of the writer, now a successful real estate developer, sends the writer—and everyone on his Rolodex—a prospectus for his next project. As the writer reads it, he sees that his friend's biographical summary contains several misrepresentations, minor acts of self-aggrandizement, typical of the man, apparently still and forever beyond his control. Now, however, after years of occasionally pointing out such anomalies or teasing his friend, the writer can't stomach it.

Why? He tries to think it through. To interact with his friend the developer in any way requires complicity in a web of small lies. But this was always true. Time is short? Yes/no/not particularly: he still has a life before him. The writer tries again. "All right. My mother died; this is what's true. Anything false, therefore, attacks not simply The Truth but *that* truth." He thinks it over. Of course he himself lies, if not as shamelessly as his friend. His mother sometimes lied, the usual social lies. But the sheer number of his friend's lies crosses some threshold, is aggressive, seeks not simply to deter detection but to force compliance. Actively denies, then, the relentless effort at clarity in his mother's writing. More, the goal of his friend's lies is to enhance his vita. It's not just that someone so determined to inflate credentials is incapable of responding to the writer's loss. Rather, such voracious promotion of the self makes it clear the world is going to keep right on turning, with or without the writer's mother. That the writer's efforts to remember her or make some claim for remembering her are nothing in the face of his friend's utterly unstoppable, too organic impulse to thrive.

Another man, really just an acquaintance, phones, expresses his condolences, says, "And how are you doing?" There's an undertone in his question, the writer realizes, that feels not at all pro forma. And then it comes to him. The caller's son for years had various problems but seemed finally to be shaping up. Then one night this son went out for a six-pack at the local liquor store, was stopped by a robber, and, though he surrendered his wallet, was shot and killed.

∼

After his mother's death the writer has her books shipped west. It takes him weeks, but finally he incorporates them into his bookcases. Her favorites: Gerard Manley Hopkins; Gilbert White's letters from Selborne; Emily Dickinson; French naturalist Henri Fabre. Her unabridged *Webster's International*, second Edition. A number of volumes on the Puritans. An extraordinary collection of natural history: Audubon, Teale, Austin, Beston; books on galls and gall insects, the American woodcock, animal tools; *Weeds in Winter, Animal Asymmetry, The Miracle of Flight.*

Going through the books, he finds index card after index card with words or sentences noted. "Collembola," "fer-de-lance," "anaclastic," "anaclisis." And, "There is an obvious resemblance between an unreadable script and a secret code..."

Books finally shelved, the writer clears more space in a bookcase near his desk. Soon he has Kübler-Ross on death as the final stage of growth. Stephen Levine's *Who Dies? The Oxford Book of Death.* This acquisition of books surprises him not at all: just what his mother would have done, what she did whenever a subject caught her interest. On the same shelf, however, he places other books recently acquired: Reik's *Of Love and Lust.* Wilhelm Reich on the Sexual Revolution. *Sex in History*, by Tannahill. Books on various utopian sexual communities.

One day he looks over at the shelf, sees the books as if for the first time, starts to laugh. Sex and death.

∼

"I have no more secrets," Ralph says. Married twenty years, Ralph's been a stubborn and truculent husband, often selfish. His wife has seen it all from him. "She knows everything about me, everything. That's hard to live with."

The writer thinks it over. "You know," Ralph continues, "people don't like to talk about this, but there are some losses for which there's simply no consolation." The writer thinks this over too.

After a while, Ralph says, "See, what it is, your parents both dead, now there's nothing between you and the universe."

The writer smiles. Just the kind of hokey statement people can't help making; far less than he'd expect of Ralph. And yet: suddenly the words chill, for a vertiginous split second he can see it, feel it: the vast, dismaying emptiness of the galaxies, souls of the dead and unborn orbiting the stars, immensity without beginning or end.

∼

At twenty-four, the year the writer's father courted his future wife, seventeen, a freshman in college, he took her to see him perform an autopsy. The corpse turned out to be that of a beautiful little girl. To the writer's mother her future husband seemed radiantly alive as death yielded its secrets. He also took her dancing, but apparently knew only one step, simply kept pivoting her around, around, around until she was dazed, until the music stopped.

After they married, he learned that, having been raised with servants and kept out of the kitchen—her mother was raising opera stars!—his bride had no idea how to cook, and for some time thereafter they often went out for dinner.

They lived in Ghent that first year, always within sound of bells:

the very walls resonated, the tuberose begonias in the enclosed garden. Music poured down over them, held in the damp air like drops of moisture. Everything was new and strange, and for that year, alert and seeking, they studied signs, intimations. What *was* the essential Flanders? Carillon? Cobbles? Canal? Pollarded willow?

∽

Nightfall after a day of sleet, lights of rush-hour traffic on Memorial Drive out the hospital room window.

"He does eleemosynary work," the writer's mother is saying, stroke not having eliminated polysyllables, speaking of the husband of a couple whose identity the writer can't place. "Jean and Juan."

"Jean and Juan?"

She grins, as if there's some kind of game in this. "Yes, he does eleemosynary work."

"Eleemosynary work. I guess you're determined to speak charitably of them."

"Very funny."

"Sorry, Mother. You were saying? Jean and Juan."

"Yes. Jean and Juan went to Carthage."

"Carthage?"

"Yes."

"I thought Carthage went out with Gaul."

"You heard what I said."

"Carthage."

"Yes."

"But not Tunisia?"

"I told you. Carthage."

"Jean and Juan."

"Yes."

∽

In early 1974, just thirty, the writer roamed the Northwest in a battered '65 Olds Cutlass convertible with the woman he'd fallen in love with, nowhere in particular to go, wandering, wandering. They kept the top down, stopped at one beach, another, studied shorebirds through binoculars, ate in greasy spoons, camped in the fog. During these travels, not having spoken to his mother for a month, the writer called, and in the course of the conversation she told him a neighbor had killed herself.

The writer was standing in a phone booth by the coast highway overlooking the Pacific, not seeing the shape of things to come, the country too damn big, ocean too vast. "I've never really thought about suicide," the writer said to his mother. By then, widowed nearly a year after forty-five years of marriage, she was composing a meditation on the death of the beloved.

"No?" his mother replied. "That's interesting."

Eleven years later, not long after his mother's death, at a time when he came to see that words were inadequate in the face of real loss, that with his parents gone a particular dialogue was now finished, he read something his mother had been working on in that period:

> Twenty thousand waves of days
> have come over me.
> Still not enough for drowning.

∼

Sweets in the writer's childhood: chocolate cakes from Dorothy Muriel's for dessert at dinner, Pepperidge Farm cookies in the kitchen cupboard; jars of sourballs and packs of Beeman's chewing gum in the dining room cabinet; Eskimo Pies and Ice Cream Sandwiches in the freezer on the porch. All of this available to the children almost any time, a zone of parental indulgence.

The writer's parents always embraced and kissed whenever they separated or were reunited, for more than forty years slept in the same bed. His father also always hugged the children whenever he came home from work, whenever one of them was leaving. But as the writer's mother is dying, when his older sister, telling family stories, mentions that they were all breast fed as babies, it starts the writer thinking. Though able to picture his mother sitting on the piano bench beside him, metronome clicking, clicking, as she labors to discipline his playing, though he has no difficulty seeing her sew a button on one of his shirts, ferrying him to school in a rainstorm, pulling off his galoshes, making dinner/washing the dishes/straightening up the house yet another time—all these recurring acts of care, concern, tutelage—the writer can evoke not a single memory of ever being touched by his mother or of seeing her hold or embrace his brother or sisters.

In the early 1970s, after their father died, without comment the writer's sisters began to make a point of embracing their mother whenever they came to visit. Certainly such gestures were à la mode, but his mother, who said not a word about it, never initiated—seemed merely to accept—this physical contact. His brother, however, made no such effort, nor did the writer. Thus it was that during what proved to be the last ten years of her life, all through his thirties, the writer would prepare to depart after a visit to Boston, his mother leaning on her cane, walking him from her apartment down the corridor to the elevator. The writer would press the button. After several minutes the doors would open. "Bye, Mother," the writer would say, and he'd be gone.

∽

Sometimes, after her stroke, on the days she's only partly responsive, there are these amazing sudden smiles. Like a baby's, without clear reference to externals seen by adult eyes. Like a mooncalf's. Like the sun popping out from behind a cloud: warming; surprising; blinding.

∽

"You could hurt me," a woman the writer's begun seeing says several months after his mother's death. "Are you good for me?"
"Speaking as your friend or as your lover?"
"Friend."
"Friend? Well, think of me as the Liberty Bell."
"The Liberty Bell?"
"You know. Free, but cracked."

∽

There's an Armenian man in the emergency room whose ninety-year-old mother has been dying for months. Despite countless death watches, still she survives. Nearly sixty, her youngest son never moved out of the family home. And though at the hospital his siblings come and go, he seems never to leave the waiting room. "He's closest to our mother," one of the brothers tells the writer. "Very close. Never married, never had kids. When she dies he'll get the house. It's only right."

∽

At seventeen the writer went to France, to Grenoble, allegedly to study French, but considered his curriculum fulfilled when he met a Danish girl. She was perhaps twenty. With a directness the writer could not quite forgive, she took him as her lover, and they slept together at her place until the concierge threw her out for having him there. Meanwhile he'd moved out of student housing into an apartment down by the Isere, near the *teleferique*. Madame was German, her first husband a pilot shot down in combat. After the war she learned French by ear, her monsieur, cross-eyed and very short, a chef she met while he was a sergeant in the French army of occupation.

The writer got to know the family at the *piscine*, helped one of her sons learn to swim, was soon invited to live in the empty bedroom.

"Bonjour," Madame would say each morning after knocking, coming through the doorway with a bowl of chocolate and a roll. When the writer told her his Danish friend needed a place, to his astonishment Madame pointed out that of course there was a second bed in his room. Soon she came in each morning with two bowls of chocolate, two rolls, on the tray. Two "Bonjours."

"Mon cheri," Margot wrote him that fall in an air letter mailed to his family home, just before he returned to college, *"je ne suis pas enceinte."* No baby.

Going out to see friends, the writer left the air letter on his bed. Perhaps to take stock of how much of a mess he'd made since coming back from Europe, his mother came up the steep flight of stairs to his attic room, saw the letter on the bed. When he came home that day, walnut-paneled doors were slamming, and his mother was weeping.

"How could you read my letter," he shouted.

"Your father came to me pure," she screamed.

That evening as usual his father returned home from his office at the hospital, but then climbed the attic stairs. Very heavily. Very slowly. It must have been years since he'd come up.

The writer was still crying mad. "Mother shouldn't have read my letter," the writer said to his father, "she had no right," but what he wanted to say was that love and desire seemed in no way synonymous, that long since he wished he'd been kinder to Margot.

He looked at his father, who'd seen so many children die, who was so tired finishing a long day at the hospital after years of struggling with his own chronic illnesses.

"You must stop fighting with your mother," his father said quietly. "She makes mistakes, but she's your mother."

"That's not fair," the writer replied.

His father shook his head, then went slowly, heavily, back down the stairs.

"We all labor against our own cure," his father once wrote, "for death is the cure of all disease." As a young man he also said to one of his sisters, when she was in a relationship that was breaking her heart, "Love unreturned is not love."

That night the writer thought it over. Was it true that his mother was his father's first lover? Did his father really, age twenty-three, come to her "pure"? Did he lie to his future wife? And if he did or didn't, had or hadn't, what of it?

∼

Both because of his father's obligation to help his many younger siblings and the tuberculosis his mother contracted soon after the marriage (enforced quiet at a magic mountain in Switzerland for nine months, then bed rest and pneumothorax—collapse of the lung—once a week for many years), they waited until she was thirty to have the first of their four children. By the time the fourth was born she was forty, her husband forty-six. The writer does the arithmetic. They knew each other twelve years before the birth of their first child. Twenty-two years before the birth of their last child. Had known each other forty years when that child turned eighteen.

By the time their first child was born, both its paternal grandparents and its maternal grandfather had died. As for the remaining grandmother—G.—well, the writer's mother never saw her again after her wedding day, though G. lived another thirty-five years. This was not exactly a dark secret in the writer's family, but the subject seldom came up, and only at his mother's initiative. So what did the writer know?

•His grandmother weighed babies during World War I, such community work apparently just the kind of thing she liked. Always organizing people, forming clubs, presiding.

•In 1925 G. took her teenage daughters to Europe for the Grand Tour after pressing her husband to fund the venture, but then for unknown reasons suddenly wanted to get back to the United States, leaving her daughters in London unchaperoned to complete the itinerary (to shop for snakeskin jackets and crocodile shoes with painfully pointed toes).

◆More than once G. came into a daughter's classroom, upbraided the teacher, took her child home.

◆As the ship was about to depart with the writer's mother and father on their honeymoon to Europe, there was a fist fight on the dock between his father and one of G.'s brothers, instigated, apparently, by G.

◆Even his mother's sister, a very social being, seldom saw her mother. Whenever G. did visit her mansion in the country, the story went, the household would soon be in chaos, servants fighting with each other.

◆Terminally ill, G. came back to Boston. Not having seen her for thirty-five years, after thinking it through—agonizing about it—the writer's mother decided not to go to the hospital.

G. was said to have died berating the student nurse who was caring for her, which the writer's mother found perfectly in character.

Perhaps the story the writer's mother told most frequently about her childhood—which is to say only four or five times in all over the years—was of taking the streetcar to Symphony Hall with her sister when they both were young. Somehow they lost the fare for the ride home or failed to get the available free transfer. When they finally arrived, having walked all the way back, their mother laughed at them, and, subsequently, if they told her that yes, they could do something, she'd respond, *"I know, I know, Symphony Hall."*

∼

Several months after his mother's death, a former neighbor invites the writer to lunch to celebrate his new book. Afterwards, she walks over to his house with him. Upstairs, under the eaves, they lie on the double bed.

"I'm not myself," the writer says, cat watching them. "I'm crazy."

"I'm married," she replies. "But you know that. What don't you know?"

He laughs. "Where did you grow up?"

"Laredo. Texas. Why?"

"I have a hang-up. I can't make love to someone without knowing where they grew up."

"I have some stipulations of my own," she says. "Don't ever call my house. And don't tell anyone."

"Fair enough."

"But you can write about me."

"Thank you. Anything else?"

"I feel guilty."

"There is feeling guilty and there is being alone."

After they make love both are laughing. For him, however, all strong emotions are bound together now: that is, any strong emotion triggers grief. "Hi, Mom," the writer says, like the football players on the sideline when the camera closes in.

She laughs.

"Shhh," the writer says, "don't wake the children."

"You don't have any children."

"I know."

"You're crazy. I mean it. Really crazy."

"True," the writer says. "True. But I told you that already. I'm just not myself."

∼

A year before her death, the writer's mother, talking with her youngest child, L., her second daughter, keeps bestowing praise on her granddaughter, who at nineteen seems busy being or becoming everything Nana wants in a young woman, everything this child is not, was not. Enthusiastic participation in the mainstream, a positive attitude, apparent compliance with Nana's norms, though once, staying overnight, she invites a date up after her grandmother is asleep. Coming out of a dream, the writer's mother drifts into the living room and sees the two of them on the balcony surveying the river below, embracing until she turns on the living room light and stalks off, waiting for her granddaughter's apology.

Nana and her daughter L. live two thousand miles apart, see each other rarely but talk every Sunday morning on the phone. Now, during one of L.'s rare visits home, just after Nana once more corrects her pronunciation and asks that in any case she speak up, L. begins to cry, accuses her mother of being endlessly and relentlessly critical. A dutiful child until seventeen, when she went away to college, L.'s never made this kind of outburst before, though it is also true that in nearly twenty years she hasn't spent more than a few days at a time at home.

Later his mother complains to the writer, who's also visiting: "Tell me, what does she want me to say? That I love her?"

To love: a verb never used within the family. Too obvious to need being said. To be taken for granted, presumably, after the proof of actions. A given. Tainted by popular overuse. Spurious, commercial, like Mother's Day or Father's Day.

∼

"How are you?" the doctor asks the writer's mother.
"Dreary. What remains to be done?"
"Do you know what day it is?"
"I don't care to know what day it is."

∼

After his mother's death, the writer calls her younger brother, a man of sixty-five, with several questions. "Poor Alfred," his mother always said when referring to him. Alfred, whom the writer's met only once or twice, and not for years: he did not come to see his sister as she was dying, for whatever reason, though they'd always kept in touch. On the phone with the writer, in any case, Alfred is genial, says he'll write back to him, and does. "I regret not being able to provide more information concerning the break between your mother and your grandmother. I was ten years younger than your mother—only eight—when the break occurred, and nobody discussed it with me. As I grew up, that rift was something there, done, a fact no one seemed inclined to broach or explain.

"When I was young my mother always seemed very strong, strong-willed. Unable to go to college for financial reasons, she was determined her children not be deprived. As a result, we three were constantly impelled in a cycle of concerts and lessons—piano, ballet, elocution, singing. Keeping all this in motion took a forceful, organized, capable woman. Suffice to say I don't recall ever having been asked if I wanted these lessons. But that's not so uncommon either, I'd guess."

∼

Back in Boston a year after his mother's death, walking with an acquaintance near Harvard Square, the writer bumps into the physician in charge of his mother's case the last five months of her life, the first time the writer's seen him not in a white lab coat, not inside the hospital. Always, the previous year, the writer and his siblings addressed him as Doctor Haley, referred to him as Doctor Haley when speaking about him with each other, though he was roughly their contemporary. But in his lab coat he evoked their father, no doubt, and perhaps in that context it seemed this surrogate father had the power to save, or, they wanted to endow him with the power to save.

As the writer registers the thought that in gray slacks, tweed jacket, and cashmere sweater the doctor seems smaller, almost an impostor, the doctor extends a hand to his friend. "Richie Haley here," he says. Startled, the writer remembers that all through his childhood grown-ups called his father, referred to his father as Doctor, even his medical colleagues. Now, standing there, hearing the absence of the honorific, the writer acknowledges what he really always knew as his mother was dying: the good doctor is only human.

~

The writer has a fan, or, a fan for whom he is periodically a fixation. Able to walk only with crutches, she researches the writer's life, learns as much as she can, calls him on the phone, obsesses about him, waits at certain cafés or bookstores hoping to bump into him.

Hearing of his mother's illness, she sends a get-well card, encloses a photo, and writes, "As you might have guessed, I'm most grateful to you for bringing your son into the world."

The writer reads the card to his mother. She's riddled with tubes, is wearing an oxygen mask, vapor condensing on her cheeks.

"Poor thing," his mother says, inhaling heavily, pausing, inhaling again. "But what have I done for her lately?"

~

"I try to respect her privacy," his mother said. *Respecting your privacy*: the gospel of his childhood. From his mother's *Webster's*: "...State of being apart from the company or observation of others; seclusion... Private or clandestine circumstances; secrecy..."

The writer's mother grew up with servants. She'd pass on an anecdote about them once in a while—about May, for instance, who'd chant, "Piss-a-bed, piss-a-bed, hie for shame, the dogs of the country will know your name," who took them to church with her on Sundays—but her essential point about their presence was that all family quarrels were played out before a Greek chorus. The most brazen person, his mother always said—clearly referring to her own mother—would always win.

Privacy. As far as L. was concerned, it meant that for fifteen years her mother did not visit her home. It's true L. was "living with someone," that Nana had no wish to legitimize the relationship by her presence, true that in the last years, travel increasingly difficult, there was much she was content not to have to know out of a kind of fastidiousness. Perhaps also, however, perhaps also she was attempting to give her daughter the gift she herself had never received.

∽

The plane ride back to California after his mother's death. Scrambling out of Harvard Square through the Portuguese and Italian neighborhoods of East Cambridge to avoid rush hour on Storrow Drive, slicing behind MIT, past the Museum of Science, up the ramp by Boston Garden, onto the Southeast Expressway for ten seconds and off again, through Callahan Tunnel to Logan Airport, and then, poof, a lumbering liftoff through the seal of low gray clouds. Heading west, uphill all the way, until at last the jet became one of the many smudges staining the sky south of San Francisco.

Met at the airport by Henry, who'd left Boston in 1966 for what he hoped was the last time to become a freak, a hippie. Born again at thirty-five, Boston suddenly no longer the hundreds of thousands of specifics he'd experienced in a life there—the bleachers in Fenway watching Yaz hit yet another homer; making out in high school on the banks of the Muddy River, hidden in the forsythia—but the "East Coast," the dead past. Soon Henry had hair to his shoulders, a button on his peacoat reading *Nirvana Now*. Much of the time he lived in his car, or camped on Jenner Beach studying the seal pods. In this period he also experienced messianic vegetarianism and savored the snares of spiritual materialism when Ram Dass confessed he hadn't really seen stigmata in the palms of a fellow guru (though it did cross Henry's mind that Dass *had* seen the stigmata but *then* chose to lie...).

By the eighties, still in California, Henry was a born-again capitalist, working long hours, complaining about bureaucrats, genially predicting doom earthquakes off the top of the Richter scale, skin cancer for sunbathers, nuclear winter, stock market meltdown, mass terminal cholesterol. The stress of such threats Henry countered by lying naked on the couch while a (clothed) therapist appraised his "body armor," Henry's having been developed early with the help of an alcoholic father who abandoned his family. Periodically he'd call to arrange for his son and daughter to meet him downtown for lunch. One time, Henry and his sister took the MTA to Boylston Street and walked over to Jake Wirth's, the old beer hall. They waited for hours, staring at the sawdust on the floor, but their father never showed up. Never called again.

As for his mother, Henry saw her for the last time as he left Boston in 1966, subsequently spoke with her only rarely. When he learned she'd died, he flew back to Massachusetts, rendezvoused with his sister, went to their mother's apartment. Seeing the terrible disorder, mounds of her personal papers, photographs, and letters, without a word he and his sister began taking load after load down to the incinerator.

So it's Henry who picks the writer up at the airport after his mother's death, as they pass downtown heading onto the Bay Bridge, sky bright blue, not a cloud in sight, tankers lying at anchor waiting for the tide to change. Henry who has transcended the data of his experience in favor of a liberating conclusion, Henry whose intuition his therapist has confirmed, that anything to do with parents is ipso facto pathological.

∾

Autopsy: examination of the self. In 1937, in a text on postmortem examination technique, the writer's father argued that for relatives of the deceased an autopsy is "a form of philanthropy not fully appreciated, and yet possible for people of any economic status," with the additional benefit of "a more complete explanation than is otherwise possible of the development of the fatal disease... This may have direct bearing on the health of other members of the family."

∾

Seth, one of his father's many younger brothers. Seth lived with the writer's parents not long after they married, when they returned from Europe. They put him through medical school, gave him the second bedroom in their small apartment. In some ways he functioned as their first child, and though in the world's terms he became a great success, in the family mythology Seth was a fallen angel. The charges against him? Seth left their home without permission, married without notifying them, went west. Went native: in their view failed to measure up to his great potential by surrendering to venal hungers—the desire for money and political power, the need to impress. Later, Seth also divorced. All through his childhood the writer identified with Seth; his parents' categorical criticism seemed to a recalcitrant and oft-disciplined child to suggest failure on their part, unacknowledged truths. The writer was disabused only when, turning twenty, on his first trip to California, he encountered his uncle. It was a living lesson in genetics, how similar and yet how unlike each other siblings could be: he saw aspects of his father in his uncle's every gesture or word, but as in a funhouse mirror.

Now, after his mother's death, the writer calls Seth. After they chat for several minutes, Seth says that the writer's father was a genius but modest, then quickly implies he himself's that kind of a man. This he follows with a joke about the fellow with the long beard in the nudist camp. "Somebody has to be able to go to the store" the punch line, all to set the writer at ease, presumably.

Finally the writer is able to ask what it was like to live with his parents so many years before. "You have to remember," his uncle says, "your mother already had tuberculosis when your father met her. The white plague. One of its symptoms is extreme irritability in the early stages. She was beautiful, brilliant, impatient. Very, very demanding of others, including me. She was the apple of your grandfather's eye, and he must have been wondering who'd take on and protect a headstrong girl with so much ability. Your father was the answer to his prayers. Your grandfather could see they'd be like swans, mated for as long as they lived. He encouraged the marriage, which itself was enough to make his wife G. hate your father.

Anyway, she and your mother were already fighting all the time. Your grandmother wanted to run your mother's life, but no one was going to do that."

~

"What are *you* doing here?" his mother says as the writer comes into the hospital room.

~

Several months after his mother's death the writer meets Carol. Twenty-two, from Salt Lake—stress on Salt, she explains—father a Mormon businessman. Having come to San Francisco, she's repudiated her childhood role models, all her girlfriends from high school long since married with children. Though clearly bound into the family romance, she has little good to say about her parents. Just barely, the writer stops himself from admonishing her to cherish them. When they make love she's so young, so healthy, so tough in her determination to carve out her own life that the writer thinks of the Beatles line, "She's the kind of girl you want so much it makes you sorry."

Carol's often frowning, thinking things through, has cropped her hair, wears long earrings, is independent, cool. Because she's a dancer, they go to see a thin update of *West Side Story*, which seems to absorb her completely. As the onscreen action moves to Spanish Harlem, the writer leans over to her. Despite the verve of the break-dance sequences, something in the film's banal plot is making him terribly lonely. "I used to be Puerto Rican," he whispers, but she just shrugs.

"See you," Carol calls out as she prepares to leave the next morning. How can she know that all change, anything like a disappearance, leaves him splayed?

"What does that mean?"

"What?"

"'See you.'"
Carol turns as she reaches the door. "It's just a phrase," she says.

∽

The writer searches, checks with his siblings. No, no pictures of his parents' wedding, nor can they remember ever seeing any. Further, no pictures of their mother's parents, either one.

∽

Even on the days she's feeling stronger, the writer's mother finds it hard to speak on the phone, and visitors just overwhelm. The writer stops by the nearby house of one of his mother's old friends, accordingly, to report on her condition. Already past eighty, this woman is still quite articulate, vital, undaunted.

After they speak about his mother's prognosis, her friend tells him that several years earlier she'd been in a coma for ten months. Laughing, she says that everyone gave up on her. "Good thing they didn't bet their lives on it," she adds, because one day she simply woke up, was once more back in the world. She shrugs.

Her story: told without a sense that she felt any particular stake in its outcome. Without a hint of information about the Other Side. Without at all suggesting the writer's mother will have the same roll of the dice.

∽

The writer asks his aunt, his mother's sister: "Why was it always 'Poor Alfred' that my mother said when referring to him? What was the problem?"

His aunt cackles. Once an extraordinarily beautiful woman, a model, actress, star in musical comedy, she's bent, wizened, seems to be wearing a wig à la Louis XIV. "Alfred," she says. "A successful doctor, four healthy children, etc., etc. All very fine, very fine. But your grandmother made him live at home during college. She didn't want him to have dates, go to parties. Your mother and I escaped early. Your grandmother wasn't about to let that happen a third time. She wanted to engineer poor Alfred's marriage, and she did." She pauses. "Though who knows, perhaps it was all for the best."

~

After a setback, his mother cannot feed herself, lacks sufficient arm strength to lift the fork. At the same time, her thinking is again quite coherent, a great relief to her children: she seems once more "herself." The writer and his mother speak of one of her acquaintances. "I marvel," his mother begins, "but mind you, she's done quite well with what she has," and they both grin at the calumny of such faint praise.

Several moments later, the orderly brings in dinner, and the writer begins to help his mother eat. A bite at a time, bite after bite, until he is certain they'd both prefer the nurse do it from now on.

~

There's a picture of the writer's mother taken perhaps a year before her stroke. She's looking right at the camera, waiting calmly, on her lips just the hint of a smile. She knows what she knows, offering in the biographical note for a new book that during her life she's portrayed wife/mother/widow/grandmother, considers these characterizations her leading roles, has in addition enacted actress/singer/poet/translator. She also plays the eccentric grande dame, reserving the right to speak in her own idiom. "I'll be there presently," she says, accent ever more mid-Atlantic.

Age seventy-two, in many ways she's beyond obligation, though she well knows the ambiguities of what she calls "an almost frightening freedom":

> ...nobody's made me cry in years.
> (I miss the hug coming after the tears.)

In her life as a widow, little left to lose, there's writing and its cool clarity, the solitude she loves, and readings/concerts/performances. These various removes she'd always sought, the discipline of Art and its pellucid passions, some saving distance from the noisy chaos of life.

∼

Though never explicitly stated, it was the writer's father's vision that his children would help each other and care for his wife after he died, and in fact they did just this, though as they grew up it was simultaneously if seldom acknowledged that their mother never saw her mother again after age eighteen, that their father's younger brother was persona non grata, that with relatives there were always inevitable hard choices to be made. Even so, the children fulfilled their father's unspoken wish despite the usual good reasons to the contrary. The writer's older sister, for instance, liked people, loved to dance, dated earlier and more than her mother approved of. By the time she was twenty her parents had broken off a number of her relationships: the sailor she went out with in high school, the dancer she met in Mexico after her freshman year of college, a medical student whose tenure ended when they were discovered "making out" in the living room late one evening. Her senior year of college she married a man one of whose principal virtues was that he had no trouble at all—perhaps even enjoyed—standing up to her parents.

∼

Survivors' tales. The writer's mother loved them, dealt with them in poetry again and again in the years after her husband's death. Her most powerful, perhaps, being a solution to the tormenting question of what happened to the innocent left-behind beasts after Noah loaded up the two-by-two and sailed off. In *her* version—rejoice! rejoice!—no living thing was lost.

∼

His mother lies there, eyes intermittently open, occasionally raising her eyebrows as if in response to something said, but not speaking. Playing possum? "She's had a tough course," the nurse says.

The clouds are low, gray, without hope: Boston as Prague. Silent, inscrutable, his mother's become a Rorschach test, open to speculation, withheld response awakening all the primary conflicts. The writer begins to cry. "You're a good son," the woman at the reception desk says as he leaves.

∼

Though he's utterly lost, the writer time and again refrains from trying to patch things up with his former wife. It was only after they separated that she told him, the first time ever, he thought, that she loved him. Actually, what she said was, "You know I've always loved you."

One night, up late, he remembers the first time she came to Boston with him. They were still just wandering, staying in friends' apartments, heading down to Nantucket in the middle of winter, out to the Berkshires, back into the city. Finally they went to have her meet his mother, who commenced an interrogation as soon as they were seated, sherry and cheese on the low table in front of the living room sofa. The writer's wife-to-be, then twenty-two, answered several peremptory questions—about family, college, plans for the future—but finally, clearly making a decision, began to respond more and more softly, until she was nearly inaudible, and then, smiling politely, ceased to answer his mother at all.

∼

As the writer grew up there were very few adult visitors to his parents' home: never a party, no overnight guests, someone for dinner only rarely, no clan gatherings. There were a number of reasons for this. To begin with, his father was working at the hospital nearly every day of the week, seldom coming home until evening. Parties just didn't much interest him, nor did he have any desire to rise socially: he was doing what he loved. Entertaining colleagues he could take care of at lunches at the hospital. As for family, his wife had long since cut herself off from most of her relatives, and the weight of his many siblings led over time to a policy of distance where possible. Phoning rather than visiting. There were stories about the early years of marriage, the writer's mother singing lieder at Sunday afternoon receptions, but this was long in the past. Now there was generally only Richie, Jonah the Tailor's hapless son-in-law and deliveryman, who always seemed to be leering at the writer's mother, to be trying to invent a reason to get into the house, the writer's mother just as persistently, year after year, telling Richie through the kitchen window and storm window to just leave things on the porch.

Occasionally one of his father's foreign counterparts—an Englishman, a Swede—or one taciturn and saturnine American doctor, a man of enormous integrity, would come for sherry. The writer and his siblings would sit with their father and the guest in the music room, making conversation, and then, suddenly, his father would say, "Ah, there she is," and their mother—hours of cleaning house behind her—would come sweeping down the stairs as they all rose. Just once, his mother tried to draw out the laconic American doctor, waxing rhapsodic when he said he'd grown up in Vermont in the Depression, asking what it had been like. "Outhouses, no plumbing, a well, the runs every spring," the doctor replied.

There was also the writer's trumpet teacher, perhaps thirty when the writer was fifteen. His mother then in her late forties. Following years of lessons, the writer and his teacher had passed to a quasi-collegial relationship: after a rehearsal or weekend Pops concert his teacher would stop at the house and they'd work on duets together, his teacher no longer accepting payment. Each time, after they'd played for a while, sitting in front of the music stand with the enormous Clarke bible of trumpet exercises in front of them, they'd hear the French doors start to open and his mother would appear. His teacher, Italian from New Orleans, with an easy smile and southern accent, would nod his head and courteously respond to her questions, though he never initiated any exchange. Nor did he rise when she came in, though clearly this was her unspoken expectation. "Demand," his teacher might have termed it, had he not been far too gallant to bring up the subject.

∼

The writer's Uncle Hugh, husband of his mother's sister. When he married, Hugh was already a high roller, always a deal on the horizon, servants, limousines. At his mansion, ice cream for kids was brought in by the cook, flambé. "I can't see why you want to know about your grandmother anyway." Hugh's never had children and, more germane, has a problem with information. Age seventy-five, having dedicated himself for years to advancing in 'Society'—endless charity balls, frequent dinner parties, a regular at "21" club—he's recently been indicted for fraud.

"No big deal," the writer replies, "we just want to know."

"It's really simple," Hugh says. "Your grandmother G. wanted her daughters to marry better men. Nobody was good enough. She wasn't interested in promise, of which your father obviously had an unlimited amount; she wanted social cachet. I had to date her daughter in secrecy. Friends of mine would take her out, then meet me at the Copley Plaza. Your mother would have known all about this. At seventeen she must have decided her mother could threaten her marriage. Your grandmother already ran her relatives' families, was a real power broker. Later, when Alfred was older, she controlled his social life. He was like his father, easygoing, would go to great lengths not to fight."

Hugh coughs, pauses. "Anything else?"

"No. Thanks, Hugh. That really helps."

"Oh, I'll tell you something," Hugh says. "One day, when you children were still very young, your grandmother decided to try to see you. She never had, of course. Apparently she went to that beautiful park across from your house and sat there and waited and waited until she saw you come out. Then she just watched while you played, until you children went back in."

What Hugh didn't tell the writer was that when Hugh was twenty, his aunt eighteen, that is, several years before their marriage in Boston, they secretly married up in Vermont. Their license to make love, or to make love without fear. The writer wonders. Did his mother know then about the secret marriage? Did she know her older sister was sleeping with Hugh? Did G. know? Was that part of her vendetta against her second daughter's fiancé, the fear or knowledge that they were sleeping together? Was that the source of her rage? Or did she really believe he was after their money? Sex, money: wouldn't it have been with an accusation about one or the other that she went to see his father's mentor, a very famous professor, to vilify the talented young physician who wanted to marry her not-yet-eighteen-year-old?

∽

"*Wie Geht's*, Mother," the writer says as he enters the hospital room.

"*Ganz gut*. I saw Victor," she replies, speaking of one of her dead husband's many brothers.

"You did?" Uncle Victor is three thousand miles away, she'd spoken with him on the phone earlier. Her son had dialed the number.

"Yes. Victor looked very well."

"Believing is seeing, Mother," the writer responds, and she cackles.

~

"Are you promiscuous?" Ana asks. They're in North Beach, wandering past a playground after Haka Chinese food, watching Chinese kids shooting hoops, playing softball. She doesn't wait for an answer. "I've never done this before," she says later as they get in her car, referring to the fact that they're on their first date. As they drive across the city he thinks of the question behind her statement: "But have you?" And hears the response from the song: "Well yes I have/ but only a time or two..."

When he wakes up at her place the room is pitch black, only flashing red numerals on the electric clock for illumination. Her mother committed suicide/her father died young/she believes in psychiatry/ her hair is red and short/she has very blue eyes/she calls herself an introvert/she doesn't like her sister/she likes his shoulders. She believes there should be a university for love, so people can learn how. Had said to him, "I'm old-fashioned."

When she wakes in the morning Ana asks, "Did you turn the hall light on?"

"Yes. Around two this morning."

"Why?"

"I've had one on at night since my mother died."

"Why?"

"I just have."

"But why?"

"Well, otherwise I might get lost."

"How?"

"I guess I wouldn't be able to get back."

"Back where?"

"I don't know. Just back."

~

The writer's father had an older brother who was studying philosophy in Germany. This would be in 1921 or 1922. Finishing college, the writer's father went over to join him, his goal to study with Sigmund Freud (who'd come to the United States in 1912 to deliver lectures at Clark University). When he reached Freiburg, however, he was incorrectly informed that he needed to be a physician to become an analyst—Freud was by then bitterly opposed to the scientific establishment—and so began medical school. Soon, encountering a great teacher, he became intrigued by pathology, over the years growing increasingly skeptical of psychoanalytic models.

The writer's mother intensely disliked psychiatry and psychiatrists, though she never quite explained why. When, as an adolescent, the writer became enamored of Freud, his mother bristled. What, the writer—teenage specialist in perceiving the latent, in detecting the unconscious—used to think, what was she so afraid of?

His mother's poetry. Dense. Elliptical. Nothing simple revealed, or, nothing simply revealed. At seventy-three, however, she publishes a first novel in the form of the diary of a seventeenth-century teenage girl whose parents are killed by Indians and who, kidnapped by them, is finally ransomed by whites in Boston. Working as a servant, the girl is then possessed by spirits and exorcised by the twenty-nine-year-old minister Cotton Mather. There's some laying on of hands involved in the cure.

Appraising his mother's transition to prose so late in her career, the writer supposes she was expressing both an impulse to be more explicit—and about some things more accountable, therefore?—as well as an interest in confronting the sexual element of a teenage girl's life. Not only do Mather and the girl have an intense and erotic—if technically chaste— relationship, but the girl, it turns out, had become pregnant while with the Indians. And in the sequel his mother was planning just before her stroke, the girl, as in the historical record, is drummed out of Mather's congregation some time after her exorcism—for adultery.

Not long before her death, his mother wrote a poem to celebrate the christening of the child of two lesbian acquaintances. Her own children were amazed. Wasn't this condoning just the kind of "inappropriate" behavior she'd long enjoyed deploring? Ten years past the death of her husband, having had to redefine her relationship to the wider world or be alone, their mother hooted, laughed, professed to think nothing of it.

∽

Assaults of the hospital: grinding routine, harried personnel. A nurse impatient with the writer's mother, whose oxygen mask has slipped off yet again. "She's moving around too much," the nurse says testily.

The writer feels his mother waiting for his response. Weeks passing, the hospital world ever more total, at the mercy of so much expertise, both of them increasingly lose autonomy, feel infantilized, become coconspirators against the quasi-parental hospital authorities.

"You know," the writer finally says to the nurse, "believe it or not, before I was born I asked for a mother who would move around too much while wearing an oxygen mask in the process of recovering from a stroke at age seventy-four."

Putting the mask back in place, his mother's one good eye staring up at her, the nurse replies, "You asked for it? You got it."

∽

Inez. Twenty-one, a Filipina, just finishing college and working as a receptionist in a doctor's office. Hoping to get an MA in public health sometime, but for now dreaming of getting out of her mother's house. Saving every penny.

What she likes about the writer is that he's not trying to be her lover, so she wants him to be her lover, so he becomes her lover. She stops by his house, and he listens as, like Adam, she names the things she sees. This skylight, that white wall, those Spanish tiles.

For several months she visits once a week or so. She's wise: "This is just what it is," she tells him.

∼

Neil's concerned about the writer. "I don't know how you do it," he says, meaning living alone, flying back and forth cross-country since his mother's stroke, spending day after day at the hospital when it's his turn to alternate with his siblings. The writer and Neil have worked together in the past, but just now the world of getting things done seems incredibly remote. Not unwelcome: beyond reach. As if he and his siblings are also consumed by their mother's stroke.

Neil perennially worries about everything, sees all the dangers, wants the writer to draw the proper inferences. How can he not be raising a family? "I mean, come on, stop bullshitting yourself," Neil says. "Think about it. Look who's taking care of your mother."

∼

"Make your soft palate like the skin of a drum. Calm, calm, calm. Have the sensation of each note coming towards you, not moving away. Start the sound from the ears backward, tongue wide at the sides. Make your throat like a cobweb: the vowel is the fly caught in the cobweb. To sing one must be an actor. Never be yourself when singing."

The education the writer's mother and her sister received, another element of which was the study of elocution and appropriate gestures. They'd recite: "The hand defines or it indicates. It affirms or it denies. It accepts or it rejects. It molds or it detects." Or they'd go through the catalog: *Arms*—Declaration, Negation, Rejection, Appellation, Benediction, Salutation; *Feet*—Defiance, Respect, Vulgar Ease, Indecision. Or they'd declaim once again: The prophet reveals mystically/The saint reveals spiritually... Oh, play on the light lute of love, blow the loud trumpet of war...

The writer's mother and her sister were forever being taken to the symphony, vaudeville, concerts. "If Pavlova stood still it was breathtaking," the writer's aunt told him. "She was the dying swan. Also, wearing a yellow satin dress, she did a gavotte to music by Galinke. Your mother and I went backstage. We were impressed that she didn't shave under her arms.

"We saw Isadora Duncan dance too. She ripped open her costume, exposed one breast. 'This,' she said, '*this* is beauty.' But we weren't impressed; we were brought up in the Russian Ballet. We were always in tutus, like in the Degas paintings. Our teacher was a White Russian refugee. She was nearsighted, wore a lorgnette studded with jewels. She had a baton, would bang your legs. Our toe shoes were always full of blood.

"We did a ballet at the home of Mrs. Arthur Curtis James at Newport. They had a Swiss village in the rose garden. Your mother was an oriental rose. Later there was ballroom dancing, with many White Russian refugees. God, they waltzed magnificently."

The writer's aunt coughs, chokes, recovers. She's chain-smoked since she was eighteen, since before the ballet at Mrs. Arthur Curtis James's. More, she's got a husband in legal trouble, enormous debts, social stigma. "If your mother were alive," she tells the waiter, "oh, if your mother were alive, she'd have me come to her."

Revived by the thought, his aunt begins to recite from *A Midsummer Night's Dream*, lines she and her sister learned more than fifty years before. "How now, proud Titania!" his aunt declaims. And, "Lord, what fools these mortals be."

∼

The writer's friend Felicity, whose mother, leaving a love child with her parents, ran off from a small Mormon town in the thirties. Whose mother was later found dead in San Francisco, a suicide. Felicity herself running off fifteen years later.

Inhaling deeply on her cigarette, Felicity studies the writer as if to read the effect of the death of a second parent. "You know," she finally tells him, "they say that if you're an orphan, you grieve the whole rest of your life."

The writer chews on it. Two thoughts recur:

1. How could their mother abandon her four children after demanding so much of them?

2. How would they now be able to explain why they were the way they were?

∼

His mother begins to vomit, almost chokes to death before the nurse can clear her throat, insert nasal tubes to empty her stomach of fluids. Later, after the writer's brother comes in, his mother finally opens her eyes. "How could you let them do that?" she asks him. "How could you be so cruel?"

∼

Some children and their teacher from a local private school plan a book on dying, come to speak to the writer's mother. "What are we interviewing her about?" the teacher asks as the tape begins to run.

"Death," says a student's voice.

"Fire away," his mother responds.

When they ask if she's afraid of dying, she says, "I don't think so. I feel I have led a rich life, a life of achievement. Though my work, my writing, still engages me, you reach a point, with gradual curtailments, when the prospect of continuing just isn't that interesting. I don't need more; that doesn't seem frightening. I do hope for a graceful conclusion. I want to accommodate myself to what I see in nature. Once was enough..."

Neither of the writer's parents has a grave. No gravestone, either. Nor can the writer remember any conversation with his parents, ever, about the hereafter, pro or con. It was apparently just not a subject of great interest to them. Asked by the high school students writing about dying what thoughts she had on the afterlife, his mother says, "I abstain, though I must say I really don't expect any emanations from the unknown."

His parents died within a week of each other, eleven years apart. Some winters, season winding down, spring on the way, the writer remembers the anniversaries of his parents' deaths only by accident. Or, more precisely, he begins to feel uncomfortable in late March, wonders what's eating him, suddenly realizes it's the week of the anniversary of his mother's death, his father's soon to follow.

Regarding what happens to someone after death: as his mother noted, Frost wrote, "Strongly spent is synonymous with kept." And Ezra Pound, she observed, said, "What thou lovest well, shall not be reft from thee." Beyond this, the writer inherits among his mother's unpublished papers her meditation on the continuity of matter, her "search for what cannot be taken from me, that this love happened," her thesis that the death of the beloved results in a dispersal—but not loss—of essence akin to the sudden scattering of a flock of birds. "To take pleasure in dissolution," she wrote, "as one enjoys beholding the dissolving shapes of clouds." Or loss, she posits, as a circling. Loss as reversible. Going forward into the past. Loss not unreturning infinity but circular renewal, as of the seasons.

"With the help of metaphors," she wrote, playing the windlasser, "I lift your loss on board." Of course she would confront the death of her husband, transfigure it, in art. As she wrote, "O love, my other wing."

∼

Again the writer's aunt. "It was typical of my mother G. to engineer deals that couldn't possibly come through. Your mother was to become a singer, that's what all the lessons were for, though she could have been a dancer too, but then my father finally learned of all this and said no. No one had ever mentioned it to him.

"My mother would talk to your friends, or teachers, without you knowing. Once, while my husband was in the Army during the war, she suggested I get in touch with my old beaus, actively encouraged me.

"It was always nerve-wracking when my mother visited. Constant trouble. You wonder about these genes...

"She caused the tuberculosis your mother got. She killed my father. He died of heartbreak after your mother's marriage, after the rift. My mother got a thing against your father, though she should have been thrilled. She accused your father of horrible, horrible things. It must have been terrible for him. Your mother was afraid her marriage would be destroyed.

"My mother was the type who appeared suddenly. She'd interfere with everything. My father, just to have peace, let her get away with most of it. My mother was very unusual. They've discovered more now. Perhaps now they have some medicine."

His aunt sends the writer a book, *Farinelli, Le Chanteur Du Roi*. As she says on the phone, "Farinelli was the most famous castrato of all time. He spent twelve years in the court of Spain, singing to the mentally disturbed King Philip every night. When Carlos III succeeded Philip, however, he banished Farinelli, saying, 'I don't like capon.'"

The writer's dying aunt, her obsession with Farinelli, her belated discoveries about her husband's frauds now that they no longer have the money to heat, much less repair, the mansion: what to make of her version of the past?

∽

The writer and his younger sister were back in Boston for a visit, talking with their mother about the houses she'd lived in, and suddenly there they were, the first time ever, heading over to Franklin Park to see the house she grew up in until her parents took the next immigrant jump of upward mobility. This house now in a black ghetto, the grape arbor of her childhood still in the yard. "My mother," she once wrote, "building me in/to my body, bolted me secure/and gave me freedom of a house./ ...Mother! Mother! I cried,/

I'd give my house for a key/to free me from my house!" Letting down her hair, she "gave out a hand to the climber/coming over the sill..."

The house in Roxbury. Odd, actually, that the writer and his sister ever did make the trip with their mother, so unsentimental about the past did she seem. So little past did she appear to have, almost none at all predating her marriage. Perhaps, however, her past was always like the house. Very close by, all too easy to get to.

Turning twenty, the writer left Boston, headed west, was for years pulled back again and again—no other place would ever feel so specific, so true—but always once more he went away, in large part to be free to invent himself. His mother, however, lived in Boston seventy-one of her seventy-four years, spent much of her adult life no more than several miles from where she was raised. Had to fight right there for all she had: nothing was going to just be left behind.

∾

"We are molded by those who love us," writes Anatole Broyard, "those who refuse to love us. We become their work, one they don't recognize, not what they intended..."

∾

"Am I improving?" his mother asks.
"Do I look any stronger?"
"I want to maintain my independence."
"I'm afraid you'll stop taking me seriously."

∾

The family genealogist, nephew of the writer's grandmother, answers his call. "Yes," he says, "your mother's mother would come to Boston every year to stay at the Copley Square Hotel. Not the Copley Plaza, mind you: this was a more modest establishment. In any case, your grandmother was one of the most colorful characters in my experience. A very commanding presence. She used to hold court. My parents were good listeners. She always talked with lots of exclamation points. Spoke about her grandchildren—you people, I mean—as if she saw you regularly, was just bringing us up to date."

∼

Postmortems. (As James McConkey puts it, "The dead are at the mercy of the living.") From his mother's manuscript, her meditation on the death of the beloved: "The pathologist has sent me this autopsy report: 'Your terminal episode was probably an arrhythmia, or a very recent extension of your infarction.'"

Heart (680 grams):
Right Atrium—Dilation and Hypertrophy, Moderate
Right Ventricle—Hypertrophy (0.3-0.5 cm.), Dilation, Moderate, Focal Fibrosis
Left Atrium—Dilation and Hypertrophy, Moderate
Left Ventricle—Hypertrophy (1.5 cm.) and Dilation. Old Healed Infarctions, Anteroseptal and Posterolateral (5x4 cm. and 9x7 cm. Respectively)

Continuing her dialogue with the beloved, his mother writes, "Whatever you were, you are no longer. This is the message of the funerary theatre."

She then refers to the Dutch anatomies of the Renaissance. Public invited, seating according to social rank as cadavers of the criminal and unfit were dissected: "'Only humble and unknown persons, then, and those from distant regions may rightly be claimed for dissection, that there shall be no outrage to neighbors or relatives...neither lean nor fat, and of rather large frame, that their components may be of more generous size and more distinctly visible to the onlookers...'" Questions from the audience were admissible, provided they were serious.

Going back through his mother's books, the writer locates William Hecksher's study of Rembrandt's *Anatomy of Dr. Tulp*. "The portrait as an art form," Hecksher writes, "is from the beginning closely linked with the idea of death," Rembrandt thus in the role of recording angel. Of the luminaries of Amsterdam seen in Rembrandt's painting, Hecksher argues that they "sought immortality when they commissioned Rembrandt to represent them for all times to come as a group in contemplation of death, of its various causes and effects, of its physiological and its moral aspects. Naturally such reflections would simultaneously lead to a deeper understanding of the phenomenon of life itself." Beyond this, there was in the public dismemberment of criminals the element of further punishment, such atonement cathartic for the audience, though some contemporaries deplored this blend of science, retribution, and spectacle: "Antiquity knew not these torture chambers...where these unnecessary cruelties are practiced by the living upon the dead."

∼

His mother's highrise. Just downriver from the hospital, a world of its own. His mother so close and yet so far, the life of the building goes right on. The super expediting somebody's possessions in, somebody's out, one of the elevators draped in mover's blankets. Residents headed to the basement with laundry. Concierge holding a package at the desk, forwarding a message, asking for news of his mother's condition.

His mother's apartment, the two-hundred-and-seventy-degree view she described in poems so many times. Oarsmen, joggers, setting sun, Larz Anderson Bridge, steeples, smokestacks, rising moon, rush hour traffic, gull/mallard/pigeon, skyscrapers downtown and the radar tower at Logan Airport, lovers on the river banks below caught in the "sometimes prurient lens" of her binoculars.

Her apartment, where she hung on for dear life after her husband died, until art and irony—whew—clicked back in. Then staying put, not simply self-protection but a form of fidelity. Sycamore, ailanthus, ash, apple, cherry, larch, dogwood, aster, willow, copper beech, Chinese maple, all as seen from above; snowfall of migrating moths blown up in a storm; crimson champleve beetle on the balcony railing; three dollars' worth of ladybugs to rid the podocarpus of aphids. The local and quite precise variety that sustained. As she wrote:

> ...Why should I travel? Where else would I be?
> Dream is my distance and it comes to me.

"Where are you staying?" his mother asks the writer not long after her stroke, meaning, "Not in my apartment, are you?" But where else can they/should they stay? It's for her they've come. Even so, they understand her feeling of displacement, loss of control.

As weeks become months, as the four of them return to the apartment time after time from their own homes, it seems increasingly less hers, precise shipboard packing away of things slowly undone, accumulation of tiny changes accruing to new essence. Not the same brand of soap or toilet paper, book replaced on a different shelf, a plant dying, coffee spilled. Of course they try to be careful, but often, witnessing the net effect of their presence, they feel like vandals. One night, back from the hospital next door after trying to cheer his mother up before she undergoes yet another operation, the writer has a sudden desperate craving for chocolate, ransacks the kitchen drawers, finally finds the boxes of after-dinner mints in the liquor cabinet. Eats them, all four boxes. Pours himself a Scotch, then another. Starts taking hits from the bottle.

In the morning, surveying the wreckage, thinking of *A Clockwork Orange*, he begins to clean up, and then, taking in the magnitude of the task, all the daily maintenance that has not been done the last few months, makes several phone calls. Soon, not a cleaning person but a cleaning crew arrives to work at a dizzying pace, a total of ten man-and-woman-hours performed in two and a half, and when they are done, gear back out in the hall near the elevator, writer signing a check, the apartment is spotless. Spotless, but now even less his mother's, every chair/sofa/table slightly off the mark, each piece of bric-a-brac or *objet d'art* at a new angle.

Taking stock of this transformation, the writer also begins to see that though the apartment has a beautiful view, nearly everything in it is tired, used up. Walls not painted in years and years, rugs worn through in some places: the apartment of someone getting old, without the energy to take care. How could they not have noticed? That the apartment was changing, that their mother was. As she wrote, "Presence is only a matter of close attention."

∽

The writer goes to see his mother's first cousin, whom he's located through the family genealogist. Elderly, she's eager for family, to introduce the whole side of the family that her cousin excised from her life at eighteen. Her second husband, perhaps eighty, listens courteously to this talk of tribal feuds fifty years and three thousand miles removed, asks the writer if he ever saw Ted Williams play, then leaves the room to listen to the A's game on the radio.

"Your mother," her cousin says. "She was so talented. And she had to excel. She'd say to me, 'You must study more if you want to do better,' expecting I'd want to.

"Your mother's mother, G. She was my aunt. It was so painful to watch her trying to get to see her daughter. You know, your mother and I were once very close—we had the same grandmother, of course. Your mother was scholastically brilliant, but I don't know about her heart. I watched her mother suffer.

"Your grandfather was slight, not tall." ("Short for his age, my father," the writer's mother wrote.) "A terrific guy, a hard worker. He did very well. Your grandmother was tall, heavyset, outgoing, domineering. Your grandfather tried to heal things after the break. He was a generous man, generous to your father, too. But your mother didn't go to her father's funeral. This was five years after her marriage. To us, it was unconscionable. Also, her break with her mother affected the entire family. None of us ever saw your mother again. It's only my humble opinion, but that was too much.

"Your grandmother had many faults, she just couldn't help herself. She'd do something extraordinarily good, then make a remark that undid it all. She was a very lonely woman, though she kept up

278 *Thomas Farber*

a brave front. Nobody really wanted her around. Your father went to see your grandmother when she was dying of cancer of the pancreas. Her hospital was right there near his office, but your mother never came, did she."

∽

Not long after his mother's death:

• A shopping spree. Nothing expensive, just the consoling act of buying things. Over and over again.

• A sense that the order necessary to survival of the self is barely achieved. That the superego—to pick one set of metaphors—has died, leaving only ego, id.

• "What are you going to do now?" friends ask, and he replies, "I'm going on a vision quest." They laugh. He laughs. The writer as Indian on a *rite de passage*. But what, he wonders, what does he mean?

• A conclusion that he and his siblings did a great deal to try to help their mother/worked well together/wore themselves out. Failed to save her.

∽

From the family genealogist, a Xerox of an inscription G. wrote in a book—*Peace of Mind*, by Rabbi Joshua Liebman—she gave in 1946 to her sister's family: "Hoping this will help you to mark out a philosophy of living your life to the full!" The script is large, strong, extroverted, with tremendous sweeps, loops, and curls.

Pictures of the writer's grandmother. From his mother's first cousin, a photo of G. wearing a pinafore at perhaps age ten, in, say, 1890, bangs cut straight across the forehead, hair long in back, a sturdy direct look at the camera. Another photo, G. at perhaps twenty, looking off into middle distance, fabric of her dress gathered in a strong right hand, hair bound up on the top of the head, ear, neck exposed. From the writer's uncle, a picture of G. in forceful middle age, wearing a floral outfit and pumps, in some kind of garden, hand on the neck of a very large flamingo on a stand, an enormous artificial mushroom on the ground beside her. And, from the writer's aunt, a picture of G. in old age. Eyebrows darkened, lipstick, small black hat with veil, skin of the throat yielding to gravity, smile on her face. Looking up at the camera from her soft chair, looking quite small, fading fast.

The writer studies the photos again and again, changes their order, searches for a message, to decipher character, to go past the photos as period pieces or documents of changes in fashion from the late nineteenth to mid-twentieth century.

As for the question of family resemblance, the writer calls his mother's cousin. "I would have to say," she concludes, "that no, your mother did not resemble her mother."

∽

"Drastic conditions require drastic remedies," the doctor had said, but now there appears to be nothing more to do. The writer's mother again in an oxygen mask, unconscious, antibiotics suspended—"Only prolonging a state that should not be prolonged," the doctor says. And, "Her understanding is compromised." More words, phrases: "appropriate supportive care;" "comatose;" "no turnaround;" "not retrievable medically." The writer and his siblings have formed the habit of listening hard, trying always to decipher the subtext, doctors unable or unwilling to speak without accenting what can be done, what they can do. Limiting discussion to the positive without setting the context of probability, leaving the four of them again and again to fathom the distance between words and tone, explicit versus actual content.

"Has anyone told Mother she's dying?" the writer asks.

The doctor seems discomfited, replies, "I told her we'd do all we can to keep her comfortable."

Though his mother appears to be in a deep sleep, the writer reads her some of his new stories. Starts to laugh to think of what her line describing the scene would be: *captive audience*...Periodically, her eyes open, there's a blank stare for several moments, and then the eyes close again. Are the eye movements connected to his presence? The writer squeezes her hand, asks her to squeeze in response. Nothing.

He puts his manuscript away. "Mother," he begins, "I'm going to tell you a story. Four months ago, in early December, you had a stroke." They've done this before, whenever he felt she needed some chronology in the face of so many operations, repeated stays in ICU, but always before she's been conscious. This time, he again recounts the saga: small periods of recovery, larger relapses, the several operations, the many life-threatening episodes.

Finally he reaches the present. "So, Mother, we've determined that this is enough. Sorry for all the mayhem. But that's what I want to say; I promise that now we're getting you out of here."

∽

"One, two, three, testing, testing." Uncle Alfred in 1955, tape recorder running for his mother G. She must have been seventy then, had another five years before she returned to Boston to die.

"I saw one thing in New York that impressed me apropos of the problems of young people today, and that was the play *The Young and the Beautiful*. Born of fine parents, the young heroine, who played her part very well, was nevertheless an unhappy girl of seventeen years. She had everything in life: affection, love, all the comforts and luxuries. She was beautiful besides, so that she had plenty of boyfriends. However, there was something missing. She was sheltered, really had too much. Problems do come when children are too indulged. And that was my reaction to this fine play. I think people who are economically capable of doing well by their children must never say, 'I am going to give them everything I did not have.' The best we can give our children are discipline and character. Unfortunately, they must taste life in stark reality. We must suffer, we must be deprived, because after all, out of the nest the hard, cold world will not indulge us. And then what happens? We can't take it. End result: neurosis, psychosis, and what have you. Therefore it behooves all intelligent parents to treat their children the way they were treated themselves when they were children. If they just recall that situation they will be very intelligent parents indeed."

~

For his mother, an ESTIMATED FUNERAL EXPENSE form:

SERVICES:	
Transfer of Deceased	$125
Procuring Medical & Legal Permits	$50
CARE OF DECEASED	
Embalming-Refrigeration	$85
Sanitary Care	$40
LICENSED PERSONNEL & STAFF	
Arranging, Directing & Supervision of All Details	$175
FACILITIES	
Facilities & Equipment	$150
TRANSPORTATION	
Funeral Coach-Service Car	$78
CEMETERY	
Cremation Fee	$140
Medical Examiner's Fee	$30

~

Rachel, neighbor from down the street when the writer was young. Divorcée with two children, his mother's confidante. "Yes," Rachel says on the phone, "I remember when your grandmother was dying. Your father visited her in the hospital. He'd already been monitoring her condition through his colleagues. And, knowing him, long since he would have been willing to make peace between your mother and grandmother. But on the other hand he would never have tried to make your mother do it. He respected her feelings too much. Anyway, because of your father, that's how your mother knew how she died shouting at the nurse, calling for the supervisor to discipline her. But well before your grandmother died, your mother had concluded that any contact would be inconsistent with her feelings over the years. When your mother told our mutual friend Laura that she would not be going to the hospital, she used that phrase. 'Inconsistent with my feelings over the years.' Laura, a devout Catholic, replied, 'But don't you believe in the grace of God?'"

~

Late March, the bitter end of winter, cold rain and sleet. Two weeks after the decision against further invasive tests or surgery. "She's being treated with dignity," the doctor had told him, which was to say that having been taken off antibiotics she would soon die.

At ten that night, the nurse calls to say his mother's going fast. By the time the writer arrives, catheter, urine bag, and nasal tubes are in the wastebasket, his mother on her back on the bed, sheets tucked in. Though he's known she was going to die, though she is better off dead, though her children are better off having her dead than comatose in some rest home for years and years, though more than once he'd come into his mother's hospital room to see her slumped over in the wheelchair, still the writer cannot help himself. Engulfed in his own sounds, he hears not crying but howling.

Several minutes later there's a knock on the door and a short, heavy, unshaven intern peers into the room, motions the writer to come out to the corridor.

"Sorry to disturb," the intern says. "Any questions?"

The writer thinks it over. "Yes. What did my mother die of?"

"You mean, did she die of a brain-stem stroke? Almost nobody dies of a brain-stem stroke."

"That's what I'm wondering about."

"Really, you'd have to say she died of bad luck. People use other terms: complications, infections, everything that happens once someone's in a hospital. You know, people assume doctors know more than they do. Think of it this way: as doctors we're standing on the beach at the edge of an ocean in a heavy fog. We know it's a beach, we know it's an ocean, we know it's a fog, but what's really out there? As far as your mother was concerned, it was torture in the name of trying to save her. All those operations. They were long shots, but we tried. She just had bad luck."

The intern rocks back on his heels. "Let me know if you need me," he says, and then disappears.

∼

In the wake of their mother's death, the writer's older sister mourning but also gaining strength, stepping in to occupy some of the space now vacated, perhaps intuiting that it is either do that or see it lost entirely. L., the writer's younger sister, of course also now freed in some ways, dealing with relatives and friends with great sympathy and dignity. But then often stumbling with her own grief. Unwilling to imagine letting go of anything from the apartment, for instance, but in the end unable to claim for herself a single piece of the furniture.

The wall mirror. Full length, a fixed center section and two hinged side panels. Writing the contract for the sale of their mother's apartment, they make the mistake of not exempting the mirror from the standard definition of fixtures. When L. finally realizes what's happened—she's clearing out the place, talking to the new owners, is about to take the mirror down—she tries to explain that it has sentimental value, that their mother rehearsed in front of it for years, that it couldn't really be worth very much to anyone else. Unmoved, the new owners insist a deal is a deal.

∽

The writer's friend Sharon. For years they've lived several thousand miles apart. Traveling to Los Angeles and San Francisco, Sharon was visiting him the day his brother called to say their father had died. Eleven years later, back on the East Coast, he was about to visit her when he learned his mother had suffered a stroke.

Sharon: rich and generous soul, straightforward, true, open. Old friend. And the coincidence of her presence in and around the death of both of his parents.

The writer wonders, is there something more to this, something he should understand?

∽

After his mother's death, a terrible dream that she is very ill, urgently needs help. Is dying.

∽

Laura. Commonwealth accent, bright, wry, direct. "Yes, I did ask your mother if she believed in the grace of God, but not to judge her. It was just a question. More to the point, I remember your mother once told me that the word best describing her mother was 'adamantine.'

"The torments the generations create. You have to remember, woven into the fabric of your mother's being was her sense of integrity. To give in to this willful woman was to condone her behavior. She just could not do it. She also felt her mother was superficial, fundamentally insecure, desperately seeking the approval of others.

"But think also of the price your mother paid. This tremendous struggle created a great reserve in her. If she'd been free to share her joy with her mother, that would have been quite different. It's not that your mother built a defense but that she used an inner strength not to be wounded in this regard. I have no awe in me," Laura says, "but I respected your mother's needs."

Adamantine. The writer looks it up in his mother's *Webster's*: "Incapable of being broken, dissolved, or penetrated; immovable... Like a diamond in hardness or luster." From Latin, *adamas*, the hardest metal; from Greek, *adamas, a* = not + *daman*, to tame, subdue. Also, in Middle English, confusion with the Latin verb *adamare*, to love, be attached to, hence also meaning "magnet."

∼

"Spaced out," he wrote eight months after his mother died. The first writing he'd done since her stroke, after wondering if language, so much part of his inheritance, his mother tongue, had died with the death of this parent, or if words were simply inadequate to the task of living. "Spaced out. Is stroke catching? The writer stutters as he speaks to the young nurse, who laughs. His mother is sitting up in bed, one eye under a patch, the other enlarged. Enormous. 'Sorry,' the writer says to the nurse. 'Forgive me. Sometimes I have trouble with words.' His mother's head slowly rotates to the right, the eye now taking them in. 'You see,' he continues, 'English is actually my second language.' His mother seems to begin to smile. 'That's right, my second language. My first language was desire.'"

∼

A memory of his mother. Once again on the phone with a friend, making a face when one of the children walks by, as if to say she'd like to get off but can't. As if only the needs of the other person keep her on the line.

∼

Stacy: very good friend. Parents who survived World War II in Greece; feisty, vibrant brother who died in college. Stacy, then, who does not need to try to console, who understands death so very well.

~

His mother's tuberculosis. Caused, his aunt had said, by G. The sudden termination of his mother's singing career when she was eighteen, possibly forever. Months in Davos taking a rest cure. Weekly pneumothorax. X-ray after X-ray to monitor the disease. Years of a quiet life until the bacilli finally withdrew.

According to a character in Mann's *Magic Mountain*, "Symptoms of disease are nothing but a disguised manifestation of the power of love; and all disease is only love transformed."

~

From his mother's death certificate:

MARRIED, NEVER MARRIED, WIDOWED, OR DIVORCED
Widowed
USUAL OCCUPATION
Author
KIND OF BUSINESS OR INDUSTRY
Books

~

Three months after his mother dies, the writer prepares for minor surgery. The doctor is Danish, a woman in her early forties, articulate, radiating competence, generous, sympathetic. In the preliminary examination, he lies back as instructed, and she takes his head in her hands. "Just relax," she says, though he has absolutely no inclination to resist.

That morning, he'd been reading Freud:
"The attributes of life were at some time evoked in inanimate matter... In this way the first instinct came into being: the instinct to return to the inanimate state. It was still an easy matter at that time for a living substance to die...till decisive external influences altered in such a way as to oblige the still-surviving substance to diverge ever more widely from its original course of life...before reaching its aim of death. Seen in this light...the theoretical importance of the instincts of self-preservation, of self-assertion and of mastery greatly diminishes... What we are left with is the fact that the organism wishes to die only in its own fashion..."

∼

One last picture of the writer's grandmother. G. at perhaps fifty, at a costume ball, large—hefty—confident, imposing, all rings and bracelets, head held high, not at all afraid of the camera. Quite at home where the event is staged, public. Has in fact perhaps arranged it all, is hostess, patron, trustee. Will be in no hurry to leave such a wonderful party.

∼

Often, the image of his mother lying there those last few days. Quite still, eyes closed, fold of white sheet under her arms. "Comatose" being the doctor's word, apparently meaning "unable to hear, unconscious, beyond reach." The writer's brother nonetheless talking to her for hours each afternoon, determined to elicit some response, to find the way to get through. After all, was their mother not still alive? Still right there. Still within reach? Still breathing in, breathing out? How to know their mother was not hearing every last word? How prove the contrary? How many times had the doctors been no more than half right? The writer's brother desperate not to abandon their mother for want of the kind of effort she'd always expected—demanded—of her children, of herself.

∼

The writer calls his mother's cousin. The year before, she'd said her older brother would know more than she would about the rift between the writer's grandmother and mother. Her brother was very busy, she said, but would be free soon.

"I'm sorry," she tells the writer now when he calls. "My brother's not well. Alzheimer's, I'm sorry to say. With him, at this point, most of the past is lost. I mean, it's all still in there in his memory, but there's really no access to it. Here and not here, if you see what I mean."

∼

In the words of Wright Morris, "Anything processed by memory is fiction."

∼

Toward the end of his text on autopsy technique, the writer's father speaks of restoration of the body after a postmortem examination. Incision lines, for example, are closed by stitches, body cavities "dried and cleaned," their external openings (anus, vagina) plugged with cotton, then "stuffed with sawdust sufficient in amount to restore the external contour of the abdomen."

The writer's father also speaks of autopsy techniques in special conditions—in a private home, or during time of war, for example—and cautions that "No trace of the autopsy be left in the home after the examination has been completed. In homes where fireplaces or coal stoves are available it has been recommended that ground coffee be thrown on a shovel full of burning coals to suppress the odor occasioned by the autopsy. The ingenuity and tact of the pathologist are important in the successful performance of a private autopsy, particularly when relatives or undertakers are present."

∽

The writer is absolutely sure this happened thirty years ago. He was fourteen, the summer after his freshman year of high school. The days were incredibly humid, incredibly hot, and there were frequent thunderstorms with lightning, canopies of the trees opulently thick and green, swaying in the sudden squalls. He and his mother were in the kitchen. There was a red and white checkerboard tablecloth, the old gas range had six burners, there were six chairs at the table. There was a stainless steel bowl on the counter overflowing with grapes, and a bowl of raw peas his mother had just been shelling. She was weeping as she spoke, saying her mother had come back to Boston to die, that she was trying to decide whether or not to go see her. She was telling her son this, but not asking his opinion, not asking to be consoled. Just telling him, though this in itself was extraordinary: neither he nor his siblings ever heard their parents argue, never discussed with their parents or heard them discuss any issue troubling one or the other. Never, except perhaps some years before when their father was ill, before it was clear he'd survive. Perhaps then part of a hard truth was conveyed. But now his mother was speaking about her mother to her son, and he remembers her tears, remembers looking out the kitchen window toward the lilacs, toward the fence, toward the elm trees beyond, yet cannot for the life of him summon up how he replied if at all, how the conversation continued, attenuated, ended. But it was in the kitchen, the lilacs were out the window, he was fourteen, and his mother was weeping.

Thirty years later, thirty years later the writer wonders what, what did his mother fear she'd lost when her mother died?

(1993)

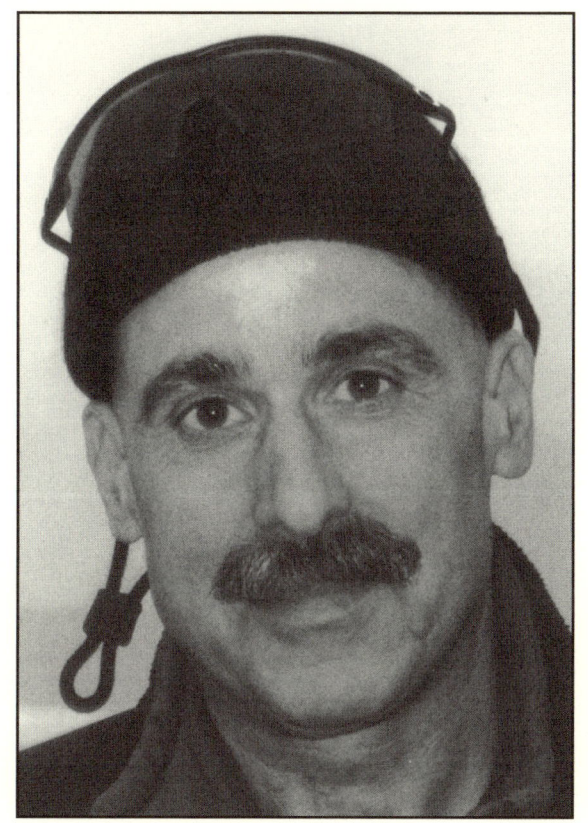

Awarded Guggenheim and (three times) National Endowment for the Arts fellowships for fiction and creative nonfiction, Thomas Farber has been a Fulbright scholar, recipient of the Dorothea Lange–Paul Taylor Prize, and Rockefeller Foundation scholar at Bellagio. He is currently Senior Lecturer at the University of California, Berkeley.